LIFEBOAT

EARTH'S LAST GAMBIT

VOLUME 2

FELIX R. SAVAGE

LIFEBOAT
EARTH'S LAST GAMBIT, VOLUME 2

First published in the United States of America in 2017 by
Knights Hill Publishing.

Cover art by Christian Bentulan
Interior design and layout by Felix R. Savage

ISBN-10: 1-937396-25-8
ISBN-13: 978-1-937396-25-1

LIFEBOAT

EARTH'S LAST GAMBIT

VOLUME 2

FELIX R. SAVAGE

CHAPTER 1

Jack Kildare checked the star sights. He lined up the ship's telescope on a bright star, measured its right ascension and declination, and punched the angles into the computer. Then he repeated the process. Then he repeated it again. He'd performed this routine every day for the last two years. Yes, of course the computer could do it, but Jack had had systems fail on him before. Anyway, he wanted the practice.

The star sights told Jack precisely where the *Spirit of Destiny* was right now.

43,040,922 kilometers from Jupiter.

Further from Earth than any humans had ever gone before.

"The Prince of Wales is moving to the moon," Alexei Ivanov said, floating beside Jack on the *SoD's* bridge.

"Didn't his ex already move to," Jack snapped his fingers, "what are they calling it?"

"Camp Eternal Light."

"Right. That's going to be bit awkward."

"Not really. There are eight hundred people there. They won't bump into each other every day."

"Alexei, I'm not sure this moon base actually exists."

"It exists," the gaunt, bearded Russian cosmonaut argued. "It's a complex of five domes, igloos really, shielded with regocrete—concrete made from lunar regolith—"

"I know what regocrete is. You're always banging on about it."

The moon base existed, all right. Jack was just winding Alexei up. The thing Jack didn't like about it was that it had been built and monetized by private aerospace companies … and the entire private aerospace sector, pretty much, was now affiliated with the Earth Party, an amorphous movement that combined the worst features of Facebook and the Glastonbury music festival. They didn't strike Jack as the right people to run a moon colony.

"The moon is rich in building materials," Alexei went on. "They're mining ice from Shackleton Crater. You can Google it."

"Maybe next time I'm bored," Jack said. This was a joke. They were always bored. "I tried to search for bug-swatting techniques the other day. Gave up after the first hour and a half." The *SoD* was now so far from Earth that signals took 47 minutes to travel one way. Despite the *SoD's* wideband Ka communications system, the internet wasn't much fun anymore.

"Why were you searching for bug-swatting techniques?"

"Need you ask?" Jack said, as a fly looped the loop in front of his face. The flies had shown up soon after they departed Earth orbit. Katherine Menelaou, the *SoD's* commander, thought their eggs must have snuck on board in a sack of soil. Jack clapped his hands on the bug, but it fluttered away, and Jack's own movement propelled him gently backwards until he bumped into the rear wall of the bridge.

The wall was a double bank of lockers. The other walls were inlaid with consoles. The *SoD's* bridge had screens instead of windows—well, it *had* windows, but the six-inch portholes just held fish-eye bubbles of space. The main screen displayed the view from the forward-facing cameras. Jupiter, bigger than any human being had ever seen it. The

SoD was racing towards the gas giant at 58,300 kph, a steel can filled with humans ... and plants ... and flies.

They could already see Europa on the screen, when the little moon orbited to this side of Jupiter.

They couldn't see the MOAD.

Not yet.

"Like this," Alexei said. He maneuvered his toes into the foot tethers in front of the copilot's couch. The bug wobbled above the consoles. They could fly in zero-gee, but always looked as if they were hammered. Alexei slowly raised one hand, then slammed it down onto the comms screen. "Got you, *svoloch.*"

The MOAD.

The Mother of All Discoveries.

The alien spaceship that had burnt into Europa orbit ten years ago.

Observably damaged, the MOAD was presumed to be a wreck. It had done nothing since its arrival except grow colder. Yet how could we ignore it? We couldn't, and that's why the *SoD* had been built, at an eyewatering price-tag of $300 billion plus cost overruns, and sent on its historic mission, with a crew of three Americans, one Russian, two Chinese, one Frenchman, and Jack, who held US/UK dual citizenship.

All of them had different reasons for being here. Curiosity might be the common factor. Duty might be another. But Jack could only speak for himself, and he was haunted by an unsettling conviction that the MOAD spelt doom. He never forgot his friend Oliver Meeks's reaction to the discovery: *If they've got the ability to travel between the stars, they also have the ability to squash us like a bug.*

3

Now Meeks was dead, but Jack was here. His gaze drifted to the set of controls high above the pilot's seat, which he wasn't allowed to touch, even though he was the pilot. The controls for the *SoD's* railguns.

Those would sort the MOAD, if need be.

Music suddenly erupted from the comms console and from the intercoms throughout the ship. Jack and Alexei groaned and clapped their hands over their ears. Mission Control continued to remind them that even at this distance, they still possessed the ability to torture the crew. "Elton John!" Alexei said darkly. "England has a lot to answer for."

The music meant that Jack's shift on the bridge had ended. Without a word—formalities of every sort had long since been discarded—he flipped in the air and flew towards the keel tube. As he brushed past Alexei, he got a pungent whiff of the other man's body odor. He knew he smelled just as bad. Two years without a shower would do that to you. They had hip baths in a small tub once a month. The rest of the time it was reusable wet wipes, which were as revolting as they sounded. The men, bearded and shaggy, now looked more like Cro-Magnons than spacefarers. At least Jack kept his beard trimmed.

He sank feet first down the keel tube. Grime from the constant touch of hands discolored the padded walls. The bright UV light from the hab threw his shadow past his head.

Another shadow blocked the light. Jack expected it to be Giles Boisselot, who'd be taking over from him on the bridge, but the shadow was the wrong shape, too small ...

"Meili!"

The *SoD's* hydroponics and electronics specialist, Qiu

4

Meili, never visited the bridge. Jack retreated to let her through. The keel tube was wide enough for two people to pass each other, but not without physical contact.

"Wow, this place stinks!" she said brightly.

Meili did not stink. She was no cleaner than anyone else, but to Jack, her body odor was a tantalizing perfume.

"I go for piss," Alexei said. "Jack, you cover for me. Five minutes."

Alexei winked at Jack as he headed for the keel tube. Jack turned in the air and flipped him the bird behind his back.

"I need to talk to you," Meili said as soon as they were alone.

They'd been sleeping together most of the way from Earth. They'd broken up a couple of months back—Meili's idea. In her highly organized way, she'd presented Jack with a laundry list of the reasons why he apparently needed a full personality transplant. In space, little niggling things about another person could take on deal-breaking dimensions. Jack hated the fact that Meili picked her nose and he wasn't too fond of her giggle, but he missed their lost closeness. He sank into the center seat and fiddled with the internal optic feeds. He wondered if she'd come to chat about their relationship.

"This is important," she said.

Internal cameras in every module monitored the astronauts. There were cameras on the bridge, too. But the only place you could *see* the feeds was right here. So the bridge was the only private place on the whole ship. Jack wondered if Meili could possibly have come for make-up sex. He dismissed the thought as too good to be true. A second later, he caught a glimpse of Giles, emerging from the secondary life support module aft of the main hab.

"Giles will be here in a minute," he said.

Meili sank through the air to his side. "The mission is in danger," she whispered.

She was hugging herself, her body language defensive: *Don't touch me.* Noted ... "What? Why?"

"I already told you!"

Jack sighed. "You mean that sabotage business?" This had been a running theme of Meili's for a while. During construction of the *SoD,* two years ago, there'd been an attempt to sabotage the ship. Meili had told him that she feared another attempt. "That's history, honestly." The saboteur had been eliminated. Jack knew this for a fact. Why? Next question, please.

Which was why Meili had always disbelieved his reassurances. Now she frowned angrily. "You're complacent."

"I assure you I'm not. Nor is anyone else," Jack said, thinking of the MOAD.

"If there's a sabotage attempt, it will start *here!* So just do this for me. Never leave the bridge unattended. OK?"

"We never do. You know that." Jack, Kate, and Alexei had staggered their shifts so that at least one of the three of them would be on the bridge at all times. "There's always one of us here, like it says in the regulations."

Something else it said in the regulations—or at least very strongly implied: *no shagging.* Jack and Meili used to sneak around during the lights-out period in the main hab, in terror of getting caught. Of course, they weren't the only ones doing that.

"Meili, if something's really bothering you, mention it to

Kate. She won't eat you, you know."

"I have!" Meili said. "She doesn't take it seriously. Just like you."

The shift change music was still playing. The sappy lyrics sneaked inside Jack's defenses, and he felt a pang of sadness. Rallying his spirits, he decided that Meili was getting a bit weird. It could happen to anyone, after two years out here. He racked his brains for some way to take her mind off her paranoia.

Alexei returned to the bridge as the music died away. "No problems?" he said, leering. Jack crossed his eyes.

Meili flew out of the bridge. Jack gave her time to get clear before following. On his way down the keel tube, he encountered Giles. The xenolinguist squeezed past him with a cheery *"Salut"* and a waft of Gallic B.O. Jack smiled, and gave Giles a friendly whack on the arse to speed him on his way. If Meili's fears turned out by some remote chance to be justified, and something ... anything ... happened while Giles was on shift, he'd be about as much use as a chocolate fireguard. But Alexei could handle anything that might arise. And nothing ever did happen, anyway.

*

Down in the engineering module, Hannah Ginsburg performed her second daily set of propulsion system status checks. The *SoD's* reactor, built in Russia, had run without a hiccup for two years. She kept waiting for something to go wrong. As an engineer, she thought constantly about risks, in order to head them off at the pass, but at the same time she *expected* trouble, and had mentally gamed out scenarios ranging from a stuck air bleed valve on the primary heat exchanger loop to life-endangering clusterfucks of various flavors. It spooked her that none of them had yet come to pass.

Well, there's still time, she told herself, with an inward smile at her own pessimism.

After all, the Juno probe had approached within photographing distance of the MOAD before it glitched out.

Mainstream scientific opinion held that a meteorite had done Juno in, but Hannah thought differently. She'd been there in the control room at JPL when Juno died.

The MOAD had done it, sure as shooting.

The ugly, broke-backed alien craft actually seemed to have a smug look on its chops as it spun around Europa, although Hannah knew that was just an artifact of the thing's design.

Revealed in new images from the *SoD's* advance landers, the MOAD resembled a sperm whale with a hole in its side. The 'grille' in front—or in back?—might be some kind of heat radiator. But it sure looked like a mouth.

Anyway.

Hannah turned from the reactor controls on the forward wall to the turbine controls on the aft wall. She believed the steam turbine was more likely to crap out than the reactor. The *SoD's* magnetoplasmadynamic (MPD) engine relied on water for reaction mass. It had been invented by a friend of Jack's, not that anyone ever mentioned that, because it was *a bit awkward* that the guy had been *murdered,* and Hannah held herself partially responsible, but if she thought about that she'd get all blue and she didn't want that. Not today.

Not ever.

She finished the turbine checks and flew across the

module.

She ducked in the air to avoid the fat conduit that ran through the center of the engineering module and into the aft bulkhead. Then she dived into the keel tube and floated aft to the turbine room. The soothing roar of the housekeeping turbine engulfed her. There were two turbine cabinets affixed to the aft wall 'below' her. One was three times the size of a jet engine. That was the drive turbine, which wouldn't be needed until they burned into Jupiter orbit. Hannah flew to the smaller housekeeping turbine cabinet.

Before opening it, she glanced up at the hole in the 'ceiling.' Her long, curly dark hair swirled across her face. All her scrunchies had worn out and her hair just would not stay in a twist-tie. She'd thought many times about cutting it all off like Kate, but perversely, she didn't want to sacrifice this symbol of her femininity …

OK, no one was spying on her.

The turbine room *did* have a door, but it wasn't a real door you could open and close. It was just a pressure door that would slam shut if the sensors detected a loss of pressure anywhere in the ship. So she could not actually shut out the rest of the crew.

But none of them ever came back here, anyway, except Skyler, and this was his exercise period.

She was safe.

She opened the locker. A sour smell wafted out.

Time to check on her bread.

CHAPTER 2

Skyler Taft walked, daydreaming about Hannah's generous curves.

In the main hab module of the *SoD,* you *could* walk, as opposed to floating. The hab was 60 meters in diameter—the height of a twenty-storey building. Its slow rotation generated 0.3 gees at the outer wall, a.k.a. the floor. This had been deemed sufficient to keep the crew healthy. But just having gravity wasn't enough, as any number of obese couch potatoes on Earth could testify. You had to exercise.

Medium-height and slight-framed, Skyler had zero interest in building muscle. Even if he sweated it out on the resistance machines like Jack, Alexei, and Peixun, he'd never be in the same league. And even if he were, Hannah wouldn't notice. She saw him as a friend, if that. So why bother? He met his exercise quota by walking.

He picked his way through avenues of staked tomato plants, between racks bristling with the leaves of sweet and white potatoes. Past dwarf avocado and lemon trees planted in canisters of ultra-lightweight rockwool. He stepped over squash and marrow tendrils crowned with flowers. He ducked under a pergola dripping with broad beans, and thought to himself, not for the first time, that this was getting ridiculous.

The mission planners had worried that the hydroponics would fail.

That the crew would die of starvation.

As it turned out, they'd had to improvise canning and freeze-drying techniques. Meili had presented them with two freaking bushels of zucchinis yesterday, and everyone had *groaned*.

The fans, whap-whapping away in the background, carried a varying menu of green and flowery scents to Skyler's nose. The floor appeared to slope up, although the spin gravity made it feel like a level surface. When he glanced straight up, he saw, first, the axis tube, encrusted with fans and LED growlights, and further away, more bushes and leafy trellises. Twenty storeys up. Hanging upside-down.

Apart from that, it felt exactly like walking through a garden.

Around and around and around.

Boring as hell, actually.

The 200-meter laps would have gone faster with some music, and one thing Skyler had brought among his personal belongings was an iPod. He had the earbuds in his ears, but he wasn't listening to anything, because exercise wasn't his *only* reason for walking.

Oh, no.

Skyler worked for the NXC—the National Xenoaffairs Council. The NXC had grown, in the years since the MOAD's discovery, to wield as much power in the United States as the CIA used to. They had enough power to get him on board the *SoD*, anyway.

So he never stopped working.

Walking, working.

Walking, working.

Approaching the herb garden, he slowed his steps.

From up ahead, he heard the voices of Meili and her compatriot, Xiang Peixun, speaking Chinese.

He pressed a button on his iPod. *Record.*

*

Meili squatted over a tray of chives, thinning them by hand. She placed the sprigs she pulled out of the cottonwool-like substrate into a sack to be added to the compost.

Xiang Peixun moved around behind her, slapping a coil of irrigation tubing from one hand to the other.

"Shift-change is probably the right time to do it," he said.

He had seen her going forward to the bridge. And coming back five minutes later. He thought she'd been doing a practice run.

He'd never know she had been trying to warn Jack, without actually telling Jack anything, which was, she admitted, kind of self-defeating, because why *should* Jack believe her, any more than Kate had believed her, when she hadn't given them any facts to back up her fears? But she simply could not risk Xiang finding out that she'd let the cat out of the bag.

"Anyway, we have to decide how to do it," he said. "There's not much time left. We can't keep putting it off."

Sharing a ship with Xiang was like being in a cage with a tiger. Meili remembered her granny taking her to the zoo in Shanghai when she was a child. She'd wriggled between people's legs to press her nose against the glass window of the tiger enclosure. Back and forth he'd paced, swinging his beautiful striped loins. She'd felt sorry for him, imagining how he must long to return to the jungle.

Meili had been a fearless child. She'd once been a fearless astronaut.

But fear and apprehension had come to dominate her life as the *SoD* neared Jupiter … and the day neared when she would have to act.

The tiger, after all, was not an object of pity. He was a ruthless predator.

"You're not just the gardener. You're also the electronics specialist. Say you have to check for fungus behind the consoles, and you need my help."

"It won't work."

"I need *your* help to pull this off," Xiang pressed, standing right behind her. His body odor overwhelmed the delicate scent of the chives. "If you don't help me, you know what? You'll be finished. Your family will be finished. We'll *all* be finished. You know that, right?"

"But it's impossible," Meili blurted. "One of them is always on the bridge." She hunched her shoulders, head down.

She meant Jack, Alexei, and Kate, the troika who really ran this ship. And it *did* make her angry that the 'multinational' *Spirit of Destiny* mission was really just a Western mission in disguise. She and Xiang were camouflage for that ugly truth. The *SoD* consortium was using them as pawns in a mission designed to benefit the West and only the West. But did that justify the orders she and Xiang had been given?

She didn't think so. She hunched over her work, obstinately silent, while Xiang paced behind her, working himself up into a righteous strop. She was a tortoise, her back rounded like a shell. He was a tiger.

Yet she could not fail to hear the fear seething under the surface of his lecture about *our duty* and *it's the right thing to do.* Because if they didn't carry out their orders, it would be his neck, too. His family, also, would be unpersonned, exiled to whatever godforsaken village their ancestors came from, if they didn't wind up in the camps.

Finished with the chives, she shuffled on her haunches to the tray of rosemary. Hannah had said she was going to bake bread today, and she'd like some rosemary to put on top. Even the *food* on this ship was Western …

Footsteps squeaked on the plastic flooring. Skyler came out from behind a rack of lettuces. He smiled and lifted a hand. "Oh, hello Skyler," she said gladly, before noticing he had his iPod on.

*

Hannah opened the housekeeping turbine cabinet and sniffed her sourdough bread starter. She'd bought it online a couple of months before they left Earth. She'd told the others it came from her Jewish grandmother.

Hannah was nothing if not thorough, so she'd actually taught herself to bake. She could now laugh at herself for tackling it so earnestly: thumping dough in the small hours, falling-down tired after long days of training, in her little apartment in League City, Texas. Baking wasn't *that* hard. She now turned out decent loaves by rote.

But she hadn't brought that starter because she couldn't live without her sourdough, as she jokingly told the others.

What is a bread starter, after all? It's live yeast.

She reached in under the turbine, into the dark warmth.

The secondary heat exchanger loop ran right through this cabinet, swaddled in silver insulation.

Hot going out. Cold coming in.

Hannah had hollowed out a hole in the insulation of the hot pipe. A metal canister sat in the hole, wired in place.

There was a little stirring motor inside it.

She'd used up nearly all her personal mass allowance bringing this stuff on board.

A tube led from the canister to the return pipe, where she'd cut away enough of the insulation to coil the tube around it several times.

The whole Rube Goldberg setup dripped its precious output into another canister.

Hannah took this second canister out of the locker. She glanced over her shoulder once more, and then transferred its contents into her squeeze bottle, which had her name on it above the *SoD* logo. Everyone had one of these bottles. The only way to drink in freefall was through a straw, like a baby.

200 milliliters, she eyeballed the volume of the liquid.

Yep, she was going to have to run the still today.

The distillation stage always filled Hannah with terror. It meant vapor trickling out of the locker, spiking the humidity. She was pretty sure that no one ever noticed a few potatoes missing. After all, it's not like they didn't have bushels of the things. And she was always careful not to be seen siphoning water out of the irrigation pipes. But the humidity sensors … she'd never figured out how to spoof those.

It was just as well Kate Menelaou never noticed what was going on around her.

Hannah closed the turbine cabinet and flew back up into the engineering module. On the way, she sealed her lips around the straw of her squeeze bottle and sucked in a mouthful of high-proof potato liquor, which she estimated to be equivalent to 0.2 of one standard unit of alcohol. She allowed herself one unit per day. She was systematic about it. She was an engineer, after all. She was also a high-functioning alcoholic, but no one knew that, and as long as her system held together, they never would.

She raised her mug to the photo of her sister's family that hung over the dollar meter. Bethany had wanted her to get help. She didn't understand that Hannah could cope just fine.

Look at me, Bee-Bee. This is not a fuck-up. This is a woman who designed and built a still, in secret, aboard a freaking *spaceship*.

She took one more sip, swallowing so much this time that she almost coughed.

The liquor burned sweetly in her belly. The demons of anxiety in her brain quieted.

She placed the squeeze bottle in its webbing holder, and popped a sprig of fresh mint into her mouth. Chewing, she started to put together a new charcoal filter for the still. Her baking hobby also gave her a source of charcoal. *Whoops*, left that loaf in the oven too long …

*

Kate Menelaou sat in her office, nibbling on a hunk of Hannah's delicious sourdough bread, procrastinating before she tackled her daily Calvary of paperwork.

Well, bits-and-bytes work.

Everything from LOX and LH2 inventory levels to the blood pressure, heart rate, and cognitive test results of each crew member had to be logged, tracked, and fired off home to Mission Control, every day.

But what did all that data really *say*?

It said nothing about the crew.

It did not describe how the eight of them, after an initial period of friction and shifting alliances, had separated into three antagonistic camps.

Camp One: the Professionals (as Kate thought of them)—herself, Jack, and Alexei. They were the only ones who really knew what they were doing.

Camp Two: the Amateurs. Hannah, Skyler, and Giles ... oh dear, Giles. The xenolinguist tried so hard, but he just wasn't cut out to be an astronaut. He'd spent more time in think tanks than neutral buoyancy tanks. As for Hannah and Skyler, Kate had pretty much given up trying to turn them into team players.

Camp Three: the Chinese. Kate winced at the very thought of Peixun and Meili. Her wince expressed shame, because try as she might, she just hadn't been able to overcome her own antipathy for the Chinese, which they certainly sensed. But come on! As a major in the USAF, she'd been beaten over the head with the threat that China posed to US interests. Now she was expected to turn around and get all smoochy with them? And they didn't even meet her halfway. They did their jobs in silence, and nattered to each other in Chinese when they thought no one was listening.

She glanced up as Skyler hurried around the field of dwarf wheat next to her office. At first his head was at right angles to hers. The angle narrowed until he was standing right way up in front of her desk. This was her office: a desk next to the wheat plot, in the No. 2 Potter space—the nook underneath Stairway 2—with a ruggedized laptop on it.

"Ma'am!"

"What's kickin', Skyler?" He was the only person who still called her *ma'am* without fail. She smiled warmly at him.

His return smile could have melted the Arctic ice sheet.

Good-looking kid. Reminded her of Jim Morrison, not that she was old enough to actually remember The Doors, thank you very much.

"Smoking gun," he said quietly. "Maybe."

He slid her his modified iPod. It plugged into the USB port of her laptop. She downloaded the .wav file he pointed out, while he explained, "They were talking about taking over the ship."

"Really, Skyler?" She hiked an eyebrow. Kate Menelaou hadn't got this far in life by believing everything she heard. "And you know this, because you speak fluent Mandarin?"

"Ma'am, I'm the first to admit my Mandarin is shit. But I have been studying it. Um, Meili's been giving me lessons, actually."

"Meili recently came to me with some concerns about potential sabotage. I think I mentioned that to you. Why would she do that, if she's conspiring to take over the ship?"

"She's having second thoughts?" Skyler offered.

Kate wrinkled her nose. "I'm still not seeing where the fire is in all this smoke."

"Kongzhi," he insisted. "That means *take control.* At the twenty-eight second mark."

She dropped the .wav file into her encryption software, which had been supplied by Skyler's outfit, the NXC. "I'll shoot it to your guys, and we'll get a real translation. *Then* we'll discuss it."

The dwarf wheat rippled in the breeze from the fans. The constant roar of the air circulation assured Kate that everything was OK with the ship. If she ever got an oh-shit-I'm-millions-of-kilometers-from-Earth

moment—and yes, even she got those—she just stilled

herself and listened to the comforting noise of human technology around her. She did not believe Xiang Peixun and Qiu Meili would do anything that put the *SoD* at risk. After all, they were all in the same boat, literally.

She said to Skyler, hoping to cool the hot gleam in his eyes, "You know what I think about sometimes? I think about how many years we wasted being afraid. Remember all the dire predictions before we set out? The reactor would blow up. A micro-meteoroid would hole our water tanks, and we'd die of thirst. The hydroponics would fail, and we'd starve."

She nodded ironically at the natural bounty around them. The hab used to be boring white. Now it was green.

"Hello, Houston?" she said rhetorically. "A spaceship turns out to be a *perfect* environment for farming. Growlights beat the sun hollow, and plants love low gravity. We're doing pretty good ourselves: apart from the muscle atrophy, we're healthier than most people on Earth. Bottom line, the Chicken Littles were wrong. We have the technology to go interplanetary. We have had it for *decades*. It just took the MOAD to give us a kick in the pants."

Skyler said, "Yeah, but ma'am, *we* is a slippery word in this context. Who invented these technologies? Us and the Russians. The Chinese didn't. And don't think they are not aware of that. It was a major motivation for CNSA in joining the project."

Kate sighed. "You're preaching to the choir. I told them if they let CNSA in the door, our IP will walk *out* the door."

"We have to maintain our technological lead," Skyler said. He toyed with the silver peace symbol he wore on a short thong around his neck. "This mission is how we stay ahead of the pack."

Kate pursed her lips. She knew that Skyler's agency saw their quest for the MOAD through the narrow filter of the 21st-century tech race. The NXC reasoned that an alien spacecraft, however banged-up, had to contain a treasure trove of potentially game-changing technologies. "With you all the way, bud," she said. "Don't worry." But she felt a twinge of annoyance that a thirty-something Jim Morrison lookalike was effectively calling the shots on *her* boat.

"For them, this is a chance to leapfrog right over the United States." Skyler licked his lips. "All they'd have to do is kill us in our beds."

Kate scoffed. She thought that he needed to cool down. "You're an astrophysicist," she said. "Go look at some stars." The problem was, the *SoD* really didn't need an astrophysicist. Skyler was here because the NXC wanted eyes and ears on board, not because he had a Ph.D. from Harvard. "Or go visit Hannah. She could use some company."

A few minutes later, Kate shouted for Xiang Peixun. The burly Chinese astronaut jogged around the hab and stood in front of her desk, expressionless.

"Hi, Peixun. Need you to run LOX, LH2, and water inventory checks for me," she said pleasantly. He was the primary life support specialist. He ran these checks every day without being told to. But that wasn't the point. She judged him—in fact, she judged every crew member—by their compliance with her orders, and her judgement was unforgiving.

CHAPTER 3

Music pounded through the main hab, signalling another shift change. Motorhead! Jack rolled his eyes. Moscow calling.

For the first few months of their voyage, each shift change had showcased an American or Russian contribution to the musical canon. Gershwin vs Tchaikovsky, Bernstein vs Stravinsky, Bruce Springsteen vs Rimsky-Korsakov. About a week before the *SoD* neared the orbit of Mars, that had started to change. The crew had been subjected to Gustav Holst's 'Mars, the Bringer of War' three times a day, every day, for ten days. It remained to be seen if 'Jupiter, the Bringer of Jollity' would accompany their insertion into Jupiter orbit next month.

Since they passed Mars's orbit, however, the musical selections had alternated schizophrenically between insipid oldies from the guys in Houston, and heavy metal from their counterparts in Star City. It was the firm belief of the *SoD*'s crew that the Russians had done a secret deal with Giles. The xenolinguist loved this stuff. Everyone else loved to hate it.

Jack stood at the foot of Staircase 3, one of the staircases that spiraled up the forward wall of the hab, shading his eyes against the growlights. "If you like to gamble, I tell you I'm your man," he sang under his breath, despite himself.

Kate climbed Staircase 2, upside-down, opposite Jack. She clung onto the handrail as she fought the shifting gravity field.

A few minutes after Kate vanished into the keel tube, Alexei's feet poked out of it. The top of Staircase 3 rotated around to him. He slid out of the tube, stepped onto the top stair, and padded down to Jack, without using the handrail. Show-off.

Jack met him with a steely glower. "Best of three," he gritted.

Alexei's lip curled. "I will bury you."

Jack had spent the last several hours transplanting potato seedlings, and wanted to take it out on somebody. "Put your money where your mouth is, Russki."

"You'll regret this, English dog," Alexei promised.

In silence—although in Jack's head, 'Ace of Spades' had changed into the *Rocky* music—the two of them sauntered to the walking track that ran around the middle of the hab. They found a bit of the track without zucchinis or strawberries impinging on it.

"Here she comes," Jack breathed.

A rope-end swept towards them along the track, spinwards. It hung from the central axis of the hab. Jack had let it down a few minutes ago after he finished with the potatoes.

With a grunt, he ran and jumped. You could jump quite high in 0.3 gees. He got his hands on the rope and his feet on the knot tied at the bottom. He immediately started to rise higher. Put a weight on the end of a rope and it turns into a bola. He was the weight. Alexei trotted along the track below, squinting up at him.

"Geronimoooo!" Jack leapt off the rope.

Down he drifted. It was the dream of flying you'd had when you were little, the one you didn't want to wake up from. He stuck out his arms like a kid playing airplane. The track rose up at him. His bare feet struck—and he lost his balance. Caught himself on one hand.

Alexei tipped his head back and howled like a wolf. "Ha! Loser! Now watch how a real man does it."

Jack jogged along the track, out of breath, watching Alexei rise on the rope. Three meters. Four meters. Madman!

"Oh shit," Alexei bawled in Russian as he let go of the rope. He, too, landed in a heap, and Jack duly gloated over him, before running after the rope to make a second attempt.

If you stuck the landing, you won a point. One point equaled one dollar of imaginary *SoD* money. Jack now had $204 of imaginary *SoD* money in his imaginary *SoD* bank account. He and Alexei traded imaginary dollars for bandwidth to download pics of (possibly imaginary) actresses.

But even that wasn't really the point. The point was they had been trapped in a fucking tin can for two years.

From up on the rope, he spotted Meili heading for the kitchen with a basket of lima beans. Maybe some exercise would take her mind off her worries. "Meili!" he shouted. "Come and play!"

*

Sitting on the lid of his coffin, with his back to the aft wall of the hab, Skyler watched Jack and Alexei playing their stupid rope game. Men in their forties, dicking around like teenagers! And now, would you look at that? They'd got Meili to join in. Skyler tch'ed disapprovingly to himself. He knew about the Jack-Meili thing—knowing stuff like that was his job—and he privately approved of the fact that Meili had broken it off. He hoped this did not portend a reconciliation. Skyler admired the quiet, highly competent Chinese woman, and believed she deserved better than Jack Kildare.

Their psychological assessment results didn't put it so bluntly, but Jack and Alexei were both the classic, Type A test pilot type. They had an emotional age of fifteen and an unhealthy fascination with big, phallic rockets. Kate was the rare and even more deadly female of the species.

It irked Skyler that Kate thought *he* was some kind of warmongering shit-stirrer. Had it never occurred to her that *they*, the 'professionals,' were the ones who'd made their careers dropping bombs on people? Jack had served in Iraq, so had Kate, and Alexei had fought in Russia's dirty war in Chechnya.

If he could count on them to be on his side, that would be one thing.

He sighed, mentally acknowledging that he was in a shitty mood. When he visited Hannah in Engineering earlier, she'd blown him off. Literally chased him out, saying she was busy. They used to shoot the breeze for hours, and those were the best times Skyler had ever had on board the *SoD*, but recently she barely even greeted him at meals. Their friendship seemed to have withered away to nothing.

He thought sometimes about having it out, laying his cards on the table, opening his heart, pick your cliché …

An alarm went off, faintly.

*

An alarm went off, loudly. Hannah dropped her new charcoal filter. Warning lights flashed on the housekeeping turbine status display.

Shaft overspeed.

Her fingers boogied on the control panel. Nothing happened. She'd lost her electronic controls.

She had no idea what could've caused the failure, but she didn't need to understand it to react to it. Overspeeding, the turbine was accumulating too much steam in its drum. Pressure was building up. That had to be stopped, or the steam drum would explode in a cloud of superheated plasma.

Sure, it was *only* the housekeeping turbine.

An explosion wouldn't destroy the ship.

The crew would just die for want of the electricity that kept their life-support systems running.

She braced her feet against the port wall. Hauling on the heavy lever, she manually closed off the feed of steam to the turbine.

The lights blinked, and came back on dimmer, as the ship's systems automatically switched over to running off the fuel cells.

Hannah bounced back to the starboard wall. The reactor was running at 15% of max output during this coast phase of their journey.

Should she shut it down?

The risk-averse technician in her said yes. But that technician had trained on the ground. Out here in deep space, shutting down the reactor would have far-reaching consequences. It would take days before it was safe to reboot it. They'd have to survive on the power stored in the fuel cells for that long. She glanced quickly at the fuel cell status indicators. Not a single one of them stood above 50%.

'Below' her, in the turbine room, a sudden *crack!!* rang out.

Hannah's heart missed a beat. She was turning in the air when the intercom squealed. "Hannah!" It was Kate, on the bridge. "We've lost all electronic controls. Do you have controls? Confirm."

With relief Hannah remembered she didn't have to make this decision on her own. "Kate, no, I do not have electronic controls. I've manually shut down the housekeeping turbine. Do you want me to shut down the reactor?"

Kate swore like a sailor. Hannah glanced down. She was afraid she knew what had made that cracking sound. *Her still.* She wanted to find out how bad the damage was, even in the midst of a life and death situation. "Are we exceeding the capacity of the primary heat exchanger?" Kate demanded.

"No. The reactor's only running at fifteen percent. The radiators can dump that much heat over the side."

"Then do not shut it down. This is bad enough without losing criticality. Son of a hairy-assed bitch!"

A wheeze and a clangorous thud interrupted Kate's cursing. Hannah flinched, and glanced up. Her mouth dropped open.

*

Jack, clinging to the rope, flinched at the alarm that shrilled faintly from Engineering.

"What the fuck was that?" Alexei shouted up at him.

"Sounds like we've just found a new failure mode," Jack yelled back, not sure yet whether to be frightened.

The noise of fans died back to a quiet hum. The lights blinked, then came back on, not as bright as before.

OK. Be frightened.

Another alarm shrilled, this time from someplace forward.

Alexei took off running towards the bridge.

Jack, still riding the rope, realized he was swinging higher and higher. *Shit!* This was why you didn't stay on the bloody rope for more than a minute or so! It was wrapping around the central axis.

Two alarms. Two problems.

Three, actually, counting the problem of his own present position.

The garden had shrunk to a green carpet, and he was now too high to drop off the rope without breaking an ankle, or worse. He was never going to live this one down.

Round and round.

Faster and faster.

Nearing the axis tunnel that ran through the center of the hab, he saw a dark head emerge from the opening that led to the secondary life support module. Xiang Peixun.

Jack took one hand off the rope to wave at Xiang, upside-down. He shot the Chinese astronaut a sickly smile.

Xiang, halfway out of the keel tube, paused to goggle at the alarming sight of Jack whizzing round and round on the end of a rapidly shortening rope, conserving angular momentum like billy-oh.

Xiang rested his elbows on the lattice and grinned. All he needed was a bucket of popcorn.

Jack understood that if he smashed into the axis tunnel at this speed, he'd damage himself rather badly. Therefore, he decided not to. At the last possible minute, he released the rope. His momentum carried him over the top of the axis. He reached down and grabbed the lattice with both hands, nearly pulling his arms out of their sockets. Then he switched his grip and let his remaining momentum carry his legs around so he was sprawled across the axis, between two banks of growlights. Zero-gee embraced him.

"And for my next trick, getting down from here," he gasped. Xiang grinned and did a golf clap.

Abruptly, a volley of ponderous booms echoed through the ship.

Jack did not wonder for long what had caused the noise. He knelt on top of the axis, staring aghast at Xiang.

CHAPTER 4

Xiang Peixun was trapped in the pressure door.

It had slammed shut on his waist.

Jack plunged through the nearest hexagonal gap in the lattice, into the axis tunnel. He pushed off with one bare foot and flew headlong down the tunnel towards Xiang.

Pinched between the pressure door and the bulkhead, Xiang couldn't even get the breath to scream. His arms and head jerked. Bloody foam bubbled from his mouth and nose.

"Hold on, mate," Jack cried. He'd trained in advanced medical support. It had to be said that the instructors had not covered 'stuck in a pressure door.' But he knew he had to prevent Xiang from spasming and doing himself an even worse injury. It looked like he may have bitten through his tongue already. "I've got you!"

Crouching in the end of the keel tube, he gently seized Xiang's shoulders to steady them.

The entire top half of Xiang's body came away in Jack's hands.

The hydraulics drove the pressure door the rest of the way shut.

Xiang's guts fell over Jack's legs in a hot cascade, and the man's grimacing face nuzzled against his breastbone. Jack toppled over backwards into the axis tunnel with the severed torso of Xiang Peixun on top of him.

*

Alexei reached the forward keel tube a few seconds after the pressure door slammed shut. He stood on the stairs, panting, staring at the untarnished plug of steel.

Kate's voice quacked from the intercom speaker beside the door.

Back at the other end of the hab, Jack suddenly started yelling. No, not yelling. *Screaming.*

Ignoring Kate's voice, Alexei hurtled down the stairs and ran back the way he'd come.

When he was in Chechnya, he'd lost friends to enemy fire. And friendly fire. And bar fights. The survivor's guilt he brought home from that miserable war had lodged in his soul like a splinter.

He couldn't let it happen again.

"Where are you?" he yelled, staring up.

Warm rain spattered his face.

He wiped it away, and glanced at his fingers.

Blood.

*

Kate, on the bridge, shouted into the PA system. "All hands to your stations! Do you copy me?"

Only Hannah responded. "The pressure door just slammed shut! I didn't do that!"

"All the pressure doors are shut," Kate said grimly. "We may have a hull breach. The doors are designed to close automatically when the pressure sensors trip. What's our power status?"

"We're running on fuel cells and batteries. Emergency life support and ventilation are working."

Kate glanced at Giles Boisselot. He floated in the left seat, groaning. "Giles is with me," she said. "He's had some kind of seizure."

"A seizure, ma'am?"

"He hollered like he got poked. I gave him CPR. He's

breathing, but not responsive. Giles!" Kate leaned over and shouted into his face. "Can you hear me?"

"Ma'am! Was he grounded at the time when he had the seizure, or whatever it was?"

"Grounded?"

"Was he touching metal?"

"He was looking into the telescope viewfinder," Kate said.

"He got shocked. The circuit breakers on the secondary heat exchanger failed. That's what caused the turbine shaft to overspeed." Hannah's voice was rapid, high-pitched. But not hysterical. Hannah had the ability to use her brain under pressure. "The whole *ship* got shocked, ma'am. That's why the doors closed. We don't have a hull breach! We just have a bunch of fried pressure sensors."

"We do not know that," Kate snapped. Common sense, however, told her that if there was a big hull breach, they'd already be dead, and if there was a small hull breach, they still had time to fix it. She thumbed the main hab intercom. "Jack, Alexei, Skyler! Gimme a sitrep!"

Skyler came on the intercom. "I'm getting lighter," he said.

"Yes," Hannah said. "The hab is gradually spinning down. The fuel cells don't have the power to sustain three RPMs."

"Turn the housekeeping turbine on as soon as it's safe," Kate ordered. "How long will that take, Hannah?"

"About forty-five minutes."

"Great." Kate bit her lip. "Can you cut the power to the doors, Hannah? Then we could lever them open."

"The problem," Hannah said, and now she did sound a bit hysterical, "the problem is I can only cut the power in big blocks. If I cut the power to the doors, we also lose the lights, the ventilation, everything. The hab spins down immediately. The plant life goes airborne."

"Someone's up in the sky bleeding," Skyler interrupted. "It's falling like rain. Wait. Jack's coming down."

Jack came on the intercom. He said, "Hannah, do *not* cut the power! OK? Leave the power to the main hab *on.*"

"We need to get the doors open," Kate snapped. Giles groaned again, and the little hairs on her neck stood on end. God help her, she did not want to be stuck in here with him if he died.

"I will get the doors open," Jack said. Then he was gone, leaving Kate shouting helplessly into the intercom.

*

Jack spun away from the intercom in Medical, a.k.a. the Potter space under one of the aft staircases, where he'd brought Xiang Peixun's top half, for no good reason. The man was dead.

Alexei sprinted around the hab towards him, dragging Meili by one arm. "She was hiding in her coffin," Alexei said when they were close enough for their heads to be pointing in the same direction.

As gently as he could, Jack said to Meili, "We have to get the doors open. The locking mechanisms are fried. Hannah says it's the pressure sensors. Can you fix or replace them?"

Meili opened her mouth to speak. Then she saw Xiang Peixun's top half lying on the gurney under the stairs. Too late, Jack cursed himself for not covering Xiang up.

"Ta si le! He's dead!"

Most of Xiang's blood had come out as Jack carried him down from the axis tunnel, but enough of it had remained to soak the gurney bright red—*Chinese* red, in fact, the color of the PRC flag, as if Xiang lay on a patriotic funeral bier. With his legs missing.

"He's dead!" Meili shrieked again.

"Yes, he's fucking dead," Jack shouted. "And his legs are in the secondary life support module, and I'd quite like to get in there, because that's where the hull repair kit is, and it would be a good idea to have that, if we do in fact have a hull breach!"

"He's dead," Meili repeated for the third time. And then she started to laugh.

Alexei slapped her.

She started to cry.

Jack dictated to himself that now was no time to feel sorry for her. "Can you or can you not open the fucking doors?" he yelled.

Meili wiped her face with her hands, like a child. "Logic cards," she sobbed. "Must replace. I have, in my office." She broke down again. Jack couldn't tell if she were laughing or crying. There was no difference at this point, perhaps. Xiang had been her closest friend on board, obviously: they spoke the same language and were always hanging around together.

No more.

Between them, he and Alexei got Meili to her office, which was the Potter space across the hab from Medical. They made her sort through drawers of parts until she found the right components. They collected her tools. Together, they climbed the stairs to the aft keel tube and knelt in Xiang's blood while Meili removed the sensor cover and swapped out the melted logic card.

Restored, the pressure sensor registered a normal air

pressure of 7.35 psi, half of sea-level air pressure on Earth.

No hull breach. Not in here, anyway.

Before they opened the door, Jack pushed Meili behind him, so he, not she, would be the one to get Xiang's severed pelvis and legs in the face.

Oh *God,* this was bad.

Jack pushed the body parts ahead of him, with his t-shirt hiked over his face so the floating globules of blood wouldn't blind him.

Despite the horrific tragedy, their first task was to check for holes in the *SoD's* hull. They found no breach in the secondary life support module. Or the storage module.

Hannah was trapped in Engineering. She reported via the intercom that there was no breach down there, either.

Once they knew that they weren't all about to die, they turned their attention to Xiang's drifting legs.

There were body bags in the storage module. Everyone had hoped they would never be needed. Now they bagged up Xiang's bottom half. Meili helped, despite Jack's attempts to deter her. They would add his top half to the bag later, then stash him outside. There was nothing else they could do for him. No funeral. No priest on board, Christian or Buddhist or any other flavor.

Meili went back for another replacement logic board, and they freed Hannah. When the pressure door opened, Jack smelt burning. "Jesus! Hannah, what's that smell? Is everything OK back here?"

The keel tube framed Hannah's besmutted face. "Stray sparks," she explained. "Don't worry. I've got everything under control."

*

34

Back in the main hab, Skyler spoke into the intercom. "They've all gone aft. I don't know what they're doing. They didn't consider it a top priority to keep me in the loop."

"What I would like to know," Kate said, "is, are they going to let me out anytime soon? Or has Jack decided he kinda likes it when I'm not there?"

"I don't know," Skyler said, opting to let that particular fire smolder unchecked. He was more interested in finding out what the hell had just happened. "Do we know what hit us?"

"It was some kind of electrical glitch," Kate said.

"Hmm," Skyler said, guessing that she didn't have a clue. "How's Giles?"

"I am fine," Giles said, hoarsely. "Headache like I get kicked in the head. What happened?"

CHAPTER 5

What happened?

That was the question on everyone's mind when the crew assembled in the unearthly dusk of growlights running on half power. Even Hannah showed up for the meeting, to Skyler's relief. She'd restarted the housekeeping turbine. Now it was just a matter of waiting for the output to creep back up. For the time being, the *SoD* was still running on power from the fuel cells. The plants hadn't started levitating, but the hab had cooled down. A lot. Everyone was wearing their thermal shells, so they looked like a post-apocalyptic North Face advertisement. Long-unused socks covered callused feet. Meili kept saying she was afraid the strawberries would die.

They met in the kitchen, which was a space amongst the greenery with a large table in it. Exhausted, depressed crew members sprawled in six out of eight lightweight aluminum chairs. The seventh chair silently rebuked them for being alive. Kate balanced one foot on the eighth chair, addressing the troops. Skyler hid his cynicism behind a mug of coffee. Kate had broken out their precious stores of Nescafe in an attempt to cheer everyone up. It wasn't working.

"A few essential tasks, gang. First of all, we have lost the pressure sensors, optic sensors, radiation counters, a whole list of stuff out there. That all needs to be repaired or replaced." She looked at Jack and Alexei. "EVA specialists, I want that done as soon as this meeting concludes."

Alexei gave her a long, slow blink that Skyler—trained in reading body language—interpreted as insubordination. This might be about to get fun. If cracks appeared in the

'Professional' camp, it would be one positive outcome of this disaster. But then the Russian followed that up with a bland "OK."

Jack just nodded, staring at the floor.

Xiang Peixun had been their third EVA specialist, but Jack was now wearing Xiang's blood.

Jack hadn't yet had time to clean up. Nor, apparently, had Hannah. Her face was dirty and she had a scratch on her left cheek. She wore a bandage around her left hand, which might conceal another injury. Skyler wanted to ask her if she was really, truly OK. Yet he dared not importune her with his concern. She was busy saving their lives—so busy that she didn't even want to be here, and sat on the edge of her chair, poised to dart back to Engineering as soon as Kate released them.

"Next," Kate said, "we need to send a full report on the incident to Mission Control. That's going to be fun when we're limited to text-only comms. The Ka antenna is down, too. I've notified them that the emergency is over, but they want to know what caused it. So do I."

Alexei said, "It was the MOAD, obviously."

"Yeah? How do you figure, Alexei?"

"It attacked us," Alexei said. "Same thing it did to the Juno probe. We think it was a high energy radio frequency pulse. Right, Jack?"

"Right," Jack said, without looking up. "Electronic systems on the outside of the ship were affected. The interior wiring was not. Ergo, the attack came from an external source."

He may not have intended it that way, but speaking to the floor instead of meeting Kate's eyes made him look disrespectful. His British accent didn't help. He sounded arrogant, and arrogance was a red flag to USAF Major (Retired) K. Menelaou. Skyler saw her tense up. The back of her neck, exposed beneath the blunt edge of her short haircut, flushed pink. "Well, guys, you seem to have given this a lot of thought. I'll include that in my report. Anyone else have an insight, theory, or wild speculation they want to share?"

Skyler actually did have a theory of his own: this had been the sabotage attempt he'd tried to warn Kate about. He'd been right about the timing, wrong about the saboteur's target.

He really, really wanted to believe that Xiang Peixun had attempted to sabotage the steam turbine … and ended up dead himself, in a horrible accident no one could have foreseen. But the universe rarely deigned to deal out *that* much poetic justice in one serving. More likely, the saboteur had been Meili herself.

It had to hurt like hell, knowing she had inadvertently murdered her friend. She sat with her arms around her knees, red-eyed, looking about twelve. Skyler could not help feeling sorry for her. He decided that he would wait to receive the translation of that last conversation between her and Xiang before he broached the subject with Kate again.

"No one?" Kate said. "Well, the important thing to remember is we're still here. *If* this attack came from the MOAD's autonomous defense systems—" she threw a bone to Alexei and Jack— "it failed. Think about that! The MOAD hit us with everything it's got, and we're still here." She smiled broadly. "This ship is as tough as they come."

Hannah stood up. "With all due respect, Kate, no it isn't.

This ship was designed and built so fast that they didn't think of all the failure modes. Every single system was rushed through development, rushed into production, and when they hit a snag, they didn't go back and fix the design, because they didn't have time. I know. I was there. The whole ship is a creative workaround. OK, credit where it's due, Sonic is a thing of beauty." She glanced at Skyler. He froze. The topic of the MPD engine was … *sensitive.* Hannah went on, "But then I would say that, wouldn't I? I built it."

"Ha, ha," Skyler said, dizzy with relief that she wasn't going to mention Oliver Meeks, the dead man who had invented the drive.

"OK, and the reactor. I love our reactor. It takes whatever you throw at it and asks for more. But the electrical systems! Jesus! Heads need to fucking roll! Who designs a door without a fuse in the motor, that you can't open, even if there's someone *stuck* in it?" Hannah's voice broke. She turned and walked away.

Skyler realized for the first time that Hannah blamed herself for Xiang's death, because she could have cut the power to the doors. That wouldn't have saved Xiang. He had literally been chopped in half. But facts never stopped Hannah Ginsburg from blaming herself for circumstances beyond her control.

By the time he got through thinking that, Hannah had vanished between the plants.

Kate looked after her for a moment, mouth thin. Then she said, "Let's give her some alone time. We were just about finished here, anyway. Who's for another cup of coffee?"

CHAPTER 6

Jupiter floated ahead of the *SoD* like a rotting peach, ten times bigger than the moon. Jack wouldn't be able to wrap his arms around it, if it were hovering right in front of him, as it seemed to be. No depth perception in space. The gas giant was still more than 30 million klicks away. But it was 1,300 times the size of Earth.

Jack held his Nikon up, stabilizing himself with his other glove on the *SoD's* hull, until he got Jupiter centered on the screen.

Click.

Oh, you beauty.

Click click click.

He'd photographed Jupiter for the first time from the ISS. At that distance, the gas giant was just a pixel. But something *else* had shown up in those photos ... a smear that turned out to be a drive plume. Those pictures had set him and Oliver Meeks on the trail of the MOAD. Now that trail was leading them to Europa. His heart beat faster at the thought of finally reaching the alien spaceship, and prying out its secrets ... even if the truth confirmed the dark fears he and Meeks had shared.

Of course it wasn't going to be a stroll in the park all the way. They'd been lucky to get this far without interference.

Click. Click.

"Hey, Alexei!"

Jack velcroed his Nikon to his shoulder patch. He'd swaddled it in insulation to keep the batteries from getting too cold. He pulled himself hand over hand along the row of grab handles that led over the top of the bridge module.

His satchel of tools and parts floated behind him.

What he was officially doing out here: repairing the electronics. The coaxial cables of the antennas had shorted out, which could only have been caused by a power surge so big that energy splooshed out of the cables into places it didn't belong. Some of the connectors were completely slagged. Anyone want to bet it *wasn't* a high energy radio frequency pulse? Anyone? Even Mission Control accepted their theory now.

"Alexei!"

"What?" Alexei was working on the Ka antenna, chipping at melted plastic and blackened metal. When he raised his head, a reflection of Jupiter swam into his faceplate.

"Say cheese."

Click.

Best. Photo op. Ever.

"Stay there ..." Jack hooked one boot through a grab handle and extended his body backwards, aiming to get Alexei and Jupiter in the frame together.

Alexei gave a thumbs-up, still holding his multitool. Then he turned to face Jupiter and gave the gas giant the middle finger.

Clickclickclickclick.

Their laughter alerted Kate, who was monitoring their EVA from inside the bridge. "How are you doing out there, guys?"

"Almost finished," Jack said, blinking his eyes. When wearing a spacesuit, it was a mistake to laugh until you cried. "Just got to replace the cables on the Ka antenna and we'll be coming back in." This was their eighth marathon spacewalk in as many days. Every action took three times as long as it would in gravity. The lining of their spacesuits had started to rot from being sweated in and never drying out. You had to break the tension.

"Quit dicking around," Kate said. "You're taking rems out there."

"These new gloves are really great, Kate. So flexible," Alexei said. He contorted his right fist into the fig sign, giving the MOAD a special Russian fuck-you. Jack photographed that, as well, snorting through his nose in an attempt not to laugh.

"Remember you still have to check the landing craft," Kate said. "Their sensors probably got fried, too."

The landing craft: the Dragon and the Shenzhou Plus, two-person rockets that would take them down to the surface of Europa. If they got that far.

The landing craft were strapped to the truss tower, outside the storage module, behind the rotating hab that blocked Jack's view aft.

Why did the *SoD* need landing craft at all? Because it couldn't haul enough water for the round trip to Jupiter. By the time they reached Europa, the tanks would be close to empty. Not enough propellant for the trip home. But Hannah's gang at Johnson Space Center had solved the problem. They'd launched two advance landers ahead of the *SoD*. Flying electrolysis units fitted with engines, the advance landers would scoop up ice from Europa's surface and process it into reaction mass for the *SoD's* return journey to Earth.

Originally, Thing One and Thing Two—as the media dubbed them, because of their Seussian appearance—had been designed to shoot their product into orbit for the *SoD* to pick up. But that turned out to be unworkable, hence the landing craft. The crew would go down to the surface of Europa to retrieve Thing One and Thing Two's output.

Jack didn't really give a damn about walking on Europa. It was the MOAD that lured him. But he had to admit that a Dragon might be a handy thing to have along.

"We'll get to it, Kate," he promised, handing Alexei a replacement connector.

The whole refueling scheme would have been bollixed if Thing One and Thing Two hadn't made it to Europa. But they had successfully landed a couple of months ago, deorbiting straight past the MOAD, snapping pictures en route. Those pictures had caused a stir on Earth as they revealed the alien spacecraft in detail for the first time.

"Hey, Alexei," Jack said aloud. "Why didn't the MOAD mess with Thing One and Thing Two?"

"Hmm," Alexei said.

Kate took the bait. "NASA assumes the MOAD is under the control of an AI tasked with area clearance. It determined that Thing One and Thing Two were not coming in at an angle that might impact the MOAD, so it didn't HERF them."

Even Kate had started using HERF—High Energy Radio Frequency—as a verb. Jack was quite proud of coining the term.

"But what about the Juno probe?" he pushed. "The MOAD HERFed the shit out of that. It was clearly not on a collision course, either."

He crossed his eyes inside his helmet.

"The AI determined that Juno carried instruments which might have revealed sensitive information about the MOAD."

43

Kate stuck to Mission Control's party line.

"So now we're saying the MOAD could tell what instruments Juno carried? It's making decisions based on long-range observations? Just how smart is this alleged alien AI?"

"Killer, just fix the goddamn electronics," Kate said tiredly.

Killer, her nickname for him. A play on Kildare. Recently, though, it sounded less like a term of endearment, and more like an accusation.

When they were back inside, Alexei said, "What was that about? You want her head to explode? We already lost one astronaut."

"Mission Control doesn't have a bloody clue about the MOAD," Jack said. "I just want her to admit it."

"She can't admit it until they do."

"Which will be when hell freezes over." Jack sighed, peeled off his underwear, and stowed it in his laundry bag. He reached into his coffin and pulled clean Y-fronts out of the storage webbing. He remembered Xiang Peixun's blood splashing into his face, like hot spray from a water-gun. Bad scene, yeah. Bad, bad scene. But it was over now. The hab had warmed up again, the growlights were back on at full strength, and Jack had to give the potatoes some TLC before he relieved Kate on the bridge. Stay focused on the mission. It's the only way forward.

Alexei sat on the folded-back cover of Jack's coffin, fiddling with his e-cigarette. They were all supposed to be paragons of healthy living, but Alexei had never had any intention of giving up smoking. He'd brought tobacco seeds on board as part of his personal weight allowance. He used his own water allowance to grow the plants, to Kate's despair. The funny part was, by the time his first crop matured, he'd admitted that he no longer got nicotine cravings... but a good DIY scheme should never go to waste, so Alexei had plunged into vaping. A year later, he could bore for Russia about the finer points of mixing nicotine juice and crafting atomizers. Space makes people weird in all the ways they were already weird, but more so.

"About Thing One and Thing Two?" he said, exhaling a monster cloud of vapor. "The aliens could see they're not a threat, so they didn't waste power on them. That's all."

Jack deadpanned, "Oh no, man. You're shitting me. Aliens?!? The MOAD is a hulk! All the scientists say so."

Of course there were aliens. Meeks had believed there were aliens, and holding to that belief was a way of honoring him. Anyway, *aliens* was the logical conclusion to draw from the media's unanimous insistence that there weren't any. When someone hands you a pacifier, look for the monster under the bed.

"Next EVA," Alexei said, "we fix the radar dish and the display electronics for the railguns."

Exhibit A. *Of course* there were aliens. If there weren't, the *SoD* would not have been fitted with two railguns that could fire three 40-kilogram steel slugs per minute. Fancy a barrage of Mach 5 projectiles, E.T.?

That said, a fat lot of good the railgun would do them without a functioning radar set-up, not to mention the electronics that extracted and processed the data.

Electronics.

Despite all her rad-hardened systems, the *SoD* was a 21st-century spaceship, crammed with semiconductors.

One more HERF like that, and they wouldn't get close enough to use the railguns.

But there was nothing Jack could do about that, so he put on his filthy gardening shorts, took a hit off Alexei's e-cig, and went to do his duty by the Yukon Golds.

As it happened, Skyler was working in an adjacent patch, adjusting the pH of the fish tanks. Tilapia swam in cool dark water under roofs of kale. They met the crew's protein requirements. Chickens had been considered, but fish were easier to handle. They didn't shit everywhere.

"Hey, Taft," Jack said. "How are our finny friends coping?"

Skyler's expression gave nothing away. He'd come aboard the *SoD* in a puking, trembling mess, but he had smartened up a lot since then. Even when Xiang died he hadn't lost it.

He withdrew the pH meter from a tank. "The fish are OK. They're surprisingly tough. The vegetables, less so. Just look at those leaves." The kale plants were noticeably yellow. "When the oxygen pumps temporarily stopped, the pH went out of kilter. Hydroponics is inherently unstable. Take away the soil, and you take away any margin for error."

Jack moved towards him with a handful of seed potato chunks in one hand, the knife he'd been using to chop them in the other. "So what do you think? Was it the aliens?"

Skyler's mouth twitched. "If the hydroponics fail, we won't have to worry about the aliens."

"Oh, so you admit it. The NXC has lied to everyone."

"We have no idea if there are aliens on the MOAD or not. But if you're talking about the scientific consensus ..."

"Yeah."

"It's a necessary corrective. The Earth Party keeps telling

everyone there are aliens, based on no evidence whatsoever. They just want them to be there."

It annoyed Jack to think that he had anything in common with the Earth Party. "Who gives a fuck about those hippies?" he said. Skyler smiled slightly and touched the peace sign he wore around his neck. It might as well have been a neon *IRONY!!* sign. Skyler was a bit of a hippie himself. Hilarious, right? What really irritated Jack was the way he played it up to convince everyone that a Fed could be human. That wasn't in question. The issue was that there was, in fact, such a thing as a bad human.

And Jack sometimes feared he was one.

"You better give a fuck about those hippies," Skyler said, still smiling. "They occupied London, didn't they? Tore up the cobblestones and planted dandelions. Shat all over Hyde Park, indulged in a bit of undocumented shopping. Then moved on, the way they do. You come from Warwickshire, right? I heard it's a nice place. Unspoiled. Might make a good party venue."

"You really are a cunt, aren't you?" Jack said. He wiped the potato knife on his shorts. It was an oblique threat, half-arsed, and he despised himself for it. Go big or go home. But no one was going home until they'd dealt with the MOAD. One way or another.

Skyler looked at the knife. "At least I'm not a killer," he said, and walked away to the far side of the lentil patch.

Whistling *Scarborough Fair.*

Mic drop.

Cunt.

*

The problem was Jack *had* killed someone.

He'd killed the guy who was Skyler before Skyler came along.

*

He went and found Alexei, who'd gone to bed in his coffin. The coffins were cavities set into the floor, evenly spaced around the aft end of the hab. They had hammocks inside that swiveled on gimbals, so 'down' would always be *down* even when the *SoD* was under thrust. In your coffin you were meant to have the expectation of privacy.

Jack threw back the cover of Alexei's coffin unceremoniously.

"Hey!" Alexei said. "What if I was wanking, eh?"

Jack sat down on the dirty floor at the edge of the coffin. "He knows." It burst out of him. "He fucking knows."

"Chto?"

"Skyler knows I did Lance in," Jack said. He briefly related their conversation.

Alexei scratched his close-shaven head. "Let's review," he yawned. "Lance was an NXC agent." Jack nodded. "He murdered your friend Ollie to steal the MPD drive technology." Nod. "He tried to sabotage the *SoD* during construction."

"Well, maybe."

"He was …" Alexei searched for the English term. "A grade-A pillock."

"Beyond a doubt."

"So that is three and a half reasons you don't lose sleep about it. Nor I don't want to lose my sleep, either. Goodnight."

Jack started to wring his hands, stopped himself. "Here's the problem. All those 'facts' about Lance? I heard them

48

from none other than Skyler Taft."

Alexei's eyes opened wider. "You think he lied."

Jack nodded wretchedly. He had not thought of that at the time. But in the long months since then, his conscience had refused to let him alone. Lance lived in his memory like the innocent Iraqis who'd died when Jack bombed them in 2003, based on faulty intelligence. He'd never seen those villagers. They were dust before his Tornado GR-4 flashed over the horizon and away. But he had seen Lance, and the frozen face in his memory whispered, *You wronged me, Jack Kildare. You flew off the handle and I died.*

Now intrigued, Alexei sat up in his coffin. "Why would Skyler lie? What did he gain with Lance dead?"

"Need you ask? He took his place!"

"He got wrong end of that bargain. Dead man is better off than passenger in this tub."

Jack said impatiently, "It's bound to have been some internal NXC fight. These creeps are always maneuvering for advantage. But the point is, Skyler used me to put his rival out of the way." Unconsciously, he started to wring his hands again. "He set me up, and I played my part, like a good little soldier boy."

Alexei grasped Jack's hands, stilling them. "Me, too. I was a good little soldier boy." The bomber pilot momentarily looked out of the haggard cosmonaut's eyes. "But no more, eh? No more."

"No more," Jack echoed. He freed his hands from Alexei's. He wasn't as comfortable with physical contact as the Russian was. "No more good little soldier boys. But he thinks he's got me in his power. That's what I can't stand. He's holding this over my head, and he's just now let me know that if I don't play nice …"

"If you don't play nice, what'll he do to you? *What*, Jack? He'll tell Kate, maybe?" Alexei pulled a faux-horrified face.

"Maybe he already has," Jack said.

"No, he hasn't," Alexei said with certainty. On this point, Jack believed him.

Yet he said, "And what if he does?"

"What if he does? We're six hundred million klicks from home. There are no police out here."

Jack managed a smirk. "That's a better way of looking at it," he said, although he was a bit unnerved by the cold glint in Alexei's gray eyes.

He left Alexei to get his sleep and plodded towards the bridge, still worrying. It was all very well to point out that Skyler couldn't hurt *him*. But Jack's parents were elderly and alone. The NXC's power on Earth extended beyond the borders of the United States. It certainly extended into the UK. What if Skyler took it into his head to order up an 'accident' for John and Helen Kildare? Various ghastly scenarios danced in Jack's mind. The worst of it was, he knew they were all warped reflections of what he'd done to Lance Garner.

Disconnected the LOX heater in his spacesuit.

Lance's head had frozen. His eyes had burst in miniature eruptions of ice crystals. He'd died without knowing what was happening to him, or why.

It had been underhanded. Cowardly. Worthy of Lance Garner himself, when he shot Oliver Meeks in his wheelchair.

Jack could never make that up to Lance. And right now, he didn't feel like he could make it up to himself, either.

CHAPTER 7

Skyler lay in his coffin with the lid open. Peas, strung up on stakes, blocked his view of the rest of the hab. He imagined he was lying in a garden, back on Earth. The roar of the fans could be wind, and the throb of the steam turbines might be ... um ...

It was no good. He couldn't forget they were cruising towards Jupiter, straight into the crosshairs of whoever or whatever inhabited the MOAD. He felt the bottomless, hostile abyss of space cupping the *SoD* like an uncomfortable garment.

He closed the lid of his coffin. The LEDs around the inside of the lid came on, and Skyler's thoughts skipped from the threats outside the ship to the threat within.

He rolled over in his hammock and reached underneath it. His fingers found a tab of duct tape and peeled it back. He retrieved his gun.

Flopping on his back again, he held the gun up and scrutinized it with dislike. It was a Glock subcompact, the trigger grip modified so he would be able to shoot it even wearing a spacesuit. The ten-round magazine held frangible bullets that would go through a person, but not a wall. The NXC had insisted he bring it. Skyler hated guns. The damn thing had to be cleaned and lubed at regular intervals, in secret. He had often thought about just chucking it out of the airlock. I mean, if you wind up facing hostile aliens with a *Glock,* basically you are already very, very fucked.

But of course the NXC had foreseen that he might have to use the gun against his fellow crew members.

And now it looked like (as usual!) they'd been prescient.

Jack Kildare had practically threatened his life with a potato knife ten minutes ago.

Stay cool, Jack, Skyler thought. I don't want the truth to come out, any more than you do.

He sucked in a breath, stifling the beginnings of a sob.

He sat up. It was just possible to sit up in a coffin, if you were only 5'8". He stuffed the Glock into the waistband of his shorts—something the shooting instructors always told you not to do; fuck 'em. His t-shirt was too tight-fitting to hide the gun's outline. He tied a long-sleeved shell around his waist. Very preppy.

He had to find somewhere better to hide the damn thing.

If Jack suspected Skyler had a weapon, his coffin was the *first* place he'd look.

Skyler climbed out of his coffin and headed for the aft stairs.

He had a hiding-place in mind.

And maybe he had something else in mind, too, but doesn't everyone? Who on this ship wouldn't sell their soul for a cuddle right now? Don't judge.

*

Hannah was *still* cleaning up globs of mash that had baked onto the inside of the turbine cabinet when her still exploded during the HERF crisis. The gooey lumps of sugar and starch had hardened to a rock-like consistency in the heat of the turbine room. She'd just chipped off a big lump with a screwdriver when Kate Menelaou slipped out of the keel tube.

Hannah yelped in shock. Pulling herself together, she said, "Oh, hi, Kate. Are you off duty?"

What was Kate doing here? She hadn't visited

Engineering in *months!* Well, apart from weekly inspections, which Hannah had advance warning of.

Hannah kicked the turbine cabinet shut, which sent her floating in the opposite direction.

"Just thought I'd drop in," Kate said. She floated down to Hannah's level and braked her drift by catching her sleeve.

Kate Menelaou was a tall, angular woman of fifty-two, a rare female top achiever in the male-dominated astronaut corps. Her last name might be Greek but she looked more Nordic, with the bone structure that you needed to carry off a blunt-cut bob. She intimidated Hannah on every level. Ironically, Hannah was used to dealing with male bosses; she still hadn't worked out how to handle a *female* boss, apart from keeping her distance.

"Whatcha doing there?" Kate said, nodding at the screwdriver in Hannah's hand.

"Um, nothing," Hannah said. Her mind was a blank.

"Oh, that's good," Kate said. "So we can hang out and chat for a while." She drifted down over the top of the turbine cabinet. "Phew, it smells a bit in here. Where's that coming from?"

"There was, uh, a spill. I'm cleaning up."

"Great." Kate spotted Hannah's squeeze bottle duct-taped to the wall. "God, I'm thirsty," she mused. "Mind if I steal some of what you're having?"

"No," Hannah yelped.

Kate arched her blonde eyebrows.

Hannah's stomach knotted. Sheer terror left her speechless. For years and years, while she rose to the top of her profession at NASA, she had kept her drinking a secret. She'd had two simple rules. #1: No drinking at work. #2:

No drinking at home. Religiously followed, these rules confined her to 'after-work drinks,' which might last until after midnight, and end in blackouts, but which could not swallow her whole life.

But there were no tequila bars on the *SoD*. No dives. No anonymous bar stools at T.G.I. Friday's. Here, work was home and home was work and Hannah had nowhere to escape her anxieties.

So she'd cast both her rules to the winds. She'd figured everything would be fine as long as she was careful.

Like all carefully engineered systems, it had worked great until it didn't.

"Is there something you want to tell me, Hannah?" Kate said.

Hannah gave up. "Ma'am, the smell is coming from my still. It's in the housekeeping turbine cabinet. It exploded during the HERF incident. Stray sparks don't play well with alcohol." She touched the burn on her left hand. The cabinet door had absorbed the explosion. She'd gotten burnt later, when she was frantically prying the hot wire off the heat exchanger pipe. "I know it was against regulations, and clearly it was a safety hazard, so I've mothballed the project." This was a lie. Most of her waking hours since the HERF incident had been occupied with getting the still up and running again. "I apologize for violating regulations, and I'll fully understand if you want to report me to Mission Control." She stopped there, heart pounding. She felt like she might actually pass out from shame.

But Kate showed no sign of being surprised by Hannah's confession. "I assume that's the product?" she said, indicating the squeeze bottle.

Hannah nodded.

Kate worked the bottle out of the duct tape holder, tilted it to her lips, and sucked. Her face reddened. She coughed. Droplets of Hannah's precious moonshine spurted out of her mouth. "Whew!" she gasped. "Holy fucking shit! Woman, what the hell is *in* that?"

"Mostly potatoes. A bit of grain, for variety." Hannah plucked an absorbent wipe out of her pocket and automatically chased down the floating droplets. Kate helped, capturing them with her sleeve.

"Kicks like a fucking mule. Looks like I am definitely gonna have to write you up, Hannah." Kate caught a globule in her mouth. "It is a crime to not drink this on the rocks."

Hannah faced her in the air. Disbelief and apprehension warred with dawning hope. "How long have you known?"

"A few months?" Kate said. "One time, when you pinched water from the irrigation system, you forgot to turn the spigot off all the way. I got a drop right in the eye. Then there were the humidity spikes. Oh, and I spotted some bits of grain in the water for the algae tanks. I guess you flushed the residues down the crapper? It went all the way around the sterilization loop and came back." She shrugged in the air, and caught herself on the top of the turbine cabinet. "Little things, y'know?"

"But you never said anything!"

"Why would I? You do your job. You do a *great* job, if I haven't mentioned that recently. If it ain't broke …"

"But the regulations …"

"Screw the regulations," Kate said dispassionately. "We're hundreds of millions of kilometers from Earth. We almost died in that HERF attack. We may die in the next attack. Oh yeah, there's going to be another one. The analysts are pretty sure of that. But we won't know it's coming until it comes. So, in the meantime? I would dearly love a glass of your 'sourdough bread.' If you're willing to share."

The truth was, Hannah did *not* want to share. If she gave Kate some, there'd be less for her. She might run out before the still got through its current fermentation cycle.

But she dared not demur. Kate seemed to assume her still was a mere hobby, like Alexei's vaping.

Alcoholics were selfish about their booze. Ordinary people shared.

So Hannah had to act like a drinking buddy was what she'd always wanted.

"Ma'am, I would be honored. How about I go get some ice?"

*

Skyler flew through Secondary Life Support, which had been Xiang Peixun's domain. Giles had stepped up to take over the dead man's duties. He nodded amiably as Skyler passed.

Popping out into the storage module, Skyler paused to consider what he was going to say to Hannah.

You've got a lot of space back here. I was wondering, can I stash this somewhere?

Well, yes, actually, it IS a gun.

Please don't freak out. I can explain.

Please let me explain.

Please.

Oh, Hannah.

Please.

He recognized that this was a fairly desperate ploy. Asking

a woman to hide a gun for you? That had to be one of the least slick romantic moves ever. But this was *Hannah*. They'd been so close before … before Skyler wrecked it by lying to her about his own role in Lance's death. She'd asked for the truth, and he'd stonewalled her. That had badly damaged their relationship, reducing it to a hollow farce of superficial friendliness.

So he'd tell her the truth now. Roll the dice. Throw himself on her mercy.

He flew into the engineering module.

She wasn't there.

She must be in the turbine room.

He flew to the aft keel tube … and braked, gripping the edge of the tube.

He heard Kate's voice from below.

The white noise of the fans made it impossible to catch her words, but at this point, Skyler could identify each crew member by the way they *breathed*, let alone their intonations.

God*dammit*.

Swallowing disappointment, he considered going away. He could come back later, when Hannah would hopefully be alone.

But on the spur of the moment, he drifted into the keel tube. Braking with fingers and toes, he edged aft until he could catch what the women were saying.

*

"So which of them have you slept with?" Kate said. She smiled mischievously at Hannah, her eyes glassy from the moonshine.

"Oh my God," Hannah gasped. "Don't tell me you've …?"

FELIX R. SAVAGE

"Of course I have."

"But the regulations …"

"There isn't actually a regulation against sex on a spaceship. There never has been. You're just expected to be discreet. God, I could tell you stories, going back to the days of the space shuttle …" Kate sighed nostalgically. "Anyway, on a ship this size, discretion is a lot easier."

"Obviously! I had no idea."

"Jack and Meili were getting it on for a while. That's cooled off now."

"Wow." Hannah shook her head in amazement at how blind she'd been. Like a little mole, hiding away in her hole back here. "Actually, I can see that," she realized. "Jack and Meili, yeah. But *you*, Kate?"

"Oh, I haven't slept with Jack," Kate said. "I thought about it, and I'm sure he thought about it, too, after the Meili thing went south. I mean, he's attractive, right?"

"Right."

"He's got that blond beast thing going on. But ultimately, he's just not my type. Too right-stuff, too straight-edge. It must be what they teach them at English public schools."

"I don't think he went to Eton or anything."

"No, but you know what I mean. I prefer bad boys."

"So," Hannah pretended to ponder, "Giles?"

Both of them cracked up. Although she knew it was mean—poor Giles! He couldn't help being a dork, with a receding hairline no less—Hannah laughed until she cried. It had been so long since she had a good chat with another woman. All right: a *drunken* chat.

"No, I'm afraid poor Giles's only friend is Ms. Rosy Palmer," Kate sighed, wiping her eyes. They were bobbling around at ease in the turbine room, squeeze bottles in hand.

"So that only leaves one guy," Hannah said. "*Alexei?*"

Kate smirked. "It could have been Peixun."

"Apart from the fact that he's dead."

"Or Skyler."

Hannah was tongue-tied. She hadn't even thought of Skyler and Kate as a possibility. She wondered how she would feel about that.

Kate put paid to her nervous imaginings. "Skyler's cute, but that really would be cradle-robbing. No, you're right: it's Alexei. Didn't you guess? Really?"

"No, but that explains a lot."

"It does?"

"It explains why you guys can't stand each other. Who broke up with who? If it's OK to ask."

"No one broke up with anyone," Kate said, her eyes widening. "I screwed him this morning before they EVA'ed."

"Oh. My. God."

"Oh, hell yeah. He's an animal. And you're right, I can't stand him, on a personal level. That makes it spicier."

"Kate, this is eye-opening. You're *almost* as screwed-up as I am." Back on Earth, Hannah used to pick up strangers when she was drunk. It was a terrible habit she'd never been able to kick until she boarded the *SoD*. Out here, there were no strangers.

"I hope I haven't completely lost your respect," Kate said.

Hannah hastened to assure her she hadn't. "If anything, I'm in awe. Alexei scares me."

"Yeah, he can be intense. He's actually an idealistic kind of guy. Beats up on himself when he doesn't live up to his own ideals. He and I are similar in that way, I guess."

Kate's expression softened as she offered these insights into Alexei's personality. Hannah thought to herself that the mission commander was in denial. That wasn't how you talked about a friend with benefits that you couldn't stand on a personal level.

But Hannah understood. Kate was in a difficult position. As mission commander, she *couldn't* allow her relationship with Alexei to become anything more than a sexual outlet. She risked losing the crew's respect as it was, if it got out.

"I've never really gotten to know Alexei," Hannah said diplomatically.

"Sometimes I think I don't really know him, either," Kate sighed. Then her expression changed to a naughty grin. "So fess up. Which of them are you screwing?"

None of them, was the truth. Hannah did think about sex—difficult not to, when you'd been celibate for two years—but only one man appeared in her fantasies, and that was Skyler. Now, with moonshine-enhanced imagination, she pictured his quick, shy smile. His beautiful musician's hands. He had a beautiful cock, too. She'd seen him naked a couple of times … difficult not to, given the laughable provisions for privacy on the *SoD* … and wished she hadn't, because those glimpses made it even harder not to fantasize about him. He was awkward, like her, a nerd, like her, and smart as all get-out, like her. But the barriers between them were insurmountable.

"Let me guess," Kate said. She was not as unobservant as Hannah had always assumed, after all. "Our boy-Fed?"

Hannah momentarily thought about confessing her unrequited lust for Skyler. But Kate's tone of voice decided her against it. *Our boy-Fed.* As the *SoD's* resident spook, Skyler ranked even lower in the pecking order than Giles. And there was the cradle-robbing thing. Hannah didn't want Kate to lose all respect for her, just when they were getting along so well.

"Nope," she said, with a salacious leer. "Jack."

The spur-of-the-moment lie seemed like a safe one. If Jack had broken up with Meili, it was plausible that Hannah might have hooked up with him. And he *was* very straight-edge—maybe even in some sense an English gentleman ... Hannah felt sure he would defend her honor, if unfounded rumors got back to him.

"I don't blame you! He *is* hot," Kate conceded. "He makes the effort to stay in shape. His lean mass numbers are the best of anyone's."

"And he's got that sexy accent."

"No, there I have to disagree. The accent drives me batshit. I would actually do him, too, if he would keep his mouth shut before, during, and afterwards." Kate waggled her eyebrows, and Hannah succumbed to a fit of the giggles.

*

Skyler flew silently back up the keel tube. He'd heard enough.

CHAPTER 8

From then on, 'girls' night in' became a regular feature of life on the *SoD*. Kate invited Meili to join them, and although Hannah resented sharing her booze with yet another person, Meili turned out to be a cool chick once she let her hair down. She had a hidden sense of humor. And when she dished about Jack's performance in bed, it made even Hannah's eyes pop. Fortunately, it turned out that Hannah's lie about sleeping with Jack was safe: Meili and Jack were barely on speaking terms these days.

"He is *all yours,*" Meili said. "He was horrible to me when Peixun died. He doesn't have a heart for others. And he farts in bed!"

She chortled, pink in the face. Meili was not much of a drinker, mercifully for Hannah. A swallow or two of their new concoction, the Sourdough Loaf—cold tea, reconstituted fruit juice, and Ginsburg label moonshine—got her buzzed. She cried inconsolably sometimes, and blamed it on the moonshine, but always came back for another 'tiny drink'.

Kate never once mentioned the word 'alcoholism.' She seemed to accept that Hannah had built a still because she was a rule-breaker who liked a nightcap—Scotty in the engine room of the *Enterprise,* sneaking drams of whiskey!—rather than an addict who needed booze in order to function. And the more Hannah hung out with Kate, the more she came to like and believe in this version of herself. After all, it was true! She *was* a rule-breaker, a glass-ceiling-smasher, making it up as she went along. So was Kate, and so was Meili. They were historic achievers, laying down new markers for women in generations to come. And they were expected to be perfect as well?!? Can you say double standard?

All the time the *SoD* hurtled closer to Jupiter. After two years of doing not much except farming, it was hard to grasp, but they were almost there.

In six days they'd burn into Jupiter orbit.

In *five* days.

Four.

Three.

Right on cue, Mission Control started playing Gustav Holst's 'Jupiter, the Bringer of Jollity' at every shift change. It was the last thing anyone needed, as no one associated Jupiter with jollity anymore. The tune got on the crew's nerves so much that Kate begged Mission Control to quit it. "Give us Rick Astley, the Bee Gees, or even Giles's crap ... anything but this!"

Two.

That night they had a bit too much. Well, Kate and Meili had a bit too much. For Hannah, there was no such thing as too much, but she was careful not to let the other women suspect that. Meili went yawning to her coffin, saying she had to get some sleep in preparation for tying down the plants on the morrow.

Left alone, Hannah and Kate floated in the turbine room. Their foreheads touched, and their hands rested on each other's shoulders. Kate's forehead was hot. She said in a hoarse whisper, "This thing. This MOAD ... *thing.*"

She trailed off. That was all she seemed able to say. But Hannah understood. She squeezed Kate's shoulders, silently letting her know: You don't have to bear the burden by yourself. You're the commander, but I'm right here, supporting you. You're not alone.

During their two-year journey, the *SoD* had ceased to be news. Out of sight was out of mind, and the internet news aggregators had reverted to covering the Earth Party's doings in breathless detail. But now, as the *SoD* neared Jupiter, the eyes of the world were once again trained on the ship. The entire human race was watching Kate, judging her, counting on her.

No wonder she was nervous.

"We're gonna have to get so lucky to make it through this," she muttered.

Hannah put on an Obi Wan Kenobi voice. "There is no such thing as luck, in my experience."

Kate laughed, but Hannah could see she didn't get the reference. Skyler would have.

Oh, Skyler. With a bit of booze in her, Hannah saw very clearly why it would never work between them. She'd known it as far back as Johnson Space Center, actually. Skyler didn't drink.

*

Skyler used the encrypted comms setup installed on the bridge by the NXC to file his reports. Kate normally allowed him to have the bridge to himself at these times. It only took a few minutes, as he just had to type up the paragraphs he'd already composed in his head.

But the Ka communications system also enabled video transmissions, and there was a webcam over the left seat.

Skyler floated in the seat, gazing into the camera. He wasn't wearing the harness, but he had his bare toes hooked into the foot tethers. In his right hand he held a clunky object resembling a pen with a metal nib.

"So, we're at burn minus twenty-three," he said. In 23 hours, the *SoD* would perform its Jupiter orbit injection burn. "Hannah has cranked the reactor's power level up to 95%."

It hurt to say her name, but none of that pain came out in his sardonic, even tone.

"The main turbine is spun up, giving us 1.1 gigawatts of electrical output. We've topped off all the power systems. Fuel cells and batteries are fully charged. We've electrolyzed water stores to fill the reactant tanks with liquefied H2 and O2."

Which left the *SoD's* external tanks of water two-thirds empty. They'd stay that way until they recovered Thing One and Thing Two from the surface of Europa.

"One hour ago, Jack flipped the ship so that our engine bells are facing Jupiter …"

And Skyler, on the bridge, was now facing home. The ridiculous little portholes on the bridge had turned into yellow gems, glowing with the distant sun's light. The unaccustomed brightness showed up just how grubby the bridge had gotten in two years. The paint had worn off the instruments most often used. Leaf fragments, crumbs, and flies wandered in the rays from the portholes.

48 minutes ago, this very same sunlight would have bathed Director Flaherty of the NXC as he got out of his car at Langley. The most powerful man in the United States, by some reports, still drove a second-hand Crown Vic. In *another* 48 minutes, Skyler's transmission would light up Flaherty's own encrypted comms system.

"But you know all this stuff anyway."

Everything Skyler just said had already been reported by Kate to Mission Control, which meant Flaherty would have it by the time he got Skyler's message.

"So let's skip to the good part."

Skyler lifted the object in his right hand, inserted the 'nib' between his lips, and inhaled. He blew a cloud of vapor away from the camera.

"Kate's getting up to her old tricks again. What do I mean? Divide and conquer, boss. Divide and conquer. She's started this new thing of women-only meetings in Engineering. Jack calls them hen parties. British slang is awesome, isn't it? *Hen parties*. What do they talk about back there? Boys, clothes, and make-up, apparently."

Skyler wouldn't have believed it, himself, before he eavesdropped on one of these chats. Hannah was a rocket scientist. She didn't do girly stuff. Skyler *knew* her … or, he had thought he knew her. That was before he found out she was sleeping with Jack Kildare. So anything was possible, really.

But to assume that the hen parties were innocent gab-fests would be to underestimate Katharine Menelaou, a mistake Skyler was far too canny to make.

"Here's how I read it," he said to the camera. "We weren't impressed with Kate's response to the HERF incident. By *we* I mean Jack, Alexei, and myself. I'm leaving out Giles, mostly because he was shocked by the HERF and remained unconscious throughout the episode, but also because I'm not actually sure he's male."

Skyler snickered. He dragged on the e-cigarette again and blew more vapor off-screen.

"So Kate's on the back foot. She's lost the trust of her

pilot and her co-pilot, and she knows it. What can she do about that? Nothing … oh, but wait for it! *Hen parties.* Now she's got her claws into Hannah. And I don't need to remind you, sir, that in theory all crew members are equal, but the reactor and propulsion systems specialist is more equal than others. That's the genius of it. If Kate's got Hannah on her side, she can tell the rest of us to take a flying leap."

A ray of sunlight was getting into Skyler's eyes. He leaned back in the air and said to the camera, "So where is Meili in all this? I'll be honest, sir, I'm not sure. But I'm watching her very closely."

In his peripheral vision, he caught a movement. *Wrap it up.*

"That's about all I've got today, sir. I'll await your response, but I may not be able to transmit again until after the big burn."

He exhaled a last cloud of vapor, straight into the camera.

"Damn, this thing is a monster," he said. "Later, sir." He reached through the fog and hit the button to end his transmission.

Alexei Ivanov descended from the ceiling of the bridge, where he had been floating outside of the camera's field of vision. His shaved head and shredded bare shoulders gave him a dangerous aspect, like a shark slicing down through the water. "That was OK," he said, grudgingly.

"I thought it was damn good," Skyler said. *"This* is good." He held up the e-cigarette Alexei had let him borrow. "Can I keep it?"

"No," Alexei said. He took it back.

"I used to smoke," Skyler said. "I never made the transition to vaping. It's not the same, but it's good."

"You can go now," Alexei invited him, pointing to the keel tube.

"I'm waiting for them to get back to me," Skyler complained.

"How long will that take?" Alexei answered his own question. "Almost two hours." Skyler's message would take 48 minutes to reach Earth. Then there was turnaround time and the 48-minute trip back. "They'll send you an encrypted email, as usual. I will tell you when it gets here. Then you'll decrypt it in front of me or Jack. We want to know what he says. No more of this secret squirrel bullshit."

Skyler sighed. "Only if you let me borrow your e-cig again," he said.

"Fuck, you make tough bargain." Alexei grinned suddenly, and slapped Skyler on the shoulder. "Now go away. We need to prepare for the burn."

Skyler floated down the keel tube. He was cross with himself for going along with Alexei and Jack's plan to get the NXC on their side. Everything had been so much simpler when he was just an astrophysicist. God, how he missed quietly looking through telescopes at stars.

He emerged from the keel tube head first, which was not recommended, but he always forgot. The main hab wheeled around him as if he'd stuck his head into a vast spin dryer. At 3 RPMs, the outer wall, a.k.a. the floor, moved so fast that the plants blurred. However, the hub of this vast drum hardly moved at all. The tops of Staircases 1, 2, and 3, which spiraled up the forward wall, rotated slowly around the outside of the keel tube.

On the top step of Staircase 1 stood Jack.

On the top step of Staircase 3 stood Kate.

They rotated past Skyler, staring at him.

Skyler felt a sudden jolt of dread. Then he produced a cheerful smile. He got himself turned around, dropped his feet through the hexagonal lattice, and waited for Staircase 2—the only vacant one—to reach him. He slid down onto the top step, grabbing for the handrail.

"All yours," he called to Kate and Jack.

With the Coriolis force seeming to pull his head away from his feet, he waited to see which of them would go first.

CHAPTER 9

Here we go.

Here we fucking go.

Burn parameters received from Mission Control. They match the ones Alexei and I generated. More importantly, they match *each other.* Houston and Star City don't always agree, especially now the NXC is running the show in Houston, but today they're in lockstep down to five decimal places. The whole human race is singing the same song today.

Here we go.

Everything—*everything,* from the tomato plants to the kit in the labs—is tied down. At least I hope it all is. That was Meili's job. I told her to get Giles to help her. She always tries to do too much on her own.

"Here we go," Jack muttered, aloud this time.

Burn minus zero.

Tense as a runner in the blocks, he instinctively hesitated, waiting for Mission Control to greenlight the burn. The training went so deep. Without that faraway voice saying "You're cleared," he felt paralyzed.

But Mission Control was 48 minutes away.

There'd be no real-time guidance for the *SoD* on this burn. They were on their own.

He glanced left at Kate, in the center seat, and cocked one side of his mouth quizzically. He meant it as an acknowledgement of her authority. After all, she was the mission commander.

She just shrugged. "Go for it," she said.

With an inward sigh, Jack keyed in the throttle command.

Two hundred meters aft, Oliver Meeks's engine woke like a sleeping volcano. Electrical impulses belched plasma, battling the *SoD's* 40,000 kph velocity. Thrust gravity settled like an intangible blanket over Jack, feather-light. He watched the position, rate and fuel indicators with total absorption, blind to the breathtaking view of Jupiter that now edged onto the optic screen.

They were going to nip in front of the gas giant, using its gravitational field as a gigantic brake, so the *SoD* would plop into a nice round orbit intersecting Europa.

*

Skyler was at his station. The joke was, he didn't have a station. As Lance's replacement, he should have been on the bridge, but even Skyler admitted that the idea of him co-piloting on a crucial burn was ludicrous. So Alexei had taken the left seat, and Skyler had taken Alexei's station in the storage module.

Five empty spacesuits hung on the curved wall of the module. (Jack, Alexei, and Kate kept theirs on the bridge.) Instead of wiggling in the breeze from the fans, like Skyler was accustomed to seeing, the arms and legs of the suits hung down. Gravity, of a sort, had returned to the regions of the *SoD* that were formerly in freefall. The burn was generating 0.1 G of thrust gravity.

Skyler stood at the workbench they used for spacesuit maintenance and repair. Singing to himself—"I wrote me a letter to Syracuse; it was a letter full of lies"—he plugged his laptop into the power outlet above the workbench.

The steam turbines whined loudly. Skyler thought about Hannah, back in Engineering, watching her displays with the absorbed expression he adored on her. Then he put her out of his mind.

That was personal.

This was important.

He opened the laptop and booted it.

He'd received a reply from Director Flaherty. Jack and Alexei had forced him to decrypt it in front of them. But all it had contained was a terse acknowledgement of his report.

Flaherty had correctly deduced that Skyler could no longer guarantee the privacy of his own transmissions. After all, he'd *blown smoke* straight into the camera. Although not a prearranged signal, it had successfully conveyed to Flaherty that Skyler was transmitting under duress.

So the director had sent his *real* reply in the form of an attachment—an innocent-seeming video of his dog, Peaches, catching a stick.

Jack and Alexei had made Skyler open this, too, and had viewed it with incredulous amusement.

"This is a how-to video for us to catch the MOAD, maybe?" Alexei had said, and Jack had added: "I've got a dog—a spaniel; he can catch better than that."

Did those two really think the NXC couldn't communicate covertly with their field agent? Skyler knew exactly what to do when he saw the video. Flaherty had used steganography, hiding a file within a file, to let any prying eyes see Peaches play catch, while slipping the real message right past them.

Now, Skyler ran the video through his NSA-developed steganography decoding second-level decryption program.

It turned into *another* attachment, and a .txt file containing a wall of text.

As he read the text, his mouth dropped open in

astonishment. His heart beat faster.

*

Hannah paced in the engineering module. It was a beguiling novelty to be able to *pace* down here, instead of floating. A tenth of a gee wasn't much. She bounced off the floor at every step, and came down slowly. But it was better than sitting still. She was tense about this burn, mentally scrolling through all the things that might go wrong.

She wished she hadn't made up her mind to do this sober. She had a headache right behind her eyes. It disrupted the sense of oneness with the ship that she needed to feel.

She paced towards the reactor controls on the port wall. Then back towards the steam turbine controls on the other wall. Every round-trip, she saw the same thing:

100%.

The reactor, turbines, and MPD engine were all running flat out.

Running like honey.

Tension ratcheting down a notch, she glanced up at the personal decorations she'd hung in the module. Her sister Bethany, Bethany's husband David, and their kids Isabel and Nathan smiled from the photograph above the dollar meter. Imagine what they'd say if they could see her now! Above the hexagonal array hung an origami Star of David—a present from a class of first-graders in Israel, who were now third-graders.

Gravity couldn't flatten the grin that curved Hannah's lips upwards.

Star light, star bright, alien spacecraft in the night.

Coming to getcha.

*

"Holy crap," Skyler breathed. Astonishment shaded into anger. "You tell me this *now?*"

Director Flaherty wrote:

OK, Taft, here we go. Read this, and then install the attached program on your laptop.

Remember the power distribution units?

Sure Skyler did. Those units had been the proximate cause of the sabotage incident in low Earth orbit. During construction of the *SoD,* the ullage motors had unexpectedly fired. The *SoD* would have drifted away into space and been lost forever, if not for the quick actions of Jack Kildare. The NXC had zeroed in on the power distribution units in the ullage motors. No way those things had misfired on their own. It was sabotage, no doubt about it. But their investigation had run aground on the shoals of the *SoD's* globally dispersed supply chain. They couldn't trace the sabotage back to any one country, let alone any one individual. And they'd been further hampered by the fact that the actual, faulty PDUs from the *SoD* had vanished.

We've found them, Director Flaherty wrote. *The fucking Russians had them all along.*

Skyler closed his eyes and shook his head from side to side. Another classic entry in the annals of international cooperation.

He opened his eyes and read on.

The ISS station chief at the time was a Russian. Grigor Nikolin, remember him? He made the PDUs disappear. Sent them back home for analysis. Roscosmos determined that the PDUs, surprise surprise, were not manufactured to NASA's specs. The Chinese company that made them, which conveniently no longer exists, added a couple extra components. Some specialized control circuits ... and an antenna.

There was no reason whatsoever for those components to have an antenna—unless it was to receive radio signals.

There's our smoking gun, Flaherty went on. *Proof of sabotage. So what do the Russkis do? Motherfuckers SIT ON THE EVIDENCE for TWO FUCKING YEARS.*

Their excuse is they needed the time to analyze the software loaded into the control circuits. That's bullshit. We could have done it in a week. They were stringing the Chinese along, blackmailing them, and you can take that to the bank. Anyway, they finally came across with the goods, I'm assuming because time is getting critical.

Here's what we now know. The PDUs contained malware that could be triggered with a Wi-Fi signal, causing the ullage motors to fire. The signal would have been sent from a device that was in physical proximity to the SoD. That narrows it down to someone in the orbital construction yard or on the ISS. Unfortunately, that includes all *the present crew members except Hannah Ginsburg and you.*

Now for the guesswork.

Skyler knew what was coming next. He raised his gaze from his laptop and glanced around the storage module in horror. The air-handling system … the algae tanks that provided the crew's oxygen … the sensors that monitored air quality … the nitrogen tank under the floor of the storage module … *any* of it might be ripe for sabotage.

Assume there's malware all over that ship like flies on shit, Director Flaherty wrote. *That's what we get for outsourcing critical parts of the supply chain to China. But don't panic.*

Don't panic, boss? DON'T PANIC?

Our belief is the saboteur has orders to wait until certain conditions are met before he or she takes action. Those conditions will be related to recovery of the MOAD. So you still have time to save the day.

The attached program is a present from the NSA. It's an extremely sophisticated malware scanner.

Incidentally, this is why the Russians finally decided to share. They couldn't write anything like this. They may have the world's best hackers, but the world's best programmers work for the NSA.

The attached .exe file was named simply: BUGSWATTER.

Install the program on your laptop and run it. It'll remotely scan all laptops, iPods, Android devices, anything with Wi-Fi or Bluetooth capability. When it finds the malware trigger, it will identify the suspect device.

Your job is to deal with the device, and the person who owns it.

Skyler bit his knuckles. He'd believed for a long time that the saboteur was Xiang Peixun. So maybe the threat was already gone—chopped in half!

But Flaherty knew, of course, that Xiang was dead, and that didn't seem to reassure *him* any.

Because Xiang, obviously, hadn't taken his laptop or any other device he may have owned with him.

Skyler's gaze tracked to the bank of lockers on the opposite side of the storage module. Xiang's laptop was in there. He had also had an MP3 player. Skyler had snuck that up his sleeve when they cleaned out Xiang's coffin, thinking he might want it if his own iPod broke at some point. It was now in Skyler's own coffin. It appeared to be loaded with hundreds of Chinese pop songs and nothing else. But what if one of those songs *was the trigger?* Skyler could've inadvertently blown up the ship, scrolling through Xiang's playlists!

Teeth chattering, he installed BUGSWATTER on his laptop.

Run.

The *SoD* fell towards Jupiter, struggling like an bird in a gale. Skyler gave not a thought to the interplay of mighty forces hurling him through space. He only had eyes for the progress bar on his screen.

*

Burn plus one.

Jack flexed his shoulders, rolling out the stiffness that had set in with one full hour of ferocious concentration on his instruments. He smiled with pure pleasure at the inertial navigation display that proved they were where he wanted them to be. "We're on track for orbit insertion," he announced. "Alexei, check the star sights."

"Roger," Alexei said, swiveling the telescope's viewfinder to his eye.

Kate touched the intercom. "Reactor status, Hannah?"

Hannah's voice came from Engineering. "Steady," she said. "Need more power? I could crank this baby up to eleven."

Jack laughed, not specifically at the Spinal Tap reference, but because he recognized the note of elation in her voice. He felt the same way. The *Spirit of Destiny* was really strutting her stuff now. This huge, magnificent burn would justify the mission all on its own. Screw the taxpayers.

An alarm shrilled.

CHAPTER 10

In Engineering, several alarms shrilled at once.

Red lights strobed on the steam turbine control display.

Shaft overspeed.

It was happening again, it was goddamn happening again, and this time it was the little housekeeping turbine *and* the big-ass drive turbine, which fed the MPD engine's voracious appetite for electricity.

The fucking circuit-breakers had failed again! Both turbines were about to burst their hearts like racehorses spurred across the finish line. In Hannah's mind, the steam drums ruptured in a catastrophic explosion.

She cannoned across the module and threw her weight on the manual shutdown lever, forcing it down to the OFF position before her terrifying vision could become reality.

The shaft speed ticked lower.

And the reactor was still pumping out 100% of output.

She had mere seconds before it would overload the primary heat exchanger. A steam drum explosion would be a wet fart compared to *that* shit-show.

Voices bawled from the intercom speaker. "Hannah! HANNAH! We have lost all electronic controls! Confirm whether you still have reactor and turbine controls!"

She already knew the controls were gone, because it was happening again, like faceplanting on a curb in a drunken haze, and this time she didn't need anyone to tell her what to do. There was only *one* thing to do and she had to do it now, now, *now*—

Teeth bared, hair whipping around her face, she toppled towards the reactor controls and stabbed the manual scram

78

button.

A deafening *WHANNGGG!* reverberated through the ship as the springs drove the control rods home.

*

Skyler screamed. The noise sounded like the hand of some vengeful space god had slapped the ship.

Terror gripped him. He automatically slammed his laptop closed. And yet his first thought was of Hannah, and another detached part of his mind noted that fact, and felt proud that he was still capable of putting her first, even though she was screwing Jack. He floundered across the storage module. As he moved, he came off the floor. Floating again.

"Hannah!"

The lights went out. LEDs around the airlock and over the keel tubes came on. Skyler flew through a red-tinted twilight.

"Talk to me, Hannah! Are you OK?"

She shouted up from the engineering module. "Skyler?"

The pressure doors hadn't closed. Skyler interpreted that as a good sign for a split second, until he remembered that they'd disabled the auto-slam thing after Xiang's death.

"Are you OK, Hannah? What was that God-awful noise?"

Hannah's pale face floated in the keel tube. "I scrammed the reactor," she said.

*

"We've been HERFed again," Jack howled in fury.

Alexei whipped off his t-shirt.

Kate said to him with rising tension, "Think you could pick a better time and place for your Putin impersonation?"

Alexei swivelled to his spacesuit, hanging on the wall

behind them, and used the utility tool on its belt to poke a hole in the t-shirt. He placed the hole over the telescope's viewfinder and wadded the material up to make a donut-shaped cushion. Jack got it. Alexei wasn't going to take the risk of touching the naked metal, not when a megavolt HERF had just slammed into the ship. Horse, barn door, but it was a sensible precaution all the same. Eye to the viewfinder, Alexei said, "Roll, pitch, yaw?"

Jack read out the numbers. Emergency power fed the bridge instruments. They'd lost the lights. The faces of the other two looked spooky and haggard in the light from the screens. The fans slowed to a halt, letting the silence of space in.

Hannah said from Engineering, "We are running on battery power. I'm going to bring the fuel cells on line in a few minutes."

Something stirred in Jack's mind. He wanted to tell her to wait, but he wasn't sure what his instincts were telling him, so he held off. Didn't want to panic her. That said, she sounded remarkably together. Skyler, Meili, and Giles had all checked in. They, too, were coping well.

It made a huge difference to know—or be 99.9% sure—what was happening, even when what was happening was utterly shit.

Alexei took the star sights and confirmed what Jack already knew. They hadn't finished their burn before the HERF hit.

The *SoD* was still travelling far too fast.

"We've lost our groove." Kate slammed one fist into the other palm. "Could they hit us at a worse time?"

"I'm sure they intended to hit us precisely at the worst

time possible," Jack said. He noticed that even Kate had started referring to the MOAD as 'they.' *The aliens.* "We're going to overshoot our optimal target in front of Jupiter. We'll still enter orbit, but it's going to be a very elongated orbit."

He mathed it out roughly on the flight control computer. Alexei and Kate did the same calculations. "Son of a three-legged bitch," Kate said.

"Yeah," Jack said. He sat back and regarded the blank optic feed screen. They'd lost the external sensors, *again.* He caught himself rubbing his fingers together nervously, and wondered why he felt so edgy, as if there was something he should be doing. There was nothing he *could* do with the reactor off-line. He might as well be sitting in a broken-down Volvo on a conveyor belt.

Which led straight into Jupiter's junkyard.

Kate huffed out a hard sigh, and leaned forward to her comms console. Just like last time, they were down to basic text-only comms. "Houston, this is the *SoD,*" she murmured out loud as she typed. "Got some good news for you, and some bad. Good news: we are on track for Jupiter orbit injection. Bad news: our projected orbit is going to sling us straight into Jupiter's radiation belt."

*

"But no," Jack cried. "It doesn't have to go like that!"

An hour had passed since the HERF attack. The *SoD* had swung around the far side of Jupiter. That terminated their comms with Earth for the time being. They'd had everyone except Hannah crowding into the bridge, desperate for information and reassurance. The crew's brittle self-command had fractured at the news that they were on course to pass through Jupiter's radiation belt. Now they needed the kind of reassurance you couldn't get over an intercom, but only through face-to-face contact with other shivering, jabbering human beings. It drove Jack up the wall, and he'd escaped to the main hab.

Hannah had brought the fuel cells on line, so the growlights were back on at half power. The garden wheeled, perceptibly slower now. Microfiber nets over the plants, securing them for the burn, gave a spiderweb sheen to the greenery, reminding Jack of his mother's garden in Warwickshire when it was all covered with dew.

He crouched in the axis tunnel, looking down at their little spinning world, like a monkey on a branch. He tossed the *SoD's* orbital parameters around in his mind like dice.

"We can do it," he shouted aloud.

He turned and flew back to the bridge.

"Out," he said to Meili. "Out," to Giles. "Bugger off," to Skyler.

"Excuse me, Jack?" said Kate.

"Alexei, can you give me our internal orbital parameters?" Jack wedged himself into his seat.

"They haven't changed," Alexei said.

"I know, but it just occurred to me. We can raise our perijove." The point at which they'd be closest to Jupiter. "That way we won't have to pass through the radiation belt!" He grinned exultantly.

"Jack," Kate said. "If that were possible, I'd have told you to do it."

"It is possible," Jack insisted.

"We are going to *lower* our perijove. That'll decrease our orbital period by thirty hours. Right, Alexei?"

"Yes," the cosmonaut said.

"Hannah says she can bring the reactor back on line in forty-eight hours," Kate said. "We'll burn once to lower our perijove, and again when we swing back to perijove—"

"In the middle of the radiation belt," Jack interrupted. "Do you realize how much radiation Jupiter blasts out? It's a blizzard. It's a maelstrom. Every moment we're exposed to that, it's as if the ship is taking mini-HERFs. We can't—"

Raising her voice, Kate interrupted him right back. "I am aware of the radiation levels! You're overstating the risks."

"Yeah," said Skyler, from the keel tube. He hadn't gone away, after all. "What's a little radiation?"

"Whose side are you on?" Jack said. He heard the insult coming out of his mouth and knew he was losing the fight. He focused on Alexei, who was working the instruments, avoiding everyone's eyes. "My point is we don't have to take that risk! We'll raise the perijove instead of lowering it! Just flip the ship!"

"Just flip the ship, huh, hotshot?" Kate said. "Alexei, how much would that increase our orbital period?"

"Forty-four hours," Alexei said.

"I'm not putting my crew through that," Kate said. "People are scared, they're on the edge of panic—"

"You'd know," Jack said.

Kate's mouth thinned. Her chin jutted. "A one-eighty flip is a perilous maneuver which I will *not* approve if it's not strictly necessary, no matter how good you think you are! Am I making myself clear?"

Jack dropped his gaze—there was no sense fighting on. He'd lost.

"Crystal." He bit off the word. "I'll calculate the

parameters for a burn at our current orientation, then."

"Thank you," Kate said. She had the decency not to look smug.

Later, Jack said to Alexei, "Why the hell didn't you back me up in there? Did she threaten a pussy strike?"

"She's sexy when she is mad," Alexei said, smirking.

"Traitor!" Jack snapped at him. He was really angry.

"Jack!" Alexei said. "Are you a fucking moron? Think like a Russian! Lose in order to win. First you lose, and then you win, is this so hard to understand? If we win this battle, we have nowhere to go except throwing her out of the airlock." He let that sink in.

"High-energy electrons and protons, Alexei." Jack's eyes were dry. He rubbed them with the heels of his hands. "Those charged particles are like bullets whacking into the ship."

"We have to go to Europa anyway," Alexei said. "We'll be sitting in a blizzard of charged particles for how long, who knows?"

"That's why I would have liked to minimize our exposure before we get there."

CHAPTER 11

Three days later, Skyler started to believe he might live through this, after all. The lights were back on at full strength, the fans hummed, and he was feeding the fish, in orbit around Jupiter.

Hannah had descrammed the reactor. Cranked it up to baseload output. Re-started the housekeeping turbine.

The *SoD* was alive and well on the inside, but dead on the outside. Antennas, sensors, the works. Everything slagged in the first HERF attack had been slagged again, and then some.

An hour ago Kate had sent Jack and Alexei out on a frantic spacewalk, laden with replacement cables and connectors.

"I want the AE-35 unit fixed," she'd said.

The AE-35 unit controlled the positioning of the ship's directional antenna for the Ka comms system. They'd successfully made the emergency burn to decrease the ship's orbital period, but because they hadn't flipped the ship, the directional antenna was still pointing away from Earth, and it was slagged. So: get out there and fix it, boys.

"Have fun," Skyler had said, seeing them off at the bridge airlock.

Jack's Z-2 suit was flexible enough for him to flip Skyler the bird. Skyler just smiled.

He really hoped they could get the AE-35 unit fixed. No comms with Earth! Forget about television and the internet, they couldn't even use their ultra-basic text messaging system, so long as their antenna was pointing at Saturn. More than anything else, the loss of comms drove home the abnormality of their situation, how far away and alone they were. Skyler never would've thought he would miss the alternating selections of crappy music from Star City and Houston. He did.

And for him personally, the loss of comms couldn't have come at a worse time.

Done with feeding the fish and checking the pH levels in their tanks, he headed aft to the secondary life support module.

Slayer blasted from tinny laptop speakers, making Skyler wince. That was Giles's music, and Giles himself floated in the middle of the module, fiddling with one of the algae tanks. These tanks—which served the crucial function of supplying the crew with oxygen—took up the whole axis of the module. Air injection tubes imparted spin to their contents, so the gelatinous green masses tumbled slowly round and round.

"Hey, Giles," Skyler said. "Whatcha doing?"

When Xiang Peixun was alive, Skyler used to come back here and hang with him. His goal had been to troll Xiang into letting slip any hint that he was the saboteur. He'd never gotten anywhere. Xiang hadn't been much of a talker. Not in English, anyway. Often, Skyler had just ended up floating near him, watching the algae spin like green clothes dissolving in a washing-machine. It was soothing to watch the tanks, and know that they were producing precious oxygen for the crew to breathe. "These little guys are the most important crew members," Xiang had said more than once.

Unexpectedly, a lump rose in Skyler's throat. Tears prickled the corners of his eyes. Was he about to cry for

Xiang Peixun? Fuck it.

"Whatcha up to, Giles?" he said, more loudly, over the thrash metal riffs.

"I check for mutations," Giles shouted. He extracted a slide from Tank 5's sampling port and flew over to the lab area. Scratching his scruffy brown beard, he inserted the slide into the electron microscope.

Skyler hovered behind him, watching him work. Giles had taken over Xiang's life-support duties without making a fuss about it. He wasn't a natural at this astronaut business, any more than Skyler was, but he worked as hard as anyone on the ship. Everyone kind of took him for granted. Made fun of his taste in music—Slayer, Giles? Black Sabbath? Motorhead? *Really?* Giles got it even worse than Skyler himself did for listening to Dylan and Joan Baez. And for the same reasons, actually. A guy who listened to *that* crap would never get laid on Earth, let alone in space. Right?

Giles's Ph.D. thesis had been on using music, specifically heavy metal and punk, to model alien languages. He'd also published a widely acclaimed article arguing, with a straight face, that the 3rd movement of Bach's Brandenburg Concerto #3 was the first thrash metal song. And *look* at him: the lumpy forehead, the weirdly luxuriant leg hair, the prim little paunch. Listen to the tuneless bellowing as he sang along with 'Raining Blood.' You just couldn't take the guy seriously.

But was that Giles's strategy?

Was he, in fact, trolling them all?

BUGSWATTER, the anti-malware program Director Flaherty sent Skyler before the HERF, had found the Chinese malware trigger on Giles's iPod.

And also on Meili's laptop.

And on Alexei's.

And Jack's.

And on Xiang's MP3 player.

And also on Skyler's own iPod.

So he was back at square one, because it was obvious that whoever the saboteur was, they'd managed to install their malware trigger on a bunch of other devices as well. Covering their tracks. It was an elementary precaution, really.

And Skyler still didn't know what the malware trigger *did,* or how it even worked. On his iPod, it looked like a .wav file entitled 'Friends & Lovers.' He had considered telling everyone about it, so they wouldn't accidentally activate it. Now he once again considered telling Giles. But if the Frenchman was the saboteur, that would just let him know Skyler was onto him.

Skyler *had* to send the trigger back to the NXC for analysis.

He needed comms.

"Merde," Giles said. "I find a mutation." He raised his face from the microscope. "You want to see?"

"Oh, crap," Skyler said, jerked back to the reality that they were orbiting Jupiter with a life support system teetering like a stack of tableware on a plate-spinner's pole. "No, I've seen enough of those babies."

"Now I have to drain the tank, flush the bad stuff down the crapper, and refill it." Giles made a very French noise of annoyance.

Skyler flew aft into the storage module and fetched a vacuum-pack of freeze-dried algae. He helped Giles drain Tank 5 and sterilize it. While they watched the pumps suck out the mutated algae, Skyler reflected that the CO_2/oxygen exchange was the most fragile link in their life support system. Too much O_2 and the plants die. Too much CO_2 and we die, to put it starkly. Working back here, Giles could screw with the algae anytime he liked. He wouldn't even need malware.

But who'd sabotage the system that they themselves depended on for survival? That's what Skyler kept asking himself. His crewmates might all be nuts in their own way—they had to be nuts, to sign up for a trip to Europa—but he felt sure none of them was a suicidal fanatic, of whatever flavor. That kind of thing tends to show.

The only conclusion he could come to was that whoever's actions were going to trigger the malware, *they didn't even know it themselves.*

✳

Outside the bridge, Jack struggled to remove the AE-35 unit from its mount. They'd replaced all the slagged cables and connectors. They'd also fixed the long-range radar. Now for the AE-35 unit. This was one of the longest and most brutal spacewalks he'd ever done. He was shaking with tiredness and feeling a bit dippy.

"Daisy," he sang, "Daisy, give me your answer, do."

Alexei, floating opposite him with the replacement unit in hand, took it up. "I'm half crazy, all for the love of you."

Jupiter glowered beneath Jack's feet, a bloated sack of gas contained by its own gravity. The *SoD* was at apojove, swinging round the top end of its elliptical orbit, a million kilometers above the gas giant's atmosphere. This high above the radiation belt, they shouldn't be getting hot.

Hopefully.

Jack had the personal radiation dosimeter his father had given him in his thigh pocket. He had something else in there, too.

"It won't be a stylish marriage," he sang, over the sighing of his suit's air supply.

"We can't afford a carriage," Alexei sang, rolling the Rs in the Russian fashion.

*

Inside the bridge, Kate sat with the headphones on, listening. The men's voices came faintly through the background radio hiss of Jupiter.

"But you'll look sweet …" Jack.

"Upon the seat …" Alexei.

And then, both together: "Of a bicycle built for two!"

Laughter.

Kate shuddered. She took off the headphones and tossed them into the air. They swayed on the end of the cord.

"Couldn't they have called the AE-35 unit something less *ominous?*" she said to the empty bridge. "It's just a gyroscope. Fucking nerds."

*

Skyler got back to the bridge a few minutes before Jack and Alexei were scheduled to return from their spacewalk. He floated behind Kate, staying out of the way.

She pulled one side of the headphones off and beckoned him to listen in.

"Open the pod bay doors," Jack said, cracking up on the radio.

"That's from *2001,*" Skyler said. He grinned.

Kate rolled her eyes.

The two men tumbled into the bridge, bringing the subtle gunpowdery smell of space with them. Alexei ripped off his helmet. His gaunt, stubbled face shone with sweat. He opened the rear entry port on Jack's Z-2. Jack wriggled out of the suit, wincing as he freed his arms.

"Did you get the AE-35 unit fixed?" Kate said.

Skyler, feeling like a servant, collected the spacesuits and hung them on the wall.

Jack pushed past him and extricated a small device from his suit's thigh pocket. "Jesus, I hope this is wrong."

"What's that?" Skyler said.

"A dosimeter. According to this, that was a year's exposure in four hours." Jack put the gadget away and stretched out his fingers. They were bloody at the tips.

"Did you get the unit fixed?" Kate repeated.

"Sure," Alexei said. "Try it now."

Kate powered up the comms system and repositioned the directional antenna. A blissful smile of relief spread across her face, mirroring the relief that Skyler himself felt. "Good work, guys." Snapping on her headset, she began to speak. "Mission Control, this is the *SoD*. I apologize for the comms outage. We are alive and well …"

Hurry the fuck up, Skyler thought as Kate plunged into a detailed status update.

He had brought his laptop up to the bridge with him. He just needed to connect the USB to the data port and dispatch a copy of the malware trigger to Earth.

Jack and Alexei stripped off their t-shirts and underpants. Naked, Alexei flew out of the bridge. Skyler gathered his sweat-soaked underwear out of the air. Jack flew up to the first-aid locker. Seeing that he was having trouble opening it,

Skyler followed him and opened it for him. Anything to get him out of here faster.

"Thanks," Jack said.

Skyler pulled out a drawer and took out the sterile wipes. Jack was clutching something in his right fist, which he now transferred to his left fist. Skyler cleaned the blood off Jack's fingers, careful not to let any of it drip into the air. He took out a roll of self-adhesive bandages and scissors, snipped off a length, and wound it around Jack's right index finger. "What's that?" he said.

Jack opened his left fist. A rosary.

"I didn't know you were Catholic."

"I was an altar boy, no less."

"You're kidding."

"Don't worry, I'm extremely lapsed. My father gave me this. He's gone back to the Faith in a big way."

"A lot of people have," Skyler said. The classified updates he got from the NXC—all the news *not* fit to print—had touched on the resurgence of organized religion. The rise of the Earth Party, a quasi-religion in the NXC's analysis, with no doctrines or hierarchy, had been matched by booming attendance at churches, mosques, and synagogues.

"It's all a load of bollocks," Jack said. "But it can't hurt, right?"

He slipped the rosary over his head, freeing up his left hand. Skyler bandaged his left index finger, not very gently.

"Ow fuck," Jack gasped.

"Sorry."

"Wait," Jack said. He raised his hand to his mouth and bit off a dangling thumbnail. The whole thing. "Fingernails, who needs 'em?" he said, spitting it out and catching it.

"I thought the Z-2 gloves were supposed to be better than the old ones," Skyler said.

"I have big hands."

Sporting Egyptian-mummy fingers, Jack grabbed dry underwear and left the bridge. Skyler went back to hovering behind Kate. At last she concluded her transmission. "Ma'am, I need the bridge for just five minutes," he said.

She gave him a bleak glare. "Secret squirrel stuff?"

Controlling his temper, Skyler said, "Yup. You want to get home again, ma'am? Let me use the comms. This shit just got real, and the NXC needs to know about it."

"Oh God," Kate said. "You've found the saboteur."

Skyler spoke before he could think better of it. "There is evidence pointing to your pilot."

*

Jack traipsed through the hab, holding his bandaged fingertips out in front of him. He was searching for Meili. When he found her, she was on tiptoe staking up the tomato vines, and didn't see him at first. Her shoulder-length black ponytail bobbed as she stretched and twisted. Her fingers moved deftly, repositioning the flex ties that held the vines up. He felt a surge of tenderness for her.

He moved in behind her, reached over her shoulder, and picked a tomato. She squeaked in surprise and turned to find herself trapped. She placed a small hand on his chest as if to push him away. Her fingers bumped the crucifix hanging around his neck.

"Hi," Jack said.

She kept her hand braced on his chest, but didn't push. "We're finished, Jack," she said. "Go away."

She smelt of girl-sweat. Jack felt an overwhelming desire

to lay her down among the tomatoes and screw her silly. He stepped back. "I just wanted to ask you if there's any way to tie the plants to the floor."

Meili frowned. "They're already tied down." She gestured at the microfiber nets that covered the jungle of vegetables around them. She'd rolled back the nearest net to attend to the tomatoes.

"Those are there so the thrust gravity won't push them over when we burn. I mean, could you actually attach the nets to the floor?"

"There's nothing to attach them *to.*"

"No, I suppose there isn't. This ship was designed by people who've seen too many movies. In the movies, everything's always clean, and everything always works," Jack said sourly. Then he grinned. "Hey! Duct tape?"

Meili's eyes softened. "I've missed you," she said.

"Jesus, woman, I miss you like crazy." Jack tried to fold her into his arms, bandaged fingers and all.

Now she did push him away. He staggered backwards, flailing to keep his balance. She said, "I miss you. But we are finished. What part of this don't you understand?"

Jack was still holding the tomato he'd picked. He bit into it crossly.

"I will cover the tanks," Meili said. "That will prevent spilling, anyway." She wiped her eyes with the back of her hand and returned to her work.

Jesus.

Women.

What part of this don't I understand?

How about all of it, Meili?

Jack carried on aft to the engineering module. In no

mood for another female encounter of the perplexing kind, he just poked his head out of the keel tube and shouted for Hannah.

"What is it?" She swam up from the turbine room. "Oh! Jack!" She held onto the bulkhead, looking like a fox trapped in headlights.

Fantastic. Another woman who's happy to see me.

"Sorry to disturb you." Jack made his tone as conciliatory as possible. "It's about our next burn."

"Oh, OK." Hannah seemed relieved that was all he wanted to talk about. "We're burning at perijove, right? We'll warp the semimajor axis of our orbit to align with Europa at the new intersection point. I've gone over that calculation, and it looks good."

Jack remembered that this was the woman who'd maneuvered the Juno probe into its history-making Europa flyby. He could trust her to do what was necessary.

"Yeah," he said. "About that burn. I'm going to need to yaw the ship as we reach perijove. I'm not sure, has Kate mentioned this?"

Hannah shook her head.

"It'll take a lot of electricity." Jack steeled himself. "We've got to cut the power throughout the ship."

CHAPTER 12

In the movies, a spaceship could maneuver like a fighter jet. The *SoD* relied on reaction wheels.

Three bloody huge reaction wheels, that acted as gyroscopes.

By clutching them individually, Jack could precess the ship in any one of its three axes.

It's like driving a really big, really slow stick-shift.

Clutch.

Wait wait wait wait wait, while the reaction wheel transferred its angular momentum to the ship.

Then clutch the wheel again, transferring the angular momentum back to the wheel, and hope like hell the ship ended up where he wanted it. The exact timing was as much of an art as a science. Jack could have said he knew what he was doing but really he was just betting on where the roulette wheel would stop.

Over and over and over, while Alexei sang out the 3D numbers in an increasingly hoarse voice.

Charged particles battered at the *SoD*. Jupiter's radio noise swamped the sensors. Rounding perijove, the ship blundered at full throttle through the heart of Jupiter's radiation belt, where it didn't have to be, if Kate had accepted Jack's alternate suggestion, but never mind, here we are, doing this. Burning burning burning.

The burn was scheduled to last three hours, yawing the ship continuously to keep the engine bells pointing in the direction of travel—that's what all the precessing was about.

It took a lot of electricity to run the reaction wheels. The MPD engine was gobbling the entire output of the big turbine, so Jack had arranged with Hannah to borrow the output of the housekeeping turbine. That meant a ship-wide blackout.

Back in Secondary Life Support, Giles was manually injecting oxygen into the algae tanks, and in the main hab, Skyler and Meili were aerating the hydroponic tanks with foot pumps, hoping to avoid a repeat of the die-off last time they lost power to the hab.

The light from dozens of displays and readouts filled the bridge like an electronic sunset. The clouds of vapor from Alexei's e-cigarette, which he had ceased to hide from Kate, glowed like nebulae. Jupiter rose like a pink Death Star on the aft-facing camera feed.

"Burn plus three," Kate said, transmitting to Mission Control. Excitement sharpened her voice. "We can see Europa!"

"What?" Alexei said. "I can't see it!"

"It's one of those pixels there," Kate said. "You can see it better on the long-range radar."

Europa. The word punctured Jack's concentration. He glanced up from the axis precession controls. The burn was just about over, anyway. He instructed the computer to throttle down the engine …

A sharp *crack!* split the air, like thunder rolling very loud and very near. Sparks spat from the consoles. Alexei leapt for the fire extinguisher. The ozone tang of electrical discharges tainted the air.

The *SoD* reverberated like a barrel struck by a hammer as the reactor's control rods slammed into the core.

The controls blinked off, leaving the bridge in darkness pierced only by Jupiter-light from the portholes. Then the consoles lit up again. Reboot screens flashed.

Alexei floated, uncertainly holding the fire extinguisher..

The intercom crackled. Hannah said dejectedly, "Wasn't me this time. At a guess, the thermal fuse melted, and triggered the auto-scram. You guys OK up there?"

Jack leant into the intercom. "HERFed again," he said.

"I figured," Hannah said. "This is getting kind of boring, you know what I mean? Why don't they vary their method of attack? I mean, haven't they got nukes? Death rays? They haven't got miniature black holes that they can fire from relativistic cannon? They haven't got anti-matter scatterguns? What the fuck, you know? You come all this way, you've got a gee-whiz alien spacecraft five *kilometers* long that looks like something out of *Battlestar Galactica*, and you haven't even got *missiles?*"

Alexei cackled helplessly. Tears were running out of Jack's eyes. He managed, "Maybe it really is an AI after all."

"I had a smarter AI in my fucking Subaru," Hannah said.

"I like you, Hannah. I really like you," Jack said. "If you tell me you can restart the reactor within …" He consulted the burn parameters in his head. "Eight hours. I'll love you until the day I die."

The wise-assery went out of Hannah's voice. "No can do, Jack, sorry."

"Come on. *Please.*"

"I wish I could say yes, but It's a different story from before. Given our previous power history, the xenon pit is now fully poisoned. It's going to take forty-eight hours, minimum."

"In that case," Jack said, "we're going to overshoot Europa. We might have time to wave at the MOAD as we flash by."

"Maybe *shoot* it as we go by," Alexei suggested.

"Nah, unfortunately," Jack said. "We won't pass close enough to its orbit. We'll just slingshot and continue to circle around Jupiter until we run out of air."

Kate thumbed the intercom. "All hands, as you've probably guessed, our trip to beautiful Europa is gonna have to be postponed." She gazed at the ceiling.

"Why don't you tell them they're going to die?" Jack said.

Kate glared at him. "They are not going to die."

"If we overshoot Europa, that's it. We don't have enough reaction mass for two more burns. The extra burn at perijove already wiped out our safety margin." Jack plucked his squeeze bottle out of the webbing at the side of his seat and gulped cold tea. His bottle was different from the ones everyone else had. His parents had bought it at some online shop capitalizing on the craze for all things *SoD*-related. There was a cartoon of the ship on one side with the caption, *I can't believe the government is paying for this.*

Kate said, "Out of our original 8.2 million liter capacity, we still have one million liters left. I think we can squeeze two more burns out of that."

"You're just saying that," Jack said.

"What do you want me to say?" Kate exclaimed.

"It mightn't be utterly impossible to squeeze out two more burns," Jack conceded, trying hard to see the thing from all angles. "But you're skipping the part where we all die of radiation sickness. Every time we dive in close to Jupiter, we're taking more rems." The next words got out before he could stop them. "I told you we should have raised our perijove."

Kate tensed.

Alexei, still floating behind them, said, "Here is another possibility. We reboot the reactor and burn into Europa orbit, as planned."

"That's what I was thinking," Jack said.

"It's inconceivable," Kate said.

"You keep using that word," Alexei said.

"I do not think that word means what you think it means," Jack said, grinning.

"It's a fucking nuclear reactor. You do not fuck around with a nuclear reactor," Kate said. She reached for the intercom. "Hannah—"

Alexei transferred the fire extinguisher he was holding to his left hand. He slid his right hand over Kate's, jerking it away from the intercom. "Go," he said to Jack.

Jack licked his lips. He released his harness and flew out of the bridge.

Straight through the keel tube.

Darkness in the main hab was thick enough to stand a spoon up in.

Meili and Skyler shouted at each other, voices clearly audible. Hold it down, hold it down. I can't.

The noise of fans—the noise of *life*—had stopped. The total silence, broken only by frightened human voices, ranked up there with the worst things Jack had ever heard in space.

In the blackness, as he flew blind through the keel tunnel, things bumped against the lattice. Water splashed into his face.

He kept moving, blundered through the SLS module and the storage module, and dropped into Engineering. He collided with Hannah. Her sensual curves registered in his brain, a small jolt of delight immediately submerged by urgency. They spun apart, grabbing for supports.

"Who's that?"

"Me."

"I'm looking for my head-lamp," she said. A minute later she found it. "What's up?"

"We need to reboot the reactor," Jack said. The light was shining in his face. He shaded his eyes, saw her mouth and nose beneath the head-lamp.

"I know," Hannah said. "Unfortunately there's nothing I can do right now besides wait. The xenon pit has to decay before I pull the control rods, or we get core poisoning."

"The trouble is if we wait, we die," Jack said. "I worked at a company that developed nuclear propulsion systems. We developed this one, in fact. I'm not completely ignorant of how reactors work. You could reboot it to criticality. Skip everything we don't need. Just give me enough delta-V to make Europa orbit."

"If you're familiar with this type of system, you must be aware of what happened at a little town called Chernobyl," Hannah said. "They tried to overcome xenon poisoning by pulling the rods prematurely. It blew the lid off the reactor."

Jack tried to tame his impatience with the engineer's mindset that missed the forest for the trees. "This is a *gas*-cooled reactor. There's no risk of a coolant void."

"There is a substantial risk of damaging the core."

"If we don't try it, we're stuffed, anyway."

"If I *do* try it, and end up poisoning the core, there are several fun things that could happen." Hannah spoke rapidly, brooking no interruption. "The core itself gets damaged, or the turbines do, or the radiators, or the steam generator. Or all four. If the core goes bye-bye, we end up with no propulsion whatsoever. If we damage the turbine, we lose power output. If we damage the radiators, ditto. Damaging the steam generator would result in hot coolant gas mixing with water, and that would cause a steam explosion that would blow off the end of the ship," she finished breathlessly.

"I'd rather die that way than stick around for a slow death from radiation poisoning," Jack said, shrugging.

"I can't." Then Hannah Ginsburg's essential honesty opened the door to their survival. "I won't."

Jack pounced. "You have to."

"Has Kate greenlighted it? Is she OK?" The visible portion of Hannah's face creased into a frown. "What are you doing back here, anyway? Shouldn't you be on the bridge?"

*

On the bridge, Kate moved at last. Turning towards Alexei, she said, "Are you going to hit me with that thing?"

Alexei looked down at the fire extinguisher in his hands. He'd grabbed it in a Pavlovian reaction to the sight of sparks. Fire was the single worst thing that could happen on a spaceship, they always told you. But now he was starting to wonder about that. Worse things could happen on a spaceship than the eggheads of Roscosmos ever encompassed in their bloodless, gelded imaginations. Look at him, holding this fire extinguisher by its base, as if it were a broken vodka bottle. "No," he said.

"Good," Kate said. She leant forward to the intercom. "Hannah, whatever Jack says, I have *not* ordered a reactor reboot. Don't—"

Alexei let the fire extinguisher go into the air. He fell, slowly, on top of Kate. She flinched back from the intercom, her sentence unfinished. Alexei punched the release on her harness. Pushing off with one foot, he hauled her bodily out of her seat.

They tumbled against the aft bulkheads, wrestling. Alexei already knew how she fought, as their lovemaking had been spicy at times. It surprised him a bit that she didn't have any new tricks.

*

Hannah let the intercom go. Wildly, she demanded, "What did she mean? What's happening?"

"I don't have time to bloody explain it to you," Jack shouted. He, too, had been taken aback by Kate's abrupt—abruptly terminated—intervention. Best not to picture what was going on up there. "All you need to know is that we're going to die if you don't restart the reactor!"

Hannah folded her arms under her breasts. "No, don't explain," she said, voice shaking. "Kate's already told me about you. There's a high probability that you're the saboteur. You put malware in the ship's control systems. This HERF theory is complete bullshit. It was you all along. And now you want me to finish the job by poisoning the core, so they can blame it all on design flaws? No, sorry. I won't."

Jack's mouth dropped open. What he was hearing was so utterly insane he didn't know how to respond to it. "That's simply absurd," he said weakly.

"I don't know, it sounds plausible to me."

"It's nonsense on stilts. You can't possibly believe it."

"I don't know what to believe anymore."

"Believe me!"

"Why?"

"Because I'm trying to save this ship!"

Hannah just snorted.

The contemptuous little sound made Jack see red. He kicked off from the wall and flew towards Hannah. She thrust out her arms to fend him off. He caught her wrists. She brought up a knee. Jack twisted from the waist, so her knee landed harmlessly on his hip instead of in his groin. His momentum carried them both on a diagonal trajectory to the floor. They bounced off gently. Hannah's head-lamp came off and drifted away, spinning its beam over the reactor and turbine control panels.

"Let me go," Hannah said thinly.

"I don't think you mean that," Jack said. He pinned her wrists with his left hand and slid his other arm around her waist. His right hand took on a life of its own and dipped lower for a quick squeeze. Hannah let out a squeak. She went rigid. Oh God, *what* did I just do?

The head-lamp drifted up to the ceiling and bounced off again with a clunk in the unnatural silence. Hannah's breath blew in hot pants against Jack's neck. Every time she breathed, her breasts pressed into his chest. He was getting hard, which appalled him. He'd had it in the back of his mind all along that he might have to physically overpower her, but you couldn't hit a woman—at least, Jack Kildare couldn't. So how could he make her do what he wanted? What was left?

"Do it," he said, lips brushing her temple.

"Or what?" she said.

Or what? He couldn't let go of her until she did what he wanted. But what did he want? It was all on a continuum, was the trouble. To overpower was to dominate was to do what men and women did in bed.

Hoping that she didn't know what was going through his mind, he let their bodies drift apart. He kept hold of her wrists, though. "Just start the bloody reactor!" he grated.

Hannah writhed violently, jerking her wrists out of his grip, and thrashed away. "Get your hands off me!" she yelled. "Just because I said I was sleeping with you, it doesn't mean you have a right to ... oh my God. OK, I accept I shouldn't have lied about something like that. But you shouldn't have jumped me! I thought you were a *gentleman!*"

The only part of that that made any sense to Jack was *you shouldn't have jumped me*. Which he fully admitted was true. "I was late on the day they handed out gentleman cards," he muttered.

"Obviously!"

She'd kicked him in the nose. He tasted blood. The pain effectively killed his arousal. "I'm very sorry, all the same. That was out of bounds, wasn't it?"

"*'Out of bounds'*?! It was sexual assault!"

"I'm a nice guy," Jack said, holding his face in his hands. "I really am."

"That's what they all say," Hannah said bleakly.

Jack gave up trying to make a joke out of it. "Look, I'm sorry. I fucked up. You can report me to Mission Control later, if we're still alive ..."

"What are they gonna do, fire you?" Hannah's mirthless laugh underlined the problem. They were way beyond the reach of any sanctions. Even the shackles of good manners and civility were starting to weaken. Jack felt a wave of self-disgust. What he had just done wasn't *him*, but he'd never be able to convince her of that.

"Sorry," he said briskly. "There isn't time for this. Four and a half hours to criticality, if we skip the full power-up and reboot. We'd better get started."

"We?"

"You."

"Fine. I'll do it," Hannah said. She sounded close to tears. "But I want it noted that I'm doing this under protest, and the only reason I'm doing it at all is because you assaulted me."

"Noted," Jack sighed. He decided not to mention that there would be no one left alive to note her protests if this didn't work out.

Hannah retrieved her headlamp. She floated down to the reactor control panel. The dollar meter stood at 0.07. The hexagonal array had cooled way down. "Here goes nothing," she said, and yanked the lever to pull out one of the outermost control rods.

CHAPTER 13

Ten hours later, Kate thumbed the PA. "All hands to the bridge, please." She was so exhausted, it took her a second to remember that the PA wasn't working. She turned to Alexei. "Go get the others. If we're going to die, let's all die together."

He left the bridge without giving her any backtalk. That made her feel a little more secure. But it didn't soothe the pain of her blacked eye, or the humiliation Alexei had inflicted on her. He and Jack had overridden her authority. And, worse: she'd set herself up for this by sleeping with him. Without their existing intimacy, he'd never have dared to physically assault her like that.

Well, their insane gamble had succeeded. Gambles sometimes did. But the most dangerous part of the operation started *now*.

*

Alexei's voice floated down from the axis tunnel, loud in the unnatural silence. "Meili? Skyler?"

"Yeah, what?" Skyler shouted, soaked to the bone and shivering as the hab cooled down. He and Meili had been working flat out to save the garden for the last ten hours. They hadn't finished covering all the tanks before the HERF hit, so they had to stumble through puddles of water, in pitch darkness, and to top it all off, gravity was rapidly failing in the main hab, so the puddles were taking to the air, along with the plants. The tilapia flopped in dumb fear against the insides of their tanks, making quiet thuds. Soon they'd be flying fish, Skyler thought. He was so tired it struck him as funny.

"Burning into Europa orbit in five minutes," Alexei shouted. "Commander wants everyone on the bridge."

"No," Meili shouted, without pausing in her work. "We're not finished yet!"

Skyler floundered over and took her by the hand. "Fuck this. We're about to make history. Let's go see it."

He'd developed a new admiration for Meili as they worked side by side. If she was the saboteur, she was doing a damn good job of acting like she cared. As a matter of fact, Skyler had ceased to worry about the malware for the time being. It paled into insignificance compared to the threat of a core meltdown, or an even tastier fate, overshooting Europa and spinning around Jupiter until they died—

—both of which threats had been averted, apparently, by a successful partial reboot of the reactor. Hannah had saved them all …

… for now.

"OK," Meili said. "I want to see, too. Let's go."

*

Alexei returned to the bridge with Giles in tow. "The others are coming," he said, strapping into his seat.

"Good. Thanks," Kate said coldly.

He'd let her down. Let *himself* down. This deeply emotional, idealistic, funny man, whom she'd trusted with her body, had resorted to superior male strength to get his way. Kate's outrage went deeper than the pain of bruises. Alexei might as well have spat on the entire edifice of human civilization that got them here in the first place.

She was *never* going to forgive him for that.

And as for Jack …!

Butter wouldn't melt in your mouth, would it, Killer?

But as Hannah entered the bridge, and Kate turned to confirm that everyone was there, she noted Hannah's terrified glance at Jack, and saw how she took a place in the far left corner, as far from Jack as she could get. So, something had happened in Engineering, too.

Burn minus 0:20.

Fuck it. Worry about this shit later.

Like they taught you in the Air Force, 90% of professionalism is successfully working with assholes.

"OK, Jack," she said. "Execute Burn Three."

"Roger," Jack said. He keyed in the throttle command.

*

Skyler and Meili trailed onto the bridge as Kate gave the command to burn. He floated over to Hannah. "OK there, Hannah-banana?"

She didn't answer, but smiled tremulously and gave his hand a quick squeeze.

"Dammit, no view," he said quietly. All the camera feeds were dark. His inner romantic had hoped for a spectacular view of Europa.

Instead, all they got was a view of Jack pushing buttons, his hands flickering from one console to another, and a soundtrack of Kate and Alexei calling out numbers. They both had their laptops open, strapped to their knees with, of course, duct tape. Even Jack had a laptop propped open in front of the useless radar plot.

Meili tugged on Skyler's shoulder and tapped Hannah's arm. She whispered, "They're literally flying blind! All the sensors are out. They have nothing, nothing. This is incredible."

Skyler whispered, "The laptops?"

Hannah answered, "The computers are still down. They only had time to fix the essential flight controls. They must have figured out the whole burn on their goddamn laptops." Her lips parted in awe. Skyler felt a stab of jealousy that poisoned the experience for him.

At last the three in the hot seats fell quiet. The deep bass thrumming of the steam turbines undergirded the silence. Skyler welcomed the sound after the hideous quiet they'd endured for hours. Back on Earth, he'd always thought the noise of machinery was ugly, but out here, the sound of machinery was the sound of life. A vital bulwark against the hostile night.

He whispered to Hannah, "Did you have any trouble with the reactor?"

She put on a folksy voice. "Oh Lawd, nothin' but trouble … Seriously, Sky, when I pulled out the first rod, I thought I was killing us all." Her face wrinkled. Tears stood in her eyes. Skyler felt terrible for making her cry.

"But it went OK?" he said, desperate to cheer her up.

"Yup. My baby's tougher than I ever dreamed." Hannah backhanded the tears out of her eyes. "I only took the output up to thirty-five percent. I'm not risking any more than I have to."

Jack pushed another cluster of buttons in rapid succession. Then he seemed to freeze, poised over the consoles.

Giles said, "Are we there yet?"

Everyone laughed louder than the joke warranted. Jack swung around, smiling— "Don't relax yet. HERF number four incoming any minute now, I wouldn't wonder."

"Luckily there is nothing left to slag," Alexei added.

"That's it, guys," Kate said. "Welcome to Europa."

*

Everyone wanted to see outside. Even Jack. Especially Jack, perhaps. He had been awake for some number of hours that made his brain feel like porridge when he even tried to add them up, yet he volunteered for an EVA immediately to restore crucial sensors and antennas. He really wanted to be the first person to see Europa with his naked eyes. With luck he might even get a glimpse of the MOAD.

Kate nixed the proposal. "You'll be going out plenty," she said. "Get some sleep first." And, accurately reading his sense of urgency: "The MOAD's not going anywhere."

Jack trailed aft through the misery of spilled tanks and floating vegetation. It was just as well the lights weren't on, so he couldn't see the plants scraping over the floor like kids' balloons a few days after the fair. He bumped into plenty of them, though.

Alexei walked beside him, leaning way forward in the ultra-low-gravity gait that made a person seem to be walking into a gale. Kate had told him to get some sleep, too.

Jack wound up at his coffin by following his nose, rather than because any of the vegetable landmarks were still there. He flung it open and collapsed into his hammock. Alexei sat on the edge of his coffin.

Accepting that Alexei wanted to talk, Jack sat up again. Tiredness, until now kept at bay by adrenaline, literally dizzied him; he folded an arm on the floor and rested his head on it. "I'm knackered, mate," he mumbled.

"I can't believe I did that," Alexei said.

"Did what?"

"I hit her. She hit me, too. And ..." Alexei pulled down the collar of his t-shirt. "These are the marks of our commander's teeth."

"You definitely took one for the team," Jack yawned.

"She likes it," Alexei declared. Then he sagged. "I don't want to hit a woman. I've never *really* hit her before. It's one thing, a spicy little spank or two, but this time I was angry. I hurt her. Jesus!" The exclamation sounded less like profanity, more like an invocation. "We can't go on like this!"

Jack sat upright. Alexei's heartfelt confession ripped away the woolly blanket of exhaustion. It exposed his own rationalizations. Guilt pricked him anew. "I didn't actually hit Hannah, but ..." He shook his head. That sounded like he was pretending he hadn't sunk that low, when actually he had sunk lower. In thought, if not in deed.

Jack Kildare was not a man who thought very deeply about his own desires. Given sufficient distractions, he didn't think about them at all. It horrified him to peer into the darkness of those moments back in Engineering. *That isn't me!* And it didn't help to realize that it wasn't really anything to do with Hannah, either. It had been the situation, his frustration, his pressing need.

What that said about him, he hated to think. He bowed his head and struck his forehead with his fist. "Must. Do. Better."

"She said you were the saboteur."

"Huh?"

"Kate said you were the saboteur. I asked her who said that. Skyler, of course."

"Of course," Jack said, grateful for the change of subject. "He's trying to screw me any way he can."

112

"We'll sort him out," Alexei said. "First, we sort out the MOAD. Then we take lunch break. Then we sort out Skyler." He yawned hugely.

"No more good little soldier boys," Jack said.

"No more good little soldier boys." Alexei clasped Jack's hand briefly and stumbled off to his own coffin.

The word was apt. Jack slept like the dead.

CHAPTER 14

Hannah found Kate asleep in her seat on the bridge. The words came to her mind—*Tied to the mast.* She wished she had a blanket to tuck over the commander, but all she had was a report on the status of the reactor. She had trimmed back the output to housekeeping level. She'd been going to tell Kate that it was OK to spin the main hab and power up the rest of the ship's systems.

She surprised herself by bending over and kissing the commander on the cheek.

Kate woke up. "Ah! Oh. Hannah."

"Sorry," Hannah said, backing away in the air. "You need to sleep."

"I'll sleep when I'm dead," Kate said grimly. "We have repairs to carry out. Are those two still down for the count?"

She meant Jack and Alexei, obviously. Hannah nodded—she'd seen that both their coffins were shut, the red 'occupied' flags showing.

"Good."

Kate had a black eye. Hannah couldn't look away from it. Noticing her gaze, Kate said crisply, "Alexei punched me."

"Oh God! I'm so sorry."

"Not as sorry as he's going to be."

Hannah's heart overflowed with sympathy and indignation. "I wasn't going to tell you," she said. "But something happened..."

She started crying.

"So much for my tough-girl image," she gasped, scrubbing at the tears which could not fall in the zero-gee environment of the bridge.

"What happened?" Kate said.

"Jack tried to rape me."

Kate floated out of her seat. Her face reddened with anger. "I *knew* something happened back there."

Hannah shook her head. Her scrupulous commitment to accuracy forced her to retract what she'd just said. "I don't want to exaggerate. He kind of grabbed me and squeezed my ass. That's all it was. But oh my God, I was so frightened."

"I'm not surprised. That *is* frightening. It's completely unacceptable." But Kate's color was returning to normal. Maybe she didn't think ass-grabbing was that bad, in the grand scheme of things. And maybe it wasn't. The truth was, it wasn't really having her ass grabbed that had scared Hannah. It had been the way Jack held her wrists, holding her powerless. But in the end, nothing had happened. So maybe she was making a mountain out of a molehill.

"Sorry," she said, sniffling. "I don't want to distract you from the mission."

"No. If you don't feel safe, that affects the mission. So it is important."

But something definitely seemed off about Kate's reaction.

Suddenly. Hannah remembered her own drunken lie that she was sleeping with Jack.

Oh, no. Of course, Kate thought Hannah had been screwing Jack for months! In that alternate universe, *rape* would have been a big deal, sure, but a bit of ass-grabbing was hardly worth mentioning.

Kate said diffidently, "Hannah, just checking, but are you

sure you were, y'know, totally sober at that time?"

"Yes, of course I was!" The question panicked Hannah. It suggested that Kate had realized her relationship with alcohol was not an entirely voluntary one.

She saw a way to divert Kate from the topic and tie up the loose ends of her previous lie at the same time. "I'm through with Jack, anyway," she said. "Finito, *no maz*. It's not even because of this. I honestly believe he knew that rebooting the reactor could have killed us all, and he was willing to take that risk, anyway."

*

So it was that Giles Boisselot became the first human being to set eyes on the MOAD.

Kate, officious and peremptory as usual, had ordered him outside to fix the comms antennas. Giles had protested that he was not an EVA specialist, but he did not wish to become a target of Kate's wrath, so he suited up and endured a pre-breathe, sharing the bridge airlock with a satchel full of replacement parts.

Ruefully, he reflected that Giles Boisselot, Ph.D, of ESA, formerly *Professeur des Xenolinguistics* at the University of Nantes, frequent ornament of interdisciplinary SETI conferences, respected to the point of fan worship by everyone in his tiny and obscure field, drinking buddy of even more obscure heavy metal bands, had come a long way. He used to create symbol sets incorporating sub-sonic frequencies to analyze and compare raw stellar data captured by telescopes throughout the Northern Hemisphere. Now he was a glorified plumber / electrician!

But Giles did not complain. He'd signed up for this, after all. Moreover, he'd given much thought to the likely future of the human race after the MOAD revealed its secrets. It would be a *better* future, he had no doubt, in ways that no one at present could imagine. He relished the honor of ushering in that future, in whatever small way he could be helpful. Even if it was just mending antennas.

He spun the wheel to open the external hatch, and egressed.

A world of illimitable blackness opened around him. There was a roof to this world: a cracked white dinner plate, with a bite out of its upper edge.

Europa.

The 'cracks' he knew to be cyclopean trenches, evidence of Europa's geological activity, which sometimes produced outgassings of water vapor. The first observations of the MOAD had been mistaken for such plumes.

Europa seemed to hang alone in space, illuminated by the distant sun, which was behind the *SoD* at present, so that Giles floated in shadow. He was perplexed not to see Jupiter, and turned all around—keeping a nervous grip on the grab handle outside the airlock—in search of it, before realizing that Europa must be hiding it from view.

This, then, was a sign that the *SoD* had entered precisely the orbit desired by Mission Control! They were meant to be in an orbit as near as possible to Europa-stationary, above the side of the moon tidally locked away from Jupiter. And it looked like that's exactly where they were.

He radioed, "Kate, I think we did it. The burn parameters were exactly correct!"

"Good," Kate said. "Hurry up and fix those antennas. You're taking rems."

"But isn't it true that Europa shields us from the worst of

Jupiter's radiation?"

"Yes and no," Kate said. "The safest place on Europa is the leading hemisphere. We are orbiting towards the terminator, the line that divides the leading and trailing hemispheres. Same place Thing One and Thing Two landed. In fact we should be able to see them, when we get the optic sensors fixed. But right now our priority is restoring comms with Earth. I also need you to fix the dipole antenna so we can receive telemetry from Thing One and Thing Two," she added, in case he might have forgotten.

"I would have liked to see Jupiter," Giles sighed, working his way along the 'ladder' of grab handles that led over the top of the bridge. The module was a gray steel cylinder, with a rounded nose cone to deflect micro-impacts. Like the rest of the ridiculously named *Spirit of Destiny,* it was aesthetically null. 21st-century humanity seemed incapable of creating beautiful objects. It was just as well so much beauty remained in space, where *Homo sapiens* couldn't defile it. Giles had no very high opinion of his species, yet he wished to preserve it—a curious paradox!

"Hang on," Kate said. "You can't see Jupiter?"

"No."

"That's wrong. Jupiter should be visible above Europa's limb."

"But doesn't Europa block it out?"

"No! The distances are completely—OK, just tell me what you can see."

Giles breathed heavily. "I can see Europa."

"And?"

"She has the appearance of a crescent moon lying on her back."

"And *that's* wrong," said Kate. "At no time should Europa appear as a crescent. There's nothing to cast a shadow on it."

"But—" Giles started, prepared to insist on the evidence of his own eyes.

Then he understood what he was really looking at.

The black convexity eating into the top of Europa was, in fact, an object floating between him and the distant moon.

The dim, scattered lights which he had taken for stars were *lights,* located here and there on the object.

He stood up to see better. The movement peeled him off the bridge module. He floated up on his tether—and *now* he could see Jupiter! It peeked from above the object.

The lumpy, engorged silhouette of a thruster stood out sharply against the creamy bands of gas.

Giles Boisselot screamed.

CHAPTER 15

Kate called an all-hands meeting.

"We are close enough to the MOAD to spit on it," she said. "We were supposed to wind up in the same orbit, with a comfortable separation. Our actual separation is a couple of hundred meters."

Jack, feeling fantastic after ten hours of sleep, grinned and shrugged. The implied criticism of his seat-of-the-pants burn calculations did not rankle. "A miss is as good as a mile," he said.

"Sorry, but are we sure we aren't going to collide with it?" Hannah said.

"Our orbit is tilted a fraction of a degree further to the north," Kate said. "So no, we won't collide with it. Unless it moves."

There was some nervous laughter. Of course the MOAD wasn't going to move! It had sat here for ten years without ever doing anything.

Except HERFing human probes and spaceships, Jack thought, but he reckoned the same thing was on everyone else's mind, so he said nothing. His personal view was that the aliens had probably shot their bolt. That spacecraft was in *bad* condition. The pictures Giles had taken with his helmet camera, although low-rez, confirmed the massive hole halfway along the MOAD's length, and added detail to the pictures previously obtained by Thing One and Thing Two. It looked like an explosion had almost ripped the MOAD in half. Jack pictured the aliens holed up in there, taking potshots at the indomitable *SoD* with the only working weapon they still possessed: a radio-frequency transmitter. The aliens themselves refused to come into focus, but the general picture in Jack's imagination owed a lot to *Alien*—only in reverse. A few surviving crew members, marooned in their own ship ... stalked by some implacable menace?

He remembered Oliver Meeks's prediction that the MOAD would deliver doom to Earth, and felt a goose walk across his grave.

More realistically, the MOAD had probably suffered a steam explosion, or whatever the alien equivalent was.

And now you're in *real* trouble, E.T. Now the humans are here.

Jack couldn't wait to get in there, appropriately loaded for bear, of course.

That last part was going to be the problem.

He leaned over and whispered to Alexei, "Remind me again why we don't have guns?"

Alexei muttered, "I'm thinking about this. We might be able to make crossbows."

Jack nearly laughed out loud. Crossbows! "Wicked," he purred under his breath. His mind immediately went walkabout, foraging in the storage module for likely materials. He listened with half an ear as Kate moved on from the MOAD to other findings.

Giles, after recovering from the surprise of coming face-to-arse with the MOAD, had completed his task of repairing the antennas—both the directional antenna for comms with Earth, and the little dipole antenna for shortwave communications with Thing One and Thing Two. They'd acquired up-to-date telemetry from the two advance landers. No problems there, it seemed.

"About time something went right for a change," Skyler said. "When are we looking at recovering the reactants, ma'am?"

"I'm glad you asked," Kate said, smiling at him. *"You* will be recovering the reactants. You'll go in the Shenzhou Plus lander with Meili. It should've been Peixun, but … rest in peace. Jack and Alexei will take the Dragon. We'll need both landers shuttling up and down to fill the tanks. Probably four trips each. What's a little radiation, right, Skyler?"

Skyler's expression was a sight to behold. It clearly had never crossed his mind that he might have to crew one of the landers. Jack almost pissed himself laughing. He set Alexei off, and Meili also went into a fit of giggles. Skyler's expression turned murderous.

They were sitting around the kitchen table, with the debris of a hearty meal before them. The hydroponics were still in a shambles, so it felt like eating lunch at a table unaccountably left behind after a hurricane flattened your house. Their empty bowls testified to Meili's liberal hand with Szechuan spices, which had turned a stew of carrots, zucchini, potatoes, and reconstituted soy protein chunks into a feast. Hannah had even baked loaves of her special bread. The general feeling of ebullience after their safe arrival made laughter easy. It was Skyler's problem if he couldn't take a joke.

"I'm just saying, shouldn't the MOAD be our priority?" Skyler protested. He forgot to say *ma'am* this time, Jack noted.

"Absolutely," Kate said, and smiled, tigerishly. Jack suddenly got a sinking feeling. "But that won't take long. A few hours? Fire up the engine, boost our orbit, achieve a safe separation of a hundred klicks or so. Then, bombs away." She opened her hands as if releasing a weight. There was dead silence around the table.

Jack erupted, "You're joking. After coming all this way to investigate it, we're going to *blow it up?*"

Alexei said, "With what? I'm sorry, but shooting that thing with our railguns will be like firing an AK at an aircraft carrier."

"You would be correct," Kate said, measuring out her words, "if we only had standard slugs to work with. As it happens, we've also got a number of plutonium rounds."

"What?" Jack yelled. He'd done ammunition inventory himself a number of times. He knew for a fact that the ammo store outside the storage module only held standard steel slugs. Everyone else looked equally blindsided by this revelation—even Skyler, although he could be acting. The NXC agent, Jack knew, was very good at hiding his thoughts and feelings. And if there was a secret stash of plutonium rounds on board the *SoD*, the NXC must've had a hand in getting it there. *"Where?"* Jack demanded.

"You don't need to know that right now," Kate said. "I'll tell you when we're ready to fire them."

Jack subsided. He sprawled lower in his chair, knees wide apart, the posture of a sulky schoolboy.

The argument waxed noisy and circular.

Should we blow up the MOAD?

She said *several* plutonium rounds. I wonder if we've actually got enough.

Ollie—Jack mentally addressed his dead friend—what would you do?

He noticed that Hannah was taking no part in the

argument. She sat with her elbows on the table, chin in her hands, watching the debate as if it were a game of ping-pong.

Renewed guilt intruded on Jack's thoughts. He heaved himself forward and cut another hunk of bread, hoping that he would win some points with Hannah if he showed appreciation for her baking skills. He spread it with butter—a perishable that froze nicely, so they still had enough of it for special occasions. "This's terrific," he said, through a mouthful. "I could eat the whole loaf." Hannah shot him a wary glance and went back to watching the argument.

"Enough," Kate finally yelled. "This is an order from Mission Control. It's not up for debate."

But her upper lip glistened with a delicate sheen of sweat, and her hands made white-knuckled fists on the table. Jack had a lightbulb moment. Mission Control had not ordered any such thing. Kate had been alone on the bridge when she talked to Houston. She was making this up.

Jack had wanted her to ditch Mission Control's party line. He had wanted her to accept that *they* were the ones out here, and should be making the crucial decisions.

But this was the *wrong* decision.

Even Skyler evidently agreed with that.

"I'm just not getting it," Skyler said. "Why have they suddenly reversed an established policy?"

"Our mission," Kate said, "was to determine whether the MOAD represents a threat to humanity. It's clear that it does."

"How is that clear?" Skyler demanded. "We have not boarded the MOAD, we haven't scanned or photographed it, we haven't done any of the shit that we came six hundred million kilometers to do! This is bullshit."

"You've got a short memory, haven't you, Skyler?" Kate said. "Remember how the goddamn thing almost killed us, less than twenty-four hours ago? Yeah, that. Now tell me it's not dangerous."

Skyler fell back on, "We would need a UN resolution before we're legally allowed to fire on the MOAD. They can't have passed anything yet. The UN takes more than twenty-four hours to scratch its ass."

"Extraordinary circumstances," Kate said glibly. "Listen, Skyler, let me worry about the paperwork. As commander it's my responsibility to preserve the lives of my crew and the integrity of my ship." She turned to Jack. "Soon as we're done eating, I'd like you to execute a short burn to boost our orbit."

"No," Jack muttered.

She obviously heard him, but decided to give him a second chance. "Say again, Jack?"

Jack had a split second to decide whether to accuse her to her face of lying about the order from Mission Control. If he did, that would spell the end of the official command structure. It would be *Mutiny on the Bounty,* deep space edition.

Their wrangle over restarting the reactor had already set the stage for mutiny. Kate had said nothing about the incident since, and Jack had hoped they could draw a line under it. Least said, soonest mended. But now, already, he had to decide whether to disobey her *again.*

Don't do it, Meeks's ghost counselled him.

But the 'orders' were bullshit. Glancing around, he

confirmed that Skyler knew it, Alexei knew it, probably even Giles knew it.

Meili was nodding along with Kate, probably on the naïve assumption that their commander would not lie to them. And Hannah …

Hannah cleared her throat. "I would like to raise a related issue," she said. "That last burn drained our external tanks. We still have plenty of water for the life-support system, but as far as propulsion goes, I'm actually not sure we've got enough reaction mass to boost our orbit. So the whole thing might be moot, for the time being."

Jack grinned to himself in relief. He knew they probably had *barely* enough reaction mass for a small orbit adjustment, but it would be a close-run thing. Anyway, Hannah was giving him an out.

"The MOAD isn't going anywhere," Hannah continued. "So I think we should prioritize recovering our reactants from Thing One and Thing Two."

Kate frowned. But she seemed to recognize that Hannah had offered her an out, as well. Grudgingly, she said, "That's a good point, Hannah. I am hesitant to expose the ship and crew to the risk of another HERF. But we do need to retrieve the reactants. I can tell Mission Control that we'll have to hold off on the kill strike until we have completed that operation."

Jack felt a surge of disgust. She was still clinging to her lie! He said, "Shrapnel from a kill strike would fall out of orbit, and might well damage Thing One and Thing Two. *That's* the kind of risk I don't like. I'd rather not pilot the Dragon through a debris field, either."

"Oh really, Jack?" Kate shot back. "I thought danger was

like crack to you." She pushed back her chair. "Prepare the landers for launch."

*

Skyler found Alexei running the electric sander in the machine shop. He'd just returned from an EVA with Meili, fingertip-checking the Shenzhou Plus for any damage it might have sustained during their voyage. His muscles quivered with fatigue. Walking didn't cut it as exercise, after all. He couldn't imagine how he was going to get through four round-trips to the surface.

Alexei balanced in the foot tethers at the machine shop, which was a workbench in the storage module, equipped with basic tools. The sander whined. The extra-powerful vent over the workbench sucked metal dust away.

"What are you doing?" Skyler said.

"Sanding," Alexei said.

"Whoa, thanks, Captain Obvious." It looked like Alexei was putting a point on a four-inch length of welding rod. He had already done a bunch of them. The points glittered like needles.

Jack popped out from the storage locker next to the machine shop, which had turned into a walk-in locker as they drew down their supplies. "Found the sheet aluminum." He held two large pieces of it. "Oh, hey, Skyler. Ready to go?"

"Doesn't look like you're ready," Skyler said.

"We're just making a few last-minute preparations," Jack said.

"I wish we had PVC pipe," Alexei grumbled, ignoring Skyler.

"The aluminum will work," Jack said.

"Look, hey, guys, what are you making?" Skyler said.

Alexei snatched a meter-long length of iron from a clasp under the bench. He jammed one end of it into his shoulder like the stock of a rifle, and pointed it at Skyler's face. "Bang," he said.

Skyler despised everyone on board the *SoD* at the moment, but right now he despised Alexei most of all. The Russian enjoyed bullying those weaker than himself, and what really got under Skyler's skin was the knowledge that Alexei considered *him* weaker. Negligible, as a man and an astronaut.

He had wanted to talk to Jack and Alexei about Kate's supposed orders to carry out a kill strike on the MOAD, but now he changed his mind. "Fuck you too, Ivanov," he said dismissively, and floated towards the keel tube.

Bang.

That reminded him, actually.

CHAPTER 16

The Shenzhou Plus drifted away from the *SoD*, burping hydrazine gas from its rotational thrusters. Skyler and Meili, buckled into the red-upholstered seats, wore their spacesuits. Before today, Skyler hadn't worn his spacesuit in two years. It still smelled of vomit. The last time he wore it, boarding the SoD, he'd baptized it with puke. He had to do better on this outing, to prove that he wasn't deadweight.

At least, thank God, he didn't feel nauseated. *Yet.*

He peered at the LCD displays in the high-tech console in front of him. One of them showed an external camera feed.

He was hoping for, and dreading, a glimpse of the MOAD.

Instead, he saw the *SoD,* seeming to elongate as the two craft changed their relative positions, until the screen framed its entire length.

Outlined by sunlight glinting on its trusses, and dotted with warning lights, the *Spirit of Destiny* resembled nothing so much as the Eiffel Tower with a rotating restaurant on top. Further back, the bioshield—the steel disk that shaded the hab modules from the reactor's lethal radiation—stuck out all around the truss tower, like a platform to catch jumpers. The architectural comparison broke down at the back of the ship, where four gigantic external tanks ringed the engine. Those tanks had held the *SoD's* reaction mass. And were now as good as empty.

They had to refill those tanks, if they were ever to get home.

Meili smiled sideways at him. "It's beautiful, isn't it?"

"The *SoD?*"

"Yes."

"It is," Skyler said, surprised how strongly he agreed. "Most beautiful thing humanity has ever built."

"They'd slay me for saying this at home, but it's even more beautiful than Tianzi Mountain."

Skyler noticed that Meili had some odd little marks on her cheeks. They looked like dark red freckles. He was pretty sure she hadn't had those yesterday.

"OK, *SoD*, we have 200 meters of separation," she said into her headset.

"Shenzhou, you are cleared to de-orbit," Kate's voice said from the radio.

"Roger," Meili said. "Here we go."

She keyed in a throttle command. The Shenzhou Plus's main engine ignited with a loud, low-pitched roar. A wallop of thrust gravity smooshed them into their seats. They thrust against their direction of orbital travel, bleeding off velocity, until they began to fall down towards Europa.

Skyler was just the passenger; Meili was driving. She controlled the lander with a sure touch. An experienced pilot, she'd flown more than one manned Shenzhou launch during the *SoD* construction process. Not that this lander bore much resemblance to the original Shenzhou, which was a Soyuz knock-off.

Originally, the *SoD* had been meant to carry *two* Dragons—which would've been a massive win for SpaceX and the United States. But the Chinese had gotten their panties in a twist about that, and they'd come up with this modified Shenzhou to take one of the lander spots. NXC sources suggested they had had to enlist Russian help to build it. The new design featured a restartable engine, so

Skyler and Meili would be able to get back into orbit, which was a good thing, yup, a very good thing indeed …

Europa filled the screen, and Skyler marveled that he wasn't more scared. He trusted Meili to get them down safely. And how fucked-up was that? He worked for the NXC. She was a CNSA taikonaut, who might still turn out to be the saboteur. He'd sent the malware trigger home to Earth, but it would take them a while to analyze it. This Chinese-made landing craft might even be the vector for the malware. It might have been built to fail …

Meili engaged the retro-rockets. Inside her fishbowl helmet, strands of black hair wafted over those odd freckles. She jerked her head unconsciously to get her hair out of her face, and reported to Kate that they were on vector to land at their target coordinates. Her cool competence calmed Skyler's jitters. He was a sucker for a woman who knew what she was doing.

The camera feed turned black.

Skyler braced for a bump, like when you landed in the Mojave desert or on the plains of Kazakhstan.

He felt nothing.

Meili waved her glove in front of his helmet. "We're down!" Her voice came over the radio link. She was grinning, and Skyler grinned back.

"You stuck the landing," he told her.

"It's Europa," she said. "Gravity of thirteen percent of one gee."

Each of them weighed less than *half* as much here as they did in the *SoD's* rotating hab.

"OK," she said. "We want to absolutely minimize our time outside the lander. Remember the rems."

"Yes, ma'am," Skyler said jokingly.

"The most dangerous type of radiation is Bremsstrahlung. That's when you shield against high-energy beta particles with dense materials, like metal, and it actually makes it worse. But not to worry. Our suits aren't shielded, anyway."

"Great."

"Oh, there's the water loop, that helps a bit. But basically we should consider that we are unshielded. So we get out there, hook up the hoses, and then come back inside while we pump. Ready?"

"Ready."

They checked each other's helmet seals. Then they wriggled out of the crew module, through the pressure door behind their seats, and into the second service module, which held a basic survival kit and repair tools. They crammed into the airlock overhead. They had already been breathing pure oxygen all the way down, so there was no need to wait.

They scrabbled up into a new world.

The Shenzhou Plus incorporated extra tankage, which made it eleven meters tall, including its engine. It now sat on its tail, giving Skyler, up top, a panoramic view of Europa.

Jupiter squatted on the horizon, scary-big.

Cracked white terrain reminded him of the Arctic.

Here and there, little hills blistered the frozen expanse.

Thing Two stood a short way off, casting a columnar shadow.

Skyler started to descend the ladder. Meili's boot came down on the rung above his head. Then she said something to herself in Chinese and jumped off the ladder.

Arms spread, she floated down to the ground, staggered,

and pirouetted. Her laughter crackled into Skyler's helmet. "I did it!" she crowed. "I did it! I am the first human being to walk on Europa! *Wheeee!*"

Skyler said severely, "That was very childish." But he couldn't help smiling. Her spontaneity befitted the moment.

"I did it, I did it! *Wo zuo daole!*"

"Remember the rems," Skyler said, and then his own boots touched the ground. Virgin snow crunched under his soles, and a shock of awe overtook him. He understood Meili's euphoria. He was literally standing on another planet!

Well, moon.

Lashed by an invisible blizzard of radiation.

"C'mon, let's get pumping."

They moved in low-gravity bounds towards Thing Two. Meili really had stuck the landing. Only twenty meters separated the two craft.

Thing Two, in keeping with its Seussian nickname, resembled a cartoon space rocket. The 'rocket' was actually a tank left over from NASA's space shuttle program. It had started off full of reactants, which had powered Thing Two's voyage to Europa. When it got here, the tank had been empty. But as soon as it landed, Thing Two—remote-controlled by the probe operators at JPL—had sunk a drill deep into the ground, and started sucking up crushed ice.

Thing One, a few klicks away, had done the same.

Melt the ice with a radioisotope generator. Pump it into the electrolysis unit. Out comes LOX and LH2.

Europa, after all, was pretty much *made* of water.

The tank and electrolyzer assembly stood on top of a hexagonal shed with six stumpy legs—Thing Two's engine bell.

Each of the legs slanted out at an angle, for stability. They elevated the engine bell about five feet off the ground. The drill descended behind it. The snow and ice was all churned up back there.

Meili jumped to catch the ladder on the side of the engine bell. She climbed up, unhooked Thing Two's LOX hose, and tossed the end down to Skyler. He made the catch, and felt proud of himself for not fumbling it.

Running in big leaps, remembering the rems, he dragged the hose back to the Shenzhou. He climbed up the ladder. The metal connector on the end of the hose stuck to his gloves. Liquid dribbled from it, bubbling like hot water from a kettle, and instantly vaporized. The temperature here was -180 Celsius, cold enough to boil liquid oxygen. Clumsily, he attached the end of the hose to the port on the lander's tank.

While he was doing this, Meili, exploring around the back of Thing Two's electrolysis unit, sang out numbers that filled Skyler with relief. 1.8 million liters. The telemetry had not lied. Thing Two's tanks were full to the brim with life-giving water.

He went back for the LH2 hose, and hooked that one up.

"OK, I'm turning on the pumps," Meili said.

"Roger."

Meili reappeared around the side of Thing Two. Skyler watched her descend to the ground.

"That's weird," she said.

"What's weird?"

There was a pause. Meili ducked under the engine bell. He could only see her legs. She spoke in an entirely different

134

tone. "The engine's gone."

*

Skyler sprinted back to Thing Two. He joined Meili under the engine bell. They shouldn't've even been able to get under there. The engine should've taken up all the space. They stood in a metal cave. Their helmet lamps flashed around the roof.

No. Fucking. Engine.

"Holy shit," Skyler said. Waves of disbelief crashed over him. For some reason he remembered his eleventh birthday, when he woke up with a weight on his feet, and sat up, expecting to see the foot of his bed heaped with presents, because that's how they rolled in the Taft household back then, but it was his father sitting on his feet, stroking his leg through the quilt and crying, yes, crying, and then he told Skyler that Mom was gone. She'd moved to Bali with her *goddamn hippie* yoga instructor. You can't make this stuff up.

Ends of fuel and coolant pipes glittered, cleanly sheared off. Wiring appeared to have been excavated out of the engine housing. Shards of low-temperature plastic littered the ice underfoot.

Skyler ducked out from under the engine bell and stared around the frozen landscape. His heart pounded so hard, he felt like he might pass out.

Nothing moved.

He transmitted to Meili, "They took it."

"Who? *Who* took it?"

"The aliens." The NXC had not yet acknowledged that there might be living aliens aboard the MOAD. Belatedly, Skyler reverted to the party line— "Or their robots took it. Maybe the AI in charge of the MOAD has drones. It sent them down to the surface to … to scavenge for parts …"

"Because you could totally fix an interstellar spaceship with the components of Thing Two's drive?"

"What's your theory, then?" Skyler said, panicking.

"I don't know. I don't have a theory." Meili came out from under the engine bell. "We need to inform Kate." She started running back towards the Shenzhou.

Skyler ran after her. They climbed the ladder. Meili was talking to herself in Chinese. She might have forgotten she was transmitting. Skyler's Mandarin comprehension sucked, despite Meili's own attempts to teach him, but he caught a few words: *they were correct … impossible …* and again, *they were correct.*

Meili plopped into the Shenzhou Plus's airlock. Skyler paused, halfway in and halfway out, to take another look at the landscape.

If the MOAD had sent down a lander, wouldn't it have left some visible traces?

A thin layer of snow—actually, frozen oxygen—covered the ice, and what's more, the ice wasn't flat like a skating rink. Every tiny variation in topology sprouted ice-moss. You crushed the feathery peaks when you walked on them. He could clearly see their own tracks, leading between the Shenzhou and Thing Two. Every bootprint held a puddle of black shadow.

The other tracks were less obvious.

He wouldn't have seen them at all if he wasn't specifically looking for something of the kind.

"Meili!"

She popped her head up— "Oh God, what?"

"Look."

Another trail of shadow-puddles led away from Thing Two, to the east. The giveaway was they were equally spaced.

A couple of meters apart.

"Whatever made *those* footprints," Skyler rasped, "was at least twenty feet tall."

He shuddered and clutched Meili's arm. She gripped him just as tightly. When the monster under the bed comes out and leaves footprints on the floor, you feel like a child. They dropped into the airlock. Skyler slammed the hatch. Meili cycled the airlock, her gloves slipping on the fiddly little high-tech buttons. They fell back into the service module. By common consent they unlocked the rear entry hatches of each other's spacesuits and writhed out into the oxygen-rich, sour-smelling air of the lander. The fans roared, a welcome noise after the quiet of outside.

Skyler grabbed Meili in his arms and held her tight. The urge for human contact was simply overpowering. She wrapped her arms and legs around him. They swayed together, like children hugging, and then all of a sudden Skyler no longer felt like a child, but rather like an insanely horny man who hadn't had sex in two years. More, actually. His sex life had been flatlined since long before he boarded the SoD.

Meili kissed his neck.

"Oh," Skyler wept. "I'm about to come in my pants." He ran his hands over the taut curves of her waist and ass. His fingertips brushed the skin of her upper thighs. "Please ... don't ..." He tried to quench his arousal by telling himself he didn't want Jack Kildare's sloppy seconds; he told himself he was being disloyal to Hannah. Nothing availed. Meili worked her hand down and squeezed his hardness, tearing a groan from his lips.

"I feel like I'm going crazy," she said.

"You're telling me."

She abruptly pulled away and retreated to the other side of the service module, staring at him.

"We have to radio up to the *SoD*," Skyler said, recovering his sanity.

"I was ordered to hijack the *SoD*," Meili said.

"Oh, *that's* what that was about," Skyler said. After they restored comms with Earth, he'd finally received the NXC's translation of the last conversation between Meili and Xiang Peixun that he'd recorded on his iPod. "Peixun said you had to gain access to the bridge, and you said you couldn't. That it was impossible."

"It *was* impossible. After Xiang died, I felt like I'd been set free. They couldn't expect me to do it on my own!"

"What did they expect you to do?"

Meili's expression turned inward, as if she wasn't really talking to him, but the faraway CNSA officials who'd given her her marching orders. "Destroy the MOAD."

This, after Kate's deceitful blow-up-the-MOAD gambit yesterday! It blew Skyler's mind how many people were turning out to be short-sighted morons. Didn't they realize that the MOAD could represent the next technological leap forward for humanity? If there were aliens on board, that complicated the picture, but the promise of levelling up for free still held. Of course, it would not be so enticing if it wasn't *your* country in prime position to grab the technological goodies …

"Do they think we won't share?" he asked.

"The Communist Party believes that the politicians in

Washington are just like themselves," Meili said.

"Actually, they pretty much are," Skyler admitted.

"All they care about is staying in power. The MOAD threatens the status quo. We already had the Xian Incident." She referred to the 2018 uprising by a unit of the PLA, which had declared a new republic at China's old capital, before being bombed into oblivion. "If there is regime change, those pigs in Beijing will end up hanging by their necks. And they know it. The MOAD could trigger regime change in any number of ways. It's an outside-context problem. The outcome is unpredictable. Even in the best-case scenario, the US gets an advantage. So they try to control it the old-fashioned way. Blow it up."

"Kate says we've got plutonium rounds, but no one knew about that until yesterday."

"No, we didn't, either."

"So how were you supposed to pull it off?"

"Extract fuel from the core of the *SoD's* reactor," Meili sighed. "All you need is about two kilos of U-235. It becomes a fission bomb yielding several million tons of TNT equivalent."

"And, um, you *die,*" Skyler said. "Handling unshielded uranium tends to have that effect."

"Oh, sure. They don't care. It's not *them* dying." Meili twitched her head to get her hair out of her face. "Peixun would have done it. He would have made me do it. When he died, I cried for joy! *For joy!* I was standing in front of a firing squad, and now I can live!" She flung up her arms, echoing her pirouette out on the ice.

"You're too beautiful to die," Skyler said. He was not good at complimenting women, but he meant this compliment with all his heart.

"Thank you," Meili said. "Anyway, I want to defect to the United States. Maybe you can help me. I'm worried about my parents. Can your agency get them out of China?"

"Whoa, whoa," Skyler said.

"What's the problem? I told you everything! I've given you great intelligence!"

"Well, sure, but …" Skyler shook his head. "No, actually, you haven't told me everything. What about the malware?"

"What malware?"

Her eyebrows went up, her eyes widened, her mouth fell open. Only a trained professional like Skyler himself could fake surprise that well, and Meili wasn't a professional. She was fairly readable most of the time. He'd accurately read the tension between her and Xiang, for example—he just hadn't known what was causing it.

Now, he knew for a certainty that she'd never been told about the malware.

"It may have been your bosses' Plan B," he said. "I'm still waiting on an analysis of the trigger."

"I don't know anything about that," Meili said. "You have to believe me. I've told you everything I know." She bounced over to him and wrapped her arms around his neck again.

"Oh honey," Skyler said, burying his face in her hair. "I don't work for Immigration Services. But I'll do what I can, I promise. I've got some connections."

"I always think you're sexy," Meili said. "But Xiang wanted me to sleep with you, so I didn't. You understand? He wanted me to get information from you … But I haven't asked you anything about the NXC, your work. I ask for nothing. Just help my family."

"How did he take it when you were sleeping with Jack?"

Meili giggled. "It pissed him off! That's why I did it! Oh, Xiang was so mad. I told him, if he wants to trade sex for information, he can do it himself."

"Uh …?"

"You're so stupid! Giles is gay. And Xiang is so patriotic, he would take a cock up his ass for China." She uttered the vulgarity in a matter-of-fact tone. "But he never did it. His excuse was the Earth Party is not important."

"The Earth Party? I feel like I'm missing something."

"Giles supports the Earth Party. Actually, I support it, too." Meili touched her cheeks.

Those odd freckles.

"OK, I *am* missing something."

"I want to come to Europa, not as a Chinese, but as a human being."

A memory stirred. The NXC had noted a fad for 'micro-cupping,' not just in China but throughout Southeast Asia. Using tiny suction pumps, Earth Party supporters gave themselves temporary tattoos in the form of blood blisters. It showed their support for the movement in nations where actual *movements* of the kind the Earth Party favored—meandering, cross-country, ideally cross-border walks—were not allowed.

The micro-cupping thing had run its course in 2019 or so, but of course Meili hadn't been back to Earth since then.

"I like the freckles," Skyler said, touched. Having rejected patriotism, Meili must have cast about for a substitute identity. It was natural for her to settle on the Earth Party. The movement had gained a reputation as the first truly global political movement, no matter how poorly defined its policy aims were. It had even gained some institutional credibility as Earth Party representatives won election to national parliaments in Europe and the U.S. House of Representatives. In the NXC's view, it was a messianic movement in secular clothing: the MOAD, our 21st-century salvation. Fringe activists also borrowed the Earth Party brand to indulge in sit-ins and looting. Skyler frowned on the whole business. However he understood how the international brothers-in-arms shtick must appeal to Meili.

He drew her into his arms, meaning to tenderly reassure her that he accepted her revelations. Unfortunately, his dick was as stupid as a dog with a bone. It swelled whether he would or not.

A string of beeps from the crew module pierced the white noise of the fans.

Meili broke away. "The tanks are full."

She dropped down through the hatch into the crew module. Skyler followed.

Now they heard Kate's voice coming thinly from the headset hanging on the center console. "... come in! Shenzhou! Come in! Meili! Skyler ..."

"She must have been trying to reach us for ages!" Meili dived for the headset. Suddenly, the urgency of what they had to impart to the *SoD* returned. "Skyler, close the valves! ... Kate, I'm so sorry. This is Meili. I read you loud and clear." Putting on the headset, she winked at Skyler. "We were busy."

Skyler toppled towards the consoles. Meili jerked a thumb at an LCD display over the left seat. Goddamn touch-screens. The Chinese had seemingly determined to make the upgraded Shenzhou's control panels look like the inside of a luxury car. Everything was electronic, not mechanical, and half of the symbols on the screen were in Chinese, with no or very dubious English annotations. Skyler saw a window labeled PUMPS, and stabbed all the off buttons. The window went away.

Meili was telling Kate about their discovery in a high-pitched gabble. "Aliens! ... *Aliens!*"

When she concluded the transmission, she was scowling. "She wants us to go out again and photograph the tracks."

"At least she's not telling us to disbelieve our lyin' eyes," Skyler said. "Oh well, we would've had to go out to disconnect the hoses, anyway."

Meili shivered. "I don't want to go out again," she said, but she put on her spacesuit.

They repeated the process of egressing from the airlock.

The tracks etched into the fluffy ice carpet had not gone away, like a nightmare should.

"I'll disconnect the hoses," Skyler said. "You take the pictures."

They had prepped their camera before coming out. Meili raised it to her fishbowl helmet and snapped.

Skyler climbed halfway down the ladder, disconnected the LOX hose, climbed further down, disconnected the LH2. He trudged back to Thing Two. Now he knew it wasn't the drill that had churned up the ice around the advance lander's feet. It was the aliens. He pictured them bending their twenty-foot bodies to pry under the engine bell, and shuddered uncontrollably. He climbed up and replaced the hoses on their hooks.

Standing on the platform behind the electrolysis unit, he

followed the line of tracks with his eyes. They vanished over the horizon.

On Europa, the horizon was only a couple of kilometers away. Small moon, tight curvature.

He hurried back to the Shenzhou Plus. They returned to the crew module and transmitted Meili's pictures to the *SoD*.

CHAPTER 17

Jack and Alexei sat in the crew module of the Dragon lander, still docked with the *SoD,* waiting.

And waiting.

And waiting.

Periodically, Kate came on the radio and told them to hang on for a few more minutes.

"Elephant," Alexei said, throwing a homemade crossbow quarrel to Jack.

"Edible," Jack said, catching it.

"You lose. Elephant is not edible."

"Bet you they are, ever tried?"

Alexei had taught him a Russian game called Is It Edible? It was meant to be played with a ball. They were using a crossbow quarrel. The tricky part was catching it without puncturing the gloves of your spacesuit. Alexei had put wicked points on the things. They had the crossbows in the storage area overhead.

"My turn, anyway," Jack said. "Wheelchair." He tossed the quarrel. Alexei batted it back. "Kate." Alexei caught it. Jack cracked up. Alexei threw it back, quite hard.

At that moment Kate came on the radio again. "Guys?" Her voice crackled with tension. "Sorry to keep you waiting so long. Here it is. Meili and Skyler have found some weird shit. The engine of Thing Two is gone. Missing. And there are tracks, as in footprints, leading away from Thing Two."

"Oh God," Jack said.

"Yeah. Meili took photographs and sent me the data via the Shenzhou's uplink. I've matched the photographs with our high-rez images of the surface, which appear to show

… well, I've forwarded everything to you. Have a look for yourselves."

Alexei reached for his laptop. He'd brought his laptop and Jack had brought his Nikon on board the Dragon, in preparation for the side trip they had planned, which was an unauthorized flyby of the MOAD. They'd been planning to launch when Kate gave them the green light. Instead of de-orbiting immediately, they had planned to cruise past the MOAD first. Check it out at close range. Take some better pictures. And if a suitable place to dock the Dragon presented itself, well, you never knew …

This new information underlined just how much they didn't know, how volatile the whole situation was.

Alexei used the end of the crossbow quarrel to tap around on his laptop, since the keyboard was not designed to be used with spacesuit gloves.

The first of the pictures Kate had forwarded filled the screen.

"Got it," Alexei said.

With enhanced contrast and magnification, Jack could see a trail of black dots leading east from Thing Two. The tracks continued in a straight line for a distance marked as 56 kilometers, and then vanished.

Next picture.

Thing One, seen from orbit.

Another line of tracks led away from it, and converged on the same place where the first set of tracks vanished. Kate had marked this location with an X.

Alexei said, "Do you think they also stole the engine of Thing One?"

"It looks that way, doesn't it?" Kate said. "Do you see

what's at that location I've marked X?"

"I would say it's a hill."

"And that's what I would've thought, too, but look at that line just north of the hill. It's about two hundred meters long, and very straight. It may be a shadow … or something else." Kate's voice hardened with anger. "They *stole our shit!* Guys, they fucking took our shit and carted it back to, God knows what the fuck that is, but I want to find out."

Jack and Alexei exchanged a delighted glance. So this was what it took to get Kate on board with the spirit of exploration: *they stole our shit!*

Up until now Kate had been the consummate professional. She'd played it safe all the way, to the point of making up orders to destroy the MOAD before it could hurt the *SoD* again. But now she was *pissed.*

OK, maybe she was pissed at *them*, as much as at the aliens. Either way, this was, Jack decided, a big improvement.

"I'm sure you can see where I'm going with this," Kate continued. "I'm going to notify Mission Control right now, but what are they gonna say? Either leave it alone, or go and check it out. Those are our only choices. So you know what, I'm going to preempt their decision. You're all fueled up and ready to rock. Let's go check it out." An unpleasant edge entered her voice. "I know how much you guys love danger."

Jack grimaced. She was daring them to demur. But what she didn't know was that he and Alexei had already planned to board the MOAD (let's be truthful) and go stalking aliens through its mysterious interior, armed with DIY crossbows. In comparison with the Ridley Scott-inspired menaces he'd already imagined, component-filching, footprint-leaving aliens sounded like a pushover.

"They must have abandoned the MOAD and taken refuge on the surface," he said. "Some refuge."

"I want you to exercise due caution," Kate warned.

It was far too late for that, of course.

*

After two hours, Kate finally cleared the Shenzhou Plus to launch. She said, "Jack and Alexei are safely down on the ground. At present they're preparing to EVA from the Dragon."

Meili tasted envy as bitter as a mouthful of turnip greens. "It's not fair," she heard herself say. "Why them?"

She glanced at Skyler, in the left seat, and knew he felt the same way.

These are *our* aliens!

We discovered them!

Why should Jack and Alexei get to meet them first?

Meili had already made history by becoming the first person to walk on Europa, but she wanted more. She wanted it all. She wanted Skyler and she wanted a big house in Texas for her family and she wanted her name on streets, and a movie made about her.

"That's the way the cookie crumbles, hon," Kate said. "Your job is to get back up here with those reactants. Honestly, why would you even want their job? It's dangerous as fuck, what they're about to do." She chuckled. "I wish I would've sent Giles down with them, too. Oh, well." She reverted to CapCom-style formality. "You are cleared for launch, Shenzhou. Godspeed."

"It's not fair," Meili muttered. She sighed, and opened the throttle.

The Shenzhou soared off the surface of Europa.

Skyler grunted as the thrust gravity spanked them. They were only pulling 0.6 gees, but they'd been living in low gravity for so long that it felt like the 3G punch you experienced on lift-off from Earth. Both of them had their suits on, which helped a bit.

Watching the fuel monitor, Meili said on their suit-to-suit link, "This will not go well. Those two are not trained in diplomacy."

"And I am." Skyler punctuated his words with gasps. "I had to practice on actors wearing rubber forehead costumes. I shit you not. We went through every version of the first contact scenario they could dream up. Nobody believed there would turn out to be actual, living aliens, but that's what the NXC does, we cover all the bases." He breathed heavily. "Now watch those douchebags fuck up our one and only chance to make a good first impression on our interstellar neighbors."

Meili laughed. She liked Skyler's sense of humor. On second thoughts, maybe he hadn't been joking.

"But, on the bright side," Skyler added. "maybe the aliens will vaporize them on sight. Betcha that's what Kate is hoping for."

Meili twisted her mouth skeptically. She doubted that Kate would actually try to get her pilot and co-pilot killed. She believed Kate was a good person and a conscientious commander, and Meili rarely erred in her assessments of people. For instance, everyone hated Skyler, but Meili had always felt that he was a sweet, sensitive guy … and see, she was right! Or take Giles. Everyone else made fun of him. But he had an inside track on the Earth Party, so Meili often talked to him about the movement. He was really cool when you got to know him …

A flashing alert from the auxiliary power unit interrupted her thoughts.

Low fuel.

The APU was running in the red.

"That's not possible!" she cried in her own language.

"That reminds me," Skyler said. "When we were climbing back into the Shenzhou, you were talking in Chinese. You kept saying *impossible. They were correct. Impossible.* What was that about?"

"Oh, I was talking about the Earth Party. They've believed in the aliens from day one. That's why they set up the moon base," she said distractedly.

"Typical cargo cult behavior," Skyler said. "Sorry."

"The APU is out of fuel."

"What's an APU?"

"The auxiliary power unit! It feeds the turbopumps for the main engine—"

The main engine cut out.

The Shenzhou's acceleration gave way to a sickening mushy drift, like when you run out of gas in your car. That had happened to Meili a couple of times back home. She could be a little bit absentminded. But not about the goddamn APU! This was life and death! She *knew* its hydrazine tank had been 72% full, precisely.

"What's happening?" Skyler shouted, as they floated up against their straps.

Before Meili could answer, the main engine surged back. A pulse of acceleration threw them back against their couches. After a second or two the engine died again, jolting them forward.

Meili scanned all the consoles, desperately trying to figure out what was wrong. Could she or Skyler have inadvertently dumped the hydrazine tank on the ground? No, she'd have noticed!

Another surge, this time so violent that her helmet snapped back against her couch. The helmet's padding cushioned her head. She was going to have a sore neck.

The engine died for the third time, tossing them forward again.

Skyler was yelling and screaming in full-fledged panic. "Shut up," Meili shouted at him. "Did you touch anything? When we were on the ground, or at any point? Tell me right now!"

Reading status displays, she confirmed that the computer had switched the main engine off, because it wasn't getting any fuel, because the fucking APU was fucked. And so were they.

"The only thing I touched was that," Skyler said, pointing at the control panel for the pumps. "I turned the fueling pumps off, like you said. That's all. I didn't touch anything else."

Meili swiped a gloved finger across the special reactive touch-screen. Her heart sank as she saw what he'd done. "You turned the APU heater off." She turned it back on.

"No, I didn't!"

"I told you to turn off the *valves!* But you turned off the heater for the APU pump! So the hydrazine froze! And now the tank is full of slush, which clogs the APU pump, so it thinks it is out of fuel. Oh dammit, Skyler."

"Why are those two things on the same touch-screen

anyway?" Skyler shouted.

"I don't know," Meili said. "It's like Windows 10."

"Or iPhone updates. Remember those?"

"Every time something is updated, it's worse than before."

"I think that just means you're over thirty," Skyler said. They floated in an unearthly silence and stillness. "So what happens now?" Skyler said after a moment.

Meili half-heard him. She was trying to contact the *SoD.* "Kate, come in, come in." The mission commander did not respond. She must be busy talking to Jack and Alexei. Sadness swamped Meili. She had wanted to meet the aliens. She had wanted so much.

"What happens now?" Skyler repeated. "We're floating! Are we in orbit?"

Meili had to laugh at that. His cluelessness was both annoying and sweet. She couldn't even blame him for switching the APU heater off. He hadn't known any better. She should have been clearer in her instructions. "We're not in orbit. The SoD is 430 kilometers up. We're not even at twenty kilometers."

"But we're in freefall!"

"That means we're topping out, and—" Right on cue, the sensation of falling arrived. "Now we are going down."

"You mean we're going to crash."

Meili switched the APU off and switched it on again, repeatedly. Every time she prayed for the pump to start, and every time it failed. "The heater doesn't have enough time to work. The fuel is still frozen." Her stomach was being sucked downward. Her brain screamed *Falling, falling. Mama, catch me.* But her mother was millions of kilometers away.

Skyler said, "Well, crap. I don't want to die."

"I don't want to die, either." She almost lost control there. She had only just clawed her life back from the Communist Party. How could the universe steal it from her? She said with desperate optimism, "We might be OK. The gravity is very weak."

Subjectively, they seemed to be falling ass-first. The engine bell would hit the ground first. That was good. Meili mentally reviewed the specs of the crash couches. These, too, were good. The best. You can't 'update' a crash couch ...

"Meili," Skyler said. "I love you. I'm so fucking pissed we didn't get to spend more time together."

She caught back a sob. "I love you, too." It was the first time she had ever said this in English to anyone, although she didn't tell him that.

The APU fired.

Meili screamed in joy.

She restarted the turbopumps.

A few tense seconds later, the main engine growled into life.

"Oh thank fuck," Skyler whooped. "I believe in God now."

But they were still falling.

"Mama catch me," Meili whispered.

The Shenzhou smashed into the ground.

CHAPTER 18

Jack stood in oxygen snow and ice moss, crossbow on his shoulder, looking up at a radio mast.

It rose as high as the tall masts at Rugby Radio Station, in Warwickshire, that you used to be able to see from the A5.

A dead white, tapered rod, like an octopus tentacle electrified to perfect rigidity. From space, all you'd see would be a suspiciously linear shadow.

"Now we know how they HERFED us," he said over the radio to Alexei.

"I don't see any cables," Alexei said, walking around the far side of the mast. "No power distribution unit, nothing."

In its starkly minimalist, unadorned construction, devoid of any fussy bits, the radio mast looked so palpably alien—despite being recognizable as a radio mast, going off the receiver dishes and active antenna mounted at the top—that it seemed silly to expect it to have power cables and that sort of thing.

"I expect the support infrastructure's buried," Jack said vaguely. "Maybe over there."

Beyond the mast, a quarter-kilometer from where they'd set the Dragon down, stood a small hill. They were awaiting Kate's OK to explore around the back of there. If she didn't hurry up and get back to them, they'd go anyway. It was not smart to hang about in this radiation-soaked environment. They'd budgeted fifteen minutes for this exploration and five of those had already gone by. "Kate?" Jack said, opening a channel to the *SoD*. "Have you had a chance to look at the pictures of the mast I just sent?"

Unlike Skyler and Meili during their walk on the surface,

Jack and Alexei could communicate directly with the *SoD*, using the Dragon's transmitter as a re-broadcast station. The Shenzhou couldn't do that. Frequency mismatch. These things happen when you've got thousands of people worldwide 'cooperating.'

"Fuck it. Let's go." Alexei started toward the hill.

Jack followed, with a worried glance back at the Dragon. He didn't like leaving it alone. But what could happen to it? "Six minutes."

They bounded towards the icy bulge. From space it had looked like any one of the other blisters that memorialized old water vapor eruptions. Tiny volcanoes, in fact. *Cryovolcanoes.* But cryovolcanoes had jagged crater rims, whereas this one was flat-topped. It reminded Jack of Wembley Stadium with the roof shut.

"That's not a hill," Alexei said, echoing his thoughts. "It's an igloo."

"They've roofed over the crater."

"Ice makes a good radiation shield."

As they loped towards the roofed hill, a new star shone out in the sky to the west.

"That'll be the Shenzhou," Jack said. "Funny. We shouldn't be able to see it from here."

As he spoke, he realized the star was moving the wrong way.

Down.

It vanished over the horizon.

"That did not look good," Alexei said, staring in the direction the Shenzhou had gone.

A scarcely-perceptible tremor travelled through the soles of Jack's boots.

"Guys!" Kate's voice blared into their helmets. "Jack, Alexei, come in!"

"This is Jack," he snapped.

"The Shenzhou's gone. It crashed a few minutes after taking off." Delivering this unthinkable news, Kate sounded icy calm. "We're in trouble now. I want you to immediately stop whatever you're doing—"

Jack started to run in the direction—half-remembered, half-guessed; the whole smooth curve of the horizon looked the same—where the Shenzhou had come down.

Alexei tackled him from behind.

"Get off!" Jack shouted.

"They're dead," Alexei grated.

"They don't have to be dead! It's perfectly possible to survive a power-off fall. They crashed near here!" He threw an elbow into Alexei's midriff. Alexei's suit absorbed the impact, but the momentum of Jack's blow toppled them both over sideways. Clumsy in the micro-gravity, they rolled over and over, wrestling.

Kate shouted in their helmets, "I can see the debris field. They are dead. The Shenzhou is totaled. Parts from that thing are spread out across a square kilometer. So if you want to be a hero, Jack, how about being a hero for those of us who are still living? Get back to the Dragon. Haul ass to Thing One and pump those goddamn reactants. Without the Shenzhou, we need the Dragon more than ever. It will have to make *seven* trips to fill the *SoD's* tanks, and you will have to make more EVAs than planned. We're fresh out of wiggle room. We do not have time to screw around with alien radio transmitters! Do you read me, Jack? Acknowledge!"

Jack wound up sprawled on his back with Alexei on top of him. The sun silhouetted Alexei's helmet. Pinning Jack's upper body, Alexei panted, "Are you going to do anything stupid?"

Jack moved his head from side to side. The sun came into view, so distant, so small, and then winked out again behind Alexei's helmet. The digital clock in the heads-up area of his faceplate glowed green. "Eleven minutes," he rasped.

"Good," Alexei said. "So, we go on." He rolled off Jack and went to retrieve their crossbows from where they'd dropped them.

Kate said, "Look, we'll destroy the radio mast from orbit. I can do that, but first you have to get out of the way!"

Jack stood up. He hoped they hadn't damaged their suits rolling around like that. Thank God there was no sharp stuff on the ground, anyway—just crushed ice and oxygen snow, which now coated them both, melting off the slightly-warmer outsides of their suits and sublimating into wisps of vapor.

"Jack, do you read me? Acknowledge!"

"I read you," Jack said, staring past Alexei at the hill, or dome, or whatever the hell it was. A black dot grew on its sunlit side. Became a circle.

"So return to the Dragon," Kate said. "That's an order!"

"Something rather interesting's happening," Jack said. "Alexei, look. No, behind you."

Spiky shapes crawled out of the hole. One, two, three. *Crawled*, yes, on all fours. The motion was perfectly recognizable. When they stood up, that movement was also recognizable, and the pins they stood on were legs, impossibly long and thin.

Alexei scuffled back to Jack's side, keeping his face turned to the …

… aliens, yes, here we are, and here they are …

… aliens.

Oh my flipping God. *Aliens.*

Alexei reached for the duct-tape ammo belt he had made. He ripped out a quarrel and slotted it into the groove of his crossbow, between the two angle irons that made the stock.

Jack loaded his own crossbow. As he reached for the cocking lever, he reconsidered.

They aren't carrying weapons.

They might be friendly.

Anything's possible.

He reached over and pushed Alexei's crossbow down, so it wasn't pointing at the approaching beings. "Don't scare them," he said.

The aliens and the humans walked towards each other and stopped a couple of meters apart. The aliens had two legs. Two arms. Their oversized heads looked like they were wearing squids on their shoulders, with waving tentacles behind and elongated bits before. Twin bulges halfway up the elongated bits could have been eyes but they were blank white, dead white, just like every other part of the aliens' bodies.

The creatures stood about seven feet tall, not the twenty that Skyler had excitedly reported.

Tusks curled out of the bottoms of their headparts, and went over their shoulders to small, rectangular backpacks. Tusks? Or breathing tubes? Perhaps the aliens were wearing advanced, form-fitting spacesuits.

Or perhaps the beings inside there weren't remotely

humanoid.

"Hello," said a clear, fluting voice. "This is so thrilling. I'm afraid we don't know your names?"

Jack shouted, "Fuck!"

Alexei shouted, *"O Gospodi!"*

Kate shouted, "Who was *THAT?!?*"

Jack let out a breathless laugh. "I think it was them," he said. His radio squealed. "Alexei?"

"I'm here," Alexei said, and he reached for Jack's hand. The two men gripped each other's gloves, still holding their crossbows in their free hands. The pressure of Alexei's hand anchored Jack in the moment, a bulwark against conflicting impulses to run, to shoot, to go up to the aliens and touch them to make sure they were real. Strangely the one thing that did not occur to him was to reply. It was as if rocks or sea creatures had spoken—a marvel, not a conversational gambit.

The alien in the middle approached them with its stilted gait and tapped on Jack's helmet, drawing back swiftly as Jack reflexively swung his crossbow at it. "Hello, hello?" it said. "Is this thing on?"

Jack cleared his throat. "Um, yeah. Are you—" he pointed at it— "talking to me?"

"Well, I'm trying to," it said. It spoke English with a cut-glass BBC accent, and that was the weirdest thing of all. "If you aren't going to attack us," it went on, "perhaps you'd like to come indoors? It really isn't a good idea to stand around out here. The radiation, you know—it's extremely damaging. We're always getting cancer, and your physiology may make you more prone to cellular damage than we are, although I admit we aren't sure how your bodies work."

Jack and Alexei looked at each other. Alexei shrugged. "What the hell?" he said.

Jack felt a little delirious. He said, "Good point about the radiation. But sorry, you HERFed us three times. I mean, you attacked us with a high energy radio frequency weapon. I assume that's it over there. You almost destroyed our ship. So I hope you'll appreciate that we're not in a very trusting mood." He lifted his crossbow to his shoulder.

The aliens turned to each other, for all the world like humans conferring. Suddenly Jack's helmet filled with an intolerable high-pitched sound.

It made him remember running down the street in Nuneaton after dark, a daily ordeal when he was in primary school. Every house he passed would assault him with a high-pitched tone that felt like a screwdriver going into his young ears—so *run,* run past the houses, as if they were the lairs of wolves. Later he had found out that those noises were flyback squeal from old cathode-ray televisions. Only children with sharp ears could hear them. He must have lost the ability to hear 15,000 Hz and up by now, but this sounded just as high, and hurt just as badly. It was a cat playing the violin, it was fingernails on a blackboard. The wolves had got him.

He screamed.

Distantly, through the God-awful squealing noise, Alexei also screamed. Then Alexei raised his crossbow and loosed into the nearest alien.

The squeal raced up and down the spectrum, from one agonizing high frequency to another.

Jack wanted to rip his helmet off. He felt nauseated, crucified by the noise. Alexei had the right idea. The aliens were aiming this noise at them. Therefore, stop the aliens.

He shot at the middle one. The 'string' of the crossbow, a length of cable, twanged. The sheet aluminum bow flexed. The sanded-sharp welding rod thudded into the alien's center of mass.

The noise did not stop. If anything it got worse. Jack loaded another quarrel into his crossbow.

Alexei shot at the last uninjured alien.

"Make a run for the Dragon," Jack howled, but it was already too late. Shadows flickered on the ice all around them. More aliens had come out of the igloo while they were distracted by the first three. Because of their dead-white coloration, which camouflaged them against Europa's icy terrain, their shadows were easier to see than they were. They moved like insects rather than people at the run, popping up in sand-flea jumps with their legs tucked under them. Now it was easy to see where those widely spaced footprints had come from. They must have carried the Things' engines in pairs.

Thieving cunts, and I believed for one second that they might be friendly?

With grim methodical care, Jack loaded and shot, loaded and shot. It pleased him how well the crossbow was performing. The unbearable noise redoubled, but he used to stay focused in the cockpit of a Tornado GR-4, and he stayed focused now. Some of his quarrels found their targets; others skittered astray on the ice.

Beside him, Alexei shot his last quarrel and changed his grip on the crossbow to swing it like a sword.

Jack shifted position so they were standing back to back. *Here am I, Jack Kildare, aged forty-three, about to die in* hand-to-hand combat on Europa.

If he had had the breath to spare he'd have laughed.

The aliens closed in.

CHAPTER 19

Hannah mashed her knuckles against her mouth, watching Kate try to raise Jack and Alexei on the radio. At last the mission commander gave up and flung herself back in her seat.

"They're not responding. The last thing Jack said was, 'I think it was them.' Then both of their radios went dead."

"What do we do now?" Hannah muttered. She glanced at Giles. He looked as sickened as she felt.

"I think," Kate said, "we have to assume that we are the only survivors."

Hannah hugged herself. The three of them had gathered on the bridge as the terrifying drama of, first, the Shenzhou's crash, and secondly, Jack and Alexei's encounter with the aliens had played out on the surface. Now they had to face the possibility that they were ... *the only survivors*. Her mind crumpled, and she ordered herself to think logically.

"We have to warn Earth," Giles said, as the same words rose to Hannah's lips.

"On it," Kate said. "But hear this. We are not giving up." Her words were forceful, but her face looked raw, as if a layer of skin had been peeled from her with the loss of four crew members.

Hannah felt a wave of grief. Skyler! She bit her knuckles again, willing the emotion away. But she knew the only thing that would cushion this blow was a drink.

A *large* drink.

Fortunately, she'd brought her squeeze bottle to the bridge with her, full of moonshine and cold tea. She cradled it. It would look crass to start chugging hooch right this

second, especially in front of Giles, who didn't know about
her still ...

As if that mattered when Skyler, Meili, Jack, and Alexei
were dead!

Hannah could see each of them in her mind's eye so
clearly that it was difficult to accept they were no more.
Meili, stoic and cheerful— "Maybe just one more tiny drink
..." Jack. Hannah thought she wouldn't miss *him,* but then
she remembered him and Alexei organizing games of tag or
Simon Says, silly stuff to keep everyone smiling. Dragging
her out of her lair— "Come *on,* Hannah, I bet you're really
good at hopscotch ..." Grief lanced her. And then she
couldn't stop herself from picturing Skyler. "OK there,
Hannah-banana?" No one else ever asked if she was OK.
And she'd never told Skyler the truth. *No, I'm not OK. I need
you. I want you. I love you.*

What a monumental idiot she'd been.

Now it was too late. Nothing left to do but drink to his
memory.

And yet she cradled the squeeze bottle without taking a
sip. Even now, her self-respect mattered.

Flies wavered around her, and she batted automatically at
them. The insect population of the *SoD* had soared. All the
dying vegetation in the main hab was a feast for bugs. They
kept getting sucked into the air circulation intake, as a result
of which the circulation efficiency had dropped. The bridge
smelled sour, like a frat-house basement.

"We are not giving up," Kate repeated. "However, with
the loss of the Dragon and the Shenzhou ..." She rubbed
her forehead. "Son of a bitch. I've got one idea. It's squarely
in desperate-gamble territory, but look where we are."

"Go on," Hannah said, still ready to trust that Kate could fix this.

"We'll have to board the MOAD."

"Yes," Giles said immediately. "That's what I was thinking." He assumed a professorial tone of voice and gestured with one forefinger. "We know that the MOAD possesses a water plasma engine similar to ours. Therefore, it's not unreasonable to assume that it contains stocks of water, or LOX and LH2. We only have to procure these stocks, and we will be on our way home."

"*Only,*" Kate echoed. "But, yes, Giles. That's my idea in a nutshell. Glad to know I'm not the only crazy one around here."

Giles giggled and batted at the flies. It spoiled his donnish affect.

Hannah said, "Hang on, guys. How do we get to the MOAD without the Dragon or the Shenzhou?" Another wave of grief crashed over her. This time she capitulated to it. She raised her squeeze bottle and swallowed a mouthful of fiery moonshine. The alcohol drowned the lump of unexpressed emotion in her stomach.

"Aha," Kate said bleakly. "Remember when Skyler came aboard?"

Hannah remembered that perfectly. Skyler had been the last of the crew to board, joining them at the last minute, after the NXC agent who'd originally been sent with them died. Lance Garner's spacesuit had malfunctioned. She still wondered if it really *had* malfunctioned, or ... Anyway. Skyler had been slung up to the *Spirit of Destiny's* orbit in a Falcon Heavy, and he'd had to venture across to the *SoD* on a broomstick.

"The broomstick," she said, understanding what Kate had in mind.

"That's it," Kate said. "We've still got it. It's tethered outside the storage module."

These 'broomsticks' had been used during the construction of the *SoD*. They were LOX tanks with nozzles and handlebars attached. Hannah had never ridden one, but she remembered the construction crew joking about popping wheelies in space.

"The MOAD is only two hundred meters away from us. The broomstick could carry two people that far," Kate said. "As regards returning with the water, we'll have to cross that bridge when we come to it. I might be able to maneuver the *SoD* close enough to the MOAD to hook up the fueling hoses. But there's no point getting ahead of ourselves. First, we have to find out if there's any water there."

Hannah shook her head. "Two people? Not all of us?"

"Of course I will go," Giles said immediately.

"And me," Kate said. "You'll stay here, Hannah." Her gaze travelled briefly to the squeeze bottle in Hannah's hand, and returned to her face.

The old paranoia roared back.

She knows I'm a lush. A shitty human being.

Get help, Hannah, get help! Her sister Bethany's voice came back to her. With those words, Bethany had cut Hannah off from her family, the only family Hannah had.

She'd come to see Kate as a substitute sister, a more *fun* sister than Bethany had ever been, a naughty elder sister who got drunk with her and gossiped about their crewmates.

And now Kate had revealed that she, too, thought

Hannah was a liability. She was taking Giles instead, because she thought Hannah would scream if she saw an alien, or puke in her spacesuit, or both.

As she struggled to respond, Kate said kindly, "It isn't just the water. We're way behind on repairs. The last HERF knocked out the control machinery for the pumps and centrifuges in the SLS. If we don't get that stuff fixed, we can have all the water we like and we'll never get home. So Hannah, I'd like you to stay here and work on those repairs."

Hannah understood that Kate was trying to make her feel better about getting left behind. She swallowed hard. "I'd probably just slow you down, anyway," she muttered.

"Good. We go," Giles said. Hannah caught a smug expression on his face, and suddenly hated him intensely, although she'd never had strong feelings about him one way or the other before.

"Life support is Giles's job," she said in a last spasm of resistance. "Shouldn't he stay and do the repairs?"

"It's only his job because Peixun is dead," Kate said. "Anyway, he has to come. He's the xenolinguist."

CHAPTER 20

Light shining in my eyes.

Go away, I'm trying to sleep.

What's that smell?

Half-conscious, Jack followed the salty smell down a memory lane that brought him out on a beach in Cornwall. A camping holiday with some friends from uni. Jack there for the laughs and a girl he wanted to get off with. But the atmosphere had rapidly soured. Jack had been a bad drinker in those days. The genes of his alcoholic Irish grandfather played havoc with his normally controlled temperament. He remembered storming out of the tent at two in the morning, walking along the beach with Meeks—this was in the days when Meeks could walk—the waves crashing on the pebbles, moonlight shattering on the bay.

Oblivious to the beauty around them, they'd continued their argument. It had started with *Independence Day*, of all things. Jack had claimed it was a perfectly plausible scenario—he *loved* that film! Meeks had insisted that the aliens would have obliterated humanity long before Will Smith ever climbed into his F-18. Somehow, they'd gone from there to tumbling around on the beach, trying to punch each other's faces in.

Jack hadn't even sobered up before he realized what a complete dick he'd been. He'd apologized so extravagantly that even Meeks ended up laughing. It had never been mentioned again. First fight, last fight. But something had changed forever on that beach.

Jack stopped drinking, joined the University Air Squadron. Next stop, Iraq.

Meeks? Built a rocket car in his garage and smashed it into the side of a Welsh quarry.

Jack opened his eyes, projecting himself into a sitting position at the same time, as if the force of that crash had carried through the decades and across 600 million kilometers to …

Europa.

Right.

Um … really?

He sat on a bluey-green platform … bunk … shelf? His eyes identified familiar objects. Lockers. Ceiling lights. A hamper full of what appeared to be seaweed, except it was wriggling about like it might be alive. The floor was very dirty. At a card table in the middle of the room sat an alien.

"If this is hell," Jack said, "it's a bit underwhelming." His voice sounded shaky in his own ears. But he could hear it, and also hear the familiar noises of fans, and a generator or something else that rumbled like a diesel engine nearby. He was not wearing his spacesuit. In fact he wasn't wearing anything except his own, rather unclean, underpants. This detail convinced him he wasn't dead. He swung his legs off the shelf—his feet dangled half a meter off the floor—without taking his eyes off the alien.

"Where's Alexei?" he blurted, remembering how they'd fought back to back, swinging wildly at their attackers. That memory broke off inconclusively. He must have passed out … and woken up here. In a room that smelled like the sea. With an alien.

The alien, after all, looked much the way it had when wearing a spacesuit, except it had a face. The skin of the face was white, but not the dead white of its spacesuit. More like mushrooms. Mushroom-color too were its hands and its bare shins and feet. It did *not* have an octopus for a head. The snaky 'tentacles' were locks of hair, or something like hair, as fat as electric cords, which stood out in a shifting halo, Medusa-like, shiny black, with a coppery glint where they caught the light.

The face reminded Jack of those Japanese cartoons he'd never gotten into. An inverted isosceles triangle dominated by gigantic purplish-brown eyes. A nothing of a nose, a gash for a mouth. Ridiculously small ears like cowrie shells.

Convergent evolution, Jack thought. Start with oxygen-breathing organisms, add a requirement for opposable thumbs, and this is pretty much what you're going to get.

Yet it blew his mind to see the alien slouching with one foot tucked up on its chair, fiddling with a metal device the size and shape of a sunflower, which was nonetheless identifiable as a computer, as it had a screen in the middle, covered with squiggly marks that must be alien text.

The alien had not so much as glanced at Jack since he woke up. While he stared, the alien put down its computer, reached around its own spindly knee, curled three of its seven fingers through the handle of a cup that stood on the table, and quaffed the black contents.

Then it flicked a glance at Jack, saw him awake, and sat up straight, dropping its foot to the floor and placing its cup on the table at the same time, with a jerky movement that looked uncoordinated, but ended in poised stillness, like a dancer only *pretending* to lose her balance.

"Mind telling me where I am?" Jack said, shakily. "Oh, and if you're going to whack me into the cookpot, I'd like to know that, too. It's not dying I'm afraid of. It's not knowing what's going to happen next."

The alien foraged through the stuff on the table, which Jack mentally labeled as playing cards, a pair of pliers, metal marbles with one flat side, and a wad of clingfilm—although each of these things bore only a categorical resemblance to its earthly counterparts. The 'playing cards,' for example, were seven-sided, and could have been alien money, or leaves from an alien plant. The alien found an object that was *completely* recognizable: a wireless headset. It stood up, walked to Jack with its stiff hip-swaying gait, and offered it to him. Jack saw that the alien had pinpoint pupils, as if it had just done a line of coke.

He took the headset dubiously. Feather-light, it seemed to be made of white plastic.

The alien mimed putting it on.

"OK, OK, I see what it *is,*" Jack said. He remembered—nails on a blackboard, nails through his head. He had to find out what had happened to Alexei. If the alien wanted to communicate with him via headset, it was a risk he had to take. He fitted the disks over his ears.

"There! Hello."

It was the same BBC voice as before. Jack stared at the alien. Its lips hadn't moved.

"My name is Keelraiser. That's a literal translation. Could I know your name?"

"Jack," Jack said, into the little mic which seemed to be made of plastic, with no visible wiring or power source.

"That is a good name. It's a nickname for John, who was an apostle of Jesus. Have I got that right?"

"Yes," Jack said. "I suppose you learned all that off the TV?"

"Yes," Keelraiser's voice said in his ears. "We are very grateful for TV. Without TV, we would have died of boredom by now. When we started our journey, the shows were in black and white, and often seemed stylized or staged. Now they are in color. Is it correct to assume that the modern shows are a better approximation of life on Earth?"

"I suppose," Jack said.

"Good. It's hard to know when we are guessing right, and when we guess wrong. I expect we've made some terrible mistakes in our assumptions, and you will laugh at us. Is this a laugh?"

Keelraiser, via the headset, made a noise that sounded like a scratchy mechanical chuckle. Jack winced. "It'll do," he said. "Why don't your lips move when you talk? Why have I got to talk to you using this headset?"

"Ah," Keelraiser said. "Do you know, I made that myself. I am glad it works! I copied it from the comms device in your spacesuit. Is it correct? The fit, the functionality?"

Jack hopped off the bunk where he was sitting. The movement made his head ring. He felt momentarily nauseated, but pushed the feeling aside. He got the distinct impression that Keelraiser was pumping him for information, while volunteering nothing itself. He moved forward. Keelraiser took a skittery step backwards.

"I've had about enough of this," Jack said levelly. He stood six feet four—he had gained an inch and a half in height since they left Earth, thanks to low gravity and freefall. The alien overtopped him by a head, but it was skeletal. Its biceps were no thicker than Jack's wrists, its legs sticks. Evolution had favored humanity over these thieving cunts, Jack felt. Unless Keelraiser had titanium bones or something, Jack could snap its spine with one hand, and the biggest proof of this was the way Keelraiser had moved back, out of grabbing range. Jack doubled down on his momentary psychological advantage. "No more messing around!" he said. "Where's Alexei?"

Keelraiser's hair moved as if it had a life of its own. The shiny locks pointed in several different directions. "He is in our hydroponics garden. Do you want to go there?"

"Hell, yes I do."

Keelraiser led him towards the end wall of the room. The dirt on the floor moved came apart into beetles, which scurried aside from their feet, like patches of oil on a frying-pan. The wall melted. A door-shaped slot appeared, where there had been no door. Jack blinked.

"Smart materials," Keelraiser said, shortly. "We are significantly ahead of you in materials science."

Jack hid a smile. Who's got the biggest dick, eh? His amusement faded as he reflected that it might be suicidal to start a pissing contest with Keelraiser's people, as long as he and Alexei remained in their power. He then wondered if Keelraiser actually had a dick. The alien came off as indefinably female. But did the concepts of male and female even apply? Keelraiser wore a loose grey string tank and grey culottes that disguised its lower body. It was flat-chested. It had no nipples.

They walked along a corridor that felt, to Jack, too high and narrow. The light was very dim: nightlight-level. The air was sweltering hot and sticky. The smell of the sea got stronger. They passed other aliens who exhibited a wide variance in terms of height, build, and coloring. Some were shorter than Jack. Some had silvery or bronze-colored hair, if those locks really were hair, which Jack began to doubt. Their reactions to him also varied, from studied indifference to freeze-and-run.

Keelraiser said, "That was a bad-mannered child—" pointing after the one who'd run.

"You have children?"

Jack regretted the words as soon as they were out. Keelraiser fixed him with a gaze that seemed to communicate world-weary disappointment. Its pupils had swelled in the low light to take up half its bruise-brown irises. "Yes, we have children," it said. "This seems an appropriate time to misquote the Bard: Hath not a *rriksti* eyes? Hath not a *rriksti* hands, organs, dimensions, senses, affections, passions? Fed with the same food, hurt with the same weapons, subject to the same diseases, healed by the same means, warmed and cooled by the same winter and summer as a human is? If you prick us, do we not bleed? Well, I am not sure we *are* subject to the same diseases. But you haven't died yet, which seems to prove something."

Jack stopped and reached out, slowly, as you'd reach out to a stray dog. Keelraiser blinked—the first time he'd seen it blink at all—but did not flinch away. Jack stroked the alien's flat, white cheek with his fingers. He'd been wanting to do this ever since he first clapped eyes on the creature. Are you really real? Yes, you're real. The skin was feverishly hot. Figure a core temperature a few degrees higher than human average. A fast metabolism to go with that gracile physique. The texture of the skin—*sticky*. Jack rubbed his fingers together. A residue clung to them.

He was very frightened. He cast about for a way to show the alien that he was *not* frightened. He put his sticky fingers in his mouth, and tasted salt. "Let's see if I die now," he said.

"May I touch you?" Keelraiser said.

Jack wanted to say no, but told himself that reciprocity was the first step towards establishing a rapport with these creatures, and getting out of here alive. He shrugged.

Keelraiser stroked his cheek with a seven-fingered hand. It ran one finger over Jack's lips, and pushed the tip inside. The salt of its skin filled his mouth. The tentative touch felt less like an intrusion than an erotic overture. Jack's nerve broke, and he pulled back.

"We are fascinated by your mouths," Keelraiser said. "You use them for everything!"

"What did you say the name of your home planet is? *Rriksti?*"

"No more than the name of your planet is *Human*. Rriksti is what we call ourselves."

"And you're like us, more or less? Two arms, two legs, two eyes … two sexes? Families, schools, armies, nations? Technology, pop culture, religion, war?"

"Yes to the last," Keelraiser said. "Very much yes." It started to walk again,.

Jack persisted, "How did you end up here?"

Keelraiser swung its face to him. Its eyes were all pupil. "There was a war. Well, there was the eleven thousand seven hundred and ninth war, counting from the beginning of recorded history … give or take. No one agrees on just how warlike we are. And oddly, those who insist we are *not* warlike are the ones who won. The *Darksiders.* They defeated us *Lightsiders*, without once admitting that we were at war again. Can you imagine? There is *no* war, they said, while the missiles were flying."

"Yes, I can imagine actually," Jack said. "We do the same sort of thing ourselves."

"Their denial of truth gave us time to save ourselves. A few ships of the Lightsider fleet escaped the first bombardment. We filled them with evacuees. Stuffed them in like insects in a trap. A thousand people applied for each crew slot. I was one of those chosen. There were nine ships. Five of them escaped our system. *One* escaped the pursuit."

Keelraiser pointed up.

"That is the ship now orbiting this rotten little moon, which you call Europa."

CHAPTER 21

"I'm very sorry we shot at you," Jack said. "With, you know, crossbows. It seems silly, doesn't it? But we didn't bring any guns."

"No one was badly hurt," Keelraiser said. "No hard feelings. Is this correct?"

"Yes—well, that's very good of you …"

"Now we are in the hydroponics garden. Your friend is over there." Keelraiser stalked away.

The hydroponics garden was a tropical swamp in a cave. Rickety walkways zigzagged over pools clogged with pale, fleshy vegetation. Fish—or aquatic life of some kind, anyway—stirred carpets of algae. Oxygen pumps burbled. That, plus the ubiquitous generator rumble, were the only sounds. The rriksti working in the garden went about their tasks in utter silence. Jack wiped sweat off his face. The room where he woke must have been air-conditioned purposely to make him comfortable. Wherever the rriksti came from, equatorial temperatures must be the norm.

"They come from Proxima b," Alexei said, when Jack found him squatting on one of the walkways, trailing a stick in the water.

Jack raised his eyebrows.

Proxima Centauri was the nearest known star to Earth. It was only four and a bit lightyears away. As interstellar distances went, that was a hop, skip, and a jump. Loosely associated with the Alpha Centauri binary star system, Proxima was a red dwarf. It had a couple of confirmed exoplanets. One in the habitable zone. Proxima b.

"*That* Proxima b?"

"So they say. They showed me a projection of the stars. I've taken the star sights often enough. It's Proxima b. 'This is our home,' they said. They described a tidally locked planet. Hot and dry on one side, frozen on the other, a narrow twilight zone where all the rich fucks live. They call it *Imf*. They're an interplanetary species. Imf's got a large moon, they've colonized it. Bases also on the other planet in the system, a rocky Mars type with a 60-day orbital period. They've sent expeditions to Alpha Centauri A and even Alpha Centauri B. Bb exists, it's a water world. Primitive life."

"I apologized for shooting them," Jack said. "'Sorry we tried to kill you with homemade crossbows,' sort of thing."

"What did they say?"

"'It's all right. No one was badly hurt. ...' Maybe their EVA suits are really, really good."

Alexei swished his stick in the water. "This is shit," he said. He laid the dripping stick on the walkway and took a drink from a plastic mug beside him. Jack realized how thirsty he was.

"What's that?"

"Water. They offered me food but it tasted like ass. These sick-looking plants? Supposed to be that color. *Suizh*. It's their staple carbohydrate. Fish in the pools. These higher shelves around the pools are mushroom beds. Well, I still think it's impossible to raise fungi hydroponically, but here we are. Here they are."

Jack sat down beside Alexei and drank some of the water from the mug, grimacing at the tang of brine. He said, "They're refugees. They fled from what sounds as if it must have been an extinction-level nuclear exchange. World War

Three. Well, according to them, World War Eleven Thousand and Something. But this one was really something. They packed their people into ships and ran like hell."

"That explains it."

"Explains what?"

"Why they're barely hanging on," Alexei said. "Why they stole the engines out of our advance landers."

"The MOAD was supposed to be a colony ship," Jack said, relaying what Keelraiser had told him. "They were in the midst of a large-scale project to colonize one of the uninhabited planets orbiting Alpha Centauri B. When war broke out, they sent all these ships in different directions, hoping that at least one of them would survive. This was that one. But it was never intended to travel this far. They barely made it. Scraped in by the skin of their teeth."

Ten years ago, Jack had photographed the moment when the MOAD skidded into the Jovian system on its last gasp. If only he'd known what he was seeing through his viewfinder!

"They've been here for ten years," Alexei said, nodding glumly at the pools that shimmered in the half-light. Rriksti knelt on the walkways, tending their fish and plants. "Everything is starting to break down. They're running out of replacement parts. They have advanced fabbers, but the problem is raw materials."

"And then we sent them Thing One and Thing Two. It must have felt like Christmas."

"The ones I spoke to ... oh, there they are." Two rriksti stalked towards them, hair swirling around their heads. "Their names are Nene and Eskitul, or some damn thing like that. They laughed about it. If only you could have landed the Things a little closer to here, they said. Three out of the four rriksti who retrieved the engines died of radiation exposure."

That angered Jack—the waste of it, and the suggestion that the rriksti would mindlessly sacrifice themselves for their collective, conforming to the Hollywood image of a Borg-like alien menace, despite the evidence of individualism he'd already seen. Then again, humans did the same thing, didn't they? Soldiers did it. Not mindlessly, but for the sake of their nation, their tribe, their platoon.

Nene and Eskitul dropped to their haunches on the walkway. They gestured for Jack and Alexei to put on their headsets. The one called Nene gushed about how pleased it was to meet Jack. It gave a very different impression from Keelraiser's grave, somewhat awkward affect. Yes, these were individuals. Nene had reddish hair, wore a purple smock over its culottes, and gestured effusively with its seven-fingered hands.

Alexei took off his headset while Nene was in mid-flow. He smiled deprecatingly at the aliens. "By the way, I found out why they HERFed the *SoD*," he said to Jack.

"They were afraid of us," Jack said. He was still wearing his headset. Nene and Eskitul stiffened. Their hair stood on end.

Nene exclaimed, "It's terrible. We are so very sorry. We were just trying to say hello."

*

"They don't talk with their mouths," Alexei sighed. "They communicate by bio-radio."

"Bio-radio?"

"That stuff on their heads isn't hair. It's keratin mixed

with iron particles. They have antennas." With every piece that fell into place, Alexei seemed to be getting gloomier. Typical Russian, Jack thought. When it rains he thinks God's pissing in his eye. "They evolved with six senses, not just five. And they thought we did, too."

"Ten years is a long time to keep making a mistake like that." Jack muttered. But he considered how much they didn't understand about the rriksti. Vice versa, the same applied. The things you couldn't learn from television were precisely the fundamentals of human existence.

"We're very sorry," Nene said, wringing its hands.

Jack said skeptically, "So when you nearly broke our eardrums yesterday, that was our suit radios picking up your crosstalk?"

"Yes. We didn't mean to hurt you."

Eskitul said, "We hypothesized that your mouth movements were a non-verbal signaling mechanism." This large-framed, bronze-haired alien's voice, as simulated by the headset, sounded deep and boomy, like whale song. "Microphones? We took them for transmitters. The hair of these poor creatures must be underpowered, we thought. Each antenna strand is so thin." Eskitul's own thick, bronze bio-antennas shook gently. "And yet, how *fast* they can process information!"

Nene explained, "We thought you demodulated the sideband signals of your television broadcasts in your heads. We never guessed that you communicate by making sounds with your *mouths!*" Nene opened its own tiny, pink mouth wide.

"Oh, the research, the mentation, the competing theories!" Eskitul said. "I was a leading anthropologist. All these years.

It was a complete waste, wasn't it?" The big rriksti came closer on its hands and knees. Its luminous eyes seemed to smile at Jack and Alexei. "I've learnt more from you than I did from thousands of hours of broadcasts."

Jack said, "You've got a powerful radio transmitter out there. Why didn't you simply get in touch? Save everyone a lot of trouble."

"We tried," Nene said immediately.

"Using digital AM signals, with frequency hopping," Alexei muttered. "Not a snowball's chance of picking *that* up."

Jack scuffled away from Eskitul. He didn't like the large alien with its bronze mane wafting around its long, starved-looking face. He disliked the idea that the rriksti had overestimated humanity, and had suffered as a result. Our radio telescopes were too weak to pick up their SOSes, we took ten *years* to get out here, and when we arrived the first thing we did was to attack them with homemade crossbows. He felt ridiculously grateful that the aliens were not holding that against them. They must have taken it about as seriously as an adult would take a toddler pounding on him with its little fists.

Frustrated and ashamed, Jack picked up the stick Alexei had been messing with and plunged it into the water. It crunched into the bottom of the pool. He bore down until his hand entered the water up to the wrist. "Careful!" Nene said. The water was blood-warm. Darting touches whispered against Jack's skin, like small fish. He moved the stick around, felt it catch in something, and brought the thing up.

A half-decayed fish head.

Dripping, gleaming in the half-light, with the flesh eaten away from the cheeks and jaw, it looked like a Halloween prop.

"Protein," Alexei said.

"Good one," Jack said. He let the fish head splash back into the water. The algae knitted over the black hole it made.

"That's not all I've found, poking around in here," Alexei said. "These are all-purpose middens. I found one of *their* skulls." He did not have his headset on. He gestured at his own jawbone. The two rriksti watched the men with patient perplexity. "They bury their dead in the compost heap. It's one step up from cannibalism."

Jack took off his headset and ruffled his hair with his fingers. It had set into stiff cowlicks, as if he'd been swimming. "I'd like to see us survive for ten years on Europa, with a busted spaceship and limited resources, after the destruction of our home planet. We wouldn't be doing aquaculture, we'd be eating each other."

"They're willing to let us see everything, stick our fingers into everything. Maybe they think we're mentally incapable of understanding how it all works. Those little scavenger bugs—you saw them?" Jack nodded. "They're also protein sources. I saw this Nene person pick one up and pop it in her mouth. *Crunch.*"

The red-haired rriksti cocked its head on one side.

"Do you think she's a she?" Jack said. "I get that impression, too. Keelraiser is a she, as well, but Eskitul's a he."

"It's a very finely tuned ecosystem. No waste, maximum recycling of resources, probably some genetic engineering at the microbe and bug level." Alexei suddenly grinned. "Did they tell you they have a fucking *fusion reactor?"*

*

Nene and Eskitul willingly agreed to show the men the fusion reactor. Alexei hadn't seen it yet, either. The two rriksti led them across the hydroponic garden. The walkways creaked under the weight of the two humans. Jack put his feet where Nene indicated, his mind filled with excitement to the exclusion of all else.

A fusion reactor! Is it possible, after all?

Physicists on Earth had been struggling to achieve scalable fusion reactions for decades. Economically viable fusion reactors were always, always ten years off.

And these buggers have *done* it?!? Or was it an inaccurate translation? Fission, fusion—they sound similar but there's a world of difference. Fission is splitting atoms. It's what the *SoD's* reactor does. Fission razed Hiroshima and Nagasaki, blew the roof off Chernobyl. Fusion is joining atoms. It's what happens in the heart of the sun.

The garden ended on a ledge stacked with supplies. They walked along a tunnel leading away and up from the garden. The sweltering heat got worse. Alexei knuckled the dirty-white wall of the tunnel. "On the other side of this is ice, yes?" he said doubtfully. "Minus 170 degrees?"

"You would call this material structural aerogel," Eskitul said in its hollow booming voice. "It's 99.99% air, 0.01% organic polymer."

"It feels like styrofoam."

"Yes, but it does not melt. We also use it to insulate the reactor."

"And it doesn't exist," Alexei said. "But I guess it does, after all!" His high-pitched cackle gave away that he was just as excited as Jack was. Aquaculture and genetically engineered bugs were all right. But Jack and Alexei were astronauts, not chemists. It was the science-fictional shit that got their blood pumping.

The tunnel dead-ended in a wall. Nene stood on tiptoe and took an armful of filmy material from a shelf. "These are protective garments. Please put them on. See, we also wear them."

Both rriksti, without any signs of hesitation or embarrassment, stripped off their clothes.

Jack and Alexei surrendered utterly to curiosity. They stared at the aliens' naked bodies.

Disappointingly, they were none the wiser. Both rriksti had wrinkly bulges at their crotches, like a single large, hairless testicle.

Jack met Alexei's eyes—his gaze said clearly, *Oh fuck*.

With great reluctance, they removed their underpants.

Nene and Eskitul fell about. They clung to each other and pointed at the men's groins. Their hair danced. Although their facial expressions did not change, Jack felt no doubt whatsoever that they were laughing their heads off.

"I wonder if they know how much it matters to us *not* to have our cocks laughed at?" Jack said dryly. Yet he welcomed the aliens' hilarity, in a way. Making people laugh was the key to getting on with them, even if you had to disrobe to accomplish it.

Alexei grabbed his penis and waggled it at the rriksti, reducing them to further paroxysms. "It's a cock, deal with it! Jesus, they must have seen some porn in all their hours of watching TV."

"They probably thought it was comedy."

They put on the filmy garments. These were full-body bunny suits, with hoods that covered the face. It felt like wearing nothing at all. The garments turned out to be white on the outside, but transparent from the inside, and permeable to air. Eskitul walked towards the wall. It opened automatically, and they walked into hell.

Alexei flinched and covered his ears. Jack fell back a step, before driving the heels of his hands against his ears and moving forward into what felt like a solid storm of noise.

They followed the rriksti between cramped partitions, up twisting steel ladders, in the near-dark. Other rriksti stepped out of walls, and regarded the humans with silent attention, their hair twitching.

The humid heat was thick enough to cut with a knife. Water dripped from overhead. The noise redoubled whenever a wall opened. Jack glimpsed corroded-looking turbine cabinets. That was where the noise was coming from. Steam turbines. No shortage of water on Europa. Convert heat energy to electricity …

He'd almost concluded that there was nothing new here, after all, when they walked through another wall into a chamber filled with brilliant white light. Jack's hood darkened, reducing the light to bearable level. The air felt brittle, charged.

A star hung in the middle of the chamber.

A jet of luminous gas gouted from the star, crossed the chamber, and vanished into the far wall. The gas jet wavered to and fro in a sinuous unpredictable pattern, yet it never died, nor did the star dim at all.

Jack stared, hypnotized. He knew that he was looking—through God knows how many layers of shielding—at a fusion reaction. This was the closest any human being had ever come to gazing into the heart of a star.

When he recovered himself, he shouted, "Are we being shot full of neutrons right now?"

Neutrons, the least appealing side products of fusion, could kill you even faster than Europa's surface radiation.

"No!" Eskitul said. "The reaction is aneutronic."

"What's the fuel?" Alexei demanded.

"Lithium," Eskitul said. "The byproduct is helium 3, which is also useful."

A shadow flickered on the ceiling of the chamber. Someone was scrambling around on top of the star. The light melted the person to a skeletal silhouette. Yet Jack recognized Keelraiser.

Jack backed up for a running start and jumped towards the star. His fingertips found the side of the housing. The light beat on the insides of his eyelids. He got his elbows over something lumpy. Up close, the thickness of shielding enclosing the reactor core could be seen—shadowy curves and corners.

He clambered on top of the housing and stood next to Keelraiser. The fusion core burnt below them, as hot as the core of the sun, yet the half-seen metal under Jack's soles felt barely warm.

"How do you catalyze the reaction?" he yelled.

"Muons," Keelraiser said. It uttered its creaky chuckle at Jack's expression. "Are you an expert?"

"Not in the least." Jack thought of Hannah. "I know an expert." Hannah would go absolutely nuts for this. He couldn't wait to share this marvel with her and the rest of the crew.

In fact, he guiltily realized that everyone on the *SoD* must be worrying about him and Alexei. They'd have to return to the Dragon soon to send a sitrep. It was going to feel so great to deliver *good* news for a change!

"The reactor is operating at five percent of maximum output," Keelraiser said. "It's not even producing thrust, you see. Maximum shielding, minimum output. I am not even sure what would happen if we cranked it up anymore."

Keelraiser suddenly turned and leapt away. Jack followed, stumbling over half-seen knobbles and hoops. He glanced back at the other three. Alexei's face, bleached by the light, looked like he'd seen God.

Keelraiser closed a hand on his wrist and pulled him through the wall.

They stood in reddish shade, balanced back-to-back on a seven-sided nozzle …

… inside the engine bell of a spaceship.

"That reactor is a drive," Jack said in delight. He touched the metal overhead. It was so smooth it didn't seem to be there. Probably niobium. That's what NASA had used for the engine bells of Thing One and Thing Two. "Jesus! You're running this whole hab off a spaceship drive!"

They stood at the small end of the engine bell. The large end measured about 10 meters across. It was mostly buried in a slumped wall of ice, with just a crack of reddish light showing at the top.

"Variable shielding," Keelraiser said. "At minimum output, nothing escapes into the combustion chamber."

"We were *in* the combustion chamber!" That room full of heat and light was actually the heart of the engine.

"Yes. When we thrust, we pump propellant into the combustion chamber, and reduce the shielding. The reactor vaporizes the propellant, and it squirts out of this nozzle. Hey presto, thrust."

Keelraiser dropped onto the smooth slope of the engine bell and coasted down to the bottom, like a child on a slide. Jack followed. He slid so swiftly that he had to brake at the bottom by shoving his feet against the wall. Cold styrofoam. It squidged between his toes, like sand, and sprang back.

A rope ladder hung down from the top edge of the engine bell. Keelraiser swarmed up it.

Jack copied the rriksti, and squeezed up through the crack between the engine bell and the wall.

He now understood that they'd climbed through the engineering deck of the spacecraft on their way to the combustion chamber. Now they stood on a makeshift platform on top of the engine bell. The aerogel-coated ice wall lapped like a frozen wave around the whole ass-end of the ship; the door they'd come through must be buried somewhere under there.

Overhead, Jack made out a distant roof in the dim light. This cavern must be the original cryovolcanic crater. Up there was the ice roof the rriksti had added.

"It is cold here," Keelraiser said. "That's why we wear protective garments. The air is dry, also. You might like it! But please do not remove your hood. The water reclamation apparatus is quite noisy. It might hurt your ears."

Pipes snaked out of the ice around the ship's business end, converging on a metal box the size of Jack's childhood home. It had a Victorian aspect, because it appeared to be made of cast iron. Jack assumed this was the 'water reclamation apparatus.' Other machines, looking more authentically alien, like complicated versions of the radio mast outside, winked and blinked at the far end of the cavern. Rriksti in protective garments stared up quizzically.

Jack's attention zeroed in on the ship he was standing on top of. It was as big as a Hercules transport, not including all the propulsion-related business at the back. From the platform where he and Keelraiser stood, an arrangement of ropes led over the top of the engine bell, through the chasm between two drum-shaped propellant tanks, through a forest of metal spikes—perhaps a heat-rejection system. The fuselage of the ship projected forward, propped up on makeshift gantries, like the body of a tropical fish. Its coloration—oxidized swirls of blue, purple, and yellow—also made him think of tropical life. It had blended wings raked back from its nose.

Walk on the wing, hold the rope. Jack's protective garment caught on the rough fibers sticking out from the rope. The combination of ultra-low and ultra-high tech amused and maddened him. The ship's aging paint job flaked off at a touch.

"On Earth, there was a reusable orbiter called the space shuttle," Keelraiser said through Jack's headset. "Is this correct?"

"Yes. I flew one," Jack said.

"Then we have something else in common. I was the pilot of this shuttle." Keelraiser reached the leading edge of the wing, released the rope, and sat down with its legs dangling over the edge.

Jack sat down beside it. He felt like a gambler holding a soft hand of maybe fourteen, tempted to stand, scared to hit.

He laid his hands palm down on his thighs.

Keelraiser tweaked the two extra fingers of Jack's protective right glove, which hung empty, since Jack didn't have enough fingers to fill them. Rolling the material between its own fingers, it said, "Ten years ago, after our ship's primary drive failed, I landed this shuttle on Europa. There were five hundred and thirty-nine people aboard. Now, we are three hundred and eight."

"How did you lose so many people?" A second later Jack realized the question should have been—*how did so many of you SURVIVE?*

"Radiation," Keelraiser said. "We didn't have the right machinery to build a shelter. We used the shuttle's drive to melt a hole in the ice. But the rest of the work had to be done by hand."

Jack shook his head, awed by what these people had been through. Two hundred of them had literally worked themselves to death to save the others. Yet his gambler's instinct prevailed. "If you've been watching TV, you'll know how much you've frightened our leaders," he said. "Outright destruction of your ship was considered. And that's before they knew about you."

"Then why don't they bomb us?" the rriksti said. It made a curious facial expression, opening its little mouth wide. "What are they waiting for?"

"They're waiting for us to tell them what to do," Jack said, and in uttering the words he became fully aware of the power he possessed. The future not only of Earth but of the rriksti lay in his hands.

It was a no-brainer, of course. But advantage remained to be extracted. *Stand,* he thought. *Stand ... and wait.*

Keelraiser pleated the extra glove fingers until it ran out of material. It pulled Jack's last two fingers into its palm and held them in its big, bony, seven-fingered fist. The layers of filmy material were nothing. Just a slipperiness. The alien delicately flicked the web of skin between Jack's pinky finger and his ring finger.

It felt downright erotic. But Jack reminded himself that he had no idea what was erotic to a rriksti. He chose to interpret it as a challenge. He uncurled Keelraiser's hand, slipped his thumb in between its last two fingers, and pressed his thumbnail into the web, through the slippery layers of fabric. He worked his thumbnail gently back and forth.

Keelraiser gazed at their joined hands. Without raising its eyes, it said, "We will give you the design blueprints for the fusion reactor. This will include complete manufacturing specifications for the advanced materials used in the magnetic bottle and shielding, and specifications for the manufacturing equipment, and the machine tools you will need to build the equipment. We'll even throw in a set of user's manuals." It uttered its creaky chuckle.

Score, fucking SCORE, Jack thought. Careful to hide his elation—on the principle that the rriksti probably had a decent grasp of human facial expressions—he hmm'd, and said aloud, "What would you expect in return?"

"To be allowed to live," Keelraiser said.

"Oh come on. Dare to dream," Jack said.

The rriksti's hair danced. "A few things. Mostly raw materials."

"Name them," Jack said. "Mind you, there are significant constraints on our interplanetary shipping capacity. Chiefly that we've not got an interplanetary shipping capacity."

Although that would change once they got their hands on fusion reactors. Jack's imagination jumped ahead ten or twenty years to the day when fusion-powered spaceships entered service. He saw himself aged sixty or so, with a belly clad in Savile Row shirting and a cigar clamped in his teeth, courting Branson-esque publicity to celebrate their first launch. Jack Kildare, aerospace tycoon! Of course, he didn't imagine or wish that it would be possible to keep the rrikstis' gifts for himself. Something that big couldn't be patented. But he figured he could wangle a competitive edge of some kind. Keep some of the booty at home in the UK. He pictured a resurrection of British manufacturing for the new space age about to dawn, led by his own company—Firebird Systems, v. 2.0. A fitting memorial to Oliver Meeks.

Jesus Christ, I might get to pilot a *torchship* before I die!

That vision put all the others in the shade. It was the future he'd dreamed about as a little boy, before he actually became an astronaut and found out that it was all about manual labor and clogged-up sinuses.

He beamed radiantly at Keelraiser and said, "Let's shake on it."

"Jack!"

Alexei's cry cut through the noise of the manufacturing floor. Jack looked down and saw his friend running across the cavern, under the nose of the alien shuttle. "Up here," Jack shouted, freeing his hand from Keelraiser's. He stood up on the wing.

"There you are," Alexei shouted. He beckoned urgently.

Jack grabbed the rope and descended to the floor, sliding most of the way. They walked away from the shuttle together.

"These guys are lying to us," Alexei said. He spoke under his breath, although the aliens could not hear, and it was noisy in here, anyway. "Everything they've told us is bullshit."

CHAPTER 22

Skyler couldn't open his eyes. His eyelids were stuck shut. He strained. Eyelid muscles: they aren't good for much. At last his eyelashes peeled apart.

All that effort for nothing. He still couldn't see.

His nose throbbed. He breathed through his mouth. His panting filled the universe.

Everything hurts.

Back. Head. Legs. Nose.

Terror overtook him, the herald of returning memory. He recalled the Shenzhou's engine failure. The horrible pogoing back and forth. The long fall.

He couldn't remember the crash itself, which was probably a good thing.

He struggled against his straps for a long minute before he remembered they were there. Fumbling, he released them—

—and fell sideways, because the whole crew module was tilted at a steep angle.

His helmet lamp came on as he fell. The beam was very weak.

He landed on top of Meili's crash couch, which had torn loose from its mounting. It seemed to be welded to the dead consoles. Skyler dragged at it. He braced himself on the side wall of the module and pushed at it with his boots. It came away like the top slice of bread in a sandwich, and the sandwich filling was Meili. The lower edge of her console matched the dent in her chest like Africa matching South America. Her face was a red smear on the inside of her helmet.

Skyler hauled himself up into the service module. Do not vomit. His suit's heads-up display came on. The external pressure sensor told him the air pressure was down to 40% of normal. The crew module had lost hull integrity. Frost coated everything. His gloves left marks in the glittering white veil. Do *not* vomit. He spun the wheel and opened the airlock. Nothing had power. No alarms went off, no lights flashed. He pushed with all his strength on the wheel that opened the hatch at the other end of the airlock.

It didn't budge.

"Help," he said. "Someone help me." All the answer he got was his own breath sighing in his ears.

He heaved again on the wheel. Sweating. Grunting. Gloves slipping. Why hadn't he worked harder to stay fit when he had the chance?

The damn thing didn't move a centimeter.

He sank back into the service module. Frost-coated supplies and survival crap drifted around his ankles, lit by the weak beam of his helmet lamp. All this Chinese shit. There might be an emergency radio beacon in here and he wouldn't even know it.

He reached into his spacesuit's thigh pocket and brought out the modified Glock the NXC had given him. Its bullets would go through a spacesuit, allegedly. Would they go through an airlock? No. They were frangible bullets, designed *not* to hole a spacecraft.

He slid back through the hatch to Meili. He turned her right way over, so she was kind of lying on the tilted consoles. The blood smeared on her faceplate hid the wreck of her face. There were strands of hair caught in the blood. He remembered touching her hair. The sweet human smell of it.

I love you. That's what she'd said to him, as the Shenzhou topped out and began to fall back towards Europa. He'd said it to her, too. *I love you.*

Momentary madness, a natural reaction to the nearness of death, but there had been truth in it. There *was* truth in it. Skyler's heart belonged to Hannah, but he had loved Meili, too. Shipmate, companion, gardener, electronics expert, pilot. Cute as hell, incidentally. And now … dead.

The first human being to walk on Europa had become the first human being to die on it.

"Oh, hell," Skyler said. "Oh, Meili, honey. It's not fucking *fair.*"

He perched on the claw-like mounting of her seat and sobbed like a child. Tears melted the sticky stuff on his eyelashes, washing it down his cheeks. Snot coursed from his nose and coated his lips and chin.

As he wept, he heard a voice in his head. It sounded like Lance Garner's.

Get your shit together, man. What are you, a fudgin' pussy? You just gonna sit there and CRY?

Skyler answered, in his head, *But she's dead. And I'm going to die, too.*

And whose fault is that, huh?

Seeking the answer to that, Skyler remembered more details from the moments before the crash. Meili had kept talking about the APU. She'd assumed he must have accidentally switched the heater off. Had he? No, he couldn't have. This *couldn't* all be his fault.

He must have been right to begin with.

The malware.

It didn't exactly make sense that the Chinese would blow up their own lander, but who said the malware was Chinese, anyway? Meili hadn't known anything about it.

Skyler suddenly remembered Alexei pointing a crowbar or some shit at his face, smiling like a wolf.

BANG.

Letting Skyler know what lay in store for him.

BANG.

"Oh, you bastard," Skyler whispered. The realization stung all the worse because it came too late. Alexei had won. Skyler was stuck in a wrecked spacecraft, and he was going to die when his air ran out.

He picked Meili up and shook her frantically, willing her to be alive. Her head bobbled against the inside of her faceplate. He glimpsed a crushed eyeball, shattered teeth.

Dropping the corpse in revulsion, he saw something flutter down from the open hatch above him. He snatched it out of the air.

A piece of laminated cardboard, coated with frost.

An airline safety card?!?

Cartoon drawings. Blocks of Chinese text.

Skyler stared hungrily at the drawings.

It absolutely *was* a safety card.

In case of emergency …

Oh my God.

He leapt back into the service module, scrambled into the airlock chamber, and located the emergency release handle for the outer hatch. He pulled it in the direction shown in the drawing on the safety card.

Now, when he put his shoulder to the wheel, it spun smoothly, and the hatch popped up. The scant volume of air that remained in the Shenzhou gusted past Skyler and away.

He put his head and shoulders out.

The view was sobering.

He gazed down at Europa's icy terrain. The Shenzhou had melted out a hole where it crashed. It now sat in a frozen hollow, tilted at an angle that made the Leaning Tower of Pisa look like a plumb line.

The ice had refrozen around the bottom of the Shenzhou, and the craft's shadow hid that side of it. Peering down at the other side, Skyler saw that the engine bell was just … gone. Strewn in smithereens far and wide, presumably. The extra-long tank had split along one side like a banana, and crumpled like the hood of a car that hit an overpass.

The LOX and the LH2 for the *SoD* must have vaporized into the vacuum. That was a stroke of luck. If the reactants had caught fire, he'd be dead.

He looked up. He saw Jupiter. He looked north and south. He saw ice. West. Ice. He looked east.

He saw a spike on the horizon.

Blink.

Still there.

A spike like a church steeple, white against the black sky.

The Dragon. In this featureless wasteland, that could only be the Dragon, parked on its landing jacks, sticking up over the horizon!

Of course, of course—the Shenzhou had gone almost straight up, aiming for the *SoD,* and had come straight down!

Hope rushed in. Jack and Alexei would rescue him …

… um, *no.* If they had purposely schemed to kill him, rescuing him would be the last thing on their minds.

They'd be investigating the alien artifact Kate had found.

Maybe even talking with the aliens.

His and *Meili's* aliens.

"Oh, you just wait," Skyler muttered. "You're not as smart as you think you are, assholes."

He closed the hatch and descended into the service module. His mind was firing on all cylinders now. If five minutes ago he'd been weeping in despair, determination now energized him.

Don't count the USA out just yet, bub.

He pressed his gloves together in a prayer-like attitude, thinking hard.

The big problem—the biggest obstacle to his survival—was the radiation.

Average radiation dose when you get a CT scan: 10 milliSieverts.

Amount of radiation you'd soak up in six months on the ISS: 160 mSv.

Maximum radiation level recorded at Fukushima: 400 mSv per hour.

Average radiation dose absorbed by Chernobyl workers who died within a month: 6,000 mSv.

Effective radiation level on Europa's surface: 200 mSv per hour.

Skyler knew these figures off the top of his head, because he had taken an intense personal interest in finding out what this trip would cost him in terms of health. Bottom line, he was going to die of cancer. Even before he set foot on Europa, he'd soaked up a quarter of a Chernobyl dose. The whole crew had, just from travelling on the *SoD* for two years.

So—fuck the future. He had no expectations of a healthy

retirement at this point, anyway. All he needed to do was stay alive, mobile, and capable of pulling the trigger for ...

... how long?

How far was it to the Dragon?

"Come on," he muttered to himself. "You're an astrophysicist."

My height above ground will intercept cue-ball-smooth Europa at a given distance X. The Dragon also intercepts the horizon at a distance Y. Since the horizon intercept is a third point on a chord that connects the two heights, you add X and Y, and hey presto, you get your total distance ...

40 kilometers.

Oh, shit.

That's five hours of walking, at 200 milliSieverts an hour.

I have six hours of air. Twice that much, if I take one of the spares. Air is not a problem. But the rems are.

OK. OK, it's the Bremsstrahlung we're most worried about. High-energy beta particles hit dense materials and produce electromagnetic radiation. We need to slow those particles down, disperse them ...

Skyler foraged through the frost-coated supplies drifting around his feet. He sorted out five sheets of aluminum, 60cm x 60cm each, and five sheets of low-temperature plastic, the same size.

He layered the metal and plastic sheets alternately, and wrapped duct tape around the whole sandwich.

When he'd done that, he laughed. Shook his head. So this is what that Ph.D was good for ...

With the sandwich under his arm, he exited the airlock hatch and jumped to the ground. He remembered Meili's historic jump to the surface. *Wo dao le!* she'd screamed, spinning round and round. *I am the first human being to walk on Europa!*

Tears welled up in Skyler's eyes again. "They'll pay for this," he muttered. "I'll make them fucking pay. I promise you, honey, they will *not* get away with this."

He used the rest of the duct tape to fasten the sandwich on top of his helmet, like a giant coolie hat. It blocked out Jupiter, and he hoped it would at least partially block out the lethal hail of charged particles from the sky.

He started to walk. In this gravity, it wasn't really walking, but skipping. Lou, lou, skip to my lou …

His breath sighed like the sea in a shell.

In, out.

Lou, *lou* …

In, out.

Skip to my *lou* …

He felt so tiny in the empty plain, it hardly seemed like he was moving. When he glanced back, the Shenzhou had shrunk to a pimple. But the Dragon did not seem to have come any closer at all.

CHAPTER 23

Kate settled herself astride the broomstick. Giles wrapped his arms around her waist, and she twisted the throttle.

The broomstick puttered away from the *SoD,* bucking a couple of times before the fuel settled.

She hadn't done this in a long time. Had spacewalked regularly, to keep her hand in. But setting off from the *SoD* without a tether introduced an element of madness into a situation already fraught with known and unknown risks.

When the excrement hits the ventilator, what do you do? They'd put her through numerous apocalyptic scenarios before the *SoD* departed from Earth. Of course, none of those scenarios came close to the reality. Four crew members down. *Jesus.* But one core principle of leadership still applied. Don't just sit around chewing your fingernails. *Act.*

So that's what she was doing.

She felt uneasy about leaving Hannah on board by herself. Hannah—great girl, but an alcoholic. You cannot trust an alcoholic, end of story. Now that Kate no longer needed to butter Hannah up, she'd have to put her foot down about the still. But that was if they survived. Obtaining the water they needed to get home came first.

The MOAD loomed ahead, blocking out Jupiter and the stars. Kate flew the broomstick along the sunlit side of the gargantuan alien spaceship. Honestly? This may have been her duty, but she wouldn't have missed it for the world.

An alien spaceship! Son of a bitch!

Thrusters the size of aircraft carriers bulged out of the steel cliff that hung to their left. You could fly the whole

SoD into one of those maws, without clipping the sides.

"*C'est fantastique!*" Giles breathed. "It is *real?*"

"You bet your sweet fanny it is," Kate said, amused.

"Where do you think they have the water tanks?"

"If these are the thrusters for their in-system drive, the water tanks must be near the thrusters."

The broomstick flew slowly with two of them on board. Spitting wisps of gas, they dawdled towards the MOAD's midsection. The hull must have been five feet thick. Extruded forms stood like cottages on a metal prairie, connected by a network of pipes. Tiny craters testified to micro-impacts over the years. Some of the craters *had* craters. How long had this thing been flying, before it reached our solar system?

"How shall we get inside?" Giles said.

"My plan," Kate said, "is to gain access through the gigantic fucking hole in the side."

The hole came into view as she spoke. She swooped the broomstick towards it, rotating at the same time. Giles gulped. Now they seemed to be flying *over* the MOAD, with the sun above them.

The cratered 'landscape' of the hull ended in a cliff. The edge of the cliff swooped up towards them in twisted points and rags of metal. They flew on over the hole. Sunlight shone on twisted metal at the bottom.

"An explosion inside the MOAD," Kate speculated. "Ripped that hull like cloth. Must have been some explosion."

She shifted her weight forward, altering the broomstick's center of mass.

They dived into the hole.

Down, down, down.

Partition walls stuck up like roofless houses in a bombed city, marking the edge of the blast zone.

She executed a flat 180° spin—Giles clung to her for dear life—and used the broomstick's thrust to decelerate.

"Whee! That was fun," she said brightly, cutting the thrust and stepping off. The broomstick had its own tether. She used it to tie the little vehicle to a support pillar that no longer supported anything.

Giles breathed heavily over the radio.

They floated between walls torn off at different heights. Sunlight came down at an angle, leaving the floor in shadow. The darkness cut them off at the thighs. A short way away, impenetrable shadow fell like a curtain over the roofless corridor.

Kate removed her belt tether. She attached it to the end of Giles's tether, and tied the other end to the pillar, giving them twice the range of a single tether. "Hold my hand, Hansel," she said. "Let's not get lost."

Giles laughed, weakly. But as they floated towards the shadow, he freed his glove from hers and darted ahead. His head lamp bobbed like a firefly in the darkness ahead. "I have found writing!" he exclaimed. Kate had never heard such joy in his voice.

She joined him. He was gloating over a seven-sided plaque on the wall. Traces of paint adhered to it. To Kate, the marks looked like chicken-scratches. "It probably just says 'No Smoking,'" she commented. "Famous last words. Giles, we're looking for water, not hieroglyphics."

Exploring the MOAD with Giles was like navigating Toys 'R' Us with her nephews. He could not stay on mission.

Whenever he saw a sign, he had to photograph it. They ventured through the dark, roofless corridors to the full length of their double tether, then returned to the broomstick and set off in a different direction. Kate sucked her teeth. 43 minutes had already elapsed since they reached the MOAD. They were exposed to space here. Exposed to Jupiter's radiation. And Giles insisted on dicking around, analyzing alien signage …

"We'll have to take the broomstick and fly into the undamaged regions of the ship," she said abruptly. "We're just wasting time here."

They retraced their steps. Giles mumbled to himself about grammatical typology and Rosetta stones.

The broomstick was gone.

The loose end of its tether had been neatly tied to the support pillar.

Kate instinctively pushed Giles behind her. Her glove scuffed the place on her hip where her service weapon should be. How deep these instincts ran.

But here, her instincts were useless. No gun. And nothing to shoot. Just the loop of the broomstick's tether, undulating in the vacuum.

"They took it," she said thickly, aware that she was echoing Skyler. Poor, dead Skyler. "The fuckers fucking *took it.*"

She jerked on the tether. It stayed tied in a nice, neat clove hitch. A Navy rating couldn't do better.

"Makes you think about all the things that are the same," she said, tightly. Her rage was incandescent. "No matter where in the fucking galaxy you come from, there's only one way to tie a clove hitch. I guess that also goes for the things you were talking about. Syntax and that shit."

Giles did not answer.

She spun around.

"Giles?"

He was gone.

CHAPTER 24

"It's all bullshit," Alexei said, walking across the manufacturing floor with his arm around Jack's neck. He had seen Jack get carried away before, and sometimes that was a good thing, but it was *never* a good thing to trust without verifying. And that's what Jack was doing. He was buying everything that the rriksti were selling, like a typical gullible Westerner.

"How is it bullshit?" Jack said crossly.

Alexei glanced back at the alien shuttle. The rriksti called Keelraiser stood on the wing. Alexei could feel it watching them all the way from here.

"I am trying to work out what type of drive the MOAD uses," he said.

Jack interrupted, "We already know it's a water plasma drive, just like ours."

"They didn't come all the way from Proxima b burning water. They must get up to a significant percent of light speed. So they need an interstellar drive."

"I think that's obvious, yes. The MPD drive is for in-system deceleration. It's a giant brake."

"So what type of interstellar drive do they use? FTL? A warp drive?"

"We can ask them later." Jack twisted out from under his arm. "Jesus, Alexei, we're being really rude."

Alexei almost laughed. Jack was concerned with being *polite!* To aliens! "I already did ask them. After you left the combustion chamber—"

"Yeah, the combustion chamber!" Jack's eyes lit up. "Wasn't that flipping amazing? We were in there with a *star!*"

Alexei wanted to shake him. "I asked them," he repeated, "about their interstellar drive, and they described it to me. The engine is a scaled-up version of the muon-catalyzed fusion drive. It is fed by magnetic field generators. A scoop, formed from these magnetic fields, thousands of kilometers across, collects interstellar hydrogen for propellant."

"It's a Bussard ramscoop."

"Yes, they invented the same concept. There are only a limited number of ways to do these things."

"So what?" Jack said. "They use a magnetic ramscoop, so what? Once you've got fusion drives, you're going to the stars one way or another." His eyes were soft, dreamy.

Alexei had been aggressively questioning the aliens about everything he could think of since he woke up on a shelf with two of them staring at him. Their readiness to answer his every question only made him more suspicious. He was dismayed that Jack seemed to take them at face value. But Jack came from green and gentle England. It was a mystery how they ever raised soldiers in that place. Alexei hailed from the mean streets of Volgograd—well, not all that mean; he'd had a private education, as you more or less had to to get into the officer corps—but life had beaten into him the lesson that everyone was an antagonist until proven otherwise. And everyone lied. Everyone.

Why should aliens be any different?

He had therefore pumped them for information, hoping to catch them out in a lie. And he believed he'd done it.

"Listen. They said that the magnetic field generator failed, and this blew a hole in the MOAD, right? Then they had to take refuge on Europa."

"Yeah."

"Why did the magfield generator fail, *when it wasn't in operation?* Ramscoops don't work within our solar system. Not enough hydrogen."

"Hmm."

"If it did fail, it failed for a different reason. Not simply wear and tear. If it was wear and tear, it would fail in deep space, not conveniently on the doorstep of Jupiter."

"Hmm."

Alexei thought he was getting through to Jack. He said, "And where are all the rest of the refugees? That ship is five *kilometers* long. They said there were thousands of rriksti on board. Where are all the rest of them?"

"I was assuming they all died in the explosion." Jack frowned. "Let's ask Keelraiser."

"No, you idiot!"

But it was too late. Jack had gone bounding back across the floor.

Keelraiser slid down the rope from the shuttle's wing.

Alexei caught up. He bunched his fist, ready to punch Jack, or Keelraiser, he wasn't sure which yet. If the rriksti knew that the men knew they were lying—about what? *Something.* Something big—this could get unpredictable, fast. Their only hope of survival might lie in acting unpredictably, first.

Jack slapped his headset on top of his dirty blond curls. "I'm hungry," he told the rriksti. He smiled, lips closed. "Alexei said you offered him some food, but it was …"

"Inedible," Alexei said. He let his fist uncurl. This might turn out to be a cunning move.

"We do need food every so often," Jack said. "We tend to get short-tempered and cranky without it. I'm sure you understand. So either feed us, please, or allow us to fetch our own food from our landing craft."

Alexei suppressed a smile. They couldn't eat the aliens' food—he'd already tried—so if the rriksti wanted to keep them alive, they would have to let them return to the Dragon. Then they'd be getting out of here, even if Alexei had to tie Jack into his couch.

Keelraiser's response disconcerted him. "Then we will eat together," it said. "I apologize for our poor hospitality."

Shit, Alexei thought. They aren't going to let us go, are they? We're trapped.

CHAPTER 25

Kate gathered in the loose end of the tether that should have been attached to Giles's belt. It had been cleanly severed. She wrapped it around her right glove and untied the other end from the stanchion. The tether reel at the end was made of solid steel. It would weigh several pounds on Earth. Not a bad weapon. It was the only one she had, anyway.

She kicked off from the wall and floated into the darkness.

"Giles," she called over the radio. "Giles."

She drifted along the corridor they had explored before. Her headlamp shone on blackened, bubbled paint. Further on, swirls of acid color glowed undamaged on the walls. So this was the MOAD's interior décor. Pretty gross.

She reached an intersection. The corridor crossing this one was as broad as a subway tunnel. Weirdly, tables and sofas stood in groups in the middle of the corridor, like some kind of extraterrestrial café. Kate's heart hammered. She peeked left and right.

The walls of the corridor were lined with lockers eight feet high. Kate suddenly remembered an incident from her own high school days. Some kids had shut a girl into her own locker. She was too ashamed to shout and kick the door, apparently, so no one found her until after school, when the janitor heard her crying. Kate had been friends with the kids who did the shutting-in. They had laughed for weeks about it. She felt bad about that to this day.

Each locker had a plaque above it, etched with the chicken-scratch writing Giles had found so intriguing.

Kate chuckled bleakly. She rapped her tether reel on the nearest locker. "It's safe to come out now, Giles. Time to go home…"

The locker lit up with a soft green light.

Kate pushed off from it in fright, and because she was in freefall she kept going until she bumped into one of the sofas in the middle of the corridor.

The light grew brighter. The door of the locker was translucent. The light was coming from inside, and it silhouetted a humanoid shape.

A woman, Kate thought.

Floating suspended.

Thick locks haloed her head like a mermaid's hair.

But this mermaid had legs. Runway-model legs. Skinny arms, and a face …

A face like a huge Halloween mask, with outsize eyes, closed.

It's an alien. A motherfucking alien.

Kate gripped her tether reel. She felt absolutely terrified lest those eyes should open, and fix on her.

She glanced up and down the tunnel. The green glow from the locker with the alien woman in it illuminated more and more lockers stretching away in both directions. Hundreds of them. *Thousands.*

She pushed off from the sofa, and caught movement at the edge of her faceplate.

An alien clambered over the sofa, reaching for her.

Just like the one in the locker, but dead black all over. The thick locks on its head wriggled like an octopus's tentacles.

Kate let out a shocked little grunt, and hurled the tether reel into those repulsive tentacles.

An unbearable high tone stabbed into her ears.

Kate wanted to rip her helmet off to escape the noise. But she guessed that it was a scream. She'd hurt the thing. *Good.*

The tether reel bounced back to her. She swung it round and round like a nunchuck and let it fly again. The tether unreeled. The tether reel made solid contact.

High-pitched tones filled her ears, warbling from one intolerable frequency to the next. Kate brought her chin down on the toggle, switching her radio off.

Now she knew what had happened to Jack and Alexei.

More tentacle-headed aliens sprang at her from either side. Her quick, frightened pants filled her helmet. She swung the tether reel at their arms, at their tentacles—that was their vulnerable point, she figured.

But every time she moved, she herself moved in the opposite direction..

The aliens encircled her.

She swung at the nearest one with furious energy, and Newtonian physics propelled her backwards again.

A blow rammed into her kidneys. Agony whited out her vision. She lost consciousness.

CHAPTER 26

Slung upside-down over a bony shoulder, helmet bumping on a fleshless rump, Giles wondered if the aliens were going to kill him. The prospect did not perturb him overmuch. He had done what he wished to do before he died—he'd seen the future.

The future jolted past him, upside-down. Skinny legs stretched out like the legs of swimmers. Bright lights on the aliens' chests lit their route. Clusters of alien furniture, bolted down, suggested an orientation that the aliens ignored as they flew onward. Giles had occasionally gone scuba diving. The aliens reminded him of fish darting through a shipwreck—agile, coordinated. Tropical colors patterned their hides.

They came to a great emptiness, and flew over a glacier that slumped away through shattered decks. The glacier curved like a difficult ski slope. The MOAD must have been rotating when the disaster happened, Giles thought. Water had burst from some reservoir, and had flowed anti-spinwards. Then—the loss of atmosphere. Everything had frozen.

At the glacier's foot, the aliens braked their flight by slamming into an elastic cable. They deftly clipped onto the cable and slid along it, towards a wall scrawled with alien writing.

The wall vanished.

They all tumbled on top of each other into the dark. Giles was spun around, dropped, seized again, and dragged by one boot.

Into twilight.

Alien hands jerked at his helmet. He slapped at them, panicking. They found the locking mechanism and pulled his helmet off.

He gasped in a lungful of hot, fetid air. But—it *was* air. He wasn't asphyxiating. He lay on a filthy floor. Sludge coated his ESA-blue suit.

He rolled over.

Above him hung a cavern of stars with Jupiter in the middle, radiant.

Aliens stooped over him. They roughly removed his spacesuit—first the upper torso, then the lower torso assembly—and peeled his spandex inner garment off, leaving him naked. Their hands had seven fingers. Their fingernails were dark brown, the color of dried blood, as heavy as dogs' claws.

He was dragged by one foot again. At this stage he consciously noticed that there was gravity here. His upper body scraped over the floor. The sludge got into his mouth. It tasted like old coins. He grabbed at the leg of a table. Claw-footed. S-curved. Very Louis Quatorze.

The aliens picked him up and threw him onto another table. Plates and cups scattered onto the floor. His hand came down on a filigreed silver platter. Everything else was filthy but the plates were as clean as a bone—they might have been licked.

He scrabbled into a sitting position, and crumpled over his bare knees. The artificial gravity, however it was produced, felt like about half of a full gee.

The room was as large as Notre Dame. And that was just the central space in which he found himself. Triangular chancels jutted off this central space like the points of a star, cluttered with machinery. The transparent ceiling—if it were not merely a projection of some kind—enhanced the spaciousness. So too did the dim light and the silence. Orange lights on the various machines glowed like candles in a church.

A *desecrated* church, the floor covered with dirt that had spilled from numerous troughs of plants. Some of the plants resembled colorless lupins and gladioli. Others looked like fungi, pale excrescences the size of babies' heads.

Machinery growled, and a fan whapped somewhere, yet *silence* was the overwhelming impression, and this was because the aliens themselves were silent.

In a pious hush, they were taking apart the broomstick Giles and Kate had ridden from the *SoD*.

Detachedly, Giles studied their weird physiology. They had been patterned all over in vivid colors when they captured him, but now they looked both more human, and less. Their patterned 'hides' must have been EVA suits. Now they wore short-sleeved coats that hung open over their chests, and trousers hacked off at the knees. The garments were so dirty that their original color could hardly be deduced. Perhaps orange. Their bare feet were encrusted with dirt. The tentacles on their heads writhed like snakes. They had skin as pale as any European's, and sludge-dark eyes the size of nectarines.

In ones and twos, they drifted over to the table where he was sitting. Finding himself the center of attention, Giles lost his sense of detachment. He cringed and said, "I'm friendly."

A taller alien pushed through the crowd. It stood at least two meters and a half, and its mane of silvery tentacles added another half-meter to its height. Its triangular face remained expressionless as it punched Giles in the cheek with a large, hard fist.

Giles sprawled sideways on the table, agony flaring through his cheek and jaw. He also pissed himself in terror.

"Don't hurt me," he babbled. "Please. I am a xenolinguist. I've been waiting for this all my life. I only want to communicate—"

An electronic squeal cut him off.

Two aliens moved up on either side of the table and hauled him into a sitting position.

The silver-tentacled one now held something that looked like a 1980s boombox. The proportions were slightly off, and the cassette player buttons had obviously been printed as mere ornamental touches.

"We come in peace," the boombox blared in English. The silver-tentacled alien pointed to its own face, conveying that these were its words, although they issued from the boombox. "Is this correct?"

Giles blinked. He said, "I have the impression that my life's work has been wasted."

He smiled, despite the pain in his cheek, savoring the rich irony of this moment. He had spent years devising exotic symbol sets and holistic three-dimensional syntax structures, the likes of which human brains less able than his could not even conceive of. And now he had been captured by aliens who spoke English.

That said, their grasp of the language seemed shaky. If this were *peace*, Giles hated to think what hostility would look like.

He reminded himself that the aliens were stranded on a

badly damaged ship. No doubt they feared the *SoD* had come to destroy them. He must lay their fears to rest.

"How did you learn English?"

"From television." The silver-tentacled one holding the boombox opened and closed its mouth silently, as if to drive through Giles's presumably thick skull that it was in fact talking.

"Ah, *merde*," Giles murmured. A new and most unwelcome theory began to take shape. On TV—a medium saturated with Anglo-American cultural pathologies—people were always punching each other. The aliens must think that was the human way of saying hello. He was lucky they hadn't shot him.

"I am talking to you," the boombox said.

"I know. Can you hear me?" The aliens had tiny, delicate-looking ears. But since they apparently could not talk without electronic intermediation, perhaps they couldn't hear, either.

"This device picks up your voice. It transmits it to me. Now answer my question! Have you been in contact with those cocksuckers on the surface?"

Giles giggled. Pain starred his cheek. "You have mastered the use of obscenity; well done. Regarding your question, if there are other living beings on the surface, we did not—we don't … Four of our crew went down to the surface, but two are dead, and the other two … I don't know. We don't know what happened."

"They *have* contacted them."

"Perhaps. I do not know …"

"Fuck," the boombox said. "Fuck, fuck, fuck."

Giles couldn't help giggling again. "Do you also speak

FELIX R. SAVAGE

French, out of curiosity?"

"English is your lingua franca. Is this correct?"

"Yes, although it pains me to say so. But these personal feelings are mere nostalgia, and I disregard them on principle. Our species is rapidly progressing towards a future without linguistic barriers, without borders, without xenophobia. In other words, we have at last reached the stage where interspecies cooperation is a possibility. I represent the political grouping—the Earth Party—that is most favorably disposed towards you, and stands ready to welcome you to Earth, in a spirit of *peace,*" he emphasized.

The speech he had prepared for this moment was actually much longer. He had envisioned many variants of this moment. None of them had included himself sitting naked on an alien dining table with a possibly shattered cheekbone.

Boombox punched him again, this time in the stomach. Giles instinctively reached down to block the blow. This laid him open to a right jab that caught him squarely in the mouth.

He regained consciousness flat on his back, looking up at Jupiter through a haze of tears. He breathed, and sobbed.

The aliens sat him up once more. Blood drooled down his chin. His head felt like a swollen balloon of agony. He blotted his lips genteelly with the back of his hand.

"Aren't you going to hit me back?" Boombox shifted its device into its left hand and spread its arms over its head, as if inviting a punch. Its coat rode up to expose a pale midriff ridged with muscle. Giles noted that it had no belly button or nipples.

"What is to be gained by exchanging blows? Should we not exchange information?" Giles raised his gaze to meet the alien's eyes. He was terrified of being hit again, but on a deeper level, his resolve remained undimmed. "I am devoured by curiosity. I am completely sincere. I want to know everything about you, even if it costs me my life!"

Boombox opened its small mouth wide. Giles could not imagine what this expression meant.

"You have the advantage of me," Giles continued. "You speak English. You know a lot about us—"

This time, he didn't even see the alien's fist coming.

Pain exploded in his right side.

Knocked sprawling on the table, he fought to breathe. Every breath stabbed like a knife in his side. A broken rib, or maybe two.

Yet this time, the pain did not overwhelm his reason.

When something happens over and over again, it's a pattern.

The alien's violence must be a form of communication. It was talking to him with its fists, and if that weren't enough, it had talked to him via its boombox.

Aren't you going to hit me back? it had said, when he failed to comply with its expectations.

Reciprocity, Giles thought. I am meant to mirror its behavior, to prove myself a worthy interlocutor. It said so in plain English. I simply wasn't listening, in too much of a hurry to communicate my own message. Would I walk up to a peer and launch into a political sales pitch without so much as shaking his hand? No, of course not! *Mon Dieu,* I deserve to get punched in the face. Some xenolinguist I am.

He pushed himself up on his knees. The gravity dizzied him. His broken ribs seemed to slice his lungs every time he breathed.

At the best of times, Giles despised physical violence. He hadn't raised a hand to a fellow creature since breaking up with his first boyfriend, whom he had been compelled to slap in the face after the latter cheated on him once too often. That's not to say he did not like the *idea* of violence—he had often envisioned lingering and painful deaths for the other members of the *SoD's* crew—but recourse to his fists would be beneath a sophisticated man like him. That's what he thought.

Yet now he had no better ideas.

Boombox stood, flanked by its fellows, gravely watching his struggles.

Giles faced the alien on his knees. The height of the table put their faces on a level. Any attempt to raise his right arm tortured his ribs, so he swung his left fist at the alien's chest, and made glancing contact.

All the aliens startled. The tips of their tentacles rose and wriggled.

Giles collapsed back on his heels, waiting for them to beat him to death.

Boombox came even closer, so that the edge of the table dug into its stomach. Giles smelled a strong salty odor. The alien shrugged off its coat and tossed it to a companion, exposing its upper body. It was so thin that its skeletal structure could be seen beneath the skin. The clavicle was longer than a human's, giving its torso an exaggerated triangular form that echoed the shape of its face.

It spread its arms obligingly.

Giles closed his eyes and punched the alien in the chest. It felt like punching a hot steel wall covered with skin.

Boombox tapped its own face.

"All right, that's what you want?" Giles swung at the pale cheek. Now he felt the dark joy of hitting the one who had hurt him. He slapped the alien's face again and again, which probably hurt him more than it hurt Boombox. But he had a torn thumbnail, and it opened a shallow gash in the alien's cheek. Blood welled.

Giles noted that the blood was as red as any human's. Then he passed out.

*

He regained consciousness, still lying on the dining table. The pain in his ribs had abated to a dull throb. He felt instinctively that only moments had passed since his orgy of violence against Boombox, but the improvement in his physical condition suggested it must have been longer.

He pushed himself up on his elbows. Pain spiked through his right cheek. *That* didn't seem to have abated any.

Boombox was pacing amidst overturned chairs and tables. It had its arms folded behind its back. Its shoulders must be double-jointed. The posture made its chest puff out in a manner that would have been comical, if it were not eight feet tall with a stalking predatorial gait.

Seeing Giles awake, it abruptly began to speak.

"We fought," it said, through the pathetic improvised communications device sitting next to Giles. "It was a fight that could not be settled. The situation deteriorated until we were entrenched at opposite ends of the ship. They held the bridge. We held the drive and the primary water reservoirs. But they also held a pocket of territory amidships, which they resupplied via the hangar deck. As we approached this gas giant, they made a sortie and captured the ship's arsenal. They targeted our front lines with … a weapon your species hasn't invented yet."

Giles struggled to process this sudden flood of information. He understood that Boombox was telling him how the MOAD had ended up here.

"You know, perhaps, that a stream of muons catalyzes fusion in water?"

Giles had not known this interesting fact.

"Those cretins fired a siege-class muon cannon at our fucking water reservoirs."

Boombox unfolded its arms and flung them out. The gesture conveyed the force of an uncontrolled explosion.

"The water tanks turned into fusion bombs."

"You blew up your own ship!" Giles said in amazement.

"No! *They* blew it up." Boombox stalked back towards him. "They murdered one hundred and eighty-four of my people. The explosion disabled the primary field generator, blew a hole in the hull. The in-system drive remains operable. But we cannot operate it."

Giles said, "I—I'm sorry."

He was sorry. He had hoped that the MOAD and its passengers would be the salvation of humankind.

"Then," Boombox went on, "they fled to the surface of this ugly ice ball. In the only working shuttle. They disabled all sixty-nine other shuttles, while my people fought the fires raging on board."

Giles shook his head at this iniquity. The motion sent needles of pain through his face. He rested his elbows on his knees and cradled his face in his hands. That hurt even worse.

Boombox closed a hot, hard hand on his arm, Giles jerked his head up to see the alien's face hanging over him, its huge eyes staring at him.

"They left us to die."

"The ship, it is completely inoperable?" Giles said, tiredly. "You said something about an in-system drive ..."

"Undamaged. But inoperable."

Boombox yanked on his arm, dragging him off the table. Giles staggered in the unaccustomed gravity. The alien hauled him over to one of the star-point chancels. The wedge-shaped space seemed to grow as they entered, the side walls becoming screens filled with overlapping 3D readouts.

"This is the bridge."

Boombox's voice now came from behind them, but Giles did not take his eyes off the alien towering over him. His gaze was drawn to the bloody scratch on its cheek. Their exchange of blows had been traumatic, but it had had a purgative effect on him. He no longer felt any dislike for the alien. In fact, he wanted to apologize for hurting it.

"For ten years I have thought about little else apart from life support. We cannibalized systems throughout the ship to survive. Even so, we've been dying. You see three sevens of people here, there are two more patrolling the ship—that's all of us."

Boombox turned away and braced its hands on the edge of the console. Its leonine head drooped. Its shoulderblades poked up against the fabric of its coat, sharp, emaciated. Giles had every reason to sympathize with what he understood to be its weariness and despair. Venturesomely, he placed one hand over the large, seven-fingered one. "You've been through hell."

"For many years this was our life. Then you arrived."

Boombox swung around to face Giles, pulling its hand out from under his. "And we had hope."

Giles smiled sadly. "There is a fantastic irony in this. Do you understand irony, by the way?"

"Yes."

"I believed that *you* were *our* hope. You see, humanity has virtually destroyed Earth. The climate is changing. The seas are rising. Our carbon dioxide emissions have trigged runaway deglaciation and biodiversity loss. We're standing on the brink of a historical wave of extinctions, and even that's not the worst of it. The Arctic sea ice is melting. When that goes, we all go."

Giles's hobby was heavy metal, but that did not absorb all his intellectual energies. Pre-MOAD, his *other* hobby had been arguing online with climate deniers.

"At this crucial inflection point in our history, *you* arrived. From this fateful conjunction of looming ecological catastrophe and first contact, the Earth Party emerged. Our mission is to welcome you, to establish a framework for dialogue, to achieve harmonious relations with your species. We hoped that you might save us from self-destruction." Giles spread his hands ruefully. "Now, I see that we were naïve. You cannot even save yourselves!"

Boombox's hair danced as if an invisible wind were blowing it around. Giles did not know what this meant.

Suddenly the alien reached under the consoles and yanked open a locker. An avalanche of fabric cascaded out. Giles wrinkled his nose at the musty smell that came with it.

Boombox snatched up a bundle of orange cloth spotted with mold. "This will be too large for you, but you can roll up the legs," it said.

"What is it?"

"A uniform."

CHAPTER 27

"Alas, my Hannah, you do me wrong, to choose that retard Jack to screw," Skyler sang. "For I have loved you so long, and dream about your coochie-coo ..."

He laughed, a gasp of breath, and searched for another rhyme.

It distracted him from how shitty he felt.

He walk had become a battle with nausea.

Maybe it was the smell of vomit, which he'd never got out of his spacesuit, sickening him. That's what he tried to tell himself. But the stomach is not to be reasoned with. Our second brain is in our gut. Isn't that what they say? The microbiome does a lot of thinking for us. And Skyler's microbiome, or his paranoia, or both, was telling him that he felt like throwing up because he was taking rems.

His stupid umbrella-hat wasn't protecting him, or wasn't protecting him enough, from the lethal blizzard of charged particles bathing Europa's surface.

"Oh, Hannah, why can't you see, I want to make sweet love to you ..."

Knives of pain twisted in his stomach. He stopped to wait it out, and looked back the way he'd come.

Under the edge of his umbrella-hat, the ice field stretched to the horizon. His footsteps crossed it in a wobbly, meandering line.

He swallowed bile. His heart thudded in his ears.

He'd been walking for four hours. The Shenzhou Plus had long since vanished over the horizon.

At last the pain receded. He faced forward again, ready to keep walking, because there was nothing else to do. Panic moved sluggishly in his brain, kept at bay, ironically, only by nausea. The white spike of the Dragon had grown taller, but its base hadn't come over the horizon yet. He should have *been* there by now. Either his calculations were way off, or he had overestimated how fast he could walk.

Probably the latter. It was *hard* to walk on an ice rink covered with grainy snow.

"I want to se-ee your ecstasy … and …"

A violent wave of nausea hit him. He barfed.

His vomit hit his faceplate—liquid, just liquid, he hadn't had anything to eat in hours. He did a couple of deep knee bends, fast, to make the vomit slide down so he wasn't staring at it.

He couldn't help seeing it.

There was *stuff* in it.

Looked like coffee grounds.

He retched again.

*

Hannah floated inside an algae tank, scrubbing it out. She'd made some headway on the to-do list Kate had left her. She'd repaired the industrial-size centrifuge and used it to separate the dead algae from the water in the tanks that had been worst hit by the power outage. She'd put the dead algae in the combustion unit and reduced them to phosphate-rich ash. That would provide extra nourishment for the living ones when she restocked the tanks.

Now she was inside one of the thick, transparent Lexan cylinders, drying it with a special polishing cloth. When she climbed in here, there'd been globules of dirty water floating around. Now they were stuck all over her clothes and hair. She had a portable fan clipped to the rim of the tank, blowing air down on her, so she wouldn't smother in her own CO2.

It was hot, dirty, slimy work, and in combination with Ginsburg brand moonshine, it just about sufficed to stop her from thinking about the fact that she was alone on the *SoD.*

That Skyler was dead.

That Meili and Jack and Alexei were also dead.

That Kate and Giles had been gone for *more than four hours* and they only had six hours of air supply in their suits.

She might be the last surviving human being within 600 million kilometers.

But she had a buzz on, so life wasn't all bad.

She climbed out of the tank at last, taking her portable fan with her, and fitted the end-cap back on. "Alas, my love, you do me wrong," she sang. She'd heard Skyler singing this old chestnut around the hab in recent weeks. "To cast me out so discourteously …"

She sniffled, and hooked up the pump. Water gushed into the tank. Soon she'd have a perfect line of full tanks spinning in their axial housing, filled with billions of algae, producing oxygen for …

… me. Only me.

She grabbed her bottle off her utility belt and squeezed it, hard. Moonshine mix gushed into her mouth.

The *SoD's* noises helped her to stay calm. Everything sounded louder now that she was alone. *BRRRRRR* went the fans. *RMMMMM* went the housekeeping turbine, aft. *Clink clink* went …

… what?

What was that?

Clink.

Still holding her squeeze bottle, Hannah drifted across the module. She ducked under the algae tanks.

Clink.

Wasn't coming from the tanks.

Sounded like something hitting the outside of the module.

Clink clink.

Micro-impact, she thought, but that was nonsense. Micro-meteoroids did not *tap* on the steel skin of your home like …

… like something seeking a weak point …

… looking for the way in.

Clink.

The sound was moving slowly over the hull of the module. Hannah floated on the inside, holding her breath. Only ten centimeters of steel separated her from whatever was out there.

The sound came again, right in her ear. *CLINK!*

Hannah flinched. She kicked off from the wall of the module and flew to the keel tube. In a blind panic, she scrambled through the axis tunnel in the main hab. Flies buzzed around her. The stench of rotting vegetation made her eyes water. She flew into the bridge and manually closed the pressure door behind her, using the hand crank they'd installed after Xiang Peixun's death.

It couldn't get at her in here.

Yes, it could.

She flew to the radio and crammed the headphones over her hair. "Kate. Kate, this is Hannah. Come in. Giles. Come in."

Silence.

"Kate, come in. *Please.*"

Nothing.

Numb denial moved her hand to the channel selector. She switched the comms over to the dipole antenna they used to receive telemetry from the maimed Things, and also to talk to the Shenzhou Plus and the Dragon. She keyed in the Dragon's frequency.

"Jack? Alexei? This is Hannah on the *SoD.* Do you copy?"

They hadn't answered before, when Kate tried to reach them. They sure as shit weren't going to answer now. They were dead, dead, dead. But she couldn't help trying.

"Jack. Alexei," she said into the dead radio. "I'm alone. I'm the only person left on the ship. And something's trying to get in."

The radio squealed. She stiffened.

"Guys! Is that you?"

Distantly, faintly, she heard something.

It might have been the static hiss of Jovian space.

But it sounded like laughter.

Hannah snatched the headphones off. She floated in the foot tethers, rigid with terror.

Her gaze fell on the telescope.

She swam across to it and pressed her eye to the improvised anti-shock pad, a donut of cloth that Alexei had duct-taped to the eyepiece a lifetime ago. The telescope was already trained on the location where Kate had found the alien radio mast. Hannah blinked the distant ice plain into focus.

She expected to see the Dragon standing next to the radio mast.

Maybe she'd even see aliens moving around it.

The same aliens that were using the Dragon's radio, screwing with her mind.

What she actually saw did not compute.

A blank field of ice, with a little blur in the middle where the Dragon had melted the ice when it landed.

The Dragon was gone.

CHAPTER 28

Kate regained consciousness lying on her back.

Aliens were trying to pull her helmet off.

Dumb freaks didn't grok that the Z-2 was a one-piece suit. The helmet didn't *come* off.

She drew her left knee up and pistoned her foot into the stomach of the nearest alien, knocking it backwards. Another one jerked her upright by the helmet. She shifted her weight forward, grabbed the arm reaching around her neck, and threw the alien over her shoulder. Kate had a black belt in tae kwon do. The alien went tumbling in a ball of spidery limbs.

"Come and get it, motherfuckers," she panted, wheeling to see what was behind her. Looked like she was in some kind of control room. Stars in the ceiling. Maybe this was the MOAD's bridge. Twenty, thirty aliens surrounded her. They'd retreated when she started to fight back.

They didn't look as scary now. In fact, they looked like *people*. Tall, skinny people with freak masks on, and manes of dreads that would be the envy of any Rasta.

Convergent evolution? Some people talked about a progenitor race that could have spawned humans and aliens alike. If that were true, humanity turned out to have some extremely freaky cousins. Their large eyes, and the eyestrain-level lighting in here, suggested that their home planet imposed a requirement for low-light / no-light sensoria. Fuckers could probably see in the dark.

One of them, even taller than the others, with silvery dreads or tentacles or whatever, advanced towards her.

OK. Bring it, freak-face.

Kate had the advantage of being in her spacesuit—a mixed blessing, actually. It gave her protection, but weighed 50 kilograms, hampered her range of movement, and limited her peripheral vision.

Breathing hard, she waited.

The creature drove a punch at her helmet.

She swayed back. In her suit, she didn't have the hip flexion for a roundhouse kick, so she drove a low kick at the creature's groin. Fight dirty? Why yes, E.T. Her boot connected with a satisfying thunk, but the alien did not collapse in agony. Maybe it didn't have balls. It reached to grab her foot, missed, shifted its weight, and when she regained her balance its fist was waiting for her helmet.

Holy fuck. Her head bounced off the inner padding. Felt like her brain bounced off the inside of her skull.

She jabbed at the alien's solar plexus, but it was a weak-sauce blow. The alien dodged easily. It punched her in the helmet again.

She hoped that hurt its hand one half as much as it hurt her head.

Stars exploding in her vision, she slid bonelessly to her knees. She'd been concentrating so hard on the fight, she had not allowed herself to notice the gravity, or her own flagging energy. Now everything just kind of gave way all at once.

She thought about what would happen after she died. She wished she could warn Hannah.

Then she spotted Giles, fucking *Giles,* standing in the circle of aliens.

Wearing the same damn clothes as them and everything.

No helmet.

All other thoughts went out of her head. Her perspective on the situation turned inside-out.

The silver-tentacled alien approached her. This time, she let it come. It moved behind her and released the catches on the back entry port of her suit. She wriggled out.

"Something stinks in here," she said, sitting on her heels. The air was warm on her face but felt cool against her limbs, as the sweat soaking her thin nylon t-shirt and panties began to evaporate.

Giles limped up to her, walking with a cane. He was clearly having trouble with the gravity, too. And the aliens had given him a cane to walk with? It was too long for him. The head looked to be made of gold.

"You did very well!" He looked a bit woozy. But his eyes were bright in the dim light. "I think they are pleased with you!"

"What? All I did was kick that fucker in the nuts."

"Yes, yes!" Giles babbled about how he'd worked out that these aliens had a custom of ritually trading blows with strangers. He described how the silver-tentacled one, which he named Boombox, had knocked him around and then invited him to hit back. Kate reflected that Giles was not a military man. He must also have avoided the playground as a child. What he described didn't sound particularly exotic to her. More like a bully acting out to amuse his fan club. *Hit me, go on. Hit me if you dare, you little faggot.* If that was a ritual, it was one humans performed, too. Yes, there were probably some alien nuances going on, but she doubted Giles had grasped them, any more than she could.

She turned her head—her neck twinged painfully, after those blows to her helmet—and located the silver-tentacled alien behind her. Its feet, covered with the muck from the floor, had seven black-clawed toes. She raised her gaze to its freaky triangular face. "You're bored, aren't you?" she said. "Stuck in this wreck for ten years. You must be climbing the walls. So when a fly comes along ... you pull its wings off. It's good to know we've encountered another intelligent species."

Boombox extended a seven-fingered hand. She deliberated for a moment, but the way she felt, she wasn't getting off the floor by herself anytime soon. She allowed the alien to haul her to her feet.

It led her to a long table with plates and cups stacked messily at one end. Chairs were pulled up to the other end. Kate collapsed into one of them, with Giles on her left. Boombox and its sidekicks sat across from them. For the humans, the chairs were like high stools. Rather than sit with her feet dangling like a child, Kate crossed her legs in lotus position.

All the furniture was ornately carved, and seemed luxurious. This gang of survivors had taken over the best part of the ship, like paratroopers squatting in Saddam's palace. Kate exhaustedly plopped her elbows on the table.

"How do you make the gravity in here?" she demanded. "And can you turn it off?"

"Mass attractors," Boombox said, from a radio-like device on the table. "They can be moved, but not turned off. When the *Lightbringer* was coasting, only the officers and VIPs enjoyed gravity. Now we enjoy it."

"The *Lightbringer?*"

"The MOAD," Giles said. "That's the real name of the ship! Translated, of course."

"And these guys are?"

"The last survivors of the ship's guard," Giles again jumped in to answer her question. Of course, as a xenolinguist, he had to act like the big expert, even though his expertise was apparently superfluous, since the aliens spoke English.

He related a tale of war breaking out on board the *Lightbringer,* pitting the ship's civilian leadership against their own guards. Kate shook her head. It sounded crazy ... and 100% believable, given recent events on board the *SoD.* Just two years had been long enough to set a handful of humans at each other's throats. If they'd had these—what? *Muon* cannon?—Jack Kildare might well have blown a hole in the *SoD,* just like the opposing alien faction had apparently blown a hole in the *Lightbringer.*

"How long was their journey?" she said.

"Oh, I had trouble working that out!" Giles said. "At first they spoke in terms of years. *Thousands* of years!"

"Oh my God."

"Yes, but you see, they explained that their home planet has an orbital period of eleven days! So one year for them is just eleven days long. Calculating it, we get a journey time of sixty-one years and five months."

"Whew. That's still pretty long. Were these guys born on the ship? Or are they long-lived?"

She suddenly remembered the alien woman in the locker. A leggy Sleeping Beauty with a fright-mask face, floating in green light.

She now doubted that it had been a woman. Long hair seemed to be a unisex thing for these guys, if that stuff even was hair. In fact, as humanoid as they superficially looked, their sex or lack thereof was a big question mark.

But the locker had been real.

Thousands of lockers, stretching away into the darkness …

As she tried to phrase a question about that, Giles dropped his voice. "I don't know about their lifespans. Clearly they are superior to us in many ways, however their biology is a mystery. We don't even know if they are male or female, or perhaps hermaphroditic!"

"No, I was wondering about that."

"Perhaps they've transcended gender identity through genetic engineering."

Kate wrinkled her nose. Giles's excitement grated on her. She could cut him a bit of slack—after a lifetime of theorizing about aliens, he finally got to meet them! He must feel like a kid in a candy shop. But they weren't here to do cultural anthropology on these guys. They were here to evaluate any risk that the MOAD might present to humanity. Giles seemed to have clean forgotten about that part of their mission.

She herself felt easier in her mind, knowing that the MOAD—sorry, *Lightbringer*—really was disabled. It posed no threat to Earth. She was not impressed with Boombox and its cronies, either. Reading between the lines, they had been at the bottom of the food chain when the *Lightbringer* was fully manned. She smiled to herself, picturing them in rent-a-cop uniforms, hiding out until the shooting was over.

Wait a minute. Uniforms?

She frowned at Boombox, across the table from her. It wore the same gear as the others. A coat cut boxy in the front, with wide lapels, and longer in the back. Kinda Napoleonic. The loose Bermuda shorts suggested a more modern era—or just comfort. The whole ensemble was so dirty, you could scarcely tell it had once been orange.

Giles wore the exact same thing, but less dirty.

"Hey, Giles. Why are you wearing their uniform?"

She expected him to make some excuse, like they'd taken his spacesuit away.

She looked around the room to see, actually, what had happened to *her* suit, and what she saw was a couple of aliens taking it apart with knives. They had it laid out on a table like a corpse and they were hacking into the made-in-America soft goods, slicing out the mylar silicone joints.

"Hey!" She was on her feet. "That's my fucking suit!" Her knees gave way. She caught herself on her chair. Boombox was there, hauling her upright. It came around the table so damn *fast*, she knew it had just been playing with her before.

"They dismantled my suit, too," Giles said. "They need the raw materials! Kate, they have *nothing*. Everything is broken. The fabrication units, the electrolysis machinery, everything! They are barely surviving!"

"So what? Honestly, Giles, so the fuck what?"

He had to think about that for a minute. She hung in Boombox's grip. It held her upper arms, gently. Her back was pressed against its torso. The heat of its skin came through her t-shirt.

"They are living creatures, like us," Giles said finally.

"So what?" Anyway, she thought, they're not like us at all.

"Oh, you're a true American," Giles said, bitterly. "As Iron Maiden said: 'White man came across the sea, he brought us pain and misery …'"

"Huh?"

"You propose to do to the rriksti what your people did to the Native Americans. They weren't seen as fully human, either."

"Giles, these guys aren't Native Americans. They aren't *human.*"

A tirade burst out of Giles. Kate couldn't follow the intricacies of his argument, but he seemed to be saying that first contact was a heavy metal thing. Metal was the music of the oppressed, of the excluded, of outsiders who did not belong. This was true on the semiotic level as well, he said. The dissonances of metal trained the brain for the weirdness of alien language. Kate remembered that these had been themes of Giles's work pre-MOAD. But now he added a tinfoil-hat twist. The *Spirit of Destiny,* he asserted, had been designed by the tottering US hegemon and its allies precisely to suppress, with violence, these natural sympathies between aliens and terrestrial heavy metal fans (and, he generously allowed, other 'outsiders' of various flavors).

Kate reflected on how inadequate her briefings on her crew had been. Even the NXC had not known Giles held these radical opinions. But maybe he *hadn't* held them before they left Earth. In the two years since the *SoD's* departure, a lot of tinfoil-hat attitudes had moved into the mainstream, courtesy of the Earth Party. It had been a mistake, she thought, to allow the crew access to the internet.

And here came the Earth Party, right on cue. It was, Giles said, the voice of the oppressed and excluded. A new alternative to Earth's corrupt politics. Direct democracy via the internet.

"The people of Earth welcome the rriksti." A drop of

Giles's spittle hit her cheek. "You will *not* stop us!"

"Giles, this is my fault," she said. "I should have paid more attention. I took you for granted. I made fun of your music. Can you forgive me?" She made this desperate plea, hoping against hope, thinking of Peixun and Skyler and Meili and Jack and Alexei—five out of eight! She couldn't lose anyone else, even if it were Giles. "I've been a shitty mission commander," she blurted.

The fey light in Giles's eyes brightened. "That's OK," he sneered. "You are not mission commander anymore."

Boombox tightened its grip on her arms, lifting her up so her toes dangled off the floor. Too late, she realized that it was holding her so that Giles could hit her. Then he did.

He slapped her in the face, punched her in the stomach, punched her in the breasts. *Christ* that hurt. All the time Boombox was holding her with her feet off the floor in what was actually a torture position. Her arms seemed to be coming out of their sockets. She spat blood, felt a tooth wobble. Giles came at her again, his eyes wild, like he wanted to gnaw her throat out. Her eyes instinctively squeezed shut, and she thought about Alexei. They'd had that fight on the bridge, the night of the third HERF attack. He'd hit her, blacked her eye. Big fucking deal, in retrospect.

But at the time, she'd felt the humiliation, the loss of authority, like a knife in her heart, and so she'd made the worst decision of her life. Instead of being up-front with Alexei and Jack and walking them through her decision-making process, she'd lied about receiving orders to blow up the MOAD. She should've sat them down for a frank talk. She could have convinced them that the MOAD was a clear and present fucking danger to *us,* if not to all humanity. But after that near-mutiny, she had not felt like dialoguing with Alexei or Jack or anybody. So she'd made up those orders from Mission Control, and we all know how *that* went. She'd had to back down for fear of provoking total mutiny.

If only, if *only* she'd just *talked* to her crew, the *Lightbringer* and these psychotic aliens would now be a cloud of debris. Alexei would still be alive. And Kate wouldn't be getting beaten to death by Giles fucking Boisselot.

The blows stopped coming.

She opened her eyes.

In a daze of pain, she saw Giles fiddling with a weird gun, resembling a water-pistol with a large reservoir. One of the aliens was showing him how to use it.

Giles stared at her and babbled, "This weapon lowers the Coulomb barrier! It will turn your heart into a fist-sized ball of radioactive ions! *Tres* cool, *n'est ce pas?*"

Oh yes, Kate thought. Shoot me, please. Anything to get away from this pain.

But wait.

There was some reason why she must not die.

What was it?

Hannah.

If she died, Hannah, left alone aboard the *SoD,* would die also.

But of course, that wouldn't make a dime's worth of difference to Giles. After all, Hannah was an American, too.

Kate twisted weakly in the alien's grip. Something popped in her right shoulder. She screamed.

Boombox wrapped its big hands around her ribcage and lifted her up so her face was on a level with its own. The huge dark eyes regarded her, their expression unreadable.

She believed that the mind in there was the unknowable mind of a psychopath, if not something worse, something so bad that human language had no words for it. But she also had to believe that Boombox had pragmatic motivations, and wanted to ensure the survival of itself and its friends.

"You took our suits," she gasped. "You took our broomstick. Your buddies on the surface took the engines out of our advance landers."

"Not our buddies," said the radio on the table.

"OK, whatever. Point being, your M.O. is taking our shit. So I'm guessing you plan to take the *Spirit of Destiny*, too. Am I right?"

Giles jumped in, *"C'est ça!* With the raw materials from the *SoD*, we will make the *Lightbringer* operable again!"

"I'm not fucking talking to you, Giles!" She stared into the alien's eyes. "Boombox, you better believe me. If you kill me—if you let that faggot piece of shit kill me—you will never get the *SoD*. Do you understand? You will get *nothing*. You know why? Because I come from the United States of America. We Americans are many things but we are not stupid. The guy I work for? The president of the United States? Gave me a deadman's switch," she lied, praying that these fuckers were paranoid enough to believe it. Anyway, it was *kind of* true.

CHAPTER 29

Jack dressed for dinner with mixed feelings. A formal sit-down meal! He'd have been fine with a sandwich, or whatever the rriksti equivalent was.

"We're probably on the menu," Alexei muttered.

Jack grinned at him. At least Alexei was joking again. For a while there he'd been spazzing out, insisting that the rriksti were holding them prisoner. Even if that was true—which Jack wasn't ready to believe—throwing punches would clearly do them zero good. Jack had pleaded with Alexei to recognize that fact.

He pulled on the shorts the rriksti had lent him. "It's better than being raped to death," he said.

"Or having our skins sewn into their clothing."

Jack held up the smock that went with the shorts. "Oh dear. Is that you, Skyler?"

Alexei sniggered, putting on his own borrowed garments.

The clothing had no seams; printed, not sewn. The material felt slubby, like a raw silk shirt Jack had once been given by a girlfriend. Smocks and shorts were the same dull gray as the clothing most of the rriksti wore.

But the room they were in—Eskitul's private apartment—shouted with color. Hangings, cushions, and screens displayed the fiddly swirling patterns that the rriksti seemed to favor. This stuff must have been brought across four lightyears from Imf, but Eskitul was not interested in showing it off. Instead, it kept fetching out items related to its study of *Homo sapiens*: books, models of the Parthenon and the Pyramids, and most disturbingly, a model of a human brain, like you'd see in a science classroom, slightly

245

wrong in its proportions. Eskitul explained that it had printed these things on the basis of images captured from television. The 'books' were particularly sad. The covers looked all right—the Bible, *Das Kapital, Mein Kampf,* all the biggies—but the plasticky pages were covered with impressionistic squiggles, not actual words.

There was a mirror. Jack combed his hair and beard with his fingers. Obviously the rriksti had no such thing as an actual comb. Eskitul had made a fuss over his blue eyes, but right now they looked more red than blue. Nervous apprehension coursed through his body, giving him a brittle kind of energy. He didn't even feel all that hungry, wished they could back out of this. His own fault for pushing it.

Alexei studied a picture on the wall. "Is this Imf?"

Jack put on his headset in time to hear Eskitul answer, "Yes, this is my home." A castle perching on an impossibly steep crag. The castle's walls burgeoned outwards—gravity on Imf was allegedly about three-quarters of Earth's. A needle-nosed airplane painted a contrail across the purple sky. Airglow lit the horizon.

"Were you some kind of oligarch?" Alexei said. "Or maybe this is your ancestral pile?"

Eskitul's hair danced. "It was my family home before the Darksiders captured it, two hundred years ago. Now it is dust."

They had sorted out the difference between rriksti years and human years. The rriksti had switched to using the human definition in their involved tales of warfare. Alexei's incessant questioning had prompted Eskitul to offer a complete history of the Long War between the Darkside and the Lightside, but it was less enlightening than mind-numbing—a dry-as-dust recitation of treaties, truces, attacks, counter-attacks, and filthy betrayals by the Darksiders.

They went into the next room, where a table had been set for what promised to be an excruciatingly formal meal. Ten rriksti rose to greet them. Keelraiser sat in the middle of one long side of the table. Eskitul took the empty place between Keelraiser and Nene. Jack and Alexei were seated across from them. A young rriksti served a starter course of what appeared to be fried floor-cleaner insects.

"What did I say?" Alexei muttered.

"They eat bugs in Asia," Jack muttered back. He picked one up with the implement provided—a cross between a fork and a pair of sugar tongs—and crunched it.

Bubble-wrap. Greasy, tough bubble-wrap. Bitter as hell. Jack's mouth threatened to turn inside-out. After a minute's solid chewing, he managed to choke it down.

The rriksti munched their servings noisily. They came off as uncouth eaters, because they could not hear themselves. They'd told the men that they did possess a sense of hearing, but that their ears were nowhere near as sensitive as human ones. Jack now saw that they also possessed teeth—crowded rows of little white needles, which showed when they curled their lips back to eat. The sight of those teeth, and the noise of crunching, made for an off-putting ambiance.

Alexei leaned back in his chair, arms folded.

Jack prayed Alexei wasn't going to make a scene. He toyed with his eating tongs, but couldn't bring himself to put another insect in his mouth. The room, having no visible doors, felt crowded and claustrophobic. The salty sea smell was overwhelming. Feeling trapped, Jack lifted his gaze

FELIX R. SAVAGE

to Keelraiser, who sat directly across from him. Its eyes were very wide. It slid one hand across the table. Jack touched its fingertips.

The waiters—pages, servants, somebody's kids?—brought bowls of stew. Eskitul explained that this was a pottage of *suizh,* their staple vegetable, with fish, flavored with 'twilight spices.' Whatever twilight spices might be, they tasted like bitter lemon zest mixed with baking soda.

But Jack had been raised to be polite. Politeness meant not turning your nose up at a meal that your hosts had clearly gone to a great deal of trouble to provide. Keelraiser's evident distress provided extra motivation. Jack picked up the large spoon provided and forced himself to eat the stew. It was just about doable, if he didn't chew much.

Champagne flute-shaped glasses held a cloudy liquid. Jack took a swallow, to get the bitterness out of his mouth.

Warmth burnt in his stomach.

He took another sip. No mistake.

"Alexei!"

"I cannot believe you're eating that shit."

"This—this—try it!"

Alexei snatched his flute and gulped.

He spluttered … and beamed at the rriksti. "My friends, where did you learn to make vodka?!?"

"It is called *krak,*" Eskitul said.

"Are you serious? *Crack!* I think I'm addicted already."

The meal went rather better after that.

"This, *this* isn't bad," Alexei declared.

A gelatinous beige pudding had been served. It tasted like

248

sugar, which was a vast improvement over everything that preceded it. Both men spooned it up hungrily.

But Keelraiser looked more distressed than ever.

Jack waved his spoon. He, too, had indulged in the alien alcoholic beverage. Not having had a drink in two years, it had gone to his head a bit. "Delicious pudding," he exclaimed. "Compliments to the chef. What's in it?"

"*Suizh,*" Keelraiser murmured.

"And?"

Alexei suddenly twisted his mouth. "*O Gospodi,*" he said. Oh my God. "What?"

"Lead chloride."

"*What?*"

Alexei tossed his spoon down with a clatter. "Lead, fucking, chloride. Tastes like sugar."

Jack took another, very small mouthful of the pudding.

… Lead chloride?

Whether it was psychological suggestion or what, he suddenly felt sick.

"You're poisoning us," Alexei shouted, shoving his chair back.

Jack dragged on his arm to keep him from standing up and, Christ knows what, taking a swing at Keelraiser probably. He didn't doubt that Alexei was right. The extreme bitterness of rriksti food had a simple explanation. It was all chock-full of metal. Jesus, the rriksti had metal in their bodies, bio-antennas *made* of metal mixed with keratin. They had to ingest that somehow. Jack had been an idiot.

"I didn't want to give you our food," Keelraiser said softly.

"Then why did you do it?" Jack demanded.

"You asked."

"Are we going to die?" Alexei shouted.

Nene said, "I don't think one meal will poison you! Most of the mineral content is not bioavailable."

"To *you*. But what about to us?"

The rrikstis' hair danced. Their heads turned to and fro. Alexei's face reddened. "Oh Jesus," he said. "I wonder if the *krak* is OK. Oh, fuck it." He drained his glass. Jack hoped this would calm him down, but he was only revving up. "So what about the other lies you've been telling us? You said you took the advance lander engines for the metals. Bullshit. You have plenty of metal! Your food is full of it!"

Nene said, "There are certain rare elements that we're short of, desperately short—"

"Then why don't you scavenge them from the MOAD? You've got a shuttle, *nyet?* What's stopping you?"

Alexei folded his arms, smiling viciously. He obviously thought he'd caught the aliens out in another lie. In fact this question had occurred to Jack, too. He'd tried to rationalize it away, but now he admitted to himself that it was time to stop making excuses for these people. They had just fed him and Alexei a pudding of lead chloride.

"The *Lightbringer*," Keelraiser said quietly. "Our ship's actually called the *Lightbringer.*"

"Lovely name," Jack said. "And you aren't able to scavenge materials from it, because?"

"Because the *Krijistal* would kill us," Keelraiser said.

Eskitul poured itself another glass of alien booze. "The *Krijistal* are perhaps like your special forces," it said. "The SEALS, the S.A.S, Chuck Norris. Is this correct?"

"Well, except for that last one," Jack said. He was too

upset to smile at the misunderstanding. "And your special forces are where, doing what, exactly?"

"On the *Lightbringer,* eating corpses, trying to get around the drive key encryption with hand-coded cracking tools." Eskitul burped. "We know they're still alive because they call us on the radio, making horrible threats. They say they'll drop chunks of debris on us if I don't give myself up. But I will not give myself up! And they daren't attack us, for fear of killing me! It is a stand-off. Is this correct?" Eskitul made a laughter-like noise. The rriksti around the table nudged each other and nodded. Jack was getting the impression that, contrary to his previous assumption that Eskitul was just some kind of resident eccentric, it was actually a very important person here.

Alexei said, "I knew it! I knew it! You've been lying to us all along! That field generator didn't fail on its own, eh? What really happened? I want the truth, now, the truth!"

Keelraiser spoke. Eskitul might be the leader of the rriksti but it was Keelraiser everyone listened to. Jack listened, too, despite the horrible visions taking shape in his head. "We had a disagreement," Keelraiser said. "Our original flight plan called for us to—to orbit Europa and observe Earth—and make contact with you—your people …"

And you're lying your alien arse off, Jack thought. Maybe you weren't before, but you are now.

It was not the halting speech that gave Keelraiser away, but the contraction of the small muscles around its eyes, and the way it stared fixedly at its plate.

On the other hand, Alexei seemed to be buying this. Maybe Jack was being overly paranoid.

"However—" Keelraiser looked at Alexei— "some of us,

the ones gathered here, changed our minds. It was a *long* journey."

"Sixty years, you said."

"Yes. A lot can change in that time. A lot has certainly changed, both on Earth, and at home, and … in our hearts. We got here, and we … we no longer wanted to be here. We decided to drop the whole thing."

Jack interrupted, "Why? You'd come all this way, why change your minds at the last minute?"

"News from home," Keelraiser said. "There was another war."

"Cripes. Was there anything left to fight over?"

"Ruins," Keelraiser said. "But even ruins are worth fighting for. One of the other refugee ships only went as far as Alpha Centauri Bb, the water world we'd hoped to colonize. They occupied the advance facilities there, regrouped, built new ships."

"You said you were the only survivors!"

"We may be, at this point," Keelraiser snapped. "Twenty years ago, the group from Alpha Centauri Bb mounted a counter-attack on Imf."

"They begged us for help," Nene said.

"So our new plan was to refuel at Europa, and then turn around and go home."

Alexei let out a long breath. "And these *Krijistal* didn't like the change of plan."

"They disliked it so much that they blew up the magfield generator to stop us from going through with it," Keelraiser said flatly.

Eskitul waved its glass, slopping booze on the table. "They turned a muon cannon on the *Lightbringer's* primary water reservoirs, transforming them into fusion bombs! Can you believe the sheer, animalistic idiocy of it? They had no idea of the explosive power they would unleash! It almost sheared the ship in half! We were lucky to escape with our lives. In fact, none of us would have escaped if not for Keelraiser." Eskitul slumped against Keelraiser, wrapped an arm around its neck, and rubbed its cheek against the other rriksti's. It was the first time Jack had seen the rriksti touch each other affectionately.

Alexei smiled, his eyes half-closed. "Muon cannon, eh?"

"No longer operational," Keelraiser said.

"But the *Krijistal* are still alive?" Jack said.

"Maybe forty of them. Fifty at most."

"That," Jack said tightly, "is enough, if they're as dangerous as you claim."

He jumped up from the table. Dizziness rocked him. Too much alien booze. Too much lead chloride, maybe. He rode it out.

"They're two hundred meters from the *SoD!*" He dragged Alexei to his feet. "They're up there with Kate and Hannah!"

"Fuck," Alexei said. A second later he added: "And Giles."

"And Giles, of course. We have to warn them! *Now!*"

CHAPTER 30

Jack opened the rear entry hatch of his spacesuit. It seemed like a year since he'd last worn it. The smell wafting up from the inside of the Z-2 struck him as vile, after the salty sea-smell of the rriksti shelter. Before putting it on, he checked the contents of the thigh pockets. His personal dosimeter registered a frighteningly high number. Of course, that was whatever the spacesuit had been soaking up, in this donning chamber at the end of a tunnel leading from the manufacturing floor. He himself should have absorbed much less radiation in the lower regions of the shelter, shielded by thick ice.

There was nothing else in the pockets.

"Hey." Not that it really mattered, but— "Where's my rosary?"

Keelraiser just blinked at him.

"Alexei, the fuckers have taken my rosary. It was in my pocket."

"Maybe you dropped it," Alexei said. "Put your damn suit on."

The men planned to use the Dragon's transmitter to contact the *SoD*. There was no time to spare.

The rriksti who would be accompanying them—Keelraiser and four others—took slim, white backpacks from a pile in the corner. They put their arms through the straps and fastened more straps across their chests and waists. They put on insect-eye goggles. They pulled breathing tubes out of the backpacks and fitted these into their mouths. Then the backpacks began to spread, as if the rriksti were being doused with white paint. The stuff

254

coated each finger, each bio-antenna. They lifted up their feet to let it get around their heels and toes.

"I want a suit like that," Jack said.

"Smart materials," Keelraiser said, on his suit radio.

"Yeah, I know, you're way ahead of us in materials science."

"When we first met, we inadvertently hurt your ears. I'm now talking on a frequency that is not a harmonic of your suit radios. We'll be careful how we tune our voices, but do let us know if you get any painful interference."

"Roger," Jack said.

They tramped to the end of the tunnel. A wall melted, admitting them to an airlock chamber. Moments later they stumbled out onto the ice of Europa. Jack breathed heavily. The featureless wasteland, and the vast black sky overhead, gave him a jolt of agoraphobia. He longed to return to the warmth and safety of the underground shelter.

The radio mast speared over the brow of the hill. They'd left the Dragon near there.

Jack started around the hill at a bounding run, with Alexei on his heels. He had already opened a channel to the *SoD*. "Kate? Come in. This is Jack. Kate, do you read me?"

The rriksti outpaced them. Their form-fitting spacesuits gave them better mobility, and their gait was naturally suited to lower gravity. White on white, they blended into the ice, but each of them carried a bright red gun.

"They're armed," Jack panted. The weapons looked like AR-15s with cylindrical tanks instead of magazines.

"What's out here to shoot?" Alexei said. "Oh, I get it. They have tricked us. They're going to murder us out here, where the kids can't see." Alexei laughed. Having got the truth out of the aliens, as he believed, he was now much more relaxed. He was making fun of his own paranoia at this point.

But at the same time, Jack was getting more and more paranoid. It often worked like this for the two of them. They balanced each other out, like children riding a seesaw.

"*SoD? SoD,* do you read me?"

No answer. Fear bloomed in his chest, and he ran faster, swinging his arms for momentum.

They rounded the hill.

The radio mast stood alone.

The Dragon was nowhere to be seen.

No wonder Kate hadn't answered. Jack hadn't been broadcasting to the *SoD* at all.

He skidded to a halt.

Alexei crashed into him.

"It's gone," Jack said.

"Those fucking cunts," Alexei said, spacing the words out.

They walked towards the radio mast. Jack kept thinking maybe his eyes were deceiving him, but they weren't.

A puddle of fresh ice remained where the Dragon had stood. Smooth as glass, it mirrored the black sky.

Jack skated on one foot across the puddle.

"They launched the Dragon," Alexei said. "Maybe took it into orbit, to hook up with the *Krijistal.*"

"I can hear something," Jack said.

"Hey, shitheads!" Alexei yelled. "Feel like telling us what you did with our landing craft?"

The rriksti had raced away across the plain, leaving a trail of widely spaced footprints. Jack followed the trail with his gaze. The rrikstis' white suits camouflaged them, but he could see their shadows bobbing up and down in the distance.

"Where are they going?" Alexei said in frustration.

"Listen!" Jack said. "Can you hear that?"

Faint. Fading in and out.

"Alas … Hannah … you do … me wrong … to never … let me … squeeze … your tits …"

"Did I just hear what I think I heard?"

"For I … have loved … you so long … in fact … I want to kiss … your …"

Static drowned the weak signal.

Alexei whooped and punched one fist into his other glove.

Jack bawled, "Hot mic, Skyler! Hot mic!" He jumped up and down, laughing so hard that tears obscured his vision.

*

"Oh … Hannah … your sexy ass … is like … a pot … of ho-o-ney … "

Skyler was no longer singing. He was croaking.

He was no longer walking. He was crawling.

He'd repositioned his umbrella-hat on his back, taping it around his chest, so he crawled like a little turtle across Europa's ice, carrying his improvised shell.

Black vomit sloshed in his faceplate.

Every now and then he sat back on his heels to let it run down inside his suit, so he didn't breathe it in.

The stuff dribbling from his lips now was red.

He couldn't think about what was happening to his body.

All he could do was crawl.

And croak ditties to Hannah.

Making rhymes kept his mind off reality, kept him going.

As goes America, so goes Skyler.

Rhyme or die.

Shadows flickered across the snow.

He puked again, and crashed down face first.

Vomit went up his nose.

Dying like Jimi, like John Bonham, like Jim Morrison … on Europa.

Always wanted to be a rock star.

*

The rriksti raced back across the snow, carrying Skyler between them. Each Z-2 suit had an individual pattern of colored piping. This one had yellow bands around the legs, so it really was him.

"Hey, Skyler!" Jack yodeled. "That was a classic performance! You ought to join the Walkers!"

"He is not conscious," said Keelraiser over the radio. The rriksti shuffled past, moving as fast as their burden permitted.

"He *was* conscious …"

"How far did he walk?" Alexei said, as it dawned on both men that Skyler was very sick indeed.

"How would I know?" Keelraiser said. "Anyway, he was not walking. He was crawling."

Jack fell back, his mind legitimately blown. Skyler must have walked all the way from the Shenzhou Plus's crash site.

And when he could no longer walk, he had *crawled.*

"I didn't think he had it in him," Jack muttered. He got a lump in his throat. It seemed horribly unfair that Skyler should have embarked on a prodigious walk across Europa's surface, and made it to safety, only to wind up with acute radiation sickness. "How bad is he?"

"Hell with him," Alexei said. "Where's our Dragon?"

Ahead of them, Keelraiser said, "My friends took it to collect the rest of your reactants from the advance landers. They ought to be back soon."

The simplest possible explanation. Jack and Alexei had completely overlooked it in their eagerness to accuse the rriksti of theft.

"We need to contact the *SoD!*" Jack said.

"We tried," Keelraiser said. "Your ship is over the horizon at present. So is the *Lightbringer,* naturally."

"They'll orbit back soon. Maybe we can use the radio mast to contact them! Come on." Jack pulled on Alexei's sleeve. They chased after the rriksti, back towards the shelter.

Skyler's spacesuit, stretched out like an X, bobbled between the bearers. One of the rriksti was holding Skyler's head and shoulders up.

Acute radiation sickness was fatal, no way around it. They could give Skyler an IV of morphine, if the rriksti had morphine, and wait for the end. There was nothing else to be done for him.

But Hannah, Kate, and Giles could still be saved. At least, Jack needed to believe they could.

Impotently, he growled, "Couldn't the bloody reactants have waited? Our friends are in danger!"

Keelraiser shouted over the radio, "I fucked up! Is this correct? I fucked up! I'm sorry!"

"Sorry is not a strategy," Alexei grunted. "Tell your friends in the Dragon to radio the *SoD.* Tell Kate ..."

He trailed off. Jack realized to his shock that Alexei was

overwhelmed by emotion.

He jumped in to cover for him. "Warn them! Tell them—tell them not to leave the *SoD*, not to let anyone in."

"They've been trying, actually," Keelraiser said after a grudging pause. "No one answers the radio."

Jack and Alexei followed the rriksti back into the airlock. Air jetted into the chamber from hidden vents, white, like the breath of cows on a winter's morning. Jack pushed between the rriksti. His helmet lamp shone on Skyler's helmet. The inside of the faceplate was coated with black stuff that looked like coffee grounds. Jack's medical training told him what that was. *Blood.* Skyler had been bleeding internally, puking it up. The poor guy had no chance.

The rriksti seemed to think differently.

As soon as the chamber was pressurized, they set off down the tunnel, carrying Skyler, at their grasshopper-like run.

CHAPTER 31

A cool, refreshing sensation spread through Skyler's body. It originated from points on his forehead, his lower belly, the small of his back, his palms, and the soles of his feet. Where it spread, the pain receded. Semi-conscious, he absorbed it passively.

"Mom," he whispered. She was back. She'd run off with her *goddamn hippie* yoga instructor but she must have come back. She was hugging him, stroking his forehead. "Don't go away again," he begged.

She'd even made her special garlic bread for him. He could taste it in his mouth.

*

"He said something," Alexei whispered.

Jack nodded. "It sounded like 'Mom.'"

The two men stood awkwardly, giving the rriksti room to … do what they were doing.

It didn't involve an IV, morphine, or any recognizable medical technology at all.

They'd dumped Skyler on the manufacturing floor. Working at top speed, they'd peeled his spacesuit off, leaving him naked. The air was cool, the floor cold, but Skyler didn't seem to mind. He lay in a fetal position, and damned if that wasn't a smile on his vomit-smeared face.

The rriksti had daubed some kind of ointment on his forehead, belly, back, hands, and feet. The stuff shone on his peeling, reddened skin.

Keelraiser squatted on its thin haunches, resting one palm on Skyler's forehead. Other rriksti touched him in the same way on his back, belly, hands, and feet. These were the five who'd gone outside. The other rriksti who'd been working on the floor had left their posts to stand or kneel behind the others, as if backing them up.

The five touching Skyler had doffed their spacesuits to the waist. Gooseflesh pebbled their exposed skin. The brisk temperature in the cavern was *cold* for them.

They were motionless.

Their thousand-yard stares creeped Jack out.

"What the hell are they doing?" Alexei muttered, shifting his weight from foot to foot.

"Some kind of energy transfer," Jack guessed.

"Huh?"

"I'm just guessing. You know, that Chinese healing stuff? Something like that. Maybe?"

"Reiki?"

"Is that what it's called?"

"I'm Orthodox, you know," Alexei prefaced his next statement. "Our Patriarch said Reiki is occult, and it doesn't work anyway."

"I think you can get it on the NHS now."

Skyler moved. He curled up in a ball, ducking his head against his knees.

Keelraiser sidled around him to reach his forehead again.

Something fell out of the pocket of Keelraiser's shorts.

Jack frowned.

That looks like …

He darted forward and picked it up. As he did so he got a whiff of Skyler. Bloody diarrhea coated the man's buttocks and legs. And yet he was *smiling*.

Jack showed Alexei the object Keelraiser had dropped. "My rosary."

"So they did take it. I'm so surprised."

Jack noticed tiny dents on the flat back of the crucifix. He held it up to the light. He didn't want to say it out loud, but he'd bet money those were *teeth marks*. His rosary was made of copper, coated with tungsten … in other words, metal. And they already knew that the rriksti thought metal was tasty.

He hid the rosary in his fist.

Skyler moved again. The rriksti closed in tighter around him, and resumed their frozen poses.

In Jack's fist, the rosary felt queerly warm.

*

Skyler sat up.

He felt better.

His trek across the ice lingered vividly in his memory, like a nightmare. His muscles felt weak and achy. But if the pain and weariness had been 1,000 on a scale of 1 to 10 before, now it was more like a 3. Best of all, his nausea had gone, washed away by …

… coolness …

… his mother's touch …

… the taste of garlic.

Or *had* his hike been merely a nightmare, after all?

The jumbled shapes and colors around him resolved into humanoid forms.

Jack Kildare crouched in front of him, holding his hands and saying, "Skyler! Skyler, Earth to Skyler!"

Not a nightmare, then. Although, to be honest, many of Skyler's nightmares had Jack Kildare in them.

"You look like crap." Jack's blue eyes crinkled. He was wearing gray shorts and had his rosary around his neck, like

263

some kind of half-dressed knight crusader. "How do you feel?"

It angered and embarrassed Skyler to be seen in a state of collapse by Jack, of all people. He pulled his hands away. "Where am I?"

"The Pit of Despair. Don't even think about trying to escape," Jack said, putting on a raspy voice. He laughed.

The lighting was low, like at a jazz club, but the only sound was a background rumble of machinery. Skyler looked past Jack.

"Aliens!!!!"

"Yeah, they're aliens. They call themselves *rriksti*. That one's Keelraiser. That one's Nene. That's Riverlock. Some of them translate their names, some don't …"

Skyler shook Jack off and stood up. With renewed energy coursing through his body, he faced the silent, goblin-faced beings. *Rriksti*. Okayyyy.

"Greetings," he said. He glanced down at himself. He was wearing nothing except shit and vomit. "Jeez, I'm making a great first impression, huh?"

"You should have seen yourself when we brought you in," Jack said. "It made your arrival on board the *SoD* look like a masterpiece of diplomacy. Oh, and you were singing! That's how they found you!"

"I don't remember that," Skyler said warily. He did.

"We couldn't really catch the words," Jack said, tactfully. "Anyway, you were in bad shape." His smile faded. "They … did something for you …"

"Oh yeah, the refreshing thing," Skyler said, as if he knew all about that. For some reason, he felt a desire to change the subject immediately. His spacesuit lay on the floor nearby. He picked it up and bundled it in his arms as a fig leaf for his nakedness. "Do these aliens have showers?" he said hopefully.

"Er, not that we've seen. But we've only been here a bit."

That was good news. On the other hand, 'we' was bad news. Skyler scoped his surroundings. Aliens, alien machinery, an alien spacecraft … and Alexei goddamn Ivanov, still smirking at Jack's *Princess Bride* quote. So the Russki had survived, too.

The mission of the SoD is to investigate the MOAD and determine whether it is, or is not, a threat to humanity.

Director Flaherty's voice echoed in Skyler's ears.

Your mission is to secure as much alien shit as you can get your hands on, and return it to the United States.

The echoes faded into irrelevance. Flaherty and the rest of the big brains who devised this mission, on faraway Earth, had no goddamn idea what it was like to *be* here.

They didn't know what it was to fall out of the sky and see a brave, strong woman squashed like a sandwich filling. To make a death-defying solo trek across Europa. And then wake up with your worst enemy smirking at your disgrace.

"Congratulations," Skyler said to Alexei, choking on his own sarcasm. "You killed Meili. You almost killed me, too. But you can't win 'em all, right, soldier?"

Alexei paced towards him. "What are you talking about?"

Jack interrupted. "Meili's dead?"

"Of course she's dead. Just like you wanted."

Skyler did not really believe Jack had wanted Meili dead, but as he spoke, he realized it made sense for Jack to have been in it with Alexei. The British government had always been cozy with the Kremlin. Anyway, look at these two, always together, no daylight between them. No jury would doubt that they were conspiring together to … to grab alien shit, and kill everyone else. Yeah, probably.

"The Shenzhou crash was an accident," Jack said. "Wasn't it?"

"That's what you'd like us to think," Skyler sneered.

"You can't possibly blame us."

"Oh, you goddamn hypocrite." *God-DAY-um HUH-p'crit.*

Skyler was channeling Lance, his dead colleague, and he welcomed the visitation. Putting on Lance's ghost like a coat, he escaped the feeling of bogusness that had haunted him throughout his career with the NXC. A Taft from Boston, holder of a doctorate in astrophysics, a descendant of ambassadors and generals, couldn't be a gen-u-wine American badass. Just didn't have the bona fides. But a redneck from rural Georgia did. Lance had never held back, or maybe it was truer to say nothing held him back. Balls to the wall, finger on the trigger, take no prisoners. That was Lance.

"Do you guys speak English?" he said to the aliens.

"They can't hear you," Jack said. "They talk in the AM band. Here, use this." He pulled a slimline headset off his head, threw it at Skyler, and turned away, pressing a fist to his lips.

Skyler picked up the headset and put it on. He heard a high, sweet voice saying, "—friends?"

"It's complicated," Alexei said, obviously talking to the aliens. "He's a shithead, and also a government agent."

"But I'm not the only government agent here," Skyler said. "Wild guess, but has this guy—" thumb-jerk at Alexei— "been less than honest with you?"

"Are you different from him?" an alien said. He couldn't tell *which* alien, because their mouths didn't move when they talked.

"Different? Hell, yeah. I'm from America. *He's* Russian."

"The United States of America is a shining city on a hill. Is this correct?"

"Nice Reagan reference," Skyler said, astonished.

Alexei said, "Keelraiser, this piece of shit is trying to trap you into making some commitment to his political masters. Don't fall for it."

Skyler shot back, "As long as we're quoting Reagan, he called you guys the evil empire."

Alexei gazed at Skyler as if he were a cockroach. Skyler's face burned. A high-school debater could have come up with a better retort than that.

"I don't really care about politics," Alexei said, shrugging. "They told me to plant a Russian flag on the MOAD. I might try to do that later."

That did it. Skyler threw circumspection to the winds. "Oh, you don't really care about politics," he drawled. "Haven't you forgotten to mention something?"

"What?"

"Such as the fact that you're a GRU agent?"

The GRU: Russia's military intelligence agency. Coasted through the fall of the USSR. Institutional history stretching back to Trotsky. Oh, and the GRU commands the Spetsnaz, Russia's dreaded special forces.

Jack barked, "Do you think it's clever to smear an honest man?"

He glanced at Alexei, awaiting a denial, which didn't come. Skyler grinned. That must feel like a two-by-four upside the head. Alexei hadn't had a canned response ready, and now it was too late. His face told a tale of dawning fury and fear. He *was* a GRU agent, of course. The NXC had confirmed it way back when. And now Skyler saw how it all fit together.

"Your people packed the *SoD* full of malware," Skyler said. "There was malware in the Shenzhou. Big surprise. The engine was built in Russia. I'd kind of like to know how you triggered the APU heater to shut down. But hey, it worked, right? You killed Meili. And you almost killed me." He grinned, wildly. "That didn't quite go according to plan, obviously."

"That is a complete lie," Alexei said, too late to be in the least convincing. Jack stared at him, so transparently shocked it was almost funny.

Alexei shot a glance at Jack. Perhaps he realized at last just how much trouble he was in now. His face changed. Skyler's conscious brain was still reveling in his enemy's humiliation, but a subconscious voice spoke up: *Uh oh.* He slid his right hand inside the folds of the spacesuit bundled in his arms.

Alexei responded to Skyler's accusations in the best Russian tradition. He hurled himself at Skyler, reaching for his throat.

Skyler struggled to disentangle his arms from his Z-2. Alexei crashed into him. Both of them flew over backwards in the low gravity. Skyler just barely raised his arms—and the bundle of spacesuit wrapped around them—in time to block Alexei's strangulation grip. The hands that would've gone around his throat latched onto the Z-2.

"Jesus Christ!" Jack shouted, seemingly far away.

Skyler hit the ground on his back with Alexei on top of

him, and bounced. The impact drove the air out of his lungs. Alexei grabbed a handful of his hair and pulled his head back. Skyler had never seen anything as terrifying as Alexei's face right now. He knew for a certainty that he was looking at his own death. Warm piss dribbled down his leg. He shook his head frantically, leaving a hank of hair in Alexei's fingers.

Jack grabbed Alexei by the shoulders and dragged him backwards, yelling, "Have you lost your fucking mind?"

Skyler seized his chance, writhed and kicked. He slithered away, leaving Alexei with an armful of Z-2 …

… and Skyler with his modified Glock in his hand.

He'd just managed to dig it out of the thigh pocket of his spacesuit before Alexei pulled the whole lot away.

He scrambled to his feet and backed out of grabbing range. He levelled the gun in a textbook two-handed shooting stance. He had always hated shooting. The NXC had made him spend hours on the range.

Alexei sat on the floor, looking up at him. "Oh, here we go," he gasped. "Now, please, who's the bad guy?"

Well, that was a good question, and Skyler would've liked for Lance to answer it. After all, it was Lance himself who'd first dragged the NXC into the wetworks business. But there was a limit to how much a dead redneck could do for you. Skyler would just have to finish this filthy job himself.

He sighted down the barrel at Alexei's center of mass.

The aliens scattered, recognizing a firearm when they saw one.

Alexei started to get up. Jack started to move towards Skyler.

Skyler fired.

The report boomed through the cavern. Echoes piled on echoes.

Alexei slumped to the floor. Blood spattered from his chest, painting sloppy micro-gravity arcs in the air.

Skyler lined up the sights on Jack's chest and fired again.

The frangible bullet shattered. Instead of penetrating Jack's body like it was meant to, fragments sliced into Jack's face and chest, drawing sheets of blood.

Skyler fired a third time. His arms shook. The bullet fragmented harmlessly on the floor.

Jack tackled him head-on, snatched the gun, and threw it overhand as far as he could. Blood poured from a gash over his left eye, splatting on Skyler's face in coppery globules. "I should kill you," Jack grated. "I should," but in the moment of speaking he seemed to lose interest in Skyler. He shoved him away and dropped to his knees beside Alexei.

CHAPTER 32

"Come on mate, come on, don't you fucking dare die." Jack applied pressure to the wound in Alexei's upper chest, bearing down with the heels of both hands. He was distantly aware of the rriksti crowding him, and of stinging pains in his face and chest.

Alexei smiled weakly. "I'm not dead," he coughed. "I think I'll go for a walk."

Jack laughed, but it sounded more like a retch. "You're not fooling anyone, you know."

"I don't want to go on the cart ..."

"Oh, don't be such a baby," Jack said. It had only been a couple of months since their last Monty Python marathon on board the *SoD*. They'd had no idea what was waiting for them, none.

Alexei's eyes rolled back.

Jack's hands slipped. Blood welled out of the wound.

"He needs help! Isn't anyone going to help?!"

He'd hardly got the words out before the rriksti bowled him out of the way. They picked Alexei up, dumped him on a stretcher—two feet too long, it made the six-foot cosmonaut look like a child—and hustled down the tunnel to the warm, salty-smelling depths of the shelter. Jack followed. They dived into one of the smaller caverns that opened off the garden.

"Where are you taking him?" Jack yelled. But he'd lost his headset in the fight. He was stranded in the rrikstis' silence.

The rriksti bounded between the jigsaw partitions to a room full of alien bodies on bunks built into the wall.

"Oh, the morgue," Jack said. "Ha, ha." He was dripping

blood on the floor. Felt about ready for the morgue himself. There was one thing he had to do before he died, though, and that was kill Skyler Taft.

All in good time. The little fucker was stuck here with them, couldn't get away.

Morgue? The 'bodies' on the bunks were alive. Their heads turned and their hair stirred at the commotion.

The rriksti rolled Alexei into a spare bunk. Jack shoved between them. He expected that there would be nothing more he could do for Alexei except close his eyes.

Alexei's diaphragm fluttered.

"He's alive!"

A rriksti pushed up beside him. Nene. It held out a basket containing what appeared to be a first-aid kit. Jack pawed through the contents of the basket. Frangible bullets. Frangible goddamn bullets, brought all the way from Earth. There were no words for it. The blood flow from Alexei's wound looked sluggish, but internal bleeding was a dead certainty.

"Put pressure on the wound," he begged Nene, miming what he wanted. The rriksti bent over Alexei and braced its thin white hands on his chest. Jack found a case of scalpels. He held up a wad of stuff that might have been bandages, or clingfilm, or God knows what—it had a rainbow tint in the gloom. "I can't see a fucking thing in here," he howled.

Someone came up behind him and slapped his headset onto his head.

"Thank you! I need light! Sterile gauze. Got to clean the wound …" Jack trailed off in despair. He had advanced medical training. He wasn't remotely qualified to perform exploratory surgery. Especially not in the dark, without the right kit. "Where's your medical technology?" he demanded. "I thought you lot came from the future. Haven't you even got diagnostic imaging equipment?"

"It was all on the *Lightbringer*. We left in a hurry," Nene said.

"Damn the goddamn future," Jack said.

Another rriksti switched on a spotlight as bright as a fifty-watt bulb. That was probably hospital-strength lighting for the aliens. Nene snatched the rainbow-tinted clingfilm from Jack and pulled off small pieces. Balling them between its fingers, it packed them into Alexei's wound.

"Is that stuff like QuikClot?" Jack leaned over to scrutinize what Nene was doing.

"We need to prevent further blood loss. Is this correct?"

"We need to stop the internal bleeding. That's what's going to kill him." Stanching the external bleeding was a good thing, in theory. In practice, it would be like slapping a patch on the Titanic. The bunk's thin mattress was already soaked with blood. More blood dripped, sparkling in the spotlight. Jack's eyes stung. He realized the blood was actually coming from his own forehead.

He regained consciousness in a sitting position, slumped against a wall. He was still in the morgue, or hospital, or whatever it was. But from his new angle, he could see that the room was much larger than he had thought. It was L-shaped and now he could see down the long leg of the L. There must be half a hundred rriksti lying in the dim light, and all of them were staring at Jack with wide, dark eyes.

He used the wall to push himself upright. He shambled to the bunk where he remembered them putting Alexei.

Nene sat on a folding chair beside the bunk. "Don't wake

him," it said via the headset that sat askew on Jack's head.

Jack bent over the bunk. He listened to Alexei's breath. He felt Alexei's pulse. Slightly thready, but regular at about 60 beats per minute. He laid the back of his hand on Alexei's forehead. Didn't feel hot. Or cold. He could not understand it. Alexei should be dead. A semi-translucent bandage wrapped his chest, flattening the clotted chest hair to bloody snails.

"He is recovering," Nene said.

"Did you do that Reiki thing on him?"

"Reiki?"

Jack flapped his hands descriptively. "The laying on of hands bit."

Nene's hair stirred around its shoulders. Its nostrils widened. Jack suspected these were signs of amusement. "Oh. No." Nene held up its seven-fingered hands, palms out. "We secrete powerful antioxidants in our skin. They relieve certain symptoms. That's all."

"Ah." Jack felt like a child who'd just been told there were no fairies. He had speculated—feared / hoped—that there was something magical going on there. "Wouldn't do much for a gunshot wound, I suppose."

"The other one shot him with a sub-lethal munition." Nene touched its own long, sharp clavicle. "There is a fracture of this bone. Also, trauma to the soft tissues, blood loss, and shock. But no deep penetration. It will be some time before he regains use of the shoulder ..."

"Sub-lethal rounds!" Jack said in amazement. "How can you be sure? Sometimes internal bleeding's hard to detect ..."

"We can see it," Nene said, calmly.

274

Jack waited for more information. Came there none. Maybe the rriksti did have some kind of diagnostic imaging equipment, after all.

He stared at Alexei for a while longer, trying to judge his pallor in the terrible light. Gradually, he realized he himself was feeling quite rough. Without another word to Nene, he returned to his patch of floor and slumped down. He tipped his head back against the wall and closed his fist around his rosary. He understood now why his father had insisted he take it. The world was closing in on him.

A slight movement of air across his face; a stronger smell of salt—without opening his eyes, Jack knew Keelraiser was there. The rriksti sat down next to him, mirroring his posture.

"Your friend is recovering," it said.

"Yeah, Nene said. Thank you for treating him."

"If we were on the *Lightbringer* now ..." Keelraiser sighed, an actual sigh, blowing air out of its mouth. "If we were on the *Lightbringer* now, everything would be very different, and that is enough said about that."

Jack gazed blearily at the rows of bunks lining the walls, stacked three deep. Other rriksti sat on chairs, holding the sufferers' hands. "What is wrong with all these people?" After he said it he realized he'd called the rriksti *people*, because he'd begun to think of them that way.

"They are sick," Keelraiser said.

"Well, obviously. Is it radiation sickness?"

"No," Keelraiser said. "I lied about that. We cope better with radiation than you seem to. This crappy little moon is not much more dangerous to us than the moon of our own home planet, Imf."

"Are you ever going to *stop* lying to me?" Jack said.

There was a silence. Keelraiser stood up. "Would you come with me, please?" it said.

Jack wavered, mostly because he felt too sick to move. In the end he decided he might as well be hanged for a sheep as for a lamb. He followed Keelraiser through the dark, hot corridors. Keelraiser walked through a wall into the very same room where Jack had woken up.

This morning? Yesterday? He'd lost track of time. All he had for a clock was his hunger, which was now so intense it verged on nausea.

The room was now lit dimly, although it seemed bright after the murky corridors, and as hot as the rest of the shelter. Keeping the 'alien' comfortable had been a once-off, clearly.

"This is my room," Keelraiser said. "The walls are painted with radio-frequency shielding material, as you would call it. We call it privacy. It's a rare commodity around here."

Jack gazed at the spartan set-up with new eyes. He realized he had woken up in Keelraiser's own bed. There was no other.

Keelraiser unearthed two mugs from the mess on the card table, wiped them with its sleeve, and filled them with liquid from the sink.

"What's that?" Jack said suspiciously.

"Water. There's nothing else that is safe for us to give you."

Jack drank the whole mug off. The briny taste scarcely bothered him anymore.

"I'm sorry," Keelraiser said. It refilled the mug.

They sat down at the card table. A ventilation unit blew

warm air on the back of Jack's neck.

"Those people in the clinic are dying of malnutrition," Keelraiser said. "Shiplord would kill me for telling you this."

"Shiplord?"

"Eskitul."

Shiplord. That must be what *Eskitul* translated as. Jack hadn't been wrong: Eskitul *was* an important person around here.

"We are *extremely* short of certain metals, such as lead, cadmium, selenium, arsenic, and others," Keelraiser said. "It's a vulnerability. I am giving it to you."

Jack lifted the rosary hanging around his neck. "Others, including tungsten?"

Keelraiser stared at the crucifix. "Yes."

"This saved my life," Jack said. "The bullet hit it, fragmented. Don't fucking steal it from me again."

Keelraiser drank from its mug of water. It didn't take its eyes off the crucifix. Grudgingly, it said, "What is it?"

"A rosary. Surely you've seen them on telly."

Keelraiser shifted its shoulders in a way that suggested it had wanted a different kind of answer. "We do not understand your Christianity," it said peevishly.

"Mate, it's just a load of medieval superstition." Jack suddenly understood how the rriksti could seem to be honest and yet lie. He had just done the same thing.

"Your other religions are easier to comprehend by analogy. On Imf, the dominant cult of *Ystyggr*—" that was what it sounded like— "is similar to your Scientology."

Jack laughed out loud.

"I'm not joking," Keelraiser said.

"Sorry, no; I know ... That's quite amusing." Jack shook

his head. Alien Scientologists!

"Ystyggr is the god of X-rays."

"What?"

"Ystyggris worship the god of X-rays." Keelraiser opened its mouth wide. Its hair danced. "Our planet is bathed in X-rays. It's anthropologically obvious."

Something frightening occurred to Jack. That high reading on his personal dosimeter. And Nene's cryptic statement … *we can see it* … He leaned forward. "Can you *see* X-rays?"

"Yes," Keelraiser said. It indicated a pair of dark dots under its eyes, which Jack hadn't noticed before. "These are detector cells. They convert X-ray photons to visible photons." Up close, the dots looked like black glass beads embedded in Keelraiser's skin.

"Can I touch them?"

"Go on."

Jack reached across the table and gently laid one finger on the bead under Keelraiser's left eye. It felt like a fingernail. Smooth, hot. Delicate folds of skin around it twitched.

Keelraiser mirrored his gesture. Its heavy, dark brown fingernail rested on the skin just below Jack's left eye. It moved its finger in tiny circles, pressing gently on the eyeball through the skin. The sensation begged for Jack's full attention, which he refused to give it.

"I can see the bone in your finger," Keelraiser said. "It glows."

"I knew I'd end up glowing in the dark at some point."

"You're touching my eye. Of course I can see it."

Of course, it was an eye, of sorts. It must be connected to a branch of the optic nerve. Jack's voracious curiosity ebbed. He drew back. "No wonder I feel like shit. And there I thought it was just because I'd been shot."

"You suffered several cuts of varying severity," Keelraiser said uneasily. It folded its hands in its lap. "Nene treated them while you were unconscious. Does that upset you?"

Jack felt his forehead. The deep gash over his right eye was tender, but it seemed to be covered with a ridge of plastic. Some type of suture. "I'm not upset because of that. I'm upset because we're soaking in X-rays. This so-called shelter is a hot zone. Isn't it?"

"The X-ray environment is *less* intense than on Imf …"

"The roof of the manufacturing floor is made of metal. Isn't it? I thought there must be an ice shield up there, but there isn't. You're letting X-rays in via Bremsstrahlung."

"The manufacturing …? Oh, the shuttle bay."

"Whatever the fuck you call it." Jack folded his arms on the card table and rested his head on them. He and Alexei had thought this was basically a human-friendly environment. So much for first impressions. Food chock-full of metal. X-rays teeming in the air. He wondered what other nasty surprises lay in store. At this rate, he'd be dead before he had a chance to find out.

"There is no good way to tell you this," Keelraiser said.

"Right on cue," Jack said, without raising his head.

"The Dragon has been lost."

At that Jack opened one eye. "Crashed it, did you?"

"The *Lightbringer* attacked it with a HERF. It suffered a full power shutdown during boost."

"Yeah, that would do it."

"I didn't think they would do such a thing. I know they want to starve us into surrender. But this, this wanton destruction of resources! They've sunk to a new low."

Jack sat upright. "Reckon they saw fit to deny us the Dragon, because they don't need it anyway, now they've got the *SoD* to consume for resources? That's what I think. And my friends are up there. Wonder if your *Krijistal* have any uses for human flesh? I recall Eskitul mentioned something about eating corpses. I suppose we can only pray that they kill them before eating them. Two of them are women, if that means anything to you. What a shit-show."

"Rriksti do not eat corpses," Keelraiser said. "Eskitul was referring to recovering fluids for hydroponics."

"Oh, that puts a whole different spin on things," Jack said sarcastically.

"In any case, we'd better not waste any more time." Keelraiser stood up in its jerky unfolding manner.

"Huh?"

"We were going to take the Dragon into orbit to retrieve your ship and your friends. However, the Dragon is now a debris field. So we'll just have to take the *Cloudeater.*"

"The *Cloudeater* being?"

"My shuttle," Keelraiser said impatiently. "The one I showed you earlier."

Jack forgot how sick he felt. He jumped to his feet. "Count me the fuck in."

CHAPTER 33

The radio came alive. *"SoD,* do you read me? Over."

Hannah screamed. Fortunately, she wasn't pressing the transmit button at the time. She stabbed it. "Hello? Hello?"

"Hannah? This is Kate. I'm coming in. Over and out."

"Roger," Hannah said, her heart thumping like crazy. She had resigned herself to dying on board the *SoD.* Hanging out on the bridge with her squeeze bottle, she'd been trying to decide between committing suicide, and eking out the life-support resources as long as she could. She had transmitted a summary of her situation to Mission Control. They had begged her to hang in there. OK, she'd told them, I'll try. It would be a fun challenge, and she could keep Earth posted on her unique n+1 experiment. How long can one woman survive in a spaceship designed for eight, when something alien to our solar system *(clink—clink—clink)* is trying to get in?

Now, all that fled like a bad dream. She floated upside-down to the consoles, right way up to the airlock, wringing her hands nervously. She'd drained her squeeze bottle while she waited for something to happen. Now she was on the unpleasant downward slope towards a hangover, but still drunk.

The hatch opened.

In floated a bizarre specter. Looked like a woman …

A naked, faceless woman with dead black skin, and a trunk that curled over her shoulder to a hump on her back.

Hannah screamed again.

"It's *me,"* Kate's voice crackled from the headphones floating in the air. "Watch this."

The woman-thing pressed its fingers to the inside of its left wrist.

It changed color. Starting with the fingers and toes, the black coloration retreated, exposing pale human skin. Freckled forearms. Small breasts mottled with purple and yellow bruises. Ribs, black and blue. A shaggy strip between the legs. Kate was a natural blonde, and now she was naked. More bruises marred her face. She removed a slender breathing tube from her mouth and shrugged off a backpack about the size of a laptop.

"Behold, alien technology," she said, tossing the backpack to Hannah.

Hannah mindlessly caught it. "You're covered with bruises. What happened?"

"Aliens happened."

"Your *face* … "

"Don't even tell me how bad it looks. They dislocated my shoulder, too. Hurts like hell. I need a drink." She plucked Hannah's squeeze bottle out of the cup holder. "Oh, Hannah. You've drunk it all."

"You were gone for seven hours," Hannah said weakly.

"I know I've got some clothes in here," Kate said. She searched the drawers built into the aft wall, onehanded, pawing through their dead crewmates' possessions.

"Where have you *been?*" Hannah turned the backpack—spacesuit?—in her hands, trying to see how it worked. "Where's Giles?"

Kate found a t-shirt. It was one of Alexei's, commemorating the 2019 Baikonur 'Intergalactic' Tennis Tournament. She pulled it over her head, and jack-knifed into a pair of underpants belonging to some dead man.

"They've got him," she said.

"Th-they?"

"The aliens." Kate held Hannah's gaze, unflinching. She was smiling with her mouth, but her eyes looked like she wanted to scream.

She's lost her mind.

Whatever happened out there, it's driven her mad.

Hannah swallowed. She knew you must not disagree with the mad, or challenge their assertions. She held onto the back of the left seat. "The Dragon's gone," she said eventually. "It just vanished."

"It didn't just vanish. They HERFed it."

Kate settled into the right seat. Jack's seat. She stretched out her bare legs, fitting her toes into the foot tethers that were positioned for Jack's 6'4" frame. She cracked her knuckles, frowned for a moment at the consoles, and started pushing buttons and adjusting dials.

Hannah hovered. "Did you find any water?" she asked. She was as frightened as she'd ever been in her life. She'd have been curled in a fetal position if she hadn't been drunk, which insulated her from reality to some extent, kept her tongue from sticking to the roof of her mouth.

"Oh, lots of it," Kate said without glancing up. "Unfortunately, it's all frozen. You ought to see it, Hannah. There are glaciers in that ship. Frozen lakes. Cargo holds full of ice. Pipes burst, pumps kept running, and then they blew a massive hole in the side of the ship. That not only sucked out all the air, but the intense low-pressure boiling froze all the water that was sloshing around. It's like the Alps in there."

She typed on the keyboard for the flight control

computer. Hannah edged closer, hand over hand along the aft bulkheads, trying to see what Kate was doing.

"OK. That ought to work. God, I'm thirsty …" Kate's eye lit on Jack's squeeze bottle, in the cup holder beside the right-hand seat. She seized it and shook it to see if there was anything left inside. Hannah reflected that the last seven hours had felt like an eternity, but in fact, less than twenty-four hours had passed since they were all together. Jack's freaking tea was still there. *I can't believe the government is paying for this!* the bottle said on the side. Kate drained its contents, her throat working.

Hannah peered over her shoulder.

The station-keeping thrusters were firing.

"We're moving!" she yelped.

"Yup. Don't worry, we're not going far."

The station-keeping thrusters ran off the reactant tanks. They were used to maintain the *SoD's* position in orbit. As a rule, station-keeping burns were irregular, small, and short. Now Kate had input a new destination. The *SoD* sidled through space, so slowly that they felt no sense of motion.

"Wh-where are we going?" Hannah said.

"Need you ask?"

The thrust level indicators dropped. Wherever it was, they were there.

Kate rose from Jack's seat and returned to the center seat. She beckoned to Hannah. "Here we are." She called up the feed from the external camera mounted on the bridge.

Blackness.

Small lights shone in the dark, *moving*—not stars.

A flash of red and blue suddenly swam across the camera's field of vision, like a deep-sea fish.

Hannah clutched Kate's arm.

Something struck the truss tower with a faint boom that resonated through the empty *SoD*.

Hannah screamed under her breath. She meant it to be a proper scream, but it didn't come out because she was so frightened.

"They're hooking up electrical cables to leech off our generator capacity," Kate said.

Hannah cleared her throat. "That's not space out there. It's the MOAD, isn't it?"

Kate nodded. "We've docked with it."

"Why, Kate? Why?"

Kate twisted around and looked her in the face. She did not look mad now. She looked anguished. Her eyes glittered in their pits of swollen flesh. "I told you, they have Giles! Hannah, you cannot imagine what they did to him ... what they threatened to do to him."

Hannah lowered her gaze. She felt selfish, because right now she did not care about Giles one little bit.

"Giles is being a real shithead," Kate said, in a more matter-of-fact tone. "He always was a shithead. I just never noticed. But he is still a member of my crew. I'm still responsible for him. He's *human,* goddammit. And they are not."

Hannah nodded. She stared at the camera feed, heart in her mouth.

"By the way, I need my iPod," Kate said.

"What?"

"I was looking for it in the drawers. Have you seen it?"

"Oh." The gears in Hannah's brain tumbled, adjusting to the sudden change of subject. "Yeah. It was in your cupholder. I put it away."

She'd actually listened to a few of Kate's tracks during her long wait. *Tubthumping.* Pharrell Williams's *Happy.* Cheerful stuff, that she had hoped would cheer her up. It hadn't worked. She got the iPod out of the drawer where she had stashed it, and handed it to Kate.

"Thanks," Kate said, pocketing it.

Suddenly, a terrific boom echoed through the ship. It sounded like something had struck the *SoD* amidships with hull-crumpling force.

This time, Hannah did scream.

CHAPTER 34

The *Cloudeater* had to be chipped out of the ice before it could go anywhere. Its auxiliary power sinks had to be topped up, and the lines that powered the shelter disconnected from the turbine generators.

From the cockpit of the shuttle, Jack watched rriksti digging cables out of the floor, carrying house-sized machines out of the way.

"They do not wish to die," Eskitul said, dispassionately.

"No one does," Jack said.

"We are not so different, after all."

"News flash," Jack said, sketching airquotes. "Living beings want to stay alive. Full story at eleven."

"We have everything in common," Eskitul concluded gloomily. "Except that you have a home to return to, and we do not."

The cockpit's high ceiling and forward wall were a single smooth concavity, reflective black. Mechanical consoles angled to face the two crew seats. The control panels had far too many buttons, even by *SoD* standards. Keyboards covered with alien squiggles were huge, for fourteen-fingered typists. When you touched the wall, a transparent 'window' would spread away from your hand like a puddle. The floor, too, was transparent. There were more boost seats down there, enough for twenty. They had boarded through the main passenger cabin, which would seat another four hundred people in economy-class conditions. There was a distinctly mouldy smell. The shuttle hadn't flown in ten years. Jack hoped it still did.

On the forward wall, 3D readouts materialized and faded

away as Eskitul paced behind the pilot and co-pilot's seats.

"We will pull this out," Jack said. "We'll destroy these arseholes on the *Lightbringer*. Then we'll get it moving again."

This was his plan, insofar as he had one. If the aliens on the *Lightbringer* thought they could cannibalize the *SoD* to get it operational, it could presumably be done. He would do it himself, though it broke his heart to think of destroying the *SoD*. It would be worth it if everyone, human and rriksti, could be saved.

He planned to make an exception for the *Krijistal*. They would be taking a short trip out of an airlock.

"Water and power," Eskitul said. "Water and power. Everything else is chemistry."

Eskitul was clearly down in the dumps, and Jack decided to leave it to its thoughts. He went down through the hatch to the lower crew area, taking the weapon Keelraiser had given him. It was one of their AR-15 lookalikes, which turned out to be energy weapons. The rriksti word for them was unpronounceable so Jack was calling them blasters. You could adjust the beam power from 'sunburn' to 'kill 'em all' strength. The trigger, made for rriksti hands, was stiff. Dry-firing it, he'd confirmed that he needed both hands to complete the trigger pull. His weakened physical state had something to do with that, clearly. He was fired up by the prospect of action, but running on fumes. He wished the rriksti ground crew would hurry up.

"I want a blaster," Alexei said.

Wrapped in a blanket, Alexei slumped on a boost seat covered in clashing blue and orange patterns. Jack frowned at him. "You shouldn't even be here."

"You just try leaving me behind."

"I wouldn't dream of it." Although the operation would be dangerous, what Jack now knew about the X-ray environment in the shelter had made him acquiesce in Alexei's insistent desire to come along. He had not told Alexei about the X-rays yet. It wouldn't improve his friend's morale to know that even if he recovered from his wound, he was looking at a life expectancy measured in weeks.

Alexei tried to scratch under the splint that immobilized his right arm. "Itchy like fuck."

"That's a good sign," Jack said sadly.

Contemplating the prospect of their death from a megadose of X-rays, he decided not to be shy. Life was, literally, too short.

"Alexei."

"What?"

"*Are* you a GRU agent?"

Alexei stopped scratching. "Yes."

"Thanks for telling me," Jack said bitterly.

"I hate it," Alexei said. "I hate them." His voice rasped with passion. "I can't even say how much I hate those cunts. They *drafted* me, Jack, you understand?"

"It's the secrecy I object to," Jack said.

"Secrecy is their drug. Secrecy and power. I only want to be a cosmonaut. I mean, fuck it! Can't I bring glory to Mother Russia by travelling to Europa, landing on a motherfucking alien spaceship? Isn' t that *enough?*"

"Anything else you're not telling me?"

Alexei thought for a minute. "I think the remake of *Planet of the Apes* was better than the original."

Jack's eyes bugged out. "That turd egg? That waste of time from that pretentious prick Tim Burton with fucking

Marky Mark!? Are you trying to make me forget you're working under orders from the GRU, or are you really that fucking dumb? If you believe that piece-of-crap movie was better than the original, we were never friends! You and your GRU handlers can go to hell! Now that I know you're that fucked-up, I feel like a used condom. I could deal with being manipulated into following orders from the GRU … but you liking that Marky Mark abomination is just. Too. Much!"

"Turd egg?" Alexei squeaked, cracking up.

"Yeah, it's when you think you've laid an egg from the golden goose, but it's actually a turd."

"Oh Jesus, that hurts my collarbone."

Jack fought, and failed, to repress a grin. Alexei made people around him laugh. That's the way he was. Could a GRU agent quote large chunks of *The Princess Bride,* and use the Russian word for 'pancake' as a swear word? Yes, yes apparently he could.

Alexei was still the same man who'd had Jack's back ever since they were trainees. This changed nothing, Jack decided.

"I have to tell you something else," Alexei said.

"Oh, no."

"*Star Trek: The Next Generation* was definitely better than the original series …"

"You really are looking for a fight, aren't you?"

Alexei made a face. Then the laughter slipped out of his eyes. "Skyler was right. There is malware on the *SoD.* The GRU wrote the programs, and Russian construction workers installed them. But I have nothing to do with that anymore. It's out of my hands. This is the truth. And there was *no* malware in the Shenzhou. I did *not* kill Meili."

"If I believed you did that," Jack said, "I'd have to try this blaster out on you. It's OK, mate. I would be more surprised if there *weren't* malware on the *SoD*. There's no other explanation for the bloody flies ..."

Overhead, an eight-foot slit ripped open in the aft wall of the cockpit. Keelraiser prowled in, stark naked. Jack craned up through the transparent floor.

"Eskitul!" Keelraiser's voice came through their headsets.

The bigger rriksti turned from the readouts it was studying.

"You look ridiculous," Keelraiser said. Eskitul was wearing a ceremonial outfit that consisted of a short red toga-like garment over a stiff split skirt. To Jack's eye, it did look ridiculous. "Get off my ship," Keelraiser said. "You aren't coming. It is far too dangerous."

Eskitul's reply was a high-pitched gargle of birdsong.

Jack perched on the couch beside Alexei's. He touched the wall to make a window. The manufacturing floor was now empty of machinery. The remaining rriksti ground techs wore their spacesuits, as if they had been doused in white paint. They had depressurized the shuttle bay. Time to go. Got to go. Kate, Hannah, Giles, we're coming ... if these aliens can decide who's going.

"You're taking their bait!" Keelraiser said to Eskitul.

The Shiplord responded in the rriksti language again.

Alexei murmured, "Pilot doesn't want commander getting in the way. Commander thinks pilot will fuck up. Sound familiar?"

"There might be more to it," Jack muttered. Keelraiser had to know the two humans were down here, although it hadn't glanced down. It was speaking English, for their benefit, but Eskitul wasn't.

"Their threats are empty," Keelraiser said. "They dare not risk your death. But if they capture you, all is lost!"

Eskitul drew itself up to its full eight-foot height and made a slashing gesture. Clearly having the last word, it spoke so forcefully that harmonics squealed into the men's ears. Both Jack and Alexei ripped their headsets off.

Keelraiser bowed its head and sat down in the pilot's seat. Eskitul folded itself into the seat beside it.

"Aaaand the commander pulls rank," Alexei said, smirking.

More rriksti filed into the cockpit and descended through the hatch to the lower seating area. All of them, like Keelraiser, were naked. They carried the small backpacks which would transform into spacesuits. One, smaller than the others, with reddish hair, held out backpacks to Jack and Alexei. "Put these on. I'm Hriklif. This translates as Ditchlight. I will look after you."

Brilliant.

Jack accepted the backpack with a smile of thanks. He helped Alexei get out of his clothes. Hriklif showed the men how to don the spacesuits. You strapped the backpack on your back, clamped the air supply tube in your teeth, donned nose plugs and goggles, and pressed a patch on the bottom of the backpack. The rriksti had double-jointed shoulders, so this was child's play for them. Jack couldn't reach the place you were supposed to press. He did Alexei's, and Alexei did his.

The contents of the backpack flowed like tepid water over Jack's back, over his naked buttocks and thighs, down his legs, between his toes. The material came around the front of his body and encased his genitals. It rose up over his stomach and chest.

"Stop," Hriklif yelled. The nearest rriksti leapt to press the buttons on Jack and Alexei's backpacks. The white tide stopped at their necks, leaving their heads exposed.

Skyler scrambled down through the hatch, entirely encased in white. He looked like a classical statue that had taken up scuba diving.

"There is a problem," Hriklif said.

"I'll say there's a problem." Jack's face heated with anger. "Who let him on board?"

Hriklif pointed upwards, through the transparent ceiling. In the cockpit, Keelraiser and Eskitul sat side by side, immobile except for their twitching hair.

"Eskitul?"

"Yes," Hriklif said. "Why is it a problem?"

"Because," Alexei explained, "if I am forced to share a ship with him again, I will have to kill him."

The other rriksti, following the exchange, twittered in their own language. Their hair danced. Was it possible that they were *amused?* They understood grudges, didn't they? Holding grudges was their national sport as far as Jack could tell. And they'd seen Skyler shoot Alexei at point-blank range. Perhaps they thought it was funny for Alexei to threaten Skyler now, given that he had a broken collarbone and only one working arm. If so, they hadn't reckoned with Jack.

Skyler waved his arms, pointing to himself, to Alexei, to Jack.

"He cannot talk," Hriklif said.

"Not a problem," Alexei said. "I don't need to *hear* his

dying screams."

"Later," Jack muttered to Alexei.

Alexei shrugged, his face gray.

Jack turned to Hriklif and changed the subject, hoping it wasn't too obvious a deflection. "I do see what you mean about the comms." The rriksti had radios in their bodies, so they didn't need them in their suits. "Can we rig the headsets to work with the suits?"

"It is so strange that you use your mouths to talk," Hriklif said, sounding exhausted by the complexity of the universe.

Jack clapped it on the shoulder encouragingly. "It should be an easy hack. We just need to rig the mouthpieces of the breathing tubes to go *over* our mouths. Split the end of the tube and wrap it with these bandages you used for Alexei's splint. They hold their shape, so we can make a little cup for a mouthpiece. Pierce a hole in that and run a wire through it for the transmitter. Easy!"

The rriksti immediately got the idea. The fix was swiftly implemented. Freed from his suit to have his breathing tube modified, Skyler stared at Jack and Alexei in fright.

Jack settled his new mouthpiece over his lips. The suit's silky material flowed up over his face and sealed itself at the top of his head. Now he was looking out at the world through a murky filter. The goggles were *dark* goggles, made for rriksti eyes. He hoped the goggles were light-sensitive, or he'd be fighting blind.

He tested out his headset. "Why don't you sit down, Skyler?"

The other rriksti, suited, settled into the boost seats. Skyler scrambled to comply with Jack's advice.

"That's right. Better than being splattered over the

bulkheads. Keelraiser tells me this thing pulls some heavy gees."

Skyler sat beside Alexei. Jack heard him mutter, "Sorry, man." Alexei gazed straight ahead as if Skyler wasn't there.

The shuttle lurched forward with a screech that sounded uncommonly like grinding gears.

The wall of the shuttle bay … *melted*.

Just like I thought. It was only made of metal, after all.

Sorry. *Smart material*.

The *Cloudeater* rolled out of the shelter where it had rested for ten years, onto the ice of Europa.

Jack touched the window beside him to make it go away. He was not interested in looking at that frozen plain ever again. His thoughts circled around the *SoD*, hundreds of kilometers overhead. He prayed they wouldn't be too late.

CHAPTER 35

The *SoD* shuddered. Metallic thuds carried through the hull and rolled over the two women on the bridge.

Kate flew to the center console. She called up the internal camera feed from the storage module. Hannah peeked over her shoulder.

Giant black insects flew across the screen. Their heads—their *heads*—did they even have heads? Or just masses of wriggling tentacles?

"They look like octopuses!" Hannah cried. "Are those the aliens? They've got octopus heads! What are they doing on our ship?!?"

She clutched Kate's arm in a white-knuckled grip.

"They don't have octopus heads," Kate said. "I thought those were tentacles at first, too. But they're bio-antennas. Fuckers communicate with radio speech."

Kate sounded astonishingly calm. Now it was Hannah who felt like she was losing her mind, just looking at those things on the screen.

"As to what they're doing on our ship," Kate added, "they're stealing our electrolysis equipment."

On the screen displaying the interior of the storage module, the hatch to the electrolysis unit's compartment was closed. It looked undamaged. But a red light flashed, indicating loss of pressure inside the compartment.

"They came in through the storage module airlock, got into the compartment, and removed the hull plates from the inside," Kate said. "Remember how the hull plates on that part of the module were designed to explode outwards, in case we had a liquid hydrogen leak? Yeah. Which makes them easy to dismantle. That would've been the big boom we heard. Let's see …"

Kate brought up the feed from the storage module's external camera.

A rectangular hole gaped in the module's hull.

Aliens swarmed in and out of it. They were removing the electrolysis equipment, pipes and all, maneuvering it through the gaps in the truss tower.

"Could you not dig your nails into me like that?" Kate said gently.

"Sorry," Hannah said. She let go of Kate's arm. "This is just … I mean, holy cow."

How would the *SoD* survive without its electrolysis unit? It wouldn't, was the answer. They would never get home.

"*Why* are they taking it?" she said helplessly.

"Because that's what they do, Hannah-banana. They steal shit. It's their culture or something."

Hannah-banana. The nickname took her off-guard. It was her old Twitter handle. She suddenly remembered her old Twitter BFF, @firebirdmeeks. *A mai tai sounds good right about now …*

The NXC killed him.

No, *we* killed him.

We killed him for his technology.

And now the aliens are about to do the same thing to us.

Poetic justice, much?

Recoiling from the implication that they were doomed, she tried to think of hacks. Thing One and Thing Two had electrolysis units. But they were down on the surface. No way to get hold of those without the Dragon or the Shenzhou …

Unexpectedly, Kate smiled at her. "Guess what, though? I have a secret weapon."

She held up her iPod.

Crazy.

She is *batshit* crazy, Hannah thought, staring into the mission commander's swollen eyes, looking at the iPod, looking back at Kate, waiting for this to make sense.

"Uh, are we going to play Pharrell at them?"

"Were you listening to my music? Lucky you didn't click on this track." Kate thumbed the iPod. She showed Hannah a playlist containing a single song, entitled *Friends and Lovers.*

"What's that?"

"Come here. Closer. They might have ways of listening that we don't know about."

Hannah let Kate draw her close, although her skin crawled at the touch of the other woman's cold fingers. Kate whispered into her ear, "It's the trigger for a Russian malware program."

Hannah pulled away. "You said it was Jack!"

"What?"

"You said Jack was the saboteur. He put malware in the control systems. Didn't he?"

Kate grimaced. "No. That's what *Skyler* said. But he was wrong. The malware is Russian. The Russkis tried to sabotage the *SoD* during construction—"

"OK, now I'm totally lost."

"Remember, before the *SoD* got the greenlight, Putin announced a Russian mission to Europa? Yeah. In the end they joined the *SoD* project, but they kept right on planning their own mission. *And* tricked us into paying half their development costs. So their idea was to take the *SoD* out, then it would've been, oh, what a shame, but never mind, you can send *one* American on *our* beautiful spaceship … But the sabotage incident didn't destroy the *SoD*, so they came up with something different."

"Malware."

"Yup. This program overrides the lockouts that prevent the control rods from being completely withdrawn from the nuclear reactor. That's your wheelhouse … I'm not sure exactly what happens when the rods are pulled out. But I'm reliably assured it will be bad."

Hannah pulled away from Kate in shock. "Um, yeah. The reactor would vigorously disassemble. That's what would happen."

"Good. That's pretty much what I thought."

"Kate, you can't—you won't … how do you even know it was the Russians?"

"Because Alexei told me." Kate's eyes glittered with tears that couldn't fall in zero-gee. "I told him what Skyler said about Jack. And he confessed. The GRU gave it to him. Like—like a suicide vest. He was supposed to hijack the *SoD* on our way back to Earth, presumably after we scored some alien goodies. You know, they're crazy like foxes, those Russian bastards. Our guys never stood a chance against them. The NXC? Give me a fucking break! The Russians have been playing us all along."

Kate's voice dissolved. Hannah, forgetting everything else, opened her arms to her. She pressed Kate against her bosom and stroked her hair, the way her sister Bethany used to hug her. Kate's hair felt tacky. Bits of it were stuck together with what looked like dried blood.

"But here's the thing," Kate said, her voice muffled in

Hannah's shoulder. "Alexei hated being used like that. He was a real cosmonaut, Hannah. A real man. I loved him. I know I acted like it was just casual sex, but it was more than that. I just wish I had told *him* … "

"I understand," Hannah said.

Kate pulled away, wiping her eyes. "So anyway, he gave me the trigger. It was his way of proving his loyalty to me, to the mission, I guess. It's like, screw you, Alexei. *I* didn't want that responsibility, either …"

Hannah's gaze returned to the iPod. "How does it work?"

"You just press play," Kate said.

"I don't want to die," Hannah said.

Now it was Kate's turn to pull Hannah into a tender, sisterly hug. "Oh, I know. I *know,* Hannah-banana. But we're going to die anyway, you understand that, right? Everyone else is dead already. It's just you and me left. They're going to kill us no matter what we do. We're dead meat. But at least we can take a bunch of these motherfuckers with us. I'm just waiting for the big boss to get here. He, it, I don't even know, he said he was going to come and look at our pathetic little spaceship."

"The *Spirit of Destiny* is *not* a pathetic little spaceship," Hannah said, hoping to spur Kate into defiance. She punched buttons on the optical screen, flicking through various cameras. When she got to the feed from the aft-facing cameras behind the bioshield, she stopped. "Holy shit!"

Fifteen, twenty tentacle-headed aliens were dicking around at the back of the ship, swimming in and out of the truss tower between the radiator vanes. A fat hose undulated in the vacuum.

"Oh, looky looky," Kate said.

"They're messing with my reactor!"

"We might get the whole gang of them."

The airlock hatch suddenly clanked open.

"Here we go," Kate said on a rising note, as if they were in a rollercoaster, at the top of a hill, about to plunge down. She pushed off from the center seat, floating away from Hannah.

An octopus-headed alien descended into the bridge. This one was covered with intricate patterns in headachy metallic colors.

"Hello, Boombox, you fucking asshole," Kate said.

Her thumb moved to the iPod's touchscreen.

Hannah pushed off and flew across the bridge, straight at her.

CHAPTER 36

Hannah cannoned into Kate with bruising force. She got her fingers around the iPod and jammed her thumb on the power button, switching it off.

The consoles stayed dark.

No klaxons sounded.

Kate had not had time to trigger the malware.

The mission commander fought like a wild animal, trying to reach the iPod.

Hannah fended her off. It wasn't hard—Kate was at the end of her strength, not to mention that she was covered with bruises and had a recently dislocated shoulder. Hannah stuffed the iPod into the pocket of her sweats.

The alien grabbed Kate by the back of the t-shirt and pulled her away from Hannah. With the other hand, it lifted Hannah in the same way. Drops of blood detached from Kate's cheek—Hannah had accidentally scratched her. The alien held the women apart like kittens. "Do you humans ever do anything except fight with each other?" it said. "You really are like us."

The voice came not from the alien itself, but from an object it had brought onto the bridge, which was now floating in mid-air. This object resembled the portable stereo that had been Hannah's most treasured possession in high school. It even had SONY written on it. But it was wrongly proportioned, crudely made.

Hannah looked from the fake Sony stereo, to the alien. "Oh, I see," she said. *"Boombox."*

Strangely, now that the alien was actually holding her by the scruff of her neck, she no longer felt afraid. This had gone beyond that.

Kate glowered at her, but didn't try to grab the iPod again. Of course, she didn't want the alien to suspect they had a secret weapon.

A secret weapon of mass destruction, Hannah thought. She resolved that no matter what, she was not going to let Kate blow the *SoD* up. She'd gone through her own valley of darkness while she waited for Kate to return. She had considered suicide, and rejected it. She wasn't going to let Kate drag her back into that deadly slough.

The alien kicked off with a many-toed foot. Still holding the women, it drifted down to the consoles. "Where are the railgun controls?" said the boombox.

"Go to hell," Kate spat.

"I don't know!" Hannah said. It was half true. She hadn't been trained to operate the railguns, unlike the other Americans. "Let's talk about something different," she gabbled. She had an idea, probably derived from Hollywood movies, that it was clever to keep the bad guys talking. "Why are your people messing around behind the bioshield? They're gonna irradiate themselves! The reactor's only running at 15%, but there are still gamma rays coming out of there!"

The alien said, "We are less vulnerable to radiation than you are."

"Oh, because you're just awesome-sauce in every way?" Her mouth was running away with her.

"Our EVA suits give us some protection," the alien said.

"If that's your suit, it doesn't look very rad-proof. It looks more like something Bootsy Collins would've worn back in the '70s."

"Oh, Hannah, Hannah," Kate said.

The alien threw Kate away from itself. Kate went spinning through the air and crashed into the aft bulkheads.

"Go away," the alien said to Kate. "My people are collecting resources from your life-support area. You can help them."

Kate shot a frightened look at Hannah, and scrambled away through the keel tube.

Hannah floated in the alien's grip. Her terror roared back. She could scarcely breathe.

Its voice fuzzed from the boombox. "You are the propulsion technician of this ship. Is this correct?"

"Y-yes."

"Where are the reactor controls?"

"N-not here," Hannah said. "Back in the, the engineering module."

The alien shifted its grip to Hannah's arm, seized its boombox in the other hand, and towed her into the keel tube. It was scarcely wide enough for the thing's shoulders. They jostled, legs banging. The alien squeezed out into the axis tunnel, still gripping Hannah's wrist. Kate was sitting on the forward stairs, near the top of Staircase 2. She looked up. Their eyes met, and then Kate rotated out of sight.

The alien flew through the axis tunnel, dragging Hannah at its side. Looking down, she saw its horror-movie companions exploring the garden.

Through SLS, past the spinning algae tanks. Through the storage module. Into the engineering module, which had been Hannah's kingdom for the last two years. She had never expected to end up sharing it with an alien.

"This is it," she gasped.

The alien let go of her. She bounced off the aft wall, catching herself with her hands.

The alien touched the inside of its left wrist, if those really were wrists, if the seven-fingered appendages really were hands ... and its disco-era coloration melted away, starting at the tips of the fingers and tentacles. The tentacles turned silver. The hands, arms, and chest turned white-person color, with blue veins webbing the biceps, like an Irish person who had not exposed their skin to the sun in about ... oh, ten years, maybe?

The triangular part below the tentacles turned into a face with a small mouth and huge coffee-colored eyes.

Hannah stared, open-mouthed.

It was otherworldly.

Grotesque.

Beautiful.

The metamorphosis stopped at the alien's waist, leaving its pelvis and legs disco-colored. It had a bulge worthy of David Bowie in *Labyrinth.* Thin stripes over its shoulders also remained patterned. When it turned away to examine the reactor controls, Hannah saw that the stripes extended like braces to a rectangular patch on its back.

"This is a very primitive ship," it said, with a hint of grumbling in its boombox-mediated voice.

"Well, excuse me," Hannah said, flustered. "We've never had the opportunity of building one before, because this is the first time we've ever encountered *aliens!*"

Boombox regarded her with its huge, dark eyes. "They say there's an explosion of intelligent life coming," it said. "Everywhere, all at once. We'll probably never meet them. Every other habitable star system is too far away."

"Wh-where do you come from?"

"The name you give to our star is Proxima Centauri."

"Oh, I was a big Transformers fan," Hannah said. "Does your ship transform into a giant robot?" Boombox just stared at her. She swallowed. "Anyway. I guess that was *Alpha* Centauri."

"We have colonized Alpha Centauri."

"Okayyyy. Do you have FTL?"

"FTL means faster-than-light propulsion. Is this correct?"

"Yes. It's supposed to be impossible, but I'm just like, *anything's* possible now."

"No, we do not have FTL," Boombox said, grumpily. It peered at the hexagonal array. "How do you increase the power output from the reactor? I wish to generate maximum output."

Hannah folded her arms. She couldn't believe she was defying this awe-inspiring, beautiful creature. "Why?"

"I am asking the questions."

"Well, if you're so smart, you figure out how to do it."

The alien floated over to her. It dragged its fingers along the ceiling to stop. Hannah held her ground, or rather her place in the air. The alien's breath sighed out of its small, thin-lipped mouth, so close that she felt it, and smelt it. Like seaweed drying in the sun.

"My people are dying," Boombox said. "We require water."

"Okayyyy ..."

"We've run a hose from your external radiator system to one of our cargo holds. The hold is full of ice."

"Yeah, Kate mentioned that."

"I wish to use your reactor to direct low-pressure steam

against the ice."

"To—to melt it, OK."

"Yes."

"Then you're going to have a cargo hold full of a steam and water mixture." Hannah recalled her own struggles with the MPD engine's steam drum. She had *not* been able to figure out how to get the steam out, without the drum undergoing a rapid unplanned disassembly. In the end, the NXC had killed Oliver Meeks to get the answer. "Everything's in freefall. There is no convection. Heat doesn't circulate. How does your cargo hold not explode before you get all the ice melted?"

The silvery bio-antennas on the alien's head danced. "We are using your electrical capacity to run fans that take the steam and water mixture from the hold and dump it into a tank. Eventually, the ice is melted and evaporated, or the tank is filled. Then we disconnect the hose."

"You've thought of everything, haven't you?"

"Yes," Boombox said, smugly.

"Except it's kind of cheating. You'll be using *our* water, in the form of steam, to melt *your* water."

"Yes."

Hannah swallowed. "OK. I'm just warning you, we don't have very much water on board."

"We will not require more than you have in your tanks."

But I don't want to *give* you everything we have in our tanks, Hannah thought. There's little enough as it is. She floated over to the other wall. Before Boombox could come to see what she was doing—as if it could read English, anyway—she disabled the gauges on the reactant tanks. "All right," she said, pretending to read the gauges. "You're drawing electricity from our fuel cells." As she spoke, she switched the fuel cells off. Now they wouldn't be depleted. The *SoD* would hang onto *some* water, however much remained in the ETs in the form of liquid reactants. She stared at the electrical output meter. The aliens were drawing a couple of megawatts via their cables, but now it was all coming from the housekeeping turbine. She turned back to Boombox, and smiled. "Now, what did you want to do with the reactor?"

It stared at her for such a long time that she started to lose her nerve. She was on the verge of confessing to her deception. At last the alien said, "Turn it up to eleven."

Hannah let out a startled laugh.

"Is this correct?"

"Yes, yes, it's correct ..." She floated over to the dollar meter. "It's gonna take a while to crank it up."

"I understand. It is a primitive system."

Hannah programmed the control rods to withdraw slowly, increasing the amount of reactivity in the core. She remembered Kate's malware. She imagined the control rods withdrawing all at once. You had to figure the malware would also turn off the coolant pumps. *Boom.* A long-forgotten face flitted across her mind's eye: the Rosatom physicist she'd slept with on her first trip to Russia, where the *SoD's* reactor was built. Had he known they were fitting the ship out with a time bomb? *Goddamn.* He'd had melty dark eyes. The same color, actually, as the alien's.

Boombox reached over her shoulder. She cringed. A slender forefinger tapped the dollar meter. "This indicates the region of critical controllable reactivity?"

"Yes." She turned. The alien was right there. "You—you

know this stuff?"

"Our ship is also nuclear-propelled. However, we use a different process."

"What process?"

"Proton-lithium-6 fusion."

"Oh. My. God. You're kidding me, right? Say you're kidding me. How do you bootstrap the reaction? What's the containment vessel made of? Protons. Wait a minute. Protons ..."

"From hydrogen."

"Aha," Hannah said. She narrowed her eyes and pointed at the alien. *'That's* why you're taking our electrolysis equipment. To make liquid hydrogen."

"Yes," Boombox said. Its bio-antennas shimmied briefly.

"Don't you have any? A ship five freaking kilometers long, all the way from Proxima Centauri, and you don't have any liquid hydrogen?"

"There is a *hole* one kilometer long in our ship," Boombox said. "Everything was fried, shattered, slagged, or sucked into space. Would I be doing this if I had a large-scale power source? If I had working electrolysis equipment? If I had one single tank of LH2?"

Hannah gulped. "I don't know." She remembered Kate saying, *They steal things. It's their culture or something.* "Would you?"

"Of course not," Boombox said. It swept a bleak, dismissive gaze around her little kingdom.

She wrung her hands. What she wouldn't give for a drink right now. She mustered a skeptical tone. "And this amazing fusion reactor of yours? That's not working, either?"

"We have no fucking hydrogen! That means no proton

source! Are you really a propulsion technician, or just a *schleerp?*"

Whatever a *schleerp* was, Hannah felt pretty sure she didn't want to be one. "I am an engineer," she said. "I'm one of the best damn engineers on Planet Earth. I helped build this system." She slapped the reactor control board, noting the dollar meter inching up past 50%. "I have babied this reactor all the way from Earth, and I'm proud to say we haven't had a single accident to this day. Whether that makes me a propulsion technician by your standards, I don't know. But I do know something about nuclear reactions. And I know there is no damn way you have overcome the Coulomb barrier to the atomic nucleus."

The Coulomb barrier was *the* stumbling block to fusion power. To overcome it and fuse two nuclei together, you needed the Large Hadron Collider, or a handy sun.

Hannah folded her arms and glowered at the alien, waiting for it to refute her.

The silver bio-antennas danced. "You would be amazed to know what we can do."

"Bet I wouldn't," Hannah said. "Bet you haven't really got a fusion reactor at all. Hell, you haven't even got any good *weapons*. All the way here, I was waiting for you to throw, like, a miniature black hole at us or something." She flung out her arms and looked around the module theatrically. "You haven't even got ray-guns! What kind of aliens are you? Pfft."

Boombox's hair—she was starting to think of it as hair, because it looked like her own did when it came out of its twist-tie in zero-gee, except silver—danced so much that Hannah cocked her head on one side, smiling.

"We *have* got ray-guns," Boombox said at last in a suspiciously choked-sounding voice. "I didn't bring mine. I did not expect to be challenged."

"Why didn't you board us before?" Hannah said. "We've been here almost a week."

Boombox's dark eyes opened wider. "Would *you* board an alien ship, risking the lives of your companions against unknown forces?"

Hannah muttered, "That's what Kate and Giles did."

"And from them we learned that there was nothing to be afraid of," Boombox said. It sounded almost sad. "They did not even carry personal weapons. What were you *thinking?*"

Hannah's eyes prickled with tears. "I guess we thought, if you need a gun, you're already fucked," she said.

"On your TV, humans often meet aliens. They always fight them. This is what we were expecting."

Hannah laughed wretchedly. "Guess we should've listened to the sci-fi writers, huh? Life imitates art."

"Courage, Hannah Ginsburg," the alien said. It pronounced her name like a trill of birdsong.

"We should've known you weren't going to be friendly."

"But I *am* friendly," said the eight-foot alien with the sea-creature hair, taking up half of her kingdom with its limbs.

Hannah laughed, really laughed. "I guess aliens do sarcasm," she said.

"We will pay for everything we take."

"With what, Proxima Centauri dollars?"

"We will take you home to Earth in the *Lightbringer.*"

CHAPTER 37

Kate delved in Alexei's coffin with her one good hand. She'd already searched Alexei's desk in the Potter space under the aft stairs. The aliens hadn't noticed what she was doing, or else they just didn't care. They were completely preoccupied with the garden, wrapping up trays of plants in vacuum-proof sheeting of some kind, so they could steal those, too. Some of them had half-doffed their spacesuits and were tasting things. She hoped the terrestrial vegetation poisoned them.

Alexei's laptop *had* to be here.

Hannah had taken Kate's iPod, but that couldn't be the only place the malware trigger existed.. Alexei had to have kept a copy. Right? Kate just had to find his laptop.

She lifted out handfuls of DIY e-cigarette parts from the storage webbings on the coffin's sides. She rummaged in the drift of dirty clothes in the hammock. Alexei had been the opposite of a neat freak. Despite herself, Kate raised the dirty clothes to her nose and inhaled his smell.

They used to make love in his coffin, on the down low. Two could fit in one of these things, although it was a squeeze. Best sex she ever had—it was a wonder everyone didn't hear her muffled screams. His clutter would dig into her back and ass when they really got going. She used to give him shit for it. *Clean out your coffin, Alexei …*

She didn't want to keep going without him. This was not a surrender to weakness. Her grief mirrored her understanding of the aliens. What they had done to Alexei, they'd do to everyone on Earth, if she did not stop them.

The nearest aliens stiffened, their bio-antennas standing

on end. Kate had seen that before. That was how they reacted when their captain, that heinous sadist Boombox, was near. She looked up.

Boombox floated out of the aft keel tube into the axis tunnel, clad in its spacesuit. The patterns on that thing were less Parliament Funkadelic than Lovecraft. They hurt Kate's eyes.

OK.

Hannah's alone in the engineering module now.

Kate started to her feet, remembering how easily Hannah had fended her off before. She was in no shape to perform zero-gee tae kwon do feats. Maybe she could just *talk* Hannah into handing the iPod over …

Before she could move a step, Hannah floated out of the keel tube, wearing her Z-2.

Kate knew it was her because of the unique piping on her suit. Green lines ran around her chest and down her legs and arms.

Hannah must have seen Kate through her faceplate. She waved energetically.

"Where are you taking her?" Kate shouted.

She knew that Hannah herself couldn't hear her. In a spacesuit, you existed in your own little bubble of silence. If the other person didn't have a radio you were SOL, and Kate had nothing except a handful of Alexei's dirty underwear.

Boombox shouted through the boombox in its hand, "We're just going for drinks!"

All the aliens wiggled their bio-antennas. Kate understood their body language well enough by now to interpret this as subservient laughter.

Going for drinks? Bullshit. Boombox was kidnapping Hannah. She'd end up in the same place as Giles.

"Have fun," Kate muttered under her breath.

As soon as they were gone, Kate climbed the stairs and went aft to the engineering module.

A blue-haired alien floated in the middle of the module, taking apart Kate's iPod.

"Hello, Gurlp," Kate said. She had met this one on the *Lightbringer.* It was Boombox's chief bully-boy sidekick. "Can I have that?" The alien had removed the back of the plastic housing. The Wi-Fi might still work.

Gurlp hijacked the intercom to reply. Its English was inadequate, compared to Boombox's. "Wish understand mechanism," it complained.

"It's a music player," Kate said. "Music is something we humans like. It makes us feel good." She bit her lip, remembering one time when Mission Control had played 'Stayin' Alive' for their shift-change selection. She and Alexei had danced around the bridge together, performing clumsy zero-gee disco moves. Oh, Alexei. *Stayin' alive, stayin' alive ...* She didn't want to stay alive any longer. "Can I have that?" she repeated, reaching for the iPod.

Gurlp backhanded her across the module. "No," it said through the intercom, as she bounced off the side wall. "Need ask you about ship weapons system."

"We've already been over this." Fresh blood filled Kate's mouth. "I am *not* telling you how to fire the railguns. Why do you want to know, anyway?"

"Us enemies come. We wish blow to shit."

Hope blossomed. Kate had no idea who the enemies of these aliens might be. But the enemy of my enemy is my friend, right? "No way, Jose," she said. "My ship, my guns. Go to hell."

Gurlp casually broke the iPod in half and dropped the pieces. That's how strong they were. It drifted towards her. "Hell, what? Human place?"

"It's just a figure of speech," Kate said.

"Rriksti also this figure of speech. Us say *show hell*. Let me teach you what means this."

CHAPTER 38

The *Cloudeater* rose off the ice, hovering. Exhaust ducted from its engine provided lift.

The main engine engaged.

Felt like getting kicked by a horse, all over Jack's body.

Keelraiser hadn't been kidding. This thing pulled some vicious gees.

Jack wondered how Alexei was holding up, but he couldn't turn his head. It was all he could do to drag air in and out of his lungs. His rosary dug into his chest like a branding iron. He'd been stupid to wear it around his neck. At this level of thrust, even a wrinkle of fabric under your back would hurt. The rriksti spacesuits didn't wrinkle. But they didn't have pockets, either.

The direction of the thrust gravity gradually changed. Jack pictured Keelraiser on the bridge overhead, fighting the gees, curving the shuttle's vector to the vertical. Now they seemed to be lying on their backs. Jack stared at the ceiling, which had been the forward wall. Graphics skidded across it. He glimpsed a planet, divided into three stripes: desert-pale, mottled green and blue, and black. That must be Imf. Before the rriksti ruined it.

What did it mean for Earth's future that the rriksti had devastated their home planet? Was that just something intelligent life *did*? Meeks had theorized that first contact was the Big Filter: the moment when an intelligent species was most likely to go extinct. But the rriksti had not needed any outside help to drive themselves to the brink of extinction.

No telling how much worse things had got in the Alpha

Centauri system since the *Lightbringer* set out. As Keelraiser had said, this group of rriksti might be the only survivors of their species.

And if that was the case, Jack had a heavy responsibility to preserve their lives.

We are not so different.

His eyes watered. Tears slid towards his ears.

The gravity went away.

They were back in freefall.

The rriksti immediately slipped out of their harnesses, and Jack forgot his disturbing thoughts as he floated up from his seat.

"We have achieved an orbital height of 450 kilometers and orbital velocity of 13,700 kilometers per hour," Keelraiser said in their headsets. "I'm now going to dive down and rise back up to converge our orbit with the *Lightbringer's* orbit. This will take approximately seventeen hours."

Seventeen hours!

Jack was frustrated, but not surprised. After all, the space shuttle used to take two days to overhaul the ISS. The *Cloudeater* was a shuttle, too. Pound for pound, it probably had even worse delta-V than the *Atlantis*. You can have a star in your belly, but you still need stuff to throw out the back, and all that passenger seating didn't leave much room for tankage.

"Relax," Keelraiser added, with a hollow laugh.

The rriksti relaxed. They floated back into the passenger cabin, talked in their silent way, ate, and drank. They'd brought food on board: greasy slabs of *suizh* that looked like tofu. Around the eighth hour of their wait, the men, tormented by their growling stomachs, caved in and asked the rriksti to share their food. The aliens delightedly watched them choke the stuff down. There was a kind that tasted like old inner tubes, and another kind that set the inside of your mouth on fire. The inner-tube variety was just about palatable, when washed down with enough *krak*. It was calories. And (Jack thought to himself) what did a little metal poisoning matter, when their bodies were breaking down anyway?

Skyler ate little. He floated on the fringe of the group, staring at Alexei. Maybe he knew what was coming to him.

*

Now or never, Skyler thought, several hours later.

Darkness shrouded the passenger cabin of the *Cloudeater*. The rriksti had strapped themselves into seats to sleep. The seats were the wrong size and shape for the humans. Jack had made himself a sort of sleeping-bag by securing a blanket to the floor in one of the aisles. He'd rigged another blanket-bag for Alexei, but the Russian wasn't asleep. Maybe he was in too much pain to doze off. Skyler could see his eyes glinting in the dim red light from the monitoring screens scattered around the cabin.

Skyler floated over and landed on the seat next to Alexei. The cosmonaut turned his head. "Can't sleep?"

Skyler gestured at Alexei's splinted arm, which lay above the blanket. "How's your arm?"

"Collarbone. Hurts. But it's not the worst thing that ever happened."

"Sorry," Skyler said. "I'm really sorry."

"You already said that."

"I'm really, really fucking sorry."

Their voices were quiet. The *Cloudeater's* air circulation system kept up a background roar. Skyler hung over the armrest of the seat, which was shaped like an oblong padded bowl, to hear Alexei better. The aisle was floored in some kind of rubbery stuff with raised patterns like flowers, or explosions. Lots of petals.

"I talked with Hriklif," Alexei said. "I asked why they let you on board. Hriklif didn't understand the problem. For one person to inflict non-fatal wounds on another, it's a normal thing for them. They don't make a big deal unless one person ends up dead. It's a sensible way of thinking, very pragmatic. We can learn a lot from them, I guess."

Skyler said, "I was so fucking glad to see you alive. Thank God those were sub-lethal rounds."

"You thought they were lethal, eh?"

Skyler was tempted to lie, but he had promised himself that he'd lay his heart bare. Let the chips fall where they may. "Yes."

"Hmm," Alexei grunted. He felt around under his blanket with his good hand. Skyler watched, petrified.

"I jumped to conclusions," Skyler blurted. "I just assumed the malware had to've caused the crash. And I figured it was Russian, because I already knew you were working for the GRU, and the pieces seemed to fit together. But it wouldn't be the first time I've been wrong." He shuddered to think how close he'd come to killing a man for the wrong reasons—*again* ... "I'm sorry, dude. Really sorry."

Alexei brought his hand out from under his blanket. He held up his mod. "I have a little bit of juice left." Depressing the switch with his thumb, he inhaled. A cloud of vapor rolled along the floor, revealing the direction of the imperceptible breeze blowing from the vents. "You want?" Alexei held out the e-cigarette.

Skyler grinned in profound relief. He understood that this was Alexei's way of saying it was OK. The e-cig of peace. "Thanks." He took a drag, coughed it out. "Wonder if the rriksti smoke? We could introduce them to a new vice."

"I look forward to discovering *their* vices," Alexei said. "*Krak* is a good start …We can put this behind us, hey, Skyler? We are both professionals."

Skyler nodded. His heart soared. Being forgiven felt amazingly good. He should try it more often. "I'm a crap spy," he said, beginning to unburden himself. "I just can't take all the lying and deception anymore."

"Nor me either," Alexei said. He reached out to retrieve the e-cigarette, and gripped Skyler's hand for a moment. "The malware *was* Russian."

"Oh."

"So you were right. But it did not cause the Shenzhou crash, this I'm sure of."

Before Skyler could respond, the mound of blanket further along the aisle humped up. Jack's head popped out. "So what *did* cause the crash?"

Jack hadn't been asleep after all! He untangled himself from his blanket and drifted down the aisle towards them.

"Mechanical error, Jack," Alexei said, sitting up. Skyler straightened up, too, so their heads were all facing the same way. "Go back to sleep."

"Mechanical errors have causes." Jack pointed at Skyler. "And if I had to guess, the cause of this one was you."

Skyler froze. As if Jack's words had opened a locker in his mind, those last terrible moments in the Shenzhou Plus tumbled into his memory. *You turned the APU heater off,* Meili had said. *I told you to turn off the valves! But you turned off the heater for the APU pump! So the hydrazine froze!*

He had constructed a fantastical case against Alexei to avoid thinking about those moments.

To avoid the accusation Jack had just made.

It was YOU, Skyler.

He covered his face with his hands, as if he could blot out the memory, but it was too late. He couldn't hide from the truth.

"You're right," he babbled. "I screwed up. That stupid touchscreen technology—no, it was my fault—everything written in Chinese—but no. It was my fault. I screwed up, and Meili's dead. I'm gonna be dealing with this for the rest of my life."

"Not to worry," Jack said. "The rest of your life is likely to be quite short."

Alexei said, "Jesus, Jack. He admits he screwed up. It can happen to anyone. He didn't mean to do it. *He* almost died, too!"

Skyler wanted to hug the Russian, he was so grateful to him for defending him. But it didn't seem to make much of an impact on Jack.

"Screwing up is not an excuse." Jack's face was a mask of fury. Skyler remembered—he'd never forgotten, actually—that Jack and Meili had been an item for ages. Jack was *never* going to forgive him.

And if Jack ever found out about the other thing …

… oh, fuck. My life won't be worth a bucket of warm spit …

… as Lance might have said.

Skyler fiddled with his peace symbol in distress. "I loved Meili, too," he muttered.

This, it immediately became clear, was the wrong thing to say. Jack huffed out breath through his nostrils like a bull. He plunged into the seat on the other side of the aisle and braced his feet against the back of the one in front of it, pushing so hard that the seats creaked.

Alexei hit Jack's leg. "Jack! Jack. Remember to look on the bright side of life." He started to sing in his creaky baritone. "Don't grumble, give a whistle! And this'll help things turn out for the best …"

"Hey, Monty Python!" Skyler said, recognizing the tune. He'd often seen Jack and Alexei guffawing over a laptop screen as they indulged in a Python viewing fest. "I freaking love Python."

"If life seems jolly rotten, there's something you've forgotten," Alexei sang.

Jack smiled reluctantly. They belted out a couple of choruses of 'Always Look on the Bright Side of Life,' while the rriksti slept, deaf to the tuneless racket. At last Jack said, "It's fine, Skyler. It's never too late to get it right."

"I'm not gonna screw up again," Skyler promised.

"Did they give you one of these?" Jack went to his blankets and came back with an alien gun. It looked like the kind of assault rifle Congress was always trying to ban. Skyler could hear Lance now: *Fudgin' Congress-critters don't even know what a so-called assault rifle IS.* Oh Lance—had you ever got your hands on one of these babies, you'd have been in heaven, before you went to hell. Skyler handled the wicked-looking gun with revulsion.

"Energy weapon," Jack said. "I'll make sure you get one.

We can't bring Meili back, but we can barbecue every fucking *Krijistal* on the *Lightbringer* in her memory."

Skyler knew what he was supposed to say now—*right on, fuckin' A*—but he couldn't do it. The long conversation he'd had with himself after he shot Alexei led to precisely this choice.

This paralysis.

He thrust the alien gun back at Jack—wrong way round, earning himself a glower. "I'll leave the guts and glory stuff to you." It came out wrong, like an accusation. "I just can't do it," he tried to explain, making it worse.

Because who was to say who deserved to die? Meili had not deserved to die. Nor had Lance. Nor had Oliver Meeks. And yet all of them had ended up dead, because of Skyler.

Jack and Alexei thought these rriksti were good and the ones on the *Lightbringer* were bad, but what if it was the other way around? Skyler refrained from opening *that* can of worms, but he could not overcome his own uncertainty. His NXC training emphasized looking at things from all angles. No statements or perceptions were to be accepted at face value, without supporting evidence. Who was right, who was wrong? Who was good, who was evil? It was all so damn contingent. And Skyler no longer trusted his own judgement. He shook his head helplessly, rubbing his thumb over his peace symbol, which had taken on a new symbolic importance for him. It wasn't ironic anymore.

"What if we get it wrong? What if I screw up again?" he said, hearing a tremor of pleading in his voice.

Jack frowned. "What you mean is, just leave it to other people."

"You don't have to do it, either."

"People with testicles."

"I just can't."

Jack floated out of the seat, taking the gun with him. "No, I see that."

Alexei watched Jack with a worried scowl. "We all need to get some sleep," he said.

In a last desperate attempt to *communicate* as opposed to just talking, Skyler said, "Don't you see, guys? We're neck-deep in alligators here, OK? But randomly shooting people is not going to help. It never helps! We have to stop and think and—and analyze the evidence ..."

... and away we go down the NXC rabbit-hole, where every conclusion might just be another screw-up in the making, another fatally flawed decision from a Harvard astrophysicist who'd thought he was smarter than everyone else.

Jack floated away. "I have no idea what you're talking about," he said over his shoulder.

*

Fucking Skyler! Jack concluded that he was simply a coward. He liked guns fine when *he* was the only person holding one. But at the prospect of a battle, he suddenly developed a conscience.

Jack's own guilty conscience nagged him. *I have no idea what you're talking about,* he'd said, but he did. Skyler had been talking about Lance. He'd been talking about the way Jack murdered him, by underhandedly messing with his spacesuit. He'd been rubbing Jack's face in it. Jack gritted his teeth so hard that his jaw hurt.

Alexei had forgiven the little twat, apparently. Alexei always had had an amazing ability to move on from things.

Jack cooled down by floating around the crew area, making windows and taking pictures. The rriksti had returned his Nikon. It had been on the Dragon, but they had apparently removed it to have a look at the state of the art of human image capture technology. It still worked, anyway. He snapped photos of Europa, waxing as the *Cloudeater* flew over the icy moon's terminator, and Jupiter. He photographed the Great Red Spot, the polar auroras, and a dun-colored storm the shape of a fried egg, losing himself for a while in the gas giant's beauty.

The camera's clock, calibrated to the now completely meaningless GMT time-zone, told him that fourteen hours had passed since they launched. Not much longer to go.

The ceiling of the crew area, formerly transparent, was now opaque. Jack floated up through the hatch into the cockpit.

Keelraiser and Eskitul were not asleep. They sat strapped into their respective seats, their hair flattened over their shoulders. Perhaps that was their way of giving each other the silent treatment.

"Tell me more about the *Lightbringer's* offensive capabilities," Jack said. Just making small talk.

"At this point, zero," Keelraiser said without looking around at him.

"You said they threatened you—"

"Yes," Keelraiser said. "They threatened to drop chunks of debris on our shelter."

Jack nodded. "That would be like dropping a brick out of a Cessna flying at 300 meters and trying to hit your friend on the head. Not much of a threat."

On the other hand, if you dropped a thousand bricks,

you'd have a good chance of nailing him.

"Oh, perhaps," Keelraiser said, staring straight ahead at the forward wall. "But if they get their reactor running, they can repair everything else. The muon cannons, the railguns, the … *elsprit* … it's a method of increasing the range over which the strong nuclear force operates. It can be weaponized. Everything can be weaponized. It's enough to say that when it's fully operational, the *Lightbringer* is a planet-killer. So the question becomes: how fast can they bring the reactor online?"

"And the answer is?" Jack said.

"We don't know," Keelraiser said. "It depends on many things."

Jack floated across the cockpit and grasped the raised, scrolled back of Keelraiser's seat. From this perspective, the wall became a dizzying panorama of space. It was not just a window. It felt as if they were literally floating in space. Europa filled half the sky, Jupiter blazed overhead, and above Europa's limb, an ember-red polyhedron identified—Jack guessed—the location of the *Lightbringer,* and the *SoD.* For almost the first time in Jack's life, vertigo gripped him.

"Tell us more about the *Spirit of Destiny's* offensive capabilities," Keelraiser said, bouncing his question back to him.

Jack didn't recall telling the rriksti that the *SoD* even *had* offensive capabilities. Maybe they took it for granted. "Two railguns mounted on the truss. Controls on the bridge, auto-loading from an external ammo store. Solid metal slugs." He remembered Kate's claim that there were plutonium rounds hidden somewhere on board, and decided not to mention that.

"Field of fire?"

"Limited. Can't fire past the bridge or the reactor. Think of the guns as broadsides."

"Targeting accuracy?"

"Not great," Jack said. He was underplaying the *SoD's* capabilities, worried that the rriksti might change their minds about the operation altogether. They were not soldiers. Every passing moment made that clearer. And they were afraid, as the carousing of the rriksti in the passenger cabin proved beyond a doubt. "Look, the reason railguns freak us out is because they can throw projectiles so *fast*. Targeting is a whole different story. Over thousands of kilometers, we're not hitting anything. And that's if the *Krijistal* have even worked out how to use our guns." Fear pinched him. The *Krijistal* could have tortured the information out of Hannah, Kate, and Giles …

"They say they are on the *SoD*, and they have us in their sights," Keelraiser said.

"You're talking to them?!"

"They're threatening to fire on us."

Eskitul said in its deep melancholy voice, "They're like children. They can't help it."

"They may believe you aren't on board," Keelraiser snapped. "They may think you stayed behind on the surface, as you should have!"

Jack stared at the crimson polyhedron. The *SoD* had to be hundreds of kilometers away. Over that distance, he would rate the chances of a hit at 50%. "Are my friends still alive?" His throat constricted with dread.

"We don't know," Keelraiser said.

"Let *me* talk to these bloody *Krijistal!*"

"No," Keelraiser said immediately. "They would only lie to you."

And that makes them different from you, how? The thought flew across Jack's mind, leaving a sulfurous contrail of mistrust..

Eskitul writhed out of its straps and rose from its seat. "They will not fire on us," it said.

"I suppose we'll find out one way or the other," Keelraiser said.

"They will allow us to approach. They wish to end this stand-off, too."

"I refuse to dock the *Cloudeater* with that ship," Keelraiser said.

"There is no need to dock. I will lead the boarding party."

Keelraiser flung its arms in the air and tilted its head back. It made a high-pitched grunting noise in Jack's headset. Jack interpreted this as the rriksti equivalent of *I bloody well give up!* He didn't care. If Eskitul said there was to be a boarding party, there would be. And they could either take Jack along, or throw him out of the airlock, because he wasn't getting left behind. "Shall we suit up now?" he said. Keen as mustard. Me, me, sir. *I'll* do that dodgy-looking bombing run.

Eskitul's hair waved. "Yes. You could use some target practice before we blow those fuckers all the way back to Imf." It added a laughing noise, which sounded like a fifty-decibel fart. Jack clutched his ears and smiled. He was starting to like the eccentric Shiplord.

CHAPTER 39

Boombox wrapped its fingers around Hannah's glove and leapt off the *SoD's* truss tower, into space.

The steel plain overhead seemed to fall towards them, but they were flying towards it. Boombox had tubes the size of salamis strapped to its wrists. They were thrusters, spewing invisible streams of cold gas. In freefall, you needed only a pinch of thrust to change your orientation. They flipped 180 degrees. Hannah's legs went over her head, and they landed with a jolt on the hull. Nearby, a group of aliens nursed a steam hose over a ragged cliff.

Kate had soft-docked the *SoD* with the MOAD, right on the edge of the vast hole in the alien ship's side. The *SoD* floated a few meters above a steel plain that stretched to the horizon, patterned like a giant silicon wafer with heat-rejection pipes and fins. The MOAD wore its circulatory system on the outside. Aft, a magnetoplasmadynamic thruster reared from the plain like a mountain. The sheer scale of the ship boggled Hannah's mind. How advanced did a civilization have to be to build something like this?

She snatched one last look at the *SoD*, silhouetted against the waxing blob of Jupiter. Every antenna and rim thruster stood out. Her heart filled with love for their battered old design disaster of a ship, which seemed so small and helpless in comparison to this monster.

Boombox pulled her over the cliff, its wrist rockets puffing.

They descended past the steam hose and the electrical

cables which were vampiring the life out of the *SoD*. Jupiter's light bathed the devastation at the bottom of the hole. They flew over that, and into darkness. An empty cargo hold, Hannah thought, although she couldn't see anything beyond the circles of weak light from Boombox's chest-lamp and her own head-lamp.

Boombox had said it would show her their ship, and the compartment they had prepared for the humans to travel in. She could make sure everything was up to her standards. She would definitely be impressed, it had said, laughing with its hair.

So far, she was mainly impressed by the scale of the ship—and the scale of the disaster that had blown its guts out. Her focus kept splitting between her external surroundings and her immediate surroundings, namely the Z-2. She had worn her spacesuit exactly once before, when she boarded the *SoD* in Earth orbit. Second time out, it was even more nervewracking than she had remembered. All this telemetry flashing in her heads-up display! The noise of her own breath filled her helmet. The suit restricted her freedom of movement, it squeezed her legs like the world's most brutal support hose, and it was so hot that sweat trickled out of her hair. EVA specialists accepted these limitations without much bitching—such is life. Hannah, however, nearly an EVA virgin, felt shocked and embarrassed that this was the state of the art of human suit technology.

Just look at Boombox, swimming easily through the vacuum in its funkadelic full-body wetsuit. Hannah wanted one of *those*.

Love or hate these aliens, you couldn't deny their suit

technology was superior.

In fact, *all* their technology seemed to be superior.

But by how much?

That was the burning question Hannah ached to answer. The future of Earth depended on it.

Boombox towed her through shattered decks. Ice clung to everything. They passed a glistening wall of what looked like Saran Wrap. That would be the cargo hold full of ice, or rather, steam and water, now. The steam hose from the *SoD* vanished into it through a DIY valve port.

They followed a secondary steam hose into a large, low-ceilinged room. Dim blue light gleamed on the frost-coated deck. Overlapping plates of steel, like the carapace of a giant woodlouse, defined a seven-sided polygon. Each side was as long as an RV. *Seven* RVs, parked nose to tail. On one side a heavily shielded box adjoined the polygon.

"This is our reactor," Boombox transmitted into her helmet.

Hannah had visited CERN, walked around the dingy jogging track of the Proton Synchrotron.

This was to that as an iPhone 12 was to a first-generation IBM mainframe.

Suited aliens worked at the injection port on the far side of the torus. "Is that where they're generating protons from our liquid hydrogen?" Hannah demanded.

"Yes."

She saw with a pang that the electrolysis equipment stolen from the *SoD* had been set up nearby. The steam hose whipped across the room. Wisps of vapor jetted into the vacuum.

Boombox landed on the floor and bent its knees to push off again. In that brief instant Hannah felt the violence of the processes concealed from sight. Vibrations from the hammering of the LH2 compressor/chiller travelled up through the soles of her feet. The floor itself seemed to contract and flex, tossing them towards the ceiling. The aliens around the injection port scattered to stations at the vertices of the torus.

"They're almost ready to start the reactor," Boombox said. "Come on. Hurry."

"Why? What's the rush?" Boombox did not answer. Hannah persisted, "You've been here ten years …"

But maybe that's exactly it, she thought. I'd want to get out of here after ten years, too.

Boombox towed her through cavernous holds, down dark corridors lined with tall lockers. The journey lasted so long that Hannah almost ceased to be amazed at the scale of the ship. At last they tumbled into a truck-sized airlock, and then into an open space filled with—a lovely shock, this—sunlight. Yes, light from the actual sun. The whole ceiling was transparent. The sun hung near the middle of the black dome, blotting out all the other stars.

"Is this the human quarters? Pretty spacious …"

Boombox unlatched the rear entry port of her Z-2. With the rush of shipboard air into her suit, a fetid smell reached her nostrils.

"Can you get out of this thing without assistance?" Boombox said, staring at her.

The answer turned out to be no. She ended up on her hands and knees, like a butterfly struggling to emerge from its pupa, knowing she had to be missing a trick. Jack and

Alexei had never needed help getting out of their suits. This was downright humiliating.

Boombox's hands fastened under her armpits. It lifted her out of the suit, into the air. Her feet pedaled off the ground. The long alien fingers moved in her armpits, tickling. An abashed laugh burst from her. "Hee hee hee. Put me down …"

Boombox set her on her feet. She caught her breath, grimacing at the awful smell.

"Now are you impressed?" said the fake Sony stereo, and Hannah's Z-2, faintly, from the floor.

"Yes, I am impressed."

The room, a good thirty meters across, had seven pointed chancels—six on one side, separated into two groups, with a gap of wall in between. One larger chancel opposed them. Same design as an alien's hand. Machinery and furniture crowded the chancels, as if this 'hand' had grabbed up all the useful stuff it could find from all over the ship. Knee-high troughs of soil haphazardly filled the circular center of the room, basking in the sunlight. Things grew in them—fungi, pale-leaved vegetables—or were spilling out of them; many of the troughs had shattered sides. Ten years in orbit. There comes a point when you can't fix things anymore. Tables covered with clutter straddled the troughs. Hoses snaked around the room, dripping water into the vegetables. Soil gritted under Hannah's bare feet.

Yes, *under her feet.*

That was the impressive part.

Her feet rested squarely on the floor, and she could feel her vertebrae compressing, shooting out twinges of pain.

"There's artificial gravity in here." It felt like about 0.5

gees. More than they had on the *SoD*. But the MOAD wasn't rotating. "Have you found the tree that anti-grav effectors grow on?"

Boombox's hair shook. "Just big lumps of iridium." It stalked between the vegetable troughs to a table covered with dirty clothes, which looked like Hannah's sofa back in League City, before she had figured out how to work her washing-machine. Presumably there was no such thing on the *Lightbringer* as a washing-machine. Boombox picked an orange tank top out of the mess and tossed it at her. The garment stank. Hannah put it on; it was better than being in her thin t-shirt and panties. It hung like a dress on her.

"Mass attractors? What a waste," she said. "Lumps of iridium that big would make you millionaires on Earth."

Boombox half-doffed its spacesuit to its waist. It set its hands to one of the troughs and pushed it to the side of the room. Pale, gladioli-like plants shivered. Soil trailed from a crack. Half-full, the trough must weigh a ton, even in half-strength gravity, but Boombox didn't sound out of breath when it next spoke. Of course, it didn't use its *lungs* to talk.

"What did you think of the reactor? When we passed through the reactor room, they were chilling it down. You may have felt the electromagnets contracting."

It was not easy for Hannah to think clearly, weary and frightened as she was. But she knew she had to convince the aliens that human beings were their intellectual equals. The fate of humanity might depend on Hannah Ginsburg's expertise.

She was an engineer. Not a nuclear physicist. But she'd spent enough time around the Rosatom boys. When they got drunk, they loved to talk about nuclear fusion: the what-ifs, the might-works. That was where she'd learned about the Coulomb barrier. And after seeing the *size* of the aliens' fusion reactor—seeing that the containment torus was *not* the size of the CERN accelerator complex, but much, much smaller—she had an idea how it probably operated.

"You must have developed a gauge field that you impose on the lithium target," she hazarded. "Inside that field, the strong force becomes strongly attractive at greater distances than normal. That's how you break the Coulomb barrier. Am I warm?"

Boombox stared at her, the bio-antennas around its face straightening out like rays. "Go on," said the voice from the boombox balancing on the dirty clothes.

"I'm reasoning backwards from the assumption that fusion occurs at temperatures well below the threshold where the entire target would fuse into a superatom, then detonate as soon as the field is turned off."

"That is a sound assumption."

"So, this field must enhance the strong force to draw protons into the nucleus at temperatures of ... oh, maybe a couple hundred thousand degrees? As opposed to ten million?"

"It's a very finely balanced thing. You cannot give the field too little power, or too much."

"Or it's hello, Mr. Superatom. And goodbye. Is that what blew a big-ass hole in your ship?"

"No. Our interstellar propulsion system malfunctioned."

"That was one heck of a malfunction," Hannah mumbled. "What about your in-system drive?"

"That still works. It is a larger version of yours."

Hannah sat on the edge of the table covered with dirty clothes, taking the weight off her spine. She hugged herself as the truth sank in. "You're only about a hundred years ahead of us. Maybe only fifty." She was using the number of years as a rough metric for the number of technical breakthroughs that separated the *SoD* from the *Lightbringer*. For instance, she had no idea how to actually generate a gauge field to increase the efficacy of the strong nuclear force. But if they let her have a proper look at the hardware, she could probably figure it out.

She felt both elated and depressed. Her emotions mirrored her innate love of advanced technology, and her relief that the aliens' technology wasn't *more* advanced. There was nothing here beyond the grasp of the human intellect. The *Lightbringer* would not shatter the arc of human history.

And yet, a part of her had hoped to find something incomprehensibly strange, instead of more proof that the universe was the same all the way down.

"What are you *doing?*" she said, as Boombox continued to push the troughs against the walls, clearing the center of the room.

Boombox straightened up. Soil smeared its face. "A VIP is coming on board. I must get the place into a somewhat less disgraceful state."

"A VIP?"

"Don't you refer to your commander as a VIP?"

"No. *Ma'am* sometimes. But mostly we just call her Kate …"

"That seems disrespectful to me. She's a formidable

human being."

"Yes," Hannah agreed. "Yes, she is." Her heart sank as the incongruities between Kate's story and Boombox's story jumped out at her afresh. Kate had said the aliens hurt her. Those bruises had been real, all right. Boombox, on the other hand, called Kate 'formidable,' and implied that she should get VIP treatment. Was this somehow the *same* story seen through two opposite sides of an imperfect human-alien linguistic interface? After all, whatever Boombox's native language was, it certainly wasn't English.

She needed Giles. He'd come with them for this very reason. "Where's Giles?" she said.

"Oh, the other one?" Boombox said. "I will bring him to join us soon."

Finished moving the troughs, it picked up a broom and began to sweep up the loose dirt. The humble broom: a piece of technology so perfectly suited for its purpose that it looked pretty much the same on Earth and Proxima b. Sitting on the table with her arms curled around her knees, Hannah wondered how many more such examples there were. Did the aliens have bicycles? Fishing rods? She already knew they had reactors and high-tech Saran Wrap.

Again wistfulness touched her. Never fully acknowledged, a childhood dream was dying. Once, a very long time ago, she'd gazed up at the stars and *known* that whatever was out there, it must be magic.

As Boombox swept, patterns came into view on the floor. The circular mosaics reminded Hannah of Roman frescoes. Pompeii meets the 1970s. Aliens were depicted in symmetrical poses like Rorschach blots, laying their hands on parts of each other's anatomy, which unfortunately was too stylized to deliver any information about alien private parts.

"Don't you have ESP or anything?" she said.

"ESP?"

"Oh, you know. Telepathic powers. Anything like that."

Boombox stood its broom against the wall. It sat on the table beside her. Its feet reached the ground, although the table was as high as a kitchen counter. *"Some* of us are extroverted," it said.

"Extroverted?"

"I am very extroverted."

"Uh, I think we have a translation glitch here."

"I am certified as a seventh-level lay cleric."

"That's nice, I guess ..."

"Others are not extroverted at all."

"No?"

"That is probably why your friends died."

The off-hand reference to Skyler, Jack, Alexei, and Meili caught Hannah like a sucker-punch in the gut. She tried to power through it, breathing deeply, willing her emotions to stay under control. It was no good. There were limits to what a person could take and keep smiling.

"They never had a chance, did they?" she said.

"I don't know. I wasn't there. But the surface of Europa is a hostile environment, even for us. Your bodies are just not made for it."

The brutal, truthful epigraph overcame her. Tears burst from her eyes. She hid her face in her knees, sobbing.

Boombox's fingers fastened in her hair. It gently raised her face and stared, apparently puzzled. Hannah kept crying.

The alien reached out and wiped one finger under her

eyes. It sniffed the finger, and then put it in its mouth.

"What are you doing?" it said at last.

"I'm crying," Hannah sobbed. "Don't you cry?"

"Not with our eyes."

"Oh." She cried harder.

"Are you hurt?"

"In here," Hannah said, placing one hand over her left breast to indicate her heart. "Yes. I'm hurt."

"I can help you."

"No, you can't. Leave me alone."

"I am extroverted."

"Whatever. Sorry. It just hurts so much."

Boombox slid one arm under her legs and deftly tilted her over backwards. She landed on her back on the dirty clothes. A musty, salty reek puffed up around her.

She struggled to sit up, panicking. Boombox's hands came down on her shoulders and forced her back. It leaned over her, bringing its face close to hers.

She flashed back on the frightening moment in the engineering module when Jack had held her powerless. *Let me go. I don't think you mean that.*

That had been bad. This was much, much worse. The thing leaning over her was not even human.

"I can help you," it said.

She wanted to scream, but there was no one to hear her. What an idiot she'd been! To come aboard an alien spaceship, alone, unarmed—oh, *damn* it, I never was the adventurous type. I shouldn't even have tried.

"Hold *still.*"

Boombox pulled her tank top aside. It ripped the neck of her t-shirt, exposing her breasts. Then it laid one large hand on her left breast, completely engulfing it.

Hannah waited in dread for something else to happen—alien rape? How much worse could this get? Don't answer that.

What happened was that a cool, refreshing sensation spread from the alien's hand into her breast. Little by little, it percolated through her body, like gradual submersion into a cool jacuzzi. Her hot, aching, weary body yearned to plunge all the way in right now. The slow spread of the feeling tantalized her. She arched her back, pushing up against the alien's hand. Boombox bore down. It had a strange expression on its face, even more inscrutable than usual; it seemed to be looking *through* her, not at her.

At last it relaxed. Leaning over her, it met her eyes. By now the delicious coolness had reached Hannah's fingers and toes and the roots of her hair. Her nipple was hard under the alien's palm. She had a funny taste of garlic in her mouth.

"Do you feel better now?" Boombox said.

"I feel *great*. What did you do?"

"You had an early-stage cancer, here." It withdrew its hand from her breast. "I am surprised you could feel it. It was very small."

Hannah sat up. She gripped her torn t-shirt together over her breasts. "I have *cancer?*"

"It was only a small one."

"But I've been tested! I had the test for the BRCA1 and BRCA2 genes. So did my sister. We were both fine." Quivering in horror, Hannah thought of Bethany. *Oh my God.* If Hannah had breast cancer, maybe Bee-Bee did, too! These genetic tests didn't guarantee anything …

The next instant, she remembered it probably wasn't genetic. She'd been in freaking *space* for two years. That would do it.

I'm going to die. I'm going to die.

But wait. Boombox had said ... "It's *gone?*"

"Yes. I took it away."

"How'd you do that?"

Boombox stretched out one hand with all seven fingers stiffly splayed. The same gesture shown in the mosaics on the floor. "I'm extroverted." it said. "I told you."

Hannah didn't know whether to laugh or cry. Was this the magic she'd yearned for? Or some kind of elaborate alien joke?

Assuming Boombox wasn't joking, an instantaneous cancer cure didn't *have* to be a supernatural feat. Any sufficiently advanced technology is indistinguishable from magic. Clarke got that right back in the 1970s. Maybe Boombox was crawling with nanites, small enough to crawl through the pores of the skin, programmed to destroy cancer cells. Earth's biotechnologists were already working on that line of research. Or maybe it was something else, something Hannah could not possibly imagine. Maybe she was wrong that the aliens were only 100 years ahead of humanity. Maybe they were *thousands* of years ahead. Or maybe their development had been asymmetrical, giving them godly powers in the arena that, after all, mattered most to biological beings: the control and maintenance of the body ...

She looked up at the tall, Olympian being before her, and started to cry again.

Hannah Ginsburg was a bit of a control freak. Surprise,

surprise. Her unhealthy love of booze complemented her need to control her environment—and most definitely her own body. As much as she might have yearned for some revelation that would save her from herself, she now felt overwhelmed by the mysteries piling up all around her. First contact sucked. She was calling it quits. It was all just too fucking weird.

Boombox regarded her for another moment. Then it ducked under the table and picked it up, Hannah and all.

"Hey!" she yelled, laughing in fright. She clung to the edges of the table as the alien carried it across the now-uncluttered expanse of the bridge.

Boombox put the table, and Hannah, down by the entrance to one of the aft chancels. "I will take you home," it said.

"Don't get my hopes up," she said wearily.

"You are an accomplished propulsion technician."

"According to my sister, I'm a great engineer but a shitty human being," Hannah said. Having thought about Bethany, she couldn't un-think about her. She had to see her family. Nothing else would begin to heal the wounds of this nightmare.

"All our engineers died in the explosion."

Hannah laughed. "So those guys bringing the reactor online right now are actually, what, they aren't technicians at all? Holy shit. I hope this thing has ejection seats."

"I want you to be our propulsion technician."

You must be kidding. Hannah almost said it, and then she thought *Kate* and then she thought *Giles.* For their sakes, she could give it a try. After all, what was the alternative?

"All right," she said, "just as long as you lay off the, uh,

342

extroverted stuff. No more messing with me. OK?"

"You may decide you want me to mess with you," Boombox said.

Hannah shook her head firmly. Once had been enough. "No."

"You will change your mind," Boombox said.

She saw the alien's huge fist draw back, but she did not have time to move before it crashed into her forehead.

CHAPTER 40

Jack clung to a strap, floating in pitch darkness, jostled between rriksti bodies. It reminded him of jump training. The tight embrace of his rriksti spacesuit also reminded him of the wetsuit he'd worn for that unforgettable adventure. "Hey, Skyler?"

"What?" said Skyler, from somewhere else in the *Cloudeater's* cargo hold. It was amazing how much fear the man could pack into one monosyllable.

"When I was in pilot training, we had to do a parachute jump into the North Sea. It was a joint effort with some troglodytes from the Parachute Brigade. Go! Go! Go!" Jack recalled, laughing under his breath. "It wasn't so much 'go' as get pushed out of the door. Anyway, I was the last one out. The rescue boat had already headed for home, as it was time for tea. I had to swim to shore, fighting off sharks with my flare pistol ..."

"This was his Chuck Norris training," Alexei told the rriksti gravely. They had never got around to correcting the record with regard to Chuck Norris, whom the rriksti believed to be a special forces unit. "For my own Chuck Norris training, I had to kill one hundred men simultaneously with a machine-gun."

"There are no sharks in the North Sea," Skyler said. "Are there?"

Jack and Alexei cracked up.

The *Cloudeater* was creeping up on the *Lightbringer* from below, backthrusting, and Jack was remembering how keen he'd been when he first joined the RAF, and what it had felt like to go into battle, when he first got to Iraq, before anyone died. He'd never shared this with anyone, as it went against the general presumption that one was just doing one's job—you were supposed to buy into all that maddening vague talk about *reducing forces* and *degrading potential*—but the fact was he had harbored a strong desire to kill Iraqis. He'd even fantasized about getting shot down and taking out ragheads bloodily, on his own, before they captured him. At root it was a primal curiosity about death. Of course that had gone away after the war, when the toll sank in, and worse yet, when the dossier revealing Blair's deception emerged, he'd begun to feel ashamed of taking part in the war at all. But the happy warrior had *not* gone away—he'd only gone to ground in some deep corner of Jack's psyche.

Now, Jack deliberately summoned that version of himself. He excised premonitions of shame and regret from his mind. Reminded himself that he most likely would not live long enough to regret this, anyway. He was psyching himself up to kill as many people as he could.

The *Krijistal* wear flower-patterned suits, or else black ones, Eskitul had said. We'll have blue bands around our limbs, so you can tell us apart.

It turned out that the rrikstis' suits were only white for purposes of camouflage on Europa. They had chameleon functionality, and right now they were stealthed black, except for the identification bands. These ironically turned out to be the shade of blue favored by the UN, which also made an appearance in the *SoD's* logo. In the blacked-out cargo hold, they were invisible, anyway.

"Velocity five meters per second," Keelraiser said calmly in their headsets, having relayed the same information to the rriksti in their own language.

Jack cradled his blaster in his free arm. It was on a tether attached to a belt around his waist. He also had wrist rockets: tubes of compressed CO_2 strapped to his forearms, for maneuvering in freefall. It was humbling to bear in mind that all this fantastic kit was merely odds and ends left over from the rrikstis' ten-year survival feat. The *Cloudeater* had had mobility pods originally, but they'd been dismantled for materials.

"Velocity three meters per second," Keelraiser said.

They were rising up alongside the gargantuan *Lightbringer*. The plan was for Keelraiser to drop them right into the massive hole in the side of the ship. It was unknown, apparently, what kind of resistance they might meet. Keelraiser refused to dock the *Cloudeater* with the *Lightbringer*. The shuttle was unarmed, so it was going to stand off, out of reach of any man-portable weapons the *Krijistal* might have.

"I see the *SoD*," Keelraiser said. "It's docked on the edge of the hole."

Alexei shouted, "Docked?!"

"There are cables connecting the two ships." Keelraiser paused. "They have begun harvesting resources from the *SoD*. There are *Krijistal* around it ..."

Eskitul's deep voice broke in. "We continue with the operation. We will board the *Lightbringer* and put an end to this. However, if the humans wish to return to their ship ..."

"They'll die," Keelraiser said. "Look at that! The *schleerps* are shooting at us!" Its voice scaled up into the rriksti frequencies and was lost to hearing.

Jack grimaced. It sounded as if Keelraiser was getting a bit windy. But Jack had made his own mind up on the spot. The situation was worse than he'd expected. There was no time to spare. "We'll get off here, Eskitul," he said. "Thanks for the lift."

"I cannot offer you any backup."

"Chuck Norris spits on backup," Alexei said.

"I completely understand," Jack said more diplomatically. "You take care of your own business. We've got this."

He pushed off and flew towards the loading door at the rear of the shuttle. It was just like a C-130. He might even get splinters in his arse sliding down that ramp, if there were any gravity. Jupiter-light shone in like a stormy sunset. Jack beheld the *Lightbringer,* a steel crag tilted at a crazy angle, close enough to hit with a well-flung rock. Jesus, Keelraiser was cutting it close! What a madman! Mad alien, I mean!

Another human-sized figure flew past Jack. That was Alexei. His rriksti suit trapped his splinted right arm against his side, leaving him free to move it from the elbow down. He held his blaster in his left hand. CO_2 vapor spurted from his wrist rockets. Jack reached for the twist-dials of his own rockets, eager not to get left in Alexei's dust.

Then he flipped in the air so he was flying backwards. He scanned the figures strap-hanging against the walls.

There.

He changed direction with a flourish of his arm, and zoomed at the small weedy figure trying to hide among the tall ones.

He grabbed Skyler's arm.

Skyler struggled wildly.

"You," Jack said, voice thick with contempt, "are *not*

getting out of this."

He kicked off from the wall and flew headlong for the exit, dragging Skyler with him.

Sparks flashed off the roof of the cargo bay.

The *Krijistal* were shooting into the shuttle.

The ramp started to close.

Jack opened the throttles of his wrist rockets all the way and hurtled out over the top of the ramp, instinctively diving to put the *SoD's* main hab between himself and the aliens.

*

The shuttle meandered onward over the vast crater in the *Lightbringer's* side.

As Jack and Skyler fell, the *SoD's* main hab rose up like a steel moon and hid the *Cloudeater* from sight.

Jack let go of Skyler. He transferred both hands to his blaster and got both index fingers around the trigger.

A black-suited alien flew over the top of the main hab, silhouetted against Jupiter.

Jack squeezed the trigger. He saw exactly what happened next in horrifying detail.

The alien started to come apart at one side of its torso, like a paper doll ripped by an angry child. Blood jetted into the vacuum, shining red, turning to spears of dark ice. The rip opened wider. Jack's invisible beam was raking across the alien's body. A linear gout of blood spurted out. The two halves of the body separated.

The top half drifted away across Jupiter's disk.

A javelin of frozen blood flew past Jack's head, followed by the alien's bottom half.

He distantly heard Skyler screaming in his headset.

He flew after the alien's top half and recovered the weapon still clutched in its hand. It looked like a Super Soaker water pistol, but Jack felt sure it did something supremely nasty.

While he was up there he had a look for Alexei. He didn't see him, but he spotted more aliens heading his way. They'd been hanging out near the storage module. Now they were spreading out to circle around the main hab.

A spot on the rim of the hab began to glow red-hot.

Then another.

Jack returned fire, first with his captured Super Soaker, then with his blaster. He didn't think he hit anything. If hitting a moving target while you yourself were moving was hard on Earth, it was an order of magnitude harder in zero-gee, where every action induced an equal and opposite reaction. Jack's first kill had been pure luck. But for the same reasons, the *Krijistal* weren't hitting him, so it was a wash.

"Alexei! Alexei, where are you?" he yelled.

"Hold still so we can kill you," purred an unknown rriksti voice.

"No thanks."

Jack flipped and dived back behind the main hab.

Skyler had not even tried to engage the enemy. He'd made straight for what must look to him like safety. He was crawling over the outside of the bridge module, heading for the airlock hatch.

Jack flew towards him, glancing at his captured Super Soaker to see if he could make out how many more shots it had in it.

The bridge airlock opened. A *Krijistal* bounded out. It grabbed the edge of the hatch for stability and leveled its weapon at Skyler.

Jack slammed into it from behind. Catching it by the gun arm, he pressed his blaster into the back of its neck and sawed its head off.

The blood spurted up so high it looked like the *Krijistal* had turned into a Golden Flower Fountain firework, except the flowers were red.

"Remember, remember, the fifth of November," Jack muttered, letting the body go.

"What?" Skyler shouted, after he stopped screaming.

"Gunpowder, treason, and plot," Jack told him. "Don't get the idea I saved your life on purpose. The bastard was in the way, that's all."

Skyler dropped feet-first into the airlock chamber. Jack joined him before the little twat could slam the hatch. Tight squeeze! He wriggled around so his head was alongside Skyler's feet.

Then they had to wait out the pressurization cycle.

"The inside of the outer hatch," said Skyler, who could see it, "is starting to glow red."

"They're wasting juice," Jack said. "Once the cycle finishes, they'll be able to come in the usual way, by opening the hatch. I wish we could lock it from the inside. I suppose the designers never envisioned this. They should have, though, shouldn't they? They should have."

The cycle finished. Jack undogged the inner hatch and hurtled into the bridge, sweeping it with his Super Soaker.

The bridge had only one occupant.

Kate.

She floated in a slowly spreading aurora of blood and fluid globules. Jack couldn't see any gaping wounds on her.

However, he had never seen such bruises and contusions on a living human being. He wouldn't even have known it was Kate if not for her short blonde hair.

"All dead, or mostly dead?" he muttered, in a trance, riding out his own horrified reaction. "If it's the former, there's only one thing to do …"

"Go through their pockets for loose change," said Alexei, in his headset. "I'm in the storage module. I hid until the fuckers got out of the way, and then sneaked in. There was one in the engineering module. I killed it. These blasters are great. Hannah's not here. The reactor is running flat out; I don't want to touch anything. Where are you?"

"Bridge," Jack said. "With Skyler." Alexei sounded pumped. A happy warrior. How was Jack going to tell him Kate was dead? The pressure door in the aft wall of the bridge was open. UV light shone down the tube from the main hab, a heartbreaking touch of normality.

"Is Kate there?" Alexei asked.

Get it over with, Jack told himself. "Alexei, she's dead, I'm afraid. I'm very sorry."

Alexei let loose a stream of Russian. The bits Jack understood were filthy, the tone highly emotional.

"Just think about how many of them you're going to kill for her," he shouted, and then Skyler waved to attract his attention.

"She's alive!" Skyler exclaimed. "Guys, she's trying to say something!"

"Fuck, you scared me!" Alexei said. "I'm coming! Stay there! I'll go through the main hab."

"No, stay where you are," Jack shouted, knowing Alexei would ignore him. He flew over to Skyler and Kate.

351

Her eyelids trembled. Her split, swollen lips seemed to be forming words.

With their rriksti suits on, Jack and Skyler couldn't hear anything from the outside world.

Jack turned the inside of his left wrist up. He found the rough spot Hriklif had showed him and pressed twice, quickly. His suit flowed down to his waist. He inhaled the rank air of the *SoD*. The familiar noise of the fans drowned out Kate's groans.

"Guard the keel tube," Jack snapped at Skyler. He flew to the first-aid locker. He tore into the trauma kit and found a syringe of auto-regulated morphine, a safe painkiller developed by DARPA. The only thing he could do for Kate right now was relieve the incredible pain she must be suffering. "Make a fist, love."

"Didn't tell them," she croaked.

"The bastards who did this to you? We're going to destroy them."

"Destroy them? After we came all this way?" Kate's lips twitched as if she were trying to smile.

Jack bowed his head and pressed Kate's fist against his forehead. "You were right. We should have nuked the bloody thing the moment we got here."

"Damn skippy."

"Go on, say it: 'I told you so.'"

She freed her hand and weakly tweaked his earlobe, an old trick of hers. "Better late than never, Killer."

Jack cast an uneasy glance up at the airlock hatch. It was about time for the *Krijistal* to burst in, if they were going to. Sure enough, the pressure indicator showed that the airlock was cycling.

In a hurry, Jack searched for a vein on Kate's horrifically bruised arm, pushed the syringe in, and pulled it back a little. Not enough blood. Missed the damn vein. He turned her over and injected her in one buttock, hating that he was hurting her more.

"Oh, that feels cold," she rasped. "Kinda like what they do, before they hit you again."

"Sssh. Don't try to talk."

"I didn't."

"This should kick in within a few seconds."

"Didn't tell them how to … operate the guns." Kate smiled. Blood welled from her lips. "Told them to … get fucked."

"You're a rock star, ma'am," Jack said. "We're going to deal with the ones trying to get in here, then we'll stand off and nuke 'em."

"No."

"No?"

Her smile faded. "They took … Hannah."

"Oh God, Kate."

"Giles … too. Aboard … *Lightbringer.*"

"We'll get them back," Jack said, praying that Eskitul's boarding operation succeeded. He withdrew the syringe from Kate's backside. Letting her go, he grabbed his blaster and frantically adjusted the beam strength.

The airlock hatch opened. An otherworldly shriek pierced the air.

CHAPTER 41

Two aliens swam into the bridge, firing their Super Soakers. The weapons made an absolutely horrible noise, as if the invisible beams emitted from their muzzles tortured the very air molecules they encountered.

Skyler dived for the keel tube.

Cowardly twat.

Molten droplets sprayed from the aft wall, adding the reek of burning plastic to the ozone smell of ionized air.

Several priorities competed in Jack's mind.

Kill kill kill, but—

Shooting up the bridge of the *SoD* would be just disastrous as getting shot by the *Krijistal,* in the longer term.

With this in mind he had already dialed his blaster's beam power back to minimum. He held down the trigger and swung the beam across the aliens' black-shrouded faces.

The beam left a visible track in the air, because the air was so damn dirty. It ignited dust and flies. It caught the empty syringe Jack had dropped and made it glow. Floating globules of Kate's blood boiled into vapor.

The aliens dropped their weapons and clutched their faces … blinded.

Now they could no longer see, they fired wildly, making red-hot holes in the aft wall.

Jack hugged the ceiling and drilled Super Soaker shots into the tops of their heads.

The Super Soaker hollowed out the insides of their skulls, vaporizing the contents into thin air. A faint blue glow dispersed. Interesting.

The aliens' suits tried to seal over the holes. Smart

material? Not so smart after all, trying to save the dead.

An indicator on the life-support console flashed. A buzzer sounded. The environmental radiation monitoring system had just picked up a spike in radioactivity.

Jack floundered over to the console and silenced the annoying buzzer. The movement caused him to rebound into the middle of the bridge. Pushing the *Krijistal* corpses away, he squinted up into the empty airlock chamber.

"Close it," Kate rasped.

She sounded a bit more together. The morphine must be kicking in. And she hadn't been hit. The day was looking up.

"I was just wondering if I should go out and head them off before they try that again," Jack said. "These water-pistol efforts seem to give off quite a lot of radioactivity."

"Screw that, Killer. Close the airlock and prepare to launch. We'll back off so they can't board us again."

"They've been stealing our water, haven't they? Have we got enough left to move the ship?"

"Dunno. Try."

Jack moved his headset's mic closer to his mouth. "Alexei! I'm up to four. I'm beating your kill count, you pussy."

No answer.

Jack's heart sank. "Kate, I'm just going to check on Alexei's progress."

"Is he *alive?*"

"I hope so," Jack muttered. He flew to the keel tube and floated down the padded tunnel, gripping his blaster in both hands in front of him.

A shadow blotted out the light at the end of the tunnel. Jack's fingers spasmed.

The blaster's stiff trigger pull saved Skyler's life. Before Jack could complete the pull, Skyler cannoned into him, empty hands stretched out to break his fall. His momentum pushed them both back into the bridge.

Jack kicked Skyler aside and flew back to the tube, just in time to drill a *Krijistal* in the face. He was not fast enough to stop it from getting off a shot.

Behind him, Kate screamed.

Skyler flew to the pressure door crank and twirled it frantically. The pressure door slid out of its housing in the aft wall and began to close..

Another *Krijistal* shouldered into the keel tube behind the one Jack had killed.

Head down on the aft wall, toes tucked through a grab handle on the ceiling, Jack squeezed off one more blaster shot through the closing door.

The heavy steel door sighed shut.

Alexei suddenly shouted in their headsets, "I'm falling back to the storage module!"

"There are fucking thousands of them!" Jack bellowed. "Are you hit?"

"It's only a scratch," Alexei grunted. "Closing the pressure door now. Oh, you fucker! *Svoloch!*"

Jack pushed off from the aft wall, flipping in the air, to check on Kate.

Hot liquid splashed into his face. He tasted blood, and dashed it out of his eyes.

Kate bucked spasmodically.

The *Krijistal's* shot had caught her on the thigh.

Arterial blood skipped across the bridge in bright red zero-gee ropes.

Jack gathered her into his arms, wedged her upper body between his chest and thighs, clamped his hands over the wound.

Blood jetted out between his fingers.

"Get me the first aid kit!" he bawled. "*SKYLER!* I need a tourniquet! Bandages! Right fucking *now!*"

Skyler didn't react. Just floated near the ceiling, eyes bugging out.

Kate died in Jack's arms.

"Oh Jesus," Jack said. "Oh, ma'am. This is a bad day."

He hugged her tightly and then let go of her. Her blood was all over the bridge. It was going to get into the electronics.

He screamed at Skyler until his voice cracked, ordering him to clean the blood up since he was completely fucking unfit for any other imaginable purpose. While he yelled, he was collecting all the loose weapons floating around—two blasters, three Super Soakers—and clipping them to his belt like some kind of piratical hula skirt. After a while he noticed that Alexei was shouting in his headset, desperate to know what had happened.

Jack laid out the facts of Kate's death. As he spoke, he distanced himself from what he was saying by wondering what had happened to Eskitul and the rest of the boarding party.

CHAPTER 42

A tumult of alien chatter roused Hannah from her despairing doze.

The voices came from the fake Sony stereo, which Boombox had left at the foot of the bunk where it laid her. The equalizer display pulsed in a range labeled 600 – 2000 KHz. These gutturals and trills must be the aliens' own language, transposed into the audible range.

She was lying in the chancel where Boombox and its fellows presumably slept, on a bunk near the back of the chancel, head-height off the ground. She sat up and slapped the top of the boombox, trying to turn it off.

Sitting up made her head hurt. She touched the tender place above her left eyebrow. Boombox had sucker-punched her. After all that shop-talk and banter, after it cured her of *cancer* ... it had just up and slugged her in the face. *Pow.*

The voices grew louder. Giving up hope of escaping once more into oblivion, Hannah lay on her stomach and propped her chin on her folded arms.

From here, she could see out between the other bunks into the center of the bridge.

A tall alien strode into her field of view, wearing a black spacesuit *under* a weird formal outfit. A bright red split skirt swished around bare, seven-clawed feet. The Roman Empire meets martial arts, Hannah thought. Nifty.

As the alien advanced, its spacesuit flowed away, exposing pale skin where its face and arms stuck out of its toga-style top, and bronze hair.

This must be Boombox's VIP, Hannah realized. Boombox hadn't been talking about Kate at all. Hannah had just misinterpreted things. Heard what she wanted to hear. *This* was the one Boombox had been waiting for.

Boombox itself strutted into her field of view, arms folded behind its back. It wore a formal outfit of its own, a dress uniform, perhaps: a Napoleonic-looking jacket, with orange Bermuda shorts flapping around its thin legs.

A horde of other aliens followed, as many as a hundred of them, some in uniforms, some in spacesuits. If Boombox had not tidied up the bridge, there literally wouldn't have been room for all of them. They stood in a crowd. Their chatter faded to silence.

The alien in the red toga headed for the forward chancel. Hannah maneuvered herself into a sitting position again. Now she could see over the heads of the crowd.

Red Toga was inspecting the machinery in the forward chancel. Holographic readouts twinkled on the walls. Looked like the power was on. They'd got the reactor online without blowing up the ship; well done, guys.

The alien voices coming from the boombox fell into a question and answer pattern. The questioner was Red Toga, based on the timing of the movements of its bio-antennas. It was mostly Boombox responding. The dynamic made Hannah think of a manager visiting the production floor, pre-disposed to find fault with everything.

Her mind kept throwing up these terrestrial analogies, but she knew it wasn't helping her to understand the aliens. They were not human. At. All.

One of Red Toga's hench-aliens pushed through the crowd, heading straight for the chancel where Hannah was hidden. This alien was 'only' about seven feet tall, neatly built, with black bio-antennas that gleamed coppery in the light from the starscape ceiling. It slid into the shadows like a knife. Hannah cringed. The alien saw her. Its bio-antennas thrashed. Alien cries exploded from the boombox, and dozens of them crushed into the chancel, staring at her.

Boombox shouldered through the crowd and lifted Hannah down from the bunk. It carried her—in its arms, cradling her like a child—to the forward chancel, where Red Toga waited.

"So you kept one," the boombox said, somewhere behind her. She assumed the speaker was Red Toga. It had a hollow, mellifluous voice.

"She is a propulsion technician," Boombox said, hugging Hannah to its chest. Its skin felt like suede, somewhat sticky. She thought about biting or scratching, but she knew that wouldn't get her far.

"Hello," said Red Toga. "I am Eskitul."

Hannah reluctantly met its big, reddish-dark eyes. Eskitul seemed melancholy and kind, but Hannah didn't trust herself to be right about the aliens anymore.

She freed one arm and pushed her tangled hair out of her face. "Eskitul," she croaked, "is that alien for *asshole?* Or *lying shithead?*"

Boombox, holding her tighter, said, "It means Shiplord. Eskitul is my commander. For ten years we have been estranged. But now the Shiplord has returned to the *Lightbringer,* and our mission can resume!"

From the way Boombox was holding her, like a man gripping a gun, Hannah sensed its excitement. This Shiplord's return was a huge deal for Boombox, and apparently for all the aliens.

She croaked, "I get it. The rest of you guys were stuck on

the surface. The *Lightbringer* didn't have enough resources to support everyone. So Boombox stayed up here, holding the fort. There was nothing else to be done … until we got here. Now you've cannibalized the *SoD's* resources to get your reactor online, you're back in business."

"Not exactly," Eskitul said. "But close enough."

"What am I missing?"

Another voice said, "Water and power are *not* everything. Ripstiggr would be helpless to operate the drive without you, Shiplord."

"Iristigut," Eskitul said. The syllables came out like a drum-roll, a warning rumble.

Boombox snapped, "I cracked the encryption years ago, for your information, Iristigut."

"Bullshit," said the unseen alien named Iristigut. "The universe would contract into a singularity before you got past that encryption, for it was designed specifically to stop you, or someone like you, from taking over."

Hannah knew this Iristigut person was speaking English for her benefit. It was trying to tell her what she was missing. She wriggled out of Boombox's arms and landed on her feet. She peered around Boombox's body to see which alien was speaking. But there was no way to tell; all of them were waving their bio-antennas.

"Enough!" Eskitul boomed. "I will end this, as it should always have been ended!"

Alien yells swallowed the end of this sentence. Hannah's gaze shot to a disturbance in the crowd. Boombox's people were piling onto the lone dissenter, this Iristigut, punching and kicking it.

Eskitul's voice rose over the clamor, calming the crowd.

The ranks of the aliens reformed as the unseen Iristigut elbowed its way out of the crowd, abandoning the argument.

Hannah felt abandoned, too. She said, "What was all that about encryption?"

Eskitul glanced down at her, with a suggestion of a sad smile in its eyes. "I am the Shiplord. That means I alone can authorize access to the *Lightbringer's* drive controls. I have the car keys, as you might put it ... *here.*" It touched the back of its neck.

"Oh boy," Hannah said. "An implant."

"A key. The encryption that safeguards this 'car' of ours against unauthorized operation is meant to be unbreakable. However, there's no such thing as an absolutely failure-proof system. I had to consider that Ripstiggr might have cracked the encryption. More probably, had I refused to return, Ripstiggr would have built a landing craft—now that the reactor is back online, the onboard shipyard can be stood up in a matter of weeks. They threatened to come down to the surface to kidnap me, and kill everyone else. So I gave myself up to save my people. This way, at least they have a chance."

Hannah laughed until she cried. She was on the verge of an emotional meltdown, anyway. It could go either way. "I thought you were all on the same side?!?"

"We are now," Boombox said, pulling her into the cage of its arms.

She felt the nearness of the aliens behind them, blocking the entrance to the drive chancel. Those were all Boombox's people. The Shiplord, for all its fancy-schmancy title, was just as much a prisoner as she was.

Yet Eskitul's proud bearing betrayed no lack of confidence. It turned to the consoles that lined the walls of the chancel. Screens and 3D holographic displays lit up, apparently tracking its gaze. Well, *that* wasn't magic. Gaze-controlled computers were only about ten years in the future of humanity.

"Reactor output ninety percent," Eskitul murmured. "Turbines operational. Working fluid sufficient."

High on the wall at the end of the chancel, a new 3D image appeared. Homesickness pierced Hannah like a knife to the belly. It was an image of Earth. That misty blue-and-white sphere cradled everything she cared about.

"Engage the main drive," Eskitul sighed.

A new group of readouts lit up. A vibration rippled into the soles of Hannah's feet—the steam turbines ramping up their output, feeding the unimaginable power of the proton-lithium-6 reactor into the *Lightbringer's* gigantic thrusters.

Contradictory emotions of hope and despair ripped into her heart like tidal forces.

The *Lightbringer* was on the move for the first time in ten years.

Heading for Earth.

Taking her with it.

Leaving the *SoD* behind, and her crew dead or dying.

That's what you get for trusting an alien, Hannah-banana.

CHAPTER 43

The *SoD* jolted. Jack's fingers slipped as he worked the drive controls console. He'd been checking on their reaction mass status—zero, as expected. He cursed and floated out of his seat. "What the hell now?" he asked.

No one answered him. Skyler huddled in the left seat, snivelling. Kate sat in the center seat, dead. Jack had strapped her in so she wouldn't float around. Her head lolled, her mouth hung open. As for the two dead *Krijistal* bumping around behind Jack's seats, their brains had been vaporized, so they weren't talking, either.

"Alexei?"

Alexei was stuck in the rear of the ship. There were eight *Krijistal* in the main hab. The internal monitoring camera feeds that Jack could access from the bridge showed them squashed into the axis tunnel. They weren't moving, they weren't talking; maybe they were dead, but that would be a risky assumption to make. Anyway, Alexei couldn't reach the bridge without going through them. He was marooned aft.

"Did you feel that?" Jack said.

Instead of Alexei, an unknown rriksti voice spoke in his headset. "Bye bye, suckers," it said sepulchrally.

"Eskitul?" Jack yelled. But the voice was wrong.

Alexei came on the radio. "The *Lightbringer's* moving." he said. "What we just felt is the *SoD* tumbling off the hull."

The bridge tilted slowly around Jack. "You know what this means?"

"Yeah," Alexei said. "Eskitul's gang got slagged. They were civilians. They never had a chance."

"I wonder what happened to Keelraiser." Jack settled his

rriksti mouthpiece over his lips.

"Fucked off back to the surface, I'm sure. If I have a working shuttle, I do the same."

"We're still connected by the umbilicals. Steam hose, electrical cables." As Jack spoke, he was digging his fingers into his left wrist. Intermittent pressure for doffing, continuous pressure for donning. The rriksti suit's smart fabric flowed up over his head and sealed itself.

"Steam hose won't hold for long," Alexei said. He sounded very tired. Jack knew he was wounded but Alexei refused to say how badly. "We're not getting a ride, Jack. They stole our water and electricity, now they're done with us. Fuck it, we're full … bye, fools. And they drive off with the gas pump hose still in the tank."

"I know," Jack said, tearing open the lockers. The *Krijistal's* shooting spree had holed their doors. The contents had been partially melted, partially vaporized. He found what he was looking for and seized it with a grunt of relief. "I'm going out," he told Alexei.

Skyler—who also had a headset on; in fact he had not come out of his rriksti suit the whole time—mooed in fright.

"If I don't come back," Jack told him, "you're in charge. Ha, ha." He tasted blood when he laughed. Shaking his head, he floated into the airlock and pulled the hatch shut after him.

Alexei said, "No, but really."

"And *you're* in charge of killing Skyler," Jack said. Curled in darkness with his awkward burden, he cycled the airlock. The sides of the chamber bumped him. He couldn't tell if he was tumbling, or the *SoD* was.

"Start the drive," Alexei said. "We'll land in the hole in the side. They will take us with them if they like it or not."

Jack didn't bother to say that there was no water left to start the drive *with*. The aliens had drained the primary tank. Alexei knew it. He was just being Russian, acting like machines could run on willpower alone. "Start it yourself," he said. The cycle finished. He undogged the outer hatch. As he rose into space, Alexei's swearing cut out. The alien headsets could barely transmit through the *SoD's* internal pressure doors, and could not transmit at all through the hull. He heard a burst of static, and then nothing.

The universe was a fast-moving 3D jigsaw of metal and darkness. Willy-nilly, his brain organized the puzzle pieces into reality. Jupiter scudded across the sky like a meteor. The *SoD* was falling towards the *Lightbringer*. Its hull bulged up at him. He clutched the grab handle outside the airlock.

The *SoD's* main hab crashed into the side of the *Lightbringer*. Jack's teeth jarred together. Steel scraped steel in a shower of sparks. The *SoD* rebounded into space.

Jack clung for dear life to the grab handle, so he seemed to be standing on his hands as the *SoD* swung away from the *Lightbringer* on the umbilicals that tethered it to the larger ship.

If the *Lightbringer* were an airplane, the *SoD* would bobble back and forth like a pendulum until the lines tore loose. But with zero atmospheric pressure in play, the *SoD* would just keep swinging around, against the *Lightbringer's* direction of travel, until it crashed into the hull again. *Then* the umbilicals would tear loose.

Jack had been told by flight instructors in the RAF that he had the best spatial perception they'd ever seen.

He hoped they'd been right.

Going on sheer instinct, he visualized the arc of the *SoD's* slow swing. They were going to strike the hull ... *there*.

Right on the edge of the hole in the *Lightbringer's* side.

A bit further forward, and they'd go *over* the cliff. The aliens would end up with unwanted hitchhikers. That'd be nice. But Jack could see they weren't going to make it.

So it was a good thing he'd brought a little helper.

The *SoD's* magnetic harpoon gun.

It was one of those gotta-have-it toys foisted on them by the eggheads at NASA. It had come in handy when they were refueling in Earth orbit, but had just been luggage ever since. At one point, Jack and Alexei had taken it on a spacewalk and played with it, shooting at garbage they released into the vacuum. It was tricky to hit anything with the magnetic grapple ...

... but the *Lightbringer* was a flipping huge target.

The *SoD* reached the peak of its swing and heeled over, falling back towards the alien ship.

Jack knelt and jammed the muzzle of the harpoon gun against the grab handle.

He was upside down.

Completely disoriented.

Not aiming. Just praying.

He fired the harpoon gun through the whole row of grab handles. The harpoon arrowed into the void, trailing its spun graphite / aramid fiber-core cable behind it. It vanished over the edge of the cliff.

The *SoD* struck the cliff with shattering force. Jack wrapped his arms around the grab handles. The impact nearly jarred him off the hull. His teeth clicked together. He tasted blood.

Relentlessly, the *SoD* rose into the void for another go-round of its wrecking ball impersonation …

The harpoon cable jerked taut.

"Come on. Come on," Jack begged. His mouth was full of blood. He swallowed it. "Hold, damn you …"

The cable vibrated, soaking up the *SoD's* momentum.

Whatever the harpoon had snagged on, below the cliff-edge, in the icy chaos of the *Lightbringer's* shattered decks, it was holding.

For now.

The barrel of the harpoon gun—a CO_2 canister in a steel housing—ground against the first grab handle, like a toggle on a duffel coat.

Jack didn't even try to retract the cable. The harpoon gun's crank-and-spool mechanism could not possibly haul the mass of the *SoD* through space. It would be enough if it held.

He began to climb down the cable.

It looked like *down,* down to the edge of the cliff, but of course it wasn't really, so he pulled himself hand over hand along the cable, ankles locked around it for stability. His guns floated out, getting in the way of his knees. Hope Alexei figures it out. We've stopped swinging. It's all I can do.

Nearly there, only a little further, and light dazzles me. What the hell? Jupiter's gotten bright.

The light is down in the hole.

The wheel of the *SoD's* main hab, above me, acquires a case of red-hot measles.

Lovely. Nothing says 'nice to see you' like fireworks.

I'll give them fireworks.

Swinging hand over hand, Jack twisted his head around to see how much further he had to go.

A four-legged spider, octopus-headed, swarmed up the tether towards him.

Not human, not human at all.

Jack took one hand off the cable and reached for the nearest of his guns. It had to be the damn blaster, which he could only fire with two hands. No time to fumble for one of the Super Soakers. He took *both* hands off the cable, swinging by his knees, and fired at the alien shape scrambling towards him.

As likely to hit a real spider, upside-down, in the dark..

The alien threw itself on him, pinning his arms in a hug.

Jack struggled, the alien came off the cable, and they both swung free, the cable slicing into the backs of Jack's knees.

He never knew if the grapple tore loose, or if the aliens below sliced the cable.

It went slack.

The *SoD* leapt into space.

Jack and the alien slid down the trailing cable, while the *Lightbringer* surged past like a metal shore, getting further away.

CHAPTER 44

Left alone on the bridge of the *SoD*, Skyler fired up the video comms system. He had a few things to say to Tom Flaherty at the NXC.

He started off by manipulating the camera with his hands, panning it around the bridge, to show the guys at Langley Kate's corpse, and the two *Krijistal* who had died with her. He provided commentary so they'd know what they were seeing, and how it had gotten this way.

While he was doing that, the *SoD* whanged into something with an almighty jolt. Skyler anxiously checked the status of the directional antenna. Whew. Undamaged.

He really wanted them to hear this, especially as he didn't figure Jack was ever coming back.

"Our mission plan was a turd sandwich, hold the bread," he said. "I know, I know, hindsight is 20/20. But *come on,* boss. You set us up for a confrontation. I'm not exempting anyone here—NASA, Roscosmos, CNSA, ESA, JAXA, there's plenty of blame to go around. Blame the weather. Blame the politicians, like you always do. But *we* convinced them to fund the mission, with that vision of a big old alien technology pie in the sky. You told them what you told me. *Now's our chance. We'll grab all the alien shit and keep it for ourselves.*

"With that kind of mindset, is anyone surprised that the aliens did exactly the same thing to us?"

He laughed mirthlessly.

The *SoD* leapt sideways.

Skyler's toes stayed in the foot tethers, but his body peeled out of his seat. He faceplanted on Kate's corpse. He recoiled from her cooling flesh, tacky with blood.

"Oh God," he said. "Oh God."

He stopped recording after that. Well, not quite. He spoke a few more words, staring into the camera, so close that he could see his own haggard reflection in its lens.

"That's about it, Tom. You don't mind if I call you Tom, do you? One last thing: *FUCK OFF. Sir.*"

He smiled.

Transmit.

A second after he pressed the button, the airlock hatch clunked open.

Skyler flew out of his sea. The *SoD* was spinning. The bridge rotated around him, so that the ceiling turned into the floor.

Jack shot up out of the airlock chamber, entangled with an alien in a dead black *Krijistal* suit.

*

Jack kicked his alien assailant off of him. They cannoned in opposite directions. The rriksti bumped into Skyler. Jack grabbed the back of the right-hand seat to break his fall. He dived over it and frantically strapped in.

"It's me!" the alien said, from the headphones of the comms console, which made its voice small and tinny. "Keelraiser!"

"Yeah, I thought it was probably you," Jack said, working the axis precession controls. The *SoD* was tumbling. He had to null out this spin. Slight surges rocked the ship as Jack clutched the reaction wheels. The lights dimmed. This maneuver gobbled electricity. Mercifully, the *Krijistal* had not drained the fuel cells. *Wait wait wait CLUTCH. Wait wait wait.*

"I am sorry," Keelraiser said.

It flew over and squatted above the main screen, at right angles to Jack. It had doffed its spacesuit to its waist. Jack reached up and struck out at it. "Be a good alien and fuck off," he said. "Skyler! Open the pressure door. Keelraiser is going to join its friends in the main hab." He was thinking he might vent the atmosphere from the main hab to kill all the rriksti on board. Wouldn't have to jettison *all* of it. Atmospheric pressure of 4.0 psi or so should sort them.

Skyler, doing as he was told for once, flew to the pressure door and turned the crank. No rriksti sprang in. A glance at the internal camera feed showed that they were still holed up in the axis tunnel. Maybe they were already dead, which would save venting the atmosphere. Deal with Keelraiser later.

"I've broken with Eskitul," Keelraiser said, floating higher, out of Jack's reach.

"They got wiped out, I suppose? I hope you don't think you're going to be safe here. I've had it with you, all of you."

"No."

Jack finished nulling out the *SoD's* spin. He punched up the external camera feed. The *Lightbringer* filled the screen. Faint coronas of red glowed around its thrusters, like the dull glow of red-hot iron. That was black-body radiation from the water plasma spewed out of the *Lightbringer's* mammoth MPD engine. The *Krijistal* were burning hard. But with that much mass to move, it would take the *Lightbringer* ages to spiral out of Europa orbit.

Good.

"Skyler, take the star sights," he ordered. "Hopefully you know how."

"Jack!" Keelraiser said. "Jack! Eskitul is *not* dead!"

That got Jack's attention. "Huh?"

"The Shiplord has reclaimed command of the *Lightbringer.*"

"What?"

"Eskitul has made peace with the *Krijistal.*" Keelraiser's mouth opened in that strange rriksti expression that seemed to combine distress and hilarity. "She has betrayed us. She's betrayed you, she's betrayed me, she's betrayed us all."

"Eskitul is a she?"

Keelraiser threw up its hands. "Not at the moment. But English has only two pronouns."

"Three. He, she, and *it,*" Jack said. *"It* is the one I favor for you lot. Go on. Tell me what happened."

"We boarded the *Lightbringer.* The *Krijistal* were waiting for us. They put up a fight, but it was … only for show. I knew what was coming when Eskitul allowed Ripstiggr to live. Ripstiggr is the acting commander of the *Krijistal.* He is very Chuck Norris. Eskitul should have killed him, but did not. This was a reward for not killing us. Oh, it is complicated. But what you must know is that Eskitul has taken command, and they're leaving."

"They've abandoned everyone in the shelter on the surface?" Skyler broke in. "Holy crap, that's cold."

"You have no idea," Keelraiser said.

"They're going home, aren't they?" Jack said. Without warning, tears heated his eyes. "Shit. I would have wanted to go. Why didn't they just take us with them?"

Keelraiser reached down and tried to pat his hair. Jack slapped its hand away.

"Fuck off." He remembered something. "The *Cloudeater?*"

"I sent it back to the surface," Keelraiser whispered.

"Hriklif isn't a pilot, but the computer can do the heavy lifting, and it's not that hard to land on an ice plain. Anyway, Hriklif is on my side."

"You saw this coming, in other words."

"Yes."

"Well, fuck you," Jack said. "Fuck you and all your Proxima b string-bean people."

"I didn't know what to do."

"I'll tell you what to do! Get out of my fucking face!"

Keelraiser started to float away. At the entrance to the keel tube, it paused. "I haven't told you the worst of it yet."

"Spit it the fuck out, then!"

"It is so *hard* to tell the truth," Keelraiser said fretfully.

"I've noticed."

"I promised myself I would not lie to you anymore," Keelraiser hissed, and then it gabbled, all at once: "I lied to you before we all did we didn't come to seek refuge we are not refugees we are not Lightsiders we are Darksiders we *won* the war and conquered Imf and now we are going to conquer Earth too and there are two more ships coming behind this one."

The two men stared at it in dumbfounded horror.

"Now you know," Keelraiser said, and dived into the keel tube, like a pale fish going down a drain.

"Shut the door," Jack said to Skyler.

He sat back in his seat.

"Well, that simplifies things," he said to no one in particular. He adjusted his headset. "Alexei? Did you hear that?"

"Yes," Alexei said.

"Do you believe it?"

"Yes. I predicted this, if you remember. This isn't Star Trek. It's a Russian science fiction movie. Everybody dies."

"No, they won't," Jack said, pulling himself together. "But the bad guys will. Are you mobile?"

"Depends what you need."

Again, Jack wondered how badly Alexei was wounded. "Stand by," he said, and floated out of his seat.

He caught Skyler by one shoulder. Skyler screamed and cowered in the air.

"I hardly touched you," Jack said in disgust. "But I'll hurt you if you don't tell me the truth, right now. Where are the plutonium rounds?"

CHAPTER 45

"The plutonium rounds are in the storage module," Skyler babbled. If Jack had known it was this easy to get him to talk, he would have physically threatened him before. "In Lance's luggage."

"Do you know that, or are you guessing?"

"Guessing," Skyler said, with a sickly smile. Blood rimmed his teeth. "But I know I'm right. That's the only place we haven't been in and out of a hundred times."

Now that Skyler mentioned it, Jack remembered Lance bringing a couple of large cases on board. He'd blocked it out, like everything else to do with Lance.

"Blin!" said Alexei, listening in. "Why didn't I think of that? All right, I'm checking now."

Jack said to Skyler, "Did you take that star sighting? Silly me, of course you didn't, because you're a useless little cunt."

He did it himself, lining up the telescope on a bright star. Wouldn't it be something if that 'star' was the Alpha Centauri system? He chuckled to himself and returned to his seat. Waiting for Alexei to find the plutonium rounds, he programmed the targeting computer. He was pleased how closely the figures from the inertial navigation units matched his star sighting.

"Got them," Alexei said. "Fuck, these things are heavy."

"They're nuclear bombs, man."

"There are two per case, two cases. They have steel plating. They're less than half a meter long, but each one must mass fifty, sixty kilograms."

Jack hesitated. He knew he was probably asking Alexei to

go beyond the limits of his strength. "You'll have to go outside to load them, I'm afraid."

"I'm already in the airlock."

"Fantastic."

Jack pored over the external camera feed. It would be lovely if the microtamped nuclear bombs would zap into that hole in the *Lightbringer's* hull, instead of blasting through from the surface. That would serve the dual purpose of destroying more of the *Lightbringer's* interior, as well as containing the blast and radiation for a few milliseconds. Not that that really mattered. He, Alexei, Skyler, and Keelraiser were dead, anyway. He frowned at the realization that he'd mentally included Keelraiser in the tally of 'people.' Oh, well. Dead was dead.

On the bright side, Eskitul and the *Krijistal* would die first. The *Lightbringer* would never bring its planet-killing armaments to bear on Earth.

Jack trained the communications laser on the hull of the *Lightbringer*. He punched the ranging function on the comms panel and triggered a squirt. 5.7 kilometers. He fed the figures into the targeting computer.

Come on, Alexei.

"Don't kill them," Skyler said.

Jack glanced to his left. Skyler slumped in the left seat. Dead Kate separated them.

All Jack could do right now was wait for Alexei to load the rounds, so to take his mind off how bad he was feeling, he said, "Why?"

"They're weak and defenseless. They're billions of miles from home."

"Did you actually hear what Keelraiser said? They came

to conquer Earth."

"Yeah, well maybe that was the plan. But their ship is messed up. Even if they make it to Earth, how're they going to conquer anything with that?"

"They'll have plenty of time to fix things along the way." Jack remembered something Eskitul had said. "Water and power. Everything else is chemistry." He added, "And DIY skills. They've got *those.* "

Restlessly, he watched the *Lightbringer* recede on the screen. His initial targeting solution was already out of date. Hurry up, Alexei.

"Well, actually, I'm mainly thinking about Hannah," Skyler said.

"I knew it."

"She's on that ship."

"Regardless, it's a threat to Earth, which needs to be eliminated. I'm not discussing this anymore." He had been trying like hell not to think about the fact that he'd be nuking Hannah and Giles, as well as the *Krijistal.* In an attempt to salve his conscience, he added, "She's probably dead already."

"But what if she's not?"

Jack leaned back in his seat and laced his hands over his eyes. When he did this, his head swam with exhaustion, and all the other things that were wrong with his body, like the grinding nausea in his gut, and the hot achy feeling in his joints, clamored for his attention. He opened his eyes and blocked it all out again by working the board, swinging the radar antenna to bear on the shrinking *Lightbringer.*

"What if Hannah's not dead?" Skyler said. "What if she's waiting for us to rescue her?"

"Then that's too fucking bad, isn't it?"

"Jesus," Skyler said. "I've never even slept with her."

"Nor have I."

"Yeah, right."

"True; and it wouldn't make any difference, anyway."

"You really are an asshole, aren't you?"

"One of the many differences between me and you is that I don't resort to name-calling when I'm out of arguments."

"I made an argument. You just didn't listen."

"Oh, they *might* not succeed in invading Earth, so we should let them have a go, because Hannah. That's persuasive."

"Aren't you supposed to be a Christian?"

Jack peered at Skyler, his gaze inevitably alighting on Kate along the way. The *SoD's* resident flies, not all crisped in the earlier gunfight, had congregated on her dead face. He waved at them, and they rose up. Kate had died a hero. And what had she died for? *Not* to let the *Lightbringer* go on its merry way to invade Earth. It had to be destroyed. She'd been right about that. He had been wrong, and she'd been right.

Skyler's thin, ravaged face shone with intensity. "Mercy," he said. "You've got to have mercy on them."

"No, I haven't."

Alexei's voice crackled into their headsets. "Done," he croaked. "Two rounds are loaded. I put ten tracer rounds ahead of each one. I'm taking a break now, guys."

"Spasibo ya u tebya v dolgu," Jack said, drawing on his small stock of Russian to let Alexei know how grateful he was. He reached up to the railgun console and powered the rails on.

Throughout the ship, system after system powered down, while a low growling sound started from far aft. The growling wound up the scale until it was an ultrasonic whine at the edge of hearing.

"You don't understand weakness," Skyler said, his face contorting with emotion.

"I do." Jack fed the figures from the radar into the targeting computer. "It means I can target them without being fired on."

"That's exactly what I mean! You're unmerciful. You're ruthless. You treated Hannah like shit. You treat everyone like shit. And before you say anything, it's not just me. Even Meili said you were an asshole. You never held her when she cried. You just walked away."

This, actually, was true. Meili used to cry sometimes for reasons she couldn't or wouldn't explain. Reasoning that he couldn't help her if she wouldn't talk to him, Jack had usually just left her to it.

"I'm a nice guy," he said. "My mother says so." His intended humor fell completely flat.

"Bet your mother doesn't know you murdered Lance."

Jack swung away from the board. "Oh, you fucking—*you* told me he was the one who killed Ollie! Was I supposed to let him get away with it?!"

Skyler grimaced. "All right, let's talk about Oliver Meeks."

"He was in a wheelchair. He was in a fucking wheelchair, and you cunts killed him."

"Maybe it wouldn't have happened if you'd been there!"

"What, was I supposed to hover around him like a mother hen? Treat him like a cripple?"

"He *was* a cripple."

"That doesn't mean someone needs a round-the-clock nanny!" This was what Jack strongly believed, and his close friendship with Oliver Meeks had been predicated on Jack's absolute refusal to treat Meeks like a cripple. But Skyler's accusation cut deep. How many times had Jack himself regretted that he had not been home that night? Lance Garner would have thought twice before drawing a gun on an able-bodied man.

"Oh, hell," Skyler said. "Fuck it, fuck it. Listen, Jack, he was strong at the end. He was incredible. You should have seen him." Skyler's voice broke. He wiped his eyes with the back of his hand. "He was in that wheelchair, pumping off rounds. He winged Lance. He was like this little battle tank, literally hell on wheels!"

Jack smiled despite himself. He could see it clearly. Admiration for Meeks softened his bitter memories of that night.

"Then he flipped out of his wheelchair and crawled under the table. I was right there. He didn't shoot me, although he could have. He told me to run. Save yourself. Run."

"Oh, Ollie," Jack muttered.

"And then ...." Skyler was really crying now. "Then he ran out of ammo. And Lance was all like, standing over him, gloating. Meeks was cursing him out. He refused to beg for mercy. That pissed Lance off. So then he was like .."

"What?"

"He—Lance—he wiped his gun off, and gave it to me. Because, you know, fingerprints. Although I didn't think of that at the time. And he was like, you do it."

"And?"

"I did it." Skyler met his eyes with tear-filled ones. "I did it."

Jack lunged at him. He moved a few centimeters before his straps cut into his shoulders, stopping him. As if it had been yesterday, he could see Meeks lying on the kitchen floor in his house in Nevada, one side of his head missing, in a pool of blood and LCD fragments. *"You* did it."

"Yep."

"And you told me Lance did it. You made me think—you made me kill him!"

"I thought Lance was a Chinese spy. I thought he was the saboteur. But he wasn't."

"No, he was just a dirty Fed," Jack said emptily. "You and him were a nice pair. As bad as each other."

"I know." Skyler wiped his eyes. He was completely losing it. A blubbering mess. "I'm as bad as he was. He affected me. *Infected* me. I used to be a nice guy, too. Before I joined the NXC ... I was normal. As normal as a Harvard astrophysicist can be. But I've gone over to the dark side of the Force." Their eyes met. "I can't go back. I can't change back to who I was. But maybe you can."

"I'm going to fucking kill you," Jack said. He heard the mindless, reflexive threat, and despised himself for it.

"Fine," Skyler said. "I don't want to live, anyway. I told Director Flaherty to go fuck himself. My life won't be worth living after he gets that."

"You told the NXC to get fucked?" Jack laughed out loud. Flecks of blood spattered the targeting screen.

"Yeah, so you might as well kill me. But have mercy on the rriksti. *Please.*"

Jack looked at his targeting board. A reticule had sprung

into being over the screen. It nearly obscured the *Lightbringer*. According to the radar return, the alien spaceship was now more than a hundred kilometers away.

Shit, shit, shit!

He targeted the gray spot he could see on the *Lightbringer*'s hull. That had to be the hole amidships. He fired a two-round burst.

With rapid *Zzzzoik!* noises, two burning red spots of light raced away.

And impacted short of the hole.

"Damn," Jack muttered. "Adjusting."

The background whine, which had dipped during the railgun firing, began climbing again.

Skyler wept, "You're killing them."

"Those were just tracer rounds." Jack fiddled with the controls. "Here we go again."

Two more burning spots of light raced away from the *SoD,* this time impacting just beyond the gray hull spot.

Have mercy.

Please.

Ignoring Skyler's entreaties, Jack continued to fire and adjust the railgun. Suddenly, the *Lightbringer* tried to take evasive action.

"Look at that whale, trying to dart around." Jack laughed so hard that tears came to his eyes. He had fired ten tracer rounds. Now he boosted the power to the rails.

With a perceptible jerk, the *SoD* launched its eleventh shot.

But the *Krijistal* had not been idle. From compartments open to space, debris of all kinds began sailing out of the ship. From scrap steel to an entire warped blast door, the

Lightbringer was throwing a screen of radar-reflecting trash behind it.

Jack gritted his teeth. He did not pray. It wouldn't be appropriate. He just watched bleakly as the plutonium round sped towards the *Lightbringer*.

The round impacted some of the lighter debris, shouldering it aside with barely a wobble. But that wobble was important, for it shifted the aim point just enough for the plutonium round to impact the warped blast door that had been tossed overboard seconds ago.

A fireball erupted alongside the *Lightbringer*. It expanded at light speed into a baby star so bright that Jupiter dimmed in comparison. Yet the fireball should have been spherical, and it wasn't. The bomb's collision with the debris had distorted the blast, sparing the *Lightbringer*.

The alien spaceship continued to recede into the dark, its engines glowing cherry-red.

"Damn it," Jack howled. "Oh, damn it all to hell."

Seconds later the port camera cut out. So did the radar, blinded by the nuclear blast.

That's it then. It's over.

Although Jack had only fired one of the railguns, and the other one was still fully loaded, he could neither aim it nor range it.

He had missed his chance to take the *Lightbringer* out, because of Skyler Taft.

It was one of those laugh or cry things.

He put his face in his hands and cried.

CHAPTER 46

On the bridge of the *Lightbringer,* Hannah curled in a lumpy armchair, watching Jupiter. The gas giant had grown perceptibly larger since the *Lightbringer* heaved itself out of Europa orbit.

Two sections of the bridge's forward wall, on either side of the drive chancel, had turned transparent. Smart materials. The aliens were a long way ahead of humanity in terms of applied nanotechnology. Eskitul had promised to teach her how it all worked, not that she had any chance of understanding it, she thought.

For now, they were relaxing.

There'd been a bit of excitement after they launched. Eskitul had given a string of orders, and the ship had surged gently this way and that. Hannah surmised that those had been evasive maneuvers. Kate must have fired on the *Lightbringer.* Hannah felt a little bit hurt by that. But she understood how Kate and Giles must feel, left behind.

Almost as bad as Hannah felt, being here.

The aliens had arranged chairs and a low table—well, low for them—in a conversation group in front of one of the viewing walls. They sat and chatted. Hannah imagined that travelling on the *Lightbringer* must once have felt a lot like a stay in a luxury hotel, with the best views in the universe.

Must've been a nice—if long—journey from Proxima b.

They called it *Imf.*

"We are Darksiders," Boombox told her.

Imf was a tidally locked planet.

"The Lightsiders pushed us out of the twilight zone, forced us to live in the dark, labor in the dark, raise our

children in the dark. So we rose up and smashed them."
This had all happened seventy years ago, according to them,
but Boombox was still gloating about it. Somehow Hannah
wasn't surprised.

"*You* do not come from the Darkside, Ripstiggr," Eskitul
said.

"No," Boombox admitted. "I grew up in the twilight zone.
But I grew up *poor.* I used to gather *jgzeriyat* from the ditches
to help put food on the table."

"Cry me a freaking river," Hannah muttered.

Boombox's hair danced. "In the twilight zone, the wind is
so strong that children fly on it."

"My nurse used to tie me to the railings," Eskitul said.

"A formative experience?" Boombox said.

Hannah hunched into herself. The aliens' reminiscences
cued memories of her own childhood. The taste of Coco
Puffs and milk on a Saturday morning, watching cartoons,
Bethany whimpering when Scooby Doo got too scary for
her … Hannah used to cover her sister's eyes until it was
'safe' for her to look. Now it turned out there really were
monsters out there, after all. Joke's on you, Hannah-banana.

Rriksti. That's what the monsters called themselves.

Their language was *Rritigul.* Transposed into the audible
range, it sounded like German with extra-long vowels, but
meaning also depended on frequency, Eskitul had told her.
They shifted frequency to add nuance, or alter the meaning
of their words altogether, the way the Chinese language
used tones. Thus, their bio-radio signals conveyed
information in *three* dimensions: sound, pitch, and frequency.
With such a fiendishly complex language under their belts, it
was no wonder they'd found it easy to learn English. Going

the other way would be next to impossible. She felt stupid just thinking about it.

Stupid, and *sick*. Her head throbbed, and the half-strength gravity made her feel as weak as if she had a fever. Maybe she did. This place must be teeming with alien bacteria and viruses. Maybe she was dying.

Or maybe she was just hungry.

One of Boombox's people laid a tray on the table. Transparent plates held various lumps, chunks, and wafers. Boombox and Eskitul used short sharp knives to chop and spear the food. Hannah's mouth watered, even though it didn't smell very pleasant. She stretched out her hand—

—and Boombox slapped it.

"Our food is not safe for you to eat."

"If you don't feed me, you're not going to have me around long," Hannah said.

"Some of your food has been brought on board. You shall have a garden of your own."

"You were planning to kidnap me all along," Hannah said with loathing.

Boombox shrugged.

The uniformed servant brought another plate. On it was a single, rather grubby Yukon Gold.

"Oh hell," Hannah said. She picked the potato up and bit into it. She knew that it was safe and even healthy to eat raw potatoes. Skyler used to snack on raw potato slices. He'd offer them to her, saying that with a bit of salt, they were as good as Kettle Chips …

Crying, chewing, she ate the whole potato.

Boombox was pouring clear liquid into ship's mugs for itself and Eskitul.

"Is that water? Can I have some?"

Eskitul said, "Oh, give her some! It is only *krak*. It doesn't poison them."

"Crack?" Hannah repeated.

"We brew it in a distillation apparatus," Boombox said. "Without *krak,* our ten-year ordeal would have been unbearable."

"A distillation apparatus?" Hannah started to laugh.

"I agree! It's funny! Reality is more bearable when it is filtered through a distillation apparatus," Eskitul said. It poured some of the clear liquid for her. "Drink! It makes everything easier. Drink!" It tipped a whole cupful down its own throat.

Hannah picked up the mug it had filled for her. She inhaled the tantalizing fumes. The contents of the scratched, battered mug smelt like home—a home she had thought lost to her forever. Her body and brain yearned for it.

Hannah's Rule #1, from her years at JPL: Never drink at work.

She had completely abandoned that rule on the *SoD,* but now was the time to revive it. If she was going to keep ahold of her mind, she had to think of this as *work*.

A new engineering challenge.

Look at all this alien shit. Transparent hull sections, gaze-controlled computers, smart walls, a freaking fusion reactor.

Your mission, Hannah Ginsburg, is to get to grips with this stuff, to *understand* it, instead of diving headfirst into a keg of alien booze.

It took every grain of her willpower, but she put the mug down—spinning justifications to mollify the screaming demon in her heart: it might not be ethanol, it might be methanol, it might kill you, don't take the risk.

The demon said that that was a risk worth taking. Hannah told it to shut the fuck up.

"No, thank you," she said to Eskitul. "Could I have some water?"

In the viewing wall, Jupiter grew larger. Eskitul explained to Hannah that it had set a course that would cross in front of Jupiter's orbital path. By skimming the top of the gas giant's atmosphere, the *Lightbringer* would reduce its velocity. When the ship exited Jupiter orbit, it would be going slow enough to fall inwards towards the sun ... and towards Earth.

"Nice," Hannah said, too mentally exhausted to think about it. She sipped the briny water they'd given her, still mourning the *krak* she had turned down. The view of Jupiter compensated somewhat for her sense of deprivation. Auroras crackled above the gas giant's north pole, an eerie web of blue lightning. She was getting a better view than the Juno probe ever had.

But wait.

Something bothered her about this trajectory.

Don't just sit there, Hannah.

Do your goddamn job.

Think.

Jupiter has four Galilean moons.

From largest to smallest: Ganymede, Callisto, Io, Europa.

Io orbits closest to Jupiter, at a distance of just 422,000 km.

"How close are we cutting it?" she asked Eskitul, nervously. "I mean, you don't want to get *too* close to

Jupiter!"

"In your units of distance, we will approach no closer than 300,000 kilometers," Eskitul said reassuringly.

So we'll be cutting inside Io's orbit.

"Where is Io right now?"

Boombox frowned.

"Io. Jupiter's innermost moon. Where is it?"

"Right there," Eskitul said. It hiccuped delicately, and gestured at the ceiling. Hannah glanced up. The dome that had held the sun at its apex now cradled a blob of sickly yellow and puke-green. That was Io, and it was *close*.

Hannah jumped to her feet. "Change course! *Now!*"

"Why?" Boombox demanded.

"The Io flux tube!" Hannah's skin crawled. Her mouth dried out with a premonition of horrible danger. As she spoke, a harmonic shrieked from the boombox. The rriksti in the drive chancel spilled out, their hair thrashing.

Boombox spun the dials of the boombox, cutting off the screech. "The electrical field sensors just overloaded!" it shouted at Hannah. "What is this Io flux tube?"

"We didn't know about it, either, until we did close fly-bys of Jupiter," Hannah gabbled. "It's an electrical current generated by Jupiter's magnetosphere. Those pretty aurorae on Jupiter's poles? Those are Io's footprints. Basically, it's a gigantic flood of charged ions. And we're about to fly straight into it!"

"Think of it as the mother of all HERFs," Eskitul explained helpfully. Its hair danced. It closed its eyes.

"Alter course!" Hannah yelled. "Ninety degrees up, or ninety degrees down. Either one will work."

"The ship is heavily shielded," Boombox said. But it took

off running to the drive chancel.

"There is nothing in our home system like this," Eskitul said to Hannah, in a conversational tone. "Our sun is a red dwarf. We never saw a gas giant until we explored the Alpha Centauri system. So this was all new to us. During our exile on Europa, we extensively observed Jupiter and its other moons. We discovered the existence of this flux tube. Clearly, the *Krijistal* did not."

"You—you *knew* about the flux tube?!" Hannah said.

"I am going to end this." Eskitul poured itself some more *krak*. She could barely pick out its words amidst the yells from the other aliens, and the shrieks of alarms going off, all channelled through the boombox's speakers. "I am sorry you had to be here."

Eskitul drained its mug and set it down just as Boombox stormed back to them. It grabbed Eskitul by one arm, hauled it out of its chair, and shook it. The speakers of the boombox sizzled with harmonics. Hannah reflexively covered her ears.

"Why don't you just alter course?!" she screamed.

Boombox threw Eskitul to the floor. The bronze-haired alien crashed into the table, knocking it over, plates and mugs, boombox and all. "You're going to kill us!" Boombox shouted.

"You deserve it," Eskitul said. "The human beings do not." It grasped Hannah's knees, as if to pull itself upright. But instead of rising, it stayed on its knees and looked up at her. "Sixty-five of your years ago, I was given the ... the honor ... of leading the conquest of Earth."

Hannah's blood ran cold, "Come to think of it," she managed, "you never did say what you were doing here in the first place."

"I lied. We all lied. We came here to conquer you."

"O—oh."

"But along the way, I changed my mind."

"You betrayed yourself," Boombox said. "You betrayed all of us. That's what comes of watching too much television."

"I *found* myself," Eskitul said. "I found that after a lifetime of war, I still had a moral core." It let go of Hannah's knees and unfolded to its full height. "I will *not* destroy another innocent people."

Eskitul's nobility moved Hannah to the point of tears. It terrified her to think that Earth's fate hung on an alien's refusal to do wrong. At the same time, it felt bizarrely right that a moral scruple should be the still point on which their survival hinged.

"So instead, you'll destroy the *Lightbringer?*" Boombox said, queerly calm. "Is that it, Shiplord?"

Eskitul paced towards the viewing wall. Spreadeagled against the eternal night, it rested its forehead on the Great Red Spot. "It is the only way to end this," its voice said from the boombox. "Consider: we will not die immediately. The magnetic flux will utterly wreck the ship's electrical systems. We will gradually spiral in towards Jupiter. But we shall have enough air and water here on the bridge to enjoy the ride. It may be *interesting!*"

"Until Jupiter's tidal forces rip us apart," Hannah yelped. She now realized just how badly she wanted to stay alive. As much as she admired Eskitul's noble gesture, she had no interest in exploring a gas giant from the inside. "Quick! Dodge above the flux tube, or below it!"

"The problem," Boombox said, "is that the drive controls are subject to the authority of the Shiplord."

"Correct," Eskitul said. "You can do nothing without me."

"Wrong. I can do this."

Boombox bent and snatched up a knife from the debris of their meal. It pounced on Eskitul from behind and seized a handful of its bio-antennas.

A hideous scream tore from the boombox. Every rriksti on the bridge rushed forward—and froze.

Boombox sank to its heels, bending Eskitul backwards over its lap. It used the eating knife to cut the Shiplord's throat.

Blood sprayed the screen, filming Jupiter red.

The lights went out.

In a fanfare of electronic whines and mechanical rattles, all the systems on the bridge powered down.

Boombox now moved even faster. It flipped Eskitul over and hacked at the back of its neck.

Hannah backed away from the horrifying scene, hands over her mouth. She bumped into some of the other rriksti, who held her.

Boombox stalked towards her. Now that the only light on the bridge came from red-stained Jupiter, Boombox was a massive, octopus-headed silhouette, reviving the terror she'd felt when she first saw the aliens. Blood dripped from its hands.

Her captors thrust her forward.

The knife flashed.

Hannah screamed.

Pain slashed across her forehead. In a flurry of

emotionally shattering impacts, she felt Boombox prying at the wound with the point of the knife, shoving *something* under her skin, *into* her, oh God help me. One of the other aliens slapped something over the wound, which infused menthol coolness into the burning agony.

They all stood like that for a few frozen seconds.

Then the lights came back on.

The air circulation and the other systems started up again.

The other aliens sprinted to the forward chancel. Boombox yelled, "Engage thrusters! 90-degree course correction! *NOW!*"

Hannah's knees crumpled. She pitched forward.

Boombox caught her. It carried her to the nearest chair and set her down. Then it sank to its knees before her. "Hail," it said. "Shiplord."

CHAPTER 47

Alexei cranked open the forward pressure door of the storage module. He took with him his rriksti blaster, and also a 1-meter length of angle iron, the stuff they'd used to make the crossbows. He'd sanded it to a point, welded a crosspiece onto it as a handguard, and wrapped duct tape around the grip.

These tasks had occupied the long minutes while he considered Kate's death. It had been therapeutic.

He floated through the secondary life-support module, clad in shipboard sweats, with a bandage wrapped around his left calf. He'd been wounded during the fight earlier. A near-miss had left an oozing, bloody abrasion on his shin, as if a patch of his skin had been vaporized. Those alien weapons were *evil*. It stung like fuck. But it was just a graze. He'd told Jack the truth about that.

On the other hand, he suspected the alien weapons emitted hefty doses of radioactivity. He might be in for a world of hurt later. But he didn't seriously expect there to *be* a 'later,' so he didn't need to think about that.

SLS was *Krijistal*-free.

Alexei opened the pressure door to the main hab.

A few minutes later, he returned in a hurry to the storage module. He flew to the first-aid locker, prepared the supplies he would need, and darted back to the main hab.

In the axis tunnel, he took the comatose aliens one by one. He pried them out of their frozen fetal postures and zip-tied them to the hexagonal lattice by a convenient arm or leg. Vomit leaked from their mouths when he moved them. Their eyes rolled, showing white. That was the first he knew rriksti eyes even had whites. In the slicks of vomit on their chins and chests, partially chewed pieces of carrot and sweet potato offered a clue to their condition. Brown globules floated in the zero-gee periphery of the axis tunnel. Another giveaway. Diarrhea. Their thin legs and buttocks were greasy with it, and the smell turned Alexei's stomach.

"Vitamin toxicity," he muttered to himself. "Perhaps vitamin A, or one of the other fat-soluble vitamins? Who knows?"

The treatment for vomiting and diarrhea was the same in any case. He had brought eight IV bags from the storage module, one for each hapless rriksti. He shook them to mix the solute pills into the water, forming a rehydration solution. Maybe the cure would be worse than the disease. But the rriksti were in hypovolemic shock. They needed to be rehydrated as a first step.

Prodding with his thumb in search of a vein, he got a comment out of the first alien. "Why help?" it wheezed in his headset.

"Oh, so you know what an IV is," Alexei said. "Maybe you can show me where you keep your veins."

It turned out that the aliens' median cubital veins were all the way on the insides of their forearms. Once he had that figured out, the next five went quickly.

Number six shrieked at him in the rriksti language and then said, "But we tried to kill you."

Alexei got its IV hooked up and sat back, bracing himself against the hexagonal lattice. He looked down to the distant floor of the hab. He saw his handmade sword standing point up in a fish tank. He had dropped it when he saw the condition the aliens were in. "It's what Kate would have wanted," he said, and moved on to number seven.

In fact, he was pretty sure Kate, were she alive, would *not* have given the aliens IVs. She would have served them each with an angle iron to the brain, and spaced their bodies.

But maybe, wherever she was now, she was smiling.

You have to believe things look different from heaven.

"Your friends left you behind," he told number eight.

"That fucker Ripstiggr. I'm not surprised," number eight said. It threw up again.

"I think you poisoned yourselves with our vegetables. Why'd you stuff your faces like that?"

"We were fucking *hungry.*"

Alexei smiled. "Have an IV. I hope you aren't allergic to isotonic chloride solution."

Strangers helping strangers—that's how you throw a spanner in the miserable deterministic gears of the universe. Every act of kindness is a fuck-you to the *siloviki*.

Even if they're not human at all.

*

As he finished his medical duties, Alexei heard someone calling his name. He looked down.

Thirty meters below and aft, Skyler rotated past, standing at the foot of Stairway 5. He had a laptop under his arm. He squinted up at the blaze of the growlights.

"What are you doing?" Alexei shouted.

"Alexei! Could you come down here for a second?"

The rriksti Alexei was attending to said, "By the way, could you turn the lights off?"

"Why?"

"They're too bright."

"Deal with it," Alexei said. The laptop under Skyler's arm

sent his thoughts skittering. He hurried down the ten-storey length of Stairway 5. Skyler met him at the bottom. He'd pulled everything out of Meili's desk, in the Potter space under this staircase. He showed Alexei a pile of electronics on top of the desk.

"The malware trigger is on all of these."

Alexei stared in wonder at Jack's laptop, with the Monty Python's Flying Circus sticker on the case.

A Chinese MP3 player.

Giles's iPod.

Skyler's own iPod.

And Meili's laptop.

Skyler opened the laptop he was carrying—his own. "This is a program the NXC gave me. I'm not supposed to show it to you, obviously, but whatever. Fuck the NXC."

Alexei found his voice. "I deleted it." He shook his head. "I gave one copy to Kate. Then I deleted my own copy. How did it get onto all these devices?"

"When you tried to delete it, that probably triggered some kind of self-preservation routine. It copied itself over the Wi-Fi to every device that was switched on. Anyway, this is all of them … except your laptop. I couldn't find that." He met Alexei's eyes. "What do you want to do?"

"What do I want to do?" Alexei laughed hollowly. "I want to take a shower, eat a steak, get drunk, go to sleep, and wake up at home."

"Me, too," Skyler said. "But apart from that."

"Delete every instance of the damn thing. But wait. If we try to delete it … it will just copy itself to any other devices around. The rriksti might get hold of it." He glanced up at the axis tunnel.

"I thought those guys were dead," Skyler said in alarm.

"No. No, they're cool ... I *think*. But we should be careful, anyway." The GRU had taught him to trust no one. Stalling, he said, "I'll go get my laptop." It was in the storage module, where he'd been using it to calculate tolerances for the crossbows he and Jack had made.

While he was back there, he took a quick peek into Engineering. The reactor was fine. Kate's iPod floated in pieces in the air. Fighting a surge of grief, Alexei wondered how that had happened, and why.

"These are the last devices," he said, tossing his laptop and Kate's broken iPod on the desk.

While Alexei was gone, Skyler had retrieved his homemade sword from the fishtank where he'd dropped it. Skyler took a practice swing at the pile of devices, not really hitting them, just being theatrical. "I checked on the fish," he explained.

"Are they alive?" Alexei was surprised.

"Yep. Tougher than we are."

"Huh." So there might be a 'later' after all. Alexei drew a deep breath. "Listen, I'm going to the bridge. I want to see what Jack is up to." He knew Kate was up there, too. He'd been stalling.

"And these devices?"

"You can dispose of them."

He imagined GRU heads, far away in Moscow, exploding at these words, and smiled bleakly to himself as he climbed the stairs.

He flew along the axis tunnel, dispensing reassurance to his rriksti patients en route. They were already feeling better, to judge from their renewed complaints about the lighting.

He shouldered through the keel tube and flew onto the bridge. "Hey, Jack—"

Kate sat in the center seat. For a heartstopping instant Alexei thought she was alive. Then he saw that she was naked, her lap covered with a blanket tucked inside her harness for decency. Flies crawled on her parted lips.

He stroked her blood-clotted hair, and kissed the dead face that he used to kiss so ardently when she was alive. He heard someone moving around above him. "Jack?" He glanced up, unashamed of the tears in his eyes.

Keelraiser floated near the ceiling.

Jack was up there, too.

Floating.

Not moving.

Alexei stared in numb shock. Globes of dark vomit floated around the pair. Clumps of Jack's hair adhered to the ceiling like dead spiders.

Alexei had taken for granted that Jack would be OK. Jack was as tough as a Russian.

On the other hand, he wasn't rad-proof.

The hair coming out, the reddish peeling appearance of Jack's skin, and above all the fact that he'd puked blood—all the symptoms indicated an absorbed dose in the fatal range.

Alexei adjusted his headset and croaked, "All dead, or mostly dead?"

"I don't know." Keelraiser lay parallel to Jack in the air, one hand flat on his belly, the other on his forehead. "Don't distract me!"

"You're doing the same thing you did for Skyler," Alexei realized with new hope.

"I am trying! But it normally takes a full hand of people.

400

And I'm not extroverted at all. I am a shitty manipulator."

Alexei ignored the last part of this, focusing on the first part. "As to that," he said, "a full hand of people is seven, yes?"

He flew off the bridge, shouting into his headset.

*

Jack floated in a hot black sea of pain. Now and then it pulled him under, and the agony drowned out thought and feeling.

At other times he could hear someone talking to him.

"*SoD. SoD,* do you read me? This is Houston, *SoD,* do you read me?"

No, I do not fucking read you, Houston. I am dying. A 36-hour X-ray bath in the alien shelter, followed by those goddamn Super Soakers spitting out rems every time I pulled the trigger, *on top* of a fairly warm career as an astronaut since the year two thousand and fucking four, and a voyage to Europa.

I've had my chips, Houston. You don't fuck with megadoses of radiation and expect to come out the other side smelling of roses.

I missed, anyway.

I was in the right place at the right time to save Earth.

And I fucking *missed.*

"*Spirit of Destiny!* Commander Menelaou! *Do you read me?*"

No, she doesn't read you, because she's dead, Mission Control. Same old story. I had a chance to save her and I stuffed it up. She's dead. Those are pearls that were her eyes and all that. No, hang on, that was Lance.

(Lumps of frozen crystals in his eye sockets. Not pearls, really. Diamonds. Murderers go to hell. Does it make any difference if you're sorry?)

"*SoD!* We have just picked up a drive plume stretching across Jupiter! Can you tell us anything about that?"

Yes. Yes, I can tell you about that. It is the drive plume of the *Lightbringer*, better known as the MOAD, and it is on its way to destroy Earth, because I screwed up.

"Don't move, Jack. Don't try to move."

Oh God, it hurts.

He couldn't move if he wanted to. His DNA was in ribbons, his cells were dividing out of control, he'd puked up his intestinal lining, and his head felt like it had been run over by a lorry.

To make matters worse, people were pawing at him, dipping their meddling fingers into the full-body agony zone that was his skin.

"It's me," the same voice whispered.

I know it's fucking you, Keelraiser. Get away from me, you deceitful, backstabbing alien piece of shit. Leave me alone to die.

"Don't be a bloody idiot," said another voice, this one so clear, and so familiar, that Jack actually forgot his torment for a moment. "I told you this would happen, if you recall. The MOAD had *extinction event* written all over it from the minute it appeared in the sky. But all is *not* lost yet. There's still time to save Earth. The *SoD* is still flyable, and you're the only one who can fly it. So stop wallowing in guilt, and let them help you! Oh, I know you have to find everything out the hard way. I did. But it actually *doesn't* make you a pathetic loser to let people help you sometimes."

"*Ollie?*"

Jack tried to open his eyes, to see if Meeks was really

there. This had the effect of reuniting his perceptions with his senses, and immersing him deeper into the sea of pain … at the very moment when it started to cool.

Oh, that's nice.

Oh, that feels good.

The taste of garlic filled his mouth.

After some time, another voice drifted into his ears. "Houston, this is Ivanov. Stop shouting at us! I am alive, but Taft is missing. I don't know where he went. And Kildare … is not in good shape."

"Just write my obituary and get it over with, why don't you?" Jack said hoarsely, heaving his eyelids up.

Alexei, at the comms console, spun around with a glad shout. He flew to Jack and hugged him. Rriksti scattered in the air.

One of them was Keelraiser.

Its eyes stared, its bio-antennas drifted limply.

It extended one seven-fingered hand and curled it into a loose thumbs-up.

Jack freed one arm and pulled Keelraiser into the hug, too.

CHAPTER 48

One of Skyler's tasks, because no one wanted an NXC agent on board, so he got all the shit jobs, had been EVA suit maintenance.

So he knew where all the spares were.

The oxygen tanks, the valves. The LOX heaters. The batteries.

He'd attached an oxygen tank to Alexei's homemade sword, two-thirds of the way up.

His feet rested on the sword's crosspiece.

Another length of angle iron, grabbed from the bench where Alexei had been working, went under the tank, crosswise. It extended far enough to the sides to support his thighs.

Batteries under the tank.

Valve and LOX heater on top.

Cobble the whole lot together with duct tape, the astronaut's best friend.

He'd converted Alexei's sword into a crude broomstick. It worked on the same principle as the one he'd ridden two years ago, wobbling all over the sky and puking in his helmet.

He wasn't wobbling now.

Felt like puking. When didn't he? But that could wait. It would *have* to wait.

He had a job to do.

He held the diaphragm for the oxygen tank in one glove. He'd modified the regulator so that a squeeze of the diaphragm would open the tank's valve. That had been the trickiest bit of the whole project.

He was wearing the wrist rockets the rriksti had given him. He opened the CO2 valves, using them like ullage motors to give himself a bit of a head start, so the LOX would settle in the tank, and bad shit wouldn't happen.

Now he was moving. Now it was safe to … *squeeze.*

The broomstick shot away from the *SoD,* with Skyler riding it like he was humping the thing, thighs clenched around the oxygen tank.

Below him, a thin rind of light heralded dawn on Europa.

With the icy little moon in darkness, Jupiter's umber glare illuminated the debris left behind by the *Lightbringer.*

Scrap metal, twisted and buckled.

And …

The drifting shape of a human spacesuit.

Just where Keelraiser had said it would be.

Skyler angled towards it, using his wrist rockets to finesse the broomstick's trajectory.

The *Lightbringer* had been thrusting away from Europa when the *Krijistal* tossed their makeshift blast screen out. So, although the *Lightbringer* had been laterally separated from the *SoD* by a hundred klicks, it had also been separated vertically. As a result, the debris had wound up in a higher orbit—a *slower* orbit—and the *SoD* had been overhauling it ever since.

Now the debris field was barely two kilometers away, directly above the *SoD.*

This is your only chance, Keelraiser had said to him. *There is a human body in the debris. If you want to recover it, you must go now.*

Skyler glanced down past his feet. The pinprick lights around the *SoD's* main hab looked very far away. He was terrified of getting left behind. He knew no one would come to save him if he didn't make it back.

Squeeze.

Cold gas streamed out of the exhaust pipe he'd taped to the oxygen tank, on the opposite side from where he rode, so he wouldn't freeze his cock off.

"Hannah? Hannah!"

No response from the drifting spacesuit. Maybe his rriksti headset wasn't compatible with the Z-2 radio. Maybe she was too sick to speak. Or, most likely: she was dead inside that thing.

Even so, he had to do this.

He hadn't expressed his feelings for her while she lived, because of the regulations, because he was scared of getting shot down, because he was trying to be a gentleman. So he'd ended up losing her to Jack. But Jack wasn't here now. It fell to Skyler to bring her home. He reveled bitterly in his own fidelity.

Gliding closer to the drifting spacesuit, he visually confirmed that it was Hannah's Z-2, the one with the green glow-in-the-dark piping. He hailed her again, but got no answer.

She rotated lazily, an X of arms and legs silhouetted against Jupiter.

They'd thrown her out with the trash.

Just one more piece of debris to deflect incoming blast waves.

It was enough to make Skyler wish Jack had hit the goddamn *Lightbringer.*

He'd done his best to talk Jack out of it, and he still believed he'd been right … but *goddamn,* those *Krijistal* were assholes.

"Hannah, it's me. I'm here …"

No response.

Had the nuke killed her? He didn't see any flame damage on her suit. She might have escaped the blast. The debris had already spread out by the time the plutonium round detonated, and explosions didn't travel far in space. But gamma rays and neutrons did. That was probably what had killed her, he told himself, clamping down on irrational hope. Either that, or she'd simply run out of air.

He rose up underneath her. His head and shoulders took the impact of the slow-motion collision.

Before she could bounce away, he got one arm around her legs.

The broomstick looped the loop while Skyler, panting and swearing, positioned Hannah on his back. She was limp and unresponsive. He'd brought pre-cut lengths of duct tape, wearing them like streamers on his arms. He taped her wrists together in front of his waist, so her arms formed a loop around him. He squeezed the diaphragm in short bursts, experimenting with the new distribution of mass, until he got the broomstick straightened out.

Then he opened the throttle and headed for home.

*

He didn't make it.

A hundred meters above the *SoD*, the oxygen tank sputtered empty.

His wrist rockets had already run out of CO_2.

In space, you keep falling forever. Skyler was still moving, but he no longer had the ability to control his trajectory, so he was going to miss the *SoD*. Eventually, he and Hannah would fall out of orbit. They would join Meili as frozen, broken corpses on the surface of Europa.

"Hey, guys!" he said into the radio, hoping against hope. "I'm out here! Can you come get me?"

The *SoD* continued to inch away along its orbital path, the main hab rotating sedately, rim lights winking.

"Guys …?"

No answer.

Well, he hadn't been expecting one.

Jack blamed him for the *Lightbringer's* escape. Alexei may have forgiven Skyler for trying to kill him, but when push came to shove, he would side with Jack. Neither of them was going to rescue him.

"Well, baby," he said to the burden on his back. "I tried." He cleared his throat. "How's about a song?"

He wasn't going to sing about his sexual fantasies. Not at a time like this. He sang instead, to the tune of 'One More Cup of Coffee':

"Your voice is soft, you make me think of Mom and apple pie. Bob Dylan won the Nobel prize, and I still wonder why." He chuckled bleakly to himself and improvised another rhyme. "Why didn't I say I love you, before the bitter end? I wanted to be your sweetie-pie, but you just wanted a friend …"

"Skyler!"

A shout cut him off.

"Skyler! Hot mic! *Hot mic!*"

Jack's voice.

Two humans in black rriksti suits swooped up from the *SoD*, wrist rockets gushing contrails.

"I also wonder why Bob Dylan won Nobel prize," Alexei said. "Your lyrics are better. Is she alive?"

"I don't know," Skyler said. "Probably not. But I had to bring her back, anyway." He felt dizzy with gratitude. "I thought you guys hated me."

"Of course we don't hate you, you dumb spook," Alexei said. "We *need* you. We all need each other now."

Tethers trailed from Jack and Alexei's belts. Two tethers each, joined together. They'd robbed the dead to extend their reach.

To save him.

They got their arms around Skyler, so they were three abreast, with Hannah riding limply on Skyler's back.

"Aren't you supposed to be sick, Jack?" Skyler croaked.

"Saved by miraculous alien antioxidants," Jack said. "And if you believe that, you'll believe anything. But I'm not complaining. Did you actually make this broomstick by yourself?"

"Yeah."

"Flipping incredible." Jack's voice held no condescension, only frank approval. "Well done, you."

Jack and Alexei retracted their tethers into the reels. The *SoD* loomed larger and closer. As Meili had said, it was the most beautiful thing ever built by humanity.

"I just figured it would work," Skyler babbled. "And I also had another idea, actually. I know how we can save the *SoD*. We can replenish the tanks with water from the surface. I know how to do it."

"Hold that thought," Jack said. "Let's get inside."

*

They had to go two by two, since the airlock wasn't big enough for four.

Skyler went first with Hannah.

409

Rriksti hands pulled them out of the chamber. Skyler controlled his instinctive flinch of fear. These guys were *Krijistal!* Or rather, they *had* been. They all needed each other now.

The rriksti cut the duct tape that held Hannah on Skyler's back. He doffed his suit to his waist and inhaled the cold, stinky air of the *SoD*. The rriksti flipped Hannah over in the air and fiddled with the rear entry port of her suit.

Skyler shoved past them and unsealed the port, shaky with dread.

The smell of diarrhea arose, mingled with the reek of blood.

Nestled tightly in the Z-2, Hannah's shoulders looked too broad and bony.

Her neck too wide.

Her hair too short.

Hardly believing his eyes, Skyler reached into the suit and got his hands under her arms.

Hannah *definitely* did not have hairy armpits.

The rriksti pulled on the Z-2's legs. Skyler pulled on the suit's occupant.

Jack and Alexei tumbled into the storage module just as Skyler went sailing backwards with an unconscious Giles Boisselot in his arms.

Most of Giles, anyway.

EPILOGUE

Jack sat in the center seat on the bridge of the *SoD*, feet up, munching a roasted sweet potato. His hair was starting to grow back. He scratched under his headset as he listened to Mission Control in Houston reading him chapter and verse.

"*Half* the crew gone. It looks pretty bad, especially to the Chinese."

The speaker was Richard Burke, the veteran director of the *Spirit of Humanity* project. He'd come on the radio after the boffins finished their spiel, to deliver some personal words of encouragement.

Jack grimaced. "I didn't plan it this way," he said, knowing Burke would never hear him. Earth was 48 minutes away, and Jack wasn't transmitting, anyway. "*Nothing's* gone according to plan." From the intercom drifted faint alien warbles—the rriksti using the ship's comms to chat as they worked.

"I'm just riding your ass, Killer," Burke said. He had adopted Kate's nickname for Jack, as if in homage to her.

"I miss her every day," Jack said. Especially because he was now sitting in her seat. They'd named him acting mission commander.

"There is a lot of anger and grief here, as you'd expect. But we're all pulling for you to bring the *SoD* safely home. In the next few hours, we'll have a quick and dirty task list for you to get started on. You've assured us that the reactor is running at housekeeping level, but we will need you to carry out visual and computer checks and send us the numbers for analysis, since ... since Hannah's not available."

Jack heard the sorrow in Burke's voice. He knew that

Burke had been close to Hannah. Their working relationship went back all the way to the days of the Juno probe. "She's not dead," he said to the empty bridge. He stuffed the sugary, partially carbonized end of his sweet potato into his mouth. "Why are you acting like she's dead?"

Maybe Burke was just being rational.

But the survivors on the *SoD* refused to accept that Hannah was lost to them forever. And Jack refused to accept that the *Lightbringer* had escaped for good.

He and Skyler could agree on at least one thing: they were going to catch that ship.

What they'd do when they caught it … well, they hadn't agreed on that.

But for the moment, they had other things to worry about.

Burke played recorded messages of hope and congratulations from the president of the United States, from the Prime Minister, from Russian President-Emeritus Putin. Jack grew bored. Half-listening, he rose in the air and focused the telescope on the surface of Europa.

" 'As painful as this is for all of us,'" he heard, "'we must consider the *Spirit of Destiny's* mission to have succeeded. The crew achieved first contact, and sacrificed their own resources so that the *Lightbringer* could start on the last leg of its journey to Earth …'"

"Jesus!" Jack howled. "What is this shit? They're not coming to say hello! They're coming to fucking *conquer* us!"

He knew there was a reason he hadn't bothered to contact Mission Control for a week after the *Lightbringer's* escape from Europa. It would have made him puke blood all over again to listen to the self-delusions of Earth's elite.

"That was from the president of the EU," Burke said, his skeptical tone confirming that even he thought it was a bit much.

"I should have guessed," Jack said.

"The EU is infested with Earth Party shills," said Giles, drifting out of the keel tube.

"Apparently they're expecting to welcome the *Lightbringer* with open arms."

"I am not surprised. I used to be one of them. I know how they think." Giles gripped the back of the left seat and bent his face to the skewer of roasted onions—the other half of Jack's lunch—that Jack had left stuck in the seat's padding. Giles had to go at the food like this because he had no hands. He was gripping the seatback with a hook Jack had made in the machine shop. The *Krijistal* had amputated Giles's arms at the elbows and his legs below the knees, so he'd fit into Hannah's spacesuit.

Strangely enough, the bastards had taken pains to ensure Giles would not die. The fabulous medical technologies Jack had been anticipating had finally made an appearance, in the form of mushroom-white, rriksti-color skin caps that covered the stumps and blended seamlessly with Giles's own skin. These finishing touches bugged Jack almost as much as the heinous cruelty of the amputations. It seemed so inconsistent.

Giles was bearing up astonishingly well. His trauma had left him with a bitter hatred for the *Krijistal*—understandable—and an equally strong hatred for the Earth Party—also understandable. But he didn't seem to be dwelling on what he'd lost. Using his hooks, he did what he could to help Jack make repairs to the *SoD* and restore the hydroponic garden.

The job was too big for the two of them. Mercifully, the ex-*Krijistal* saw fit to lend a hand. They had learned to stay away from veggies with a high vitamin A content.

Jack leaned over, pulled the skewer of onions out of the seat padding, and held it in front of Giles's mouth so the other man could eat.

On the radio, Burke was still talking. "So, now that your places in history are assured, let's get back to the technical issues. Our discussions here and in Moscow have centered around water. You've got a few hundred thousand gallons in the housekeeping water cycle, but the ETs and the bioshield tank are bone dry. Fortunately, we think we've got a way for you to retrieve ice from Europa, and get it into the tanks."

Jack smiled. "Do tell," he murmured.

"The catch is that you'll have to negotiate with the aliens remaining on Europa, and get them to help," Burke said.

"That part was easy. They want to get away from this rotten little moon as much as we do."

"You'll start by locating a nice-sized nickel iron meteoroid buried—but not too deeply—in the ice."

"There was one quite near their shelter."

"They'll have to dig it out, mix in carbon, and make crude steel."

"They already had the equipment and processes in place. Carbon from their rubbish dump. They've been manufacturing steel on a limited scale for years."

"The steel will need to be fashioned into hoops and wrapped with wire. Are you following so far? It'll all be in a PDF you can download via the text comms link. Form the rest of the iron from the meteor into inverted umbrellas that can be inserted into plugs of ice. Then the aliens will have to use their fusion reactor to energize the hoops, flinging the plugs from hoop to hoop, so that they're ultimately travelling fast enough to be flung into orbit."

Burke's voice grew livelier as he described the concept.

"It's all from a Heinlein book, actually! It's quite poetic how science fiction turns into reality, given enough time. Or maybe poetic isn't the word I'm looking for," Burke finished with a chuckle.

Giles chewed and swallowed, the lingering bruises on his temples moving like shadows. "He must have read the same book Skyler did."

"Sounds like it."

Jack leaned forward to the telescope. The *SoD* was approaching the longitude of the alien shelter. He adjusted the telescope until the mass driver came into focus.

The rings were still under construction. Rriksti, no longer invisibly camouflaged, their spacesuits keyed to the flamboyant patterns they liked best, moved around outside their shelter, positioning enormous steel hoops in a north-south line. Jack noted down the exact orientation of the telescope and pointed the *SoD's* long-range camera at the same spot. He didn't have his Nikon anymore—Alexei had taken it down to the surface to document work flows—but the *SoD's* camera had good enough resolution to capture the work site. He would send the pictures to Mission Control. Burke would know what he was looking at.

He switched off the radio as Burke began to talk about the challenge of capturing the ice chunks flung into orbit, and melting them to get them into the *SoD's* tanks. Skyler had come up with a solution for that, too. Catch the ice chunks in a big sack—the rriksti could make one of smart plastic. Run both of the fuel cells and the housekeeping turbine. Get the bioshield tank up to 80° C, and run all that water into the sealed sack with all the ice in it. Flow hot water in, melt the ice cubes, pump cold water back into the tank. Use the extra electricity to run the heaters.

"Are you going to respond to them?" Giles said.

"Nah," Jack said. "I'll just send them pictures as we go."

He switched the radio over to the channel dedicated to *SoD*-surface communications. As long as the *SoD* was above the horizon relative to the shelter, they had line-of-sight comms, using the rrikstis' radio mast as a relay. "Hey, Alexei! Come in."

"Yeah?" Alexei said, seconds later, from the surface.

"Houston says we suck. We should form the rest of the nickel iron from the meteor into umbrellas. Stick them into plugs of ice and throw the whole thing into orbit."

"That's the funniest thing I've heard all day," Alexei said. "I'll have to tell Skyler."

Skyler came on the radio. "Tell Houston *they* suck," he said. "First of all, there isn't that much iron in the meteor. We're going to make it into buckets that hold ice chunks, which can be reused after they fling the ice into orbit. So Europa's going to end up with a petite version of Saturn's F ring. So what? We'll pick it all up on the way out."

"We're staying with your plan," Jack assured him.

"Anything from Flaherty?"

"Not as such," Jack said, although he had rather had the feeling at certain points that although he was hearing Burke's voice, it was Tom Flaherty talking.

He focused the telescope on the work site again, and

cranked up the magnification. Now he could actually make out the radproof shells, like oversized Daleks, that the rriksti had made for Alexei and Skyler so they could hang out on the surface without getting sick. The shells were constructed from the aluminum hulls of Thing One and Thing Two, melted down and foamed up with hydrogen gas. The advance landers had finally played a lifesaving role, even if it wasn't the one they were designed for. Alexei and Skyler slept in their 'Daleks' when they were inside the rriksti shelter, too, to avoid getting X-rayed.

Next to the two giant pepperpots stood a lone rriksti in a blue and green patterned suit, looking up, hands shading its face from the sunlight reflected off Europa's ice.

"Hey there, Keelraiser," Jack whispered.

THE ADVENTURE CONTINUES IN BOOK 3 OF
THE EARTH'S LAST GAMBIT TRILOGY, *SHIPLORD*.

SELECTED CREW MEMBERS OF THE
LIGHTBRINGER

Commander Eskitul ("Shiplord")

Medical Specialist Nene ("Breeze")

Shuttle Pilot 1st Class Iristigut ("Keelraiser")

Atomic Engineer Hriklif ("Ditchlight")

Weapons Specialist Gurlp ("Rocky")

Sergeant 1st Class Ripstiggr ("Godsgift"), also called Boombox